# The SolGrid Rebellion

## Book Six
## of the Jack Commer Series

Michael D. Smith

For my wife Nancy

# CHAPTER ONE
## A Beagle and a Blouse at the Saturnalian
*Monday, April 13, 2076, 2025 hours*

One handsome young man in black set out plates and another placed five fresh glasses of wine on the candlelit table. As the waiters withdrew, Patrick James looked from his steak to the sixth dinner guest beside him shoving a toothy muzzle into his own meat.

*Excellent!* Trotter beamed, chewing and gulping.

How did the waiters keep from gagging? How did anyone put up with this? Of course, the management had been thoroughly charmed by Jonathan James Commer over the past six months, just as everyone in New Houston had been. Naturally JJC's Beagle Trotter would be allowed a seat at the Saturnalian.

Trotter outclassed them all tonight in his tuxedo and bow tie. Pat, Sanders, and Jonathan James wore sport coats without ties, and the women were also informal, Jackie in a clingy navy-blue dress and Suzette in orange blouse and miniskirt.

That orange blouse sat to his left. That seriously transparent orange blouse, and that devastatingly transparent orange bra, as if she were topless beside him. And her slender legs crossed in that miniskirt.

Why couldn't Pat just admit he'd fallen in love with Suzette Borman? He closed his eyes to the sound of the tuxedoed dog wolfing steak off his plate.

Thank God Trotter was Dark. They all were. Pat and Sanders had agreed to remain Dark as they worked on the SolGrid programming, and he knew only too well how averse JJC, Jackie, and Suzette were to the Grid. Only Trotter occasionally issued a comment, though this wasn't via SolGrid but through the Martian telepathic outradiance the dog had mastered decades ago.

Pat lifted his wine glass. The Saturnalian kept its gravity at a standard 1G, as Pat did at SolGrid's offices. The absurdly light surface gravity of Enceladus was fun, but he'd found he couldn't

1

concentrate on his work when every movement either went awry or had to be thought through in advance. Even setting a comm on a worktable in one-tenth gravity required some mental adjustment.

He regarded Jonathan James with unease. The young man wore a dark blue coat over a collarless purple shirt. His long brown hair was pulled back in a ponytail and his big hairy hands protruded from too-short sleeves as he fingered the stem of his wine glass. Tall, skinny JJC gave the impression of being frail until you noticed those powerful biceps and forearms. He sat with the women to either side, Jackie on his left and Suzette to his right.

That bastard thought he understood women so well. Maybe that came from frying his brains on being Emperor of Alpha Centauri for a few minutes last year, with trillions of Centaurian females running amok in his mind and worshipping him. In any case the ladies sure flocked to him now. A lot of people had underestimated JJC, Pat thought sourly. Including himself.

Pat set his wine down and tried to ignore Trotter slurping at a bowl of water. "Okay, guys, look, anyone can see something's up here."

Forks momentarily halted. JJC looked up with a smile. "Something *up* here?"

"C'mon, anyone can see something's going on here. You call this dinner, you say it's the last time we can get together, and so what's the deal?"

JJC grinned. "Why don't you just dip into your little SolGrid and find out?"

"You know damn well that's not how it works." Any idiot knew that if the others weren't participating in the Grid, Pat wouldn't find any information unless he happened upon some other person privy to whatever JJC knew. "So you call this dinner, and it's all *so* mysterious."

"I didn't *call* any dinner. I *invited* my friends here because I wanted their company. I'm not some hotshot corporate president who *calls* dinners."

Pat blinked at the insult. Okay, so he'd called a few dinners here himself as SolGrid president. But the others weren't SolGrid, just Pat and Sanders. Jackie had her own projects to attend to and had never shown any interest in the company, and Suzette had her complicated life running between her husband back on Mars and her new lover Jonathan James. Jonathan James and his damn telepathic dog.

"Okay, okay," Pat said, "I just wanted to say I know your little secret and it's damn stupid if you ask me. I can't believe it of any of you."

The others were silent. Pat had a moment of satisfaction seeing JJC blink, but Jonathan James took a sip of his golden wine and recovered, turning to the other tables to assess the noise level. Pat followed his gaze to the windows and the icy mountains beyond the small buildings of New Houston's main street. Above it all loomed the giant yellow sphere of Saturn undergoing reconstruction by the Martians.

JJC turned back. "I'm surprised, Patio. I really didn't think SolGrid could pick that up if we were Dark."

"*Grr ... uff!*" Trotter put in with a hint of warning.

Pat winced. He kept forgetting that the dog understood every word they said. He was also tired of JJC's irritating nicknaming habit. Things had definitely changed between them since their first dinner last December. He and Sanders had been deep into creating SolGrid when Jack Commer's son showed up asking for an interview. Sanders had maintained that JJC might have some insight into the software, but Pat protested that everyone knew the twenty-eight-year-old had burned his brains out messing with the fascist Alpha Centaurian Grid a few months previously. But since JJC was his old friend Jack's son, Pat reluctantly agreed they could take some time out and invite the kid to dinner.

Two things had immediately surprised Pat. First, instead of applying for a job, JJC pleaded with Pat to scrap all plans for SolGrid, but seeing that Pat wasn't budging from his fresh United System contract to build just such an application, Jonathan James began a campaign to introduce safeguards against any Alpha Centaurian-style brainwashing. Over the past few months Pat had promised a dozen add-ons which he always found excuses not to implement. There just hadn't been time with the threat of Wounded spies in Sol.

The second revelation was more astounding. It was painfully obvious that both Jackie and Sanders' girlfriend Suzette were smitten with the young man. Jackie was seventy-six but rejuvenated to mid-thirties, and she was *drooling*. Pat's own girlfriend was drooling for this brain-damaged fool. And Suzette Borman, forty-two but never rejuvenated, looking so alarmingly hard and used up, was giggling, swatting JJC's thigh, and hanging onto his shoulder. Lee Borman's wife, who'd been having an affair with Sanders Hirte for God knew how long.

Pat had recoiled in disgust at JJC's charisma. It was an unruly and much more powerful version of his father's leadership charm, and over the next months Pat had gotten more than enough of it shoved down his throat. But before long JJC was somehow part of the SolGrid group, even though he was passionately devoted to dismantling Pat's ultimate achievement.

"Look, it's obvious something's been up for a while. This opposition to SolGrid you have. And somehow you've brainwashed everyone else into it."

JJC narrowed his eyes. "Let's not use that term if you don't mind, Mr. Patster."

"Okay, okay, all I meant was that something's up, and now I know what it is."

"Here's how he found out," Sanders said, passing his comm across Jackie to JJC. "He hacked Jackie's comm. She hadn't upgraded to 9.22 yet and so it's been relatively unprotected."

"Really?" Jackie said, hand to her breast. "I thought 9.22 was optional."

"It's optional if you want your boyfriend to hack into your messages," Sanders grinned, the wild tattoos all over his face expanding and contracting.

"Dammit, Sanders!" Pat cried. "How dare you!"

"That reminds me," JJC said. "Sanders, let's get all our comms upgraded with the latest darkware."

"I just did right now," Sanders replied. "All four of us are now on the latest."

Pat pointed at JJC. "*You*--giving orders to--to--" he sputtered.

JJC shrugged.

"*Grrr!*" Trotter said. He gulped down the rest of his steak and eyed Pat's.

Pat turned to Sanders. "You're *taking* orders? From *him?*"

Sanders also shrugged.

"Dammit, you're my first assistant!"

"Aw, c'mon, Pat, you know the problems of SolGrid," Sanders said softly. "It's out of control, man, it really is. It's time we all admitted it."

"It's *not* out of control. You of all people should know that."

"Well, looks like we don't have a serious security problem after all," JJC drawled as he scrolled through Sanders' comm. "Mr. Patster here just knows from his hack that we're all sick of this crap and that we're leaving. Let's just say I've kept the *means* in my head this whole time. And Sanders' head, of course. We do things the old-fashioned way. We *talk*. So as far as I can tell, you don't know everything."

"This is *unbelievable*. So you're leaving, all of you! Even Sanders! Even *you,* Jackie! Where the hell do you think you're all going? What's all this going to prove anyway?"

JJC leaned back in his chair, again assessing other diners' ability to overhear. "Let's just say that I've got a nice, Dark place all picked out. Sanders knows exactly where it is."

Sanders nodded. "Sorry to turn in my resignation, you know, Pat. It was fun for a while." To Pat's dismay, Sanders reached into his coat pocket and withdrew a sheet of plasti-paper folded into thirds. He passed it across Trotter who sniffed it as it went by.

"Dammit, Sanders, I can't believe this!" Pat gasped, unfolding the letterhead.

*SolGrid, Inc.*
*1522 Main Street, Suite 114*
*New Houston, Enceladus*

*Office of the First Assistant*

*I hereby resign at the end of the business day, April 13, 2076.*

Pat involuntarily checked his wristwatch. 8:30 PM. "Really? You're already gone? After all we've been through together?"

"Don't take it too hard, man. You've been great to me, you really have. But I have to get out on my own now. And hell, Pat, it finally hit me just how wrong SolGrid is. How wrong the whole *concept* is. I just can't do it anymore."

The letters on the page surged in and out of focus. With trembling hands Pat laid the paper atop his salad. He turned to Jackie across the table. "You too? You're leaving the Committee and--and *everything?*"

He couldn't bring himself to add: *And me too?*

Jackie shrugged. For the first time in months Pat saw her as a beautiful woman, not just as a girlfriend who dropped in now and then to interrupt his work on SolGrid. God, she was elegant. That perfectly sculptured face, that flawless body in that tight dark blue dress. What had he been thinking all these months? Why hadn't he noticed how noble she was? He'd been so consumed with the business. Four hours of sleep was the standard. His mind was so locked into programming that a few nights ago he'd exited the office airlock with his EnviroField's AutoMode switched off, to find himself on Main Street with no air, no pressure, temperature four hundred degrees below zero. Fortunately Sanders had been right behind him and maxed his own EnviroField over him, saving his worthless life. Another quarter second and he'd have been gone.

"This--this is just something I need to do," Jackie said. "I'll take a leave of absence from the Committee. Get back to them later, after things settle down. The Ywritt won't mind. I think they need a break from us too, tell you the truth. Look, Pat, I know SolGrid's important to you, I really do. But after looking into it, after *knowing* it, there's something wrong. I can't explain exactly, but it's wrong for *me*."

"And you're going with *him,* without evening knowing where you're going?"

"Yes, dammit! It has to be secret because of SolGrid itself! Can't you understand we're all tired of being under your *surveillance?*"

"We're *all* pulling out, Mr. Pat," Suzette put in gently. "Jonathan James knows where he's going. We *trust* him."

Pat whirled to her; he'd forgotten the goddess next to him. "Yeah, I suppose you'd have to go, wouldn't you?" He was aware of the bitter disdain in his voice but the sight of her dark nipples clearly visible through the orange blouse was too much for him. He could feel her smiling brown eyes and finally looked up to meet them.

"Of course I have to go with my man, Mr. Pattycakes! And I'm sorry to report right to your dear face that SolGrid *does* suck, Patio! Sorry to be the one to tell you that, honeycakes!" She pressed warm fingers to his upper leg. Pat stared in shock.

*I love her! I love her!*

His eyes wrenched from the hand still on his leg, across her miniskirted thighs, up over the full, nearly nude breasts, and finally to that unfathomable, taunting Mediterranean face.

"We've taken a vow to fight your SolGrid, Mr. Pat. That's just the way it is!"

Pat was lost in her laughing eyes, and everyone at the table knew it, even Trotter who was nuzzling the remains of Pat's meat and potato off his plate. What had happened with her rejuvenation? How did she get to be so transcendently beautiful? She'd been *horrifying* before, even though the tough, aging creature had somehow captured Jonathan James within a week of that first dinner. The two had openly been a couple since then, and Sanders truly didn't mind. "What the hell, it was time for her to switch off," was the only comment Pat had gotten out of his first assistant. But to Pat, Sanders Hirte's former saucy girlfriend and Lee Borman's wandering wife had always seemed akin to an ex-whore meth addict.

So he'd scoffed when Suzette announced she was finally

getting her first rejuvenation therapy this spring. He'd assumed she'd be frozen at her stone-hard texture for the next two hundred years, but everyone was astonished when she'd emerged from the treatment at the end of March, just two weeks ago. Suzette was dazed to find her body, her skin, her energy, her sexuality, all reversed to age nineteen in one of the rare cases where rejuvenation actually turned the aging process backwards. Usually rejuvenation kept you at a robust late thirties or early forties, but there were varying results including people like JJC's own counselor, who so far hadn't taken well to his treatment and looked his eighty years.

The group had been thrown into disarray by Suzette's impossible beauty and the sex hormones blasting everywhere. JJC was delighted, but the fact that he'd already been besotted with her before rejuvenation only added to her own addiction to him. Jackie was secure enough to show no jealousy, but it was obvious that she, like Pat, struggled to accommodate an extremely sexually active teenager in their midst.

Pat had wondered if Sanders would turn back in Suzette's direction, but he'd seemed to shrug the entire thing off. What was he doing with that huge oversexed body these days? Was he heading over to the prostitutes on Cleaver Street? Pat had been there twice himself and each time had sworn he'd never return. Now he was contemplating leaping from this table and going for his third.

Because there was Suzette. And he *loved* her. She was so magnificent. And she *smiled* at him, half-naked right next to him, touching his leg, arousing him, for God's sake. Even as she insulted SolGrid, his sole reason for existence.

Like the rest, she knew SolGrid was broken. But how could they know how bad it really was? Pat hadn't even told First Assistant Sanders how bad it was.

He wrenched his glance from her dangerous eyes, from her lips, from the intoxicating blouse. "Look, none of you really has the slightest idea what you're talking about!" he tried, even as it sank in even further than they all knew. The entire solar system knew.

## CHAPTER TWO
### Draft One Must Die!

JJC laughed. "You know, Mr. Pat, my first thought when I got to Enceladus was to blow up your damn headquarters. Not that I'd want to hurt you personally or anyone. I figured I could do it in the dead of the night, you know. But I'm not a terrorist, and anyway Hirte says you have so many backup locations it wouldn't matter." He waved at the frozen mountains outside, at the temperatures flirting with absolute zero. "And I can't bring myself to blow up this charming little artist colony."

Pat stared at Trotter, who was fully onto Pat's plate, scarfing down the salad with his nose pulsating under Sanders' resignation letter. Pat knew it was over. He loved SolGrid. He loved the office and the state-of-the-art computer equipment in there. But it was all over anyway whether JJC blew it up or not. The endless nights working on the program, so elegant, so mesmerizing. All for nothing.

Okay, so he wasn't getting enough sleep. So he wasn't sampling the wonders of the damn artist colony. He loved New Houston anyway. Enceladus had originally been the province of Martians repairing it from the Saturn explosion of 2031 and guiding this and the other moons back into their former orbits. Then scientists arrived to probe the newly-discovered primitive life forms in the underground ocean, and somehow museums had gravitated here, science museums and art museums and then galleries and pottery studios, restaurants like the swanky Saturnalian, and endless bars. Freaky creative types in EnviroFields pranced everywhere in the one-tenth gravity, and bikers roared through town on moon motorcycles, though they actually roared by broadcasting EnviroField frequencies which anyone could turn off or on as they chose, depending on how much local color they wanted. One brainless jerk had actually hit escape velocity on his bike and had to be rescued by the USSF.

But Pat's friends were leaving, mocking him, turning on him. Suzette whom he loved. His friend Sanders Hirte. How had this Jonathan James son of a bitch gotten control of his Sanders?

Sanders had been the bouncer at Lee and Suzette's nightclub in Marsport, and Pat had snatched him up the day he'd finalized the contract for SolGrid with the United System Council. Yeah, people had squawked; nobody could understand how an apparent drifter like Hirte could become Pat's top programmer, but Pat knew Hirte's talents and was certain he had just the man for the job. It was the first week of December and they'd had to move fast to get SolGrid done by the end of the year.

"Dammit, guys, doesn't anybody remember that we're really still at war?" Pat cried. "Doesn't anyone remember the Wounded?"

JJC sat back. "Mr. Patster, we must've had this conversation a hundred times."

Hirte shrugged. "We did what we set out to do, Pat. Now we've got to come to terms with the *problems* in SolGrid."

"Nobody knew whether they were coming down our throats the next second or not!" Pat yelled. "Can't you idiots ever understand that? Sanders, *you* understood!"

"I know, man, I know, but think about the static, and the privacy violations, and the damage to SolNet itself."

"There's … no damage, really." But nobody knew better than Pat what the so-called auxiliary application SolGrid had done to the SolNet infrastructure. Even Sanders didn't know all of it. The thirty kid programmers still coding away down at 1522 Main this evening on their cute little SolGrid apps had no clue. Or the five hundred employees of the Marketing Department scattered across the solar system, in fact the largest part of SolGrid. Despite involving Hirte in much of the secondary programming, Pat had written Draft One of SolGrid himself in defiance of Section 14 of the contract. And nobody but Pat was allowed to look at the Telepathic Kernel.

People called him a genius. If they only knew he'd just memorized Phil Sperry's hack of the Alpha Centaurian Grid last summer. He'd been fully inside the Grid. All anybody had to do was *look*, and commit the damn Grid kernel to memory.

Yes, SolGrid was based at its core on the *Alpha Centaurian Grid.*

God, what if he just blurted that out? Sure, he had safeguards in place. Special human frequency blocks. Too bad they just didn't work.

Faces turned away from him. Even Trotter had his head down.

They all must have dropped him a long time ago. He'd been working nonstop since December 2nd. Even after they implemented SolGrid on the last day of December, he just couldn't let up. How much of the group dynamics had he missed? He'd tried to persuade himself that JJC might provide interesting counterarguments for him to gnaw on, that his presence in the group might be a catalyst for breakthroughs. He'd dismissed Suzette's whines as mere echoes of JJC's thinking, but hadn't realized that Jackie had also turned against SolGrid.

Sanders was the big surprise. Over the last week he'd been coming to Pat with concerns about the static, the SolNet pollution, and database decay, but Pat had assumed Hirte wanted to work on these problems. Now he'd given up.

They all had. Pat would return to Command Cubicle One tomorrow without any of them. No more dinners at the Saturnalian. No more Jackie. She wanted Jonathan James. God, the kid would take both women. Maybe share them with goddamn Sanders.

Pat reeled at the vision of the four of them groping each other in bed. Another chug of wine didn't help. "Dammit, we've outed 7,129 Wounded robots since December! Fifteen more just today! We *saved* the goddamn solar system from getting Sphered like Iota Persei last year! And what do you do? You whine and complain and run off to start some *sex commune!*"

"Wow, what's Mr. Pattycakes have on *his* mind, I wonder?" Suzette laughed, poking his thigh. "Dear Mr. Pattycakes, aren't you *romantic!*"

Trotter barked happily.

"*Dammit ...*" Pat muttered, aware of other diners following this exchange.

JJC laughed. "C'mon, this ain't no sex commune, Patio. Believe me, we're gonna pick up *followers.* If you haven't noticed, there are millions of people totally fed up with SolGrid. The only ones who still love it are the SolGrid addicts."

"*No* …" Pat moaned. He was tempted to roll into the Grid and verify what JJC was saying, but he kept up his guard. He'd only allowed himself into PublicGrid a couple times for quick tests. AdminGrid was a different matter. It had only one member. In fact, he'd been so rattled he'd forgotten to delete Hirte from EditGrid. He burst into Admin and it was like a cold bucket of water over his head.

Across the table Sanders blinked at being deleted.

"Sorry, man, sorry," Pat muttered, reluctant to relinquish the cool Admin and return to his humiliation at the dinner table. "But I can't have you in there anymore. And I demand you honor the nondisclosure agreement."

"Agreed," Sanders said. "No big deal. Anyway, we're leaving, and I'm done with any sort of Grid. JJC has this *vision,* I guess you could say."

"Look, Pat," Jackie put in, "we know SolGrid has done some good, especially in January when it began flushing out all those Wounded. But SolNet's never been right, and think about the Martians. About all that static coming into their outradiance."

"Aaah, screw the goddamn Martians," Pat said. "Bunch of wimps. I told 'em they'd feel it a little bit, but of course they have to exaggerate it all out of proportion."

"A *little* bit? It's *wrong,* Pat. It's not working, and you know it."

"But this is my *life.* This is what I was called on to *do!*"

"And anyway, if there are any Wounded left, they're probably just better at hiding now. Anyone can go Dark, obviously."

"Sure, but the patterns of millions of people on the Grid, I mean, then you *sift* the patterns and you can easily figure out who's a goddamn robot or not," Pat protested, itching to jump back into AdminGrid. What if he could follow the logic paths for isolating robotic behavior based on the input of millions of SolGrid connectees in their various random contacts with that robot, and then strengthened Scanning Matrix at Polarity Axis?

"We've gotten too paranoid, Pat. SolGrid's *destroying* us."

"Dammit, Jackie, I can't believe you turned on me like this!"

"I can't believe you turned on *me*," Jackie shot back with the slightest nod in Suzette's direction.

Somehow the sex hormone-drenched Suzette didn't pick up this inference. Pat looked away from Jackie's glare, down to the scraps on his dog-soggy plate. Did Jackie know how he felt about Suzette? Oh God, of course she did. Everyone did.

But if that were the case, what if a Pheromone Scanner Subsystem was interpolated into the Bypass Matrix and then every time someone questioned the stability of a sexual relationship, Frequency Node would take a snapshot and port it over to the resulting--

No, it would never work. Frequency Node didn't interface with--

*Dammit, stop it!*

"Look, I know SolGrid has problems. That's why I'm trying to fix them. That's why I'm working these twenty-hour days! But then you *abandon* me!"

Hirte shrugged. "There's something really, deeply *wrong* with SolGrid, dude. Something that can't be corrected. You have to know that."

"No! Draft Two will take care of all the problems! I've got it all in my head!"

"Draft Two?" JJC said with a raised eyebrow.

"Yes, Draft Two! I *know* Draft One is crap! I admit it! But Draft Two will correct everything!"

"Will it be based on that same Telepathic Kernel you won't let anyone look at?" Hirte said. "All the problems lead right back there. I've just never been able to get any further."

Pat blinked. "Of *course* I'll change the Kernel ... a little."

Sure he would, just as soon as he figured out how it worked.

Was he an idiot or what, to think he could inflict the Alpha Centaurian Grid on the whole solar system? It was all a failure. They'd gotten some Wounded, but his ex-friends here were right. Anybody could figure out how to outwit RobotScanGamma.

And there was Jackie looking so irresistible. When was the last time they'd had good sex? *Any* sex?

"All right, I'll admit it. SolGrid sucks! See, I agree with you! Okay? I've been working my ass off on it for five months now and I'm as sick of it as any of you! Okay?"

He met JJC's sad brown eyes set incongruously in that merry laughing face. Yes, Jonathan James was now the leader. All this time Pat had thought he was actually running something, but he wasn't. JJC had walked in here and grabbed it all. And it was funny because Pat loved the guy, everyone did. *He* had the charisma, not Pat. *He* had Suzette. Pat could never lead a glorious escape to a new life, a new sex commune, a place where people communicated telepathically, not with some stupidass code. JJC was a sexy rock star, and Pat was a sucky poet locked in his room writing stupid crap nobody would ever read.

Pat was thrust back to a memory of his college days he hadn't replayed in decades. Yeah, there was Edwin Ratliff, mustached, stoned, casually perched on the concrete railing of the third-floor balcony, strumming his acoustic guitar, surrounded by cooing coeds while Pat cringed in his room trying to shut out the graceful flowing notes so he could write "Mr. Waterwaterhead," the worst poem anyone had ever written anytime, anywhere, and almost as bad as Draft One of SolGrid.

Could he tweak SolGrid back to sanity? He'd always thought that someday he'd magically understand the Kernel. But it was impossible to make sense of the damn thing. Who was the first Alpha Centaurian to come up with it, eons ago? So often Pat wished he could've met him.

"When … are you leaving?" he moaned to the accompaniment of a telepathic burst of pity from Trotter to his right. Yes, a snuffling telepathic Beagle *pitying* him, here at the end of everything.

"Tomorrow morning," JJC said, grinning. "Care to join us? There's always room for one more rebel!"

# CHAPTER THREE
## Amav Declines
### *Tuesday, April 14, 2076, 0400 hours*

Joe stepped inside the steel and glass Commer home as Amav buckled her weapons belt and punched a command to cycle the front airlock. "He's up in the Turret, making some calls," his sister-in-law snapped, yanking a thigh zipper on her red flight suit.

"So you're going with us?"

Amav brushed long uncombed hair off her forehead. "No. Absolutely not."

Joe blinked. He opened his mouth but thought better of it. Her deep brown eyes were cold and he could see by the set of her jaw that it was prudent not to ask questions. "Well, I'll just get on up there."

"If you *must* know, I was set to leave at 0500 for Venus. Then this *crap* happens. I told Jack to just figure it out. I'm tired of dealing with this. I told him I'm taking the saucer and that's that. I've had this meeting with the Four set up for *weeks* now. And I'm not changing my plans for *him*." She sized him up. "So you got roped into this, I take it?"

"Well, there's no copilot for the *VI* yet, and I need some flight time. Anyway, Jack thought I could maybe talk to him or something."

"It's so *stupid*. He just *faked* his way through all that counseling. Nodding and smiling to everyone, telling everybody what they wanted to hear. And now *this*. Damn him to hell! I'm not gonna figure this one out for Jack. I just refuse!"

"Well, I guess I can understand."

"Look, Joe, I'm sorry. I'm sure you'll find him on Andertwin and then, hell, I don't know. I need to get going." Amav opened a zipper on her sleeve, checked her comm, and zipped up again. She grabbed a silver valise off a table. "Jack will keep me posted. I just can't deal with this. See you later." She slid the airlock open, shut and depressurized. Joe saw the sparkling of her EnviroField kicking in as the outer door slid

16

aside. She marched across the rock garden and opened the hatch of the twenty-foot-wide Commer saucer faintly shining in the Martian night.

"Shall I escort you to your brother Jack?" came a soft bass voice beside him.

Joe turned to the hulking Saint Bernard by his knee. "Sure, Eddie. But I know the way."

"Of course, Mr. Joe," Edward said, "but I'm heading to him myself, so it's no trouble at all." Joe noted the holster draped around the service robot's neck. It held standard USSF blaster/shattergun, superspace comm and a backup comm, as well as med kit and dagger. Joe already had all his equipment on his belt.

"This way, if you please," Edward said, leading Joe to the plastiglass elevator and pawing the up button. They rode to the fourth floor through girders and transparent panels bathed in multicolored lights. "Master Jack is quite stressed," the dog warned. "Mistress Amav is also quite stressed, as you no doubt noted yourself."

Joe nodded. Through the glass walls he could see the Commer saucer hovering, then blasting straight up. That had been a fast preflight check, if there had been one. Amav must really have wanted to blow this place. "Yeah, I did see that. I'll let Jack know she's gone."

It wouldn't do for Edward to talk to Jack, because Jack was certain he'd deactivated the speech function of the robot dog Amav had bought him for Christmas, claiming that while he appreciated having an energetic valet to keep his home life in order, even to the point of setting up and paying for plumbing services, he drew the line at a talking dog. Jack shunned humanoid robots and barely tolerated the presence of USSF technician robots working at the spaceport. He wouldn't allow them on USSF ships. But he'd acknowledged that Edward made life simpler at the Commer residence as long as there was no disconcerting speech issuing from the thing.

But Amav had reactivated the speech function to allow the dog to talk to anyone except when Jack was within earshot. Joe wondered how long it would be before something screwed up and Jack found out. Anyway, Jack got messages from Edward on his comm, so what was the difference?

On the top floor, the thirty-foot-wide plastiglass hemisphere Jack called the Turret, Joe found the Supreme Commander of the United System Space Force in his black underwear, jabbing at an image on a ninety-inch viewscreen. At Joe's urging Jack had recently ramped up his workouts and was in great shape, with huge pectorals and biceps, muscular thighs and flat stomach, his skin smooth and taut. Not bad for an old fart of seventy-three.

"To tell you the truth, Jack, I think my presence would be detrimental," came a voice from the screen. In the background Joe could hear a woman shouting: "I *never* trusted that son of a bitch! I *told* you I saw this coming!" Joe recognized Alycia's voice on the other end of the Superspace connection, and now he saw Urside Charmouth on the screen, and in the background Urside and Alycia's Illinois mansion. Those two hadn't taken rejuvenation very well, though Urside claimed they were beginning to see some results.

"So he really didn't give you any indication of this?" Jack said.

"No, as far as I knew everything was going fine. We talk every couple weeks or so. He was upset when Trotter got so sick in February, I mean, *really* upset. He said he didn't think he could live if Trotter died. You know how bonded they've been. He was really on edge, and I have to admit I was damn concerned. But once Trotter was okay, he seemed normal again."

Jack turned to Joe. "The damn thing's *twenty-three*. Why are we wasting rejuv resources on *dogs?*"

Joe shrugged. Rejuv wasn't that expensive for pets these days, and in any case Trotter had received his while still in Alpha Centauri. "I don't know, Jack, he had that weird *Garthah-/yuu* trip with the dog and Clopt. He told me this Zarj brothers thing was an incredible *sharing*. That when Clopt killed himself, it was like one major foundation pillar going for both him *and*

Trotter. But he thought he could make it as long as Trotter was okay."

"Damn." Jack turned back to the screen. "Hey, Urside, you think he could've headed for Andertwin? They've upgraded the cloaking and we just plain can't track them right now. Would he try to go back to where he bonded with the dog? Is that possible?"

"Look, I just don't know," Urside said. "This is all such a surprise."

"It wasn't to *me*. I saw this coming all along!" his wife Alycia shouted from the background. "I *knew* he was faking it!"

"Dammit, Urside, why didn't *you* see this coming?" Jack snarled as Edward nudged him with the holster of weapons. "Just set them on the table there and get my blue flight suit," he told the dog. Edward shrugged the belt onto the low table and padded into the closet.

"Jack, I've told you from Day One I'm a goddamn *artist,* not a professional counselor!" Urside flared. "Maybe you should have gotten JJC one of *those*."

"Yeah, maybe. Look, I'm sorry, Urside. I thought you guys had a *rapport*."

Urside shrugged. "I thought we did, too."

"Well, I appreciate your insight on all this, I really do. I need to sign off but please call me if you have any ideas."

"Will do, Jack, and if--"

Jack cut the call. Edward returned, pushing a light cart with his nose. Atop the cart's iridescent surface lay a bright blue flight suit and a pair of boots. "Thanks, Edward. I'll also need my flight valise. Standard military contents."

Edward wagged his tail and padded out. Joe wondered whether Jack even considered how a dog was going to pack a USSF flight valise, and whether Amav had ever revealed that all four of Edward's paws could extend into full human hand functions, that the dog could stand erect on its hind feet, and, as Amav had told Joe, could fling two thousand Ninja throwing stars to nail an outline of the *Mona Lisa* on a wall in fifteen seconds. She thought Jack was too proud to admit the need for any sort of bodyguard, but hell, he was the SCUSSF, wasn't he? Who knew what sort of crackpot might try to target the Supreme Commander's house, no matter how many security force fields and AI sensors it had? Amav also said she slept better with Edward around.

Jack had a leg through his blue pants when the viewscreen flashed.

"Hello, Jack, I've made further inquiries here and throughout the Procyon A system," said Dar, his wife K'sla at his side. The Emperor and Empress Emeritus of the Martians were still on their extended vacation on Andertwin, living in Jonathan James' old guest house. Though the familiar Martian outradiance wasn't coming over the Superspace link to Andertwin, after decades with the Martians Joe could detect the tiny lines around the two Martians' eyes and intuit the worry they felt. Both also had a trace of that scattered look all Martians had these days. Even eleven and a half light-years away, Dar and K'sla reflected the new disruptions in Martian culture.

"Yes?" Jack said, drawing his blue shirt across his back.

"Still nothing within half a light-year of Procyon A. We can penetrate '60s cloaking technology, but still nothing. Of course, we'll keep monitoring and let you know whatever we find. But I think Jonathan James isn't choosing to return here."

"Right, right. The thing is, someone must've hacked the cloaking tech and upgraded it somehow. Hell, the only stuff we *can't* break is like '71 on. So somebody, probably with a lot of USSF expertise, has been fooling with the ship's systems. If its cloaking is upgraded to '70s, it could be *anywhere*."

"Really?" Joe said. "You think he really hacked it to modern standards somehow? Is that even possible with something that old?"

"I don't know. The ship just *disappeared*. We couldn't even track it out of Sol, couldn't even trace its Star Drive."

"Wow ..." Joe said. Cloaking Star Drive trails had only been introduced last October, and was only intended to be used under combat situations. "This looks a little more serious than I'd thought."

Jack finished buttoning his shirt. "I don't know what to think. How the hell could he *do* this?" He reached for his weapons belt. Joe noted a paperback book on the table. He knew Jack still liked these sorts of books and mixed reading them with e-versions on his comm.

"*Julius Caesar?*" Joe said, hoping to break the tension. "We had to read that in high school, didn't we? Mrs. Nortel?"

"Yeah, I couldn't sleep. I was up reading it when the call came. It's kind of a page-turner once you get into it."

"You haven't had any *sleep?* Can you fly? You want me to pilot?"

"Yeah, maybe. I've just got to calm down a bit." Jack looked up to the viewscreen. "Look, Dar, keep us posted and we'll do the same for you. Just let me know if anything happens."

"Sure will, Jack. Good to see you as well, Joe. You're going to pilot the *VI?* The *VII* is still not ready?"

"Yeah, we're still aligning the Star Drive computers and there are some other glitches to chase down. On top of that I don't have a full crew yet and I haven't flown anything but my own saucer in a month. Jack's short a copilot for the *VI* so here I am."

"Well, we wish you all--"

"Hey, Dar, sorry, we've got to move on," Jack said. "We're getting a feed from Enceladus and we need to check it out. Talk to you later."

"Sure, Jack, good luck and we'll be sure to--"

Jack switched off and studied the text and images coming up. "The other hack was scrambling the records of everyone at the museum. But I had Information Services on it first thing. Looks like they've been able to reconstruct something."

Joe studied the screen. The museum had just opened at 10 AM on Enceladus, though that was 0300 hours here; he'd long ago given up trying to figure out why certain moons or planets decided to be several hours before or after Martian time. In any case thirty-five humans and six Martians had just entered the museum. A map showed where everyone had been standing.

There was a cluster of dots at the airlock to the ship itself.

"Thank God no one was hurt," Joe said, pointing to the low-level weapons readings. Twenty-five stun-level pulses.

Jack pointed to the list of people accounted for. Thirty humans, five Martians, all museum visitors and staff. "So there are six gone. One of 'em a Martian." The Info Services software began offering its best guesses for these six from the scrambled records.

"There's JJC," Jack said, pointing to the first name. Then, at the second: "*Suzette Borman?* That's crazy! What's wrong with this damn software?"

Joe regarded the image of the dark-haired, languid beauty perched on a bright red stool, leaning forward in her low-cut tank top. "Wow, they updated her photo fast," he mused. "*After* the rejuvenation, I see."

"But why the hell's the software pulling *her* up?"

Joe shrugged. "Well, she's Hirte's girlfriend and she spends a lot of time on Enceladus. You think he could have kidnapped her or something?"

"Damn, Joe, is my son a *kidnapper* too?"

Joe punched at his comm. "Lee? You there? Heading to the *VI?*"

"Yeah, Joe, you in on this deal too?" came Lee Borman on Joe's comm. "I'm heading to the spaceport. Should be there in ten."

Joe sent Lee's image to the corner of the viewscreen. "Yeah, great. I'm copiloting, or maybe piloting, or whatever."

"Lee, we're trying to figure out who's on the ship," Jack cut in. "But the records got scrambled and for some reason it's pulling up your wife's name."

"So we called to ask where she is," Joe said. "Take a look at what Info Services is guessing at."

"*Dammit,*" Lee said. "Look, guys, I haven't seen her in like a couple weeks. Tell you the truth, things have been a little tense at home, you know how that goes, and, uh ..."

"*And?*" Jack demanded.

"Well, you do know about Hirte, don't you?"

"Right, right, we know," Jack said, though of course neither he nor Joe had ever admitted this in Lee's presence.

"Well, now that she's taken up with JJC instead--"

"*What?*" exploded from both Jack and Joe.

"Yeah, yeah, she told me a while back. Like they can have this goddamn love nest out on Enceladus and I'm not supposed to do a damn thing and, you know, the Response is almost bankrupt as it is without her there to keep an eye on things, and she goes and gets all rejuvenated and who the hell thinks I have time to run the damn place?"

"God, Lee, I don't care about your stupid nightclub!" Jack said. "Are you saying you think Suzette went *willingly* with JJC?" He turned to Joe. "My son and *Suzette Borman?*"

"Well, you know what she's like, I mean, I only saw her once after she got rejuvenated, and then she's off to goddamn Enceladus again!"

"*Sanders Hirte!*" Jack cried, pointing to the third name appearing on the viewscreen. "Sanders Hirte is on the ship? With your wife? And Jonathan James?"

"That--that's not possible!" Lee sputtered. "*Is* it? Are they having some stupidass *threesome?*"

Joe pointed to the fourth name coming up. "*Jackie Vespertine?* Jack, this just can't be! The records must be totally scrambled or something."

Jack pulled up another window on the viewscreen and dragged the IDs of the four onto the USSF Sol Human Locator. The existence of this software was top secret and Joe knew Jack hated to consider its existence. By law Martians were excluded, but SHL gave the precise location of any human being in the solar system.

UNKNOWN WHEREABOUTS
UNKNOWN WHEREABOUTS
UNKNOWN WHEREABOUTS
UNKNOWN WHEREABOUTS

## CHAPTER FOUR
### Hey, the Software's Pointing to the Martian They Took

"*Damn* ..." Jack muttered. "So it's true. They're all on the ship."

"What the hell's she *up* to?" Lee moaned. "I mean, look, I give her her freedom, but *hell,* man."

"Okay, Lee, okay! I need to think. Meet you at the spaceport in a few minutes," Jack said, cutting Lee out and overriding Joe's own comm connection to Borman. "Is any of this possible? Is he really kidnapping them, or are they *with* him somehow? To do *what?*"

A fifth name came up.

"Patrick? Patrick *James?*" Jack moaned. The SHL again showed UNKNOWN WHEREABOUTS.

"*Damn,* Jack. Can this really be?"

Jack tapped the screen. "I'm rerunning the list of possibles. It's corroborating against travel records. Suzette's been on Enceladus since March 31st, Jackie since April 4th. The others haven't left the place in weeks. Dammit to hell, it's true!"

"Pat? On the ship too? I can't believe it!" Joe hadn't seen their former sensor officer since Pat quit the USSF last November. At first Joe thought the stress of dealing with the Wounded at Iota Persei had prompted Pat to bail. Jack had even lobbied to get Pat on the Committee to the Ywritt, the sentient race of bubble creatures of Iota Persei, but Pat had declined and soon they knew why. In December he'd founded SolGrid Inc. and gotten the contract with the United System for the implementation of a voluntary form of the Alpha Centaurian Grid in the Sol system. And promptly patented the telepathic software code that ran it.

"He must have kidnapped them *all* somehow. They're *hostages,*" Jack muttered, fastening his weapons belt. "We need to get moving. Are you ready?"

"Yeah, definitely. But we can't just shoot off to Procyon if we don't have any idea where he's really headed. Might be better to wait until we get some more data."

24

"Well, we can do that as well aboard ship and be ready to go."

"Yeah, you're right. I just can't believe this. About Jackie, I mean. Maybe I should call Ranna. If it's true her sister's onboard."

"Right, right, but we can wait for more confirmation as we head to the ship."

Joe still felt embarrassed, decades later, about the idiotic passion he'd once had for Jackie Vespertine. Marrying her older sister was the best thing that had ever happened to him, but there was still that awkwardness around Jackie. Both sisters had said the whole issue was long forgotten, Ranna in so many words, Jackie much more obliquely. Jackie had done well for herself in the ensuing years, exiting an unworkable marriage, picking up advanced work in exobiology and a professorship at the University of Mars, and along with Ranna becoming a member of the Committee to the Ywritt. But kidnapped? In danger? Joe reeled. "Or maybe we should get Ranna to join us. She could be back from Iota Persei in two hours."

"Huh ..." Jack said, considering. "Do you really think it's a good idea to have her onboard while we're hunting for her sister?"

"Well, you told me you wanted Amav along to be able to talk to JJC."

"I've been rethinking that. I don't think this a dangerous mission, but maybe it should just be only military personnel right now. Yeah, I thought Amav could talk with him. But I should've known she'd say the hell with that. Anyway, then I realized you'd be the best person to talk some sense into him."

"We've had some good talks, I guess. Sure I'll give it a try." Joe wondered if you could ever really know someone who'd been through so much turmoil. Maybe JJC had hoodwinked Joe as well.

He winced. The damn headache was back. He'd been having a lot of them recently, and had even wondered to Amav whether they might be a side effect of continuing rejuvenation treatments, at which point Amav had ragged at him for not seeing his doctor. Then she'd revealed she'd been having similar headaches, so Joe could return the rebuke. Even though she'd come close to tearing his head off a few minutes ago, the two had been good friends since '34. They also shared an unusual sensitivity to Martian outradiance.

"Do you think Jonathan James might be trying to head to Iota Persei?" Jack said. "That ship would never make it."

"Why would he steal that old thing? And take *hostages?*"

"Well, who knows how many are hostages? Anderson said there were three men firing shatterguns. One heavily tattooed. That has to be Hirte."

"So you think JJC and Hirte planned this together?"

Jack punched at the viewscreen. "A bouncer at a bar, of all things! Suzette's damn *lover.* Or former lover, I guess. And then Pat's first assistant! And did Pat just snap or something? Or is *he* a hostage?"

Joe knew they both had to be thinking about *three* men firing shatterguns in a crowded museum. "I assume they're all Dark? You'd think hostages would log onto to SolGrid to let everyone know where they were."

Jack dragged the five names to the SolGrid Online Indicator to check. Nothing. "Figured as much. They're either Dark or unconscious. But I've been monitoring the newsfeeds. There were a few people in the museum in the Grid at the time. All we've gotten from them is a sort of eyewitness account that corroborates Anderson's."

Joe nodded. The fact that Jack and Joe were Dark to the Grid themselves and had been since December didn't diminish the sense of criminality that being Dark implied these days. "So are you thinking to tap into SolGrid yourself?"

"Are you kidding? Damn well can't afford to, even for this. You know that."

"Yeah. I know." Joe had been tempted to take a tiny dip into SolGrid when Jack described what had happened at the museum. But it was treasonable folly for any USSF personnel to access it. At the end of December Joe and Jack had both sampled the newly-activated SolGrid, then immediately jumped out when they'd seen that the program would leak military secrets to every SolGrid user. Even Patrick James had understood that, but his software still had no real safeguards. So any USSF personnel who experimented with SolGrid were immediately dishonorably discharged. Only a few hundred did this before everyone else knew not to. Promises had been made to establish some Dark ‑ areas of the Grid, but as Pat had pointed out, that defeated the foundation of SolGrid's Telepathic Kernel.

"I guess it's crazy to think one of us could go in for just a second," Joe said. "See what came up."

"Forget it. Even one second would open up everything. Dammit, is JJC doing this just to spite me? None of this makes *sense*."

The viewscreen flashed. "Hey, the software's pointing to the Martian they took."

"*Z'B?*" Jack cried.

"No way!" Joe blurted at the travel records showing the Emperor of the Martians' visit to Enceladus to inspect the ongoing work on Saturn's ring system.

"Dammit, I'm supposed to be *notified* when the Emperor's away!"

"Amav said she was heading to Venus for this meeting with the Four anyway. Why isn't he *there?*" Z'B had walked for billions of years in the *Garr/thahg* afterlife and had returned with enough knowledge to pull the star Iota Persei through a wormhole by thought alone. "How could anyone kidnap him?"

"Well, he's been scrambled. All the Four have. You don't think Z'B could've willingly *joined* with them? Oh, God!"

"I just can't see it. He's so above all that."

"But he told me he was having trouble concentrating enough to do any Amplified Thought beyond simple tricks. Maybe that's why he headed to Saturn without telling us. They've been having all sorts of problems with AT out there."

"That's true enough." The past few months the Martian race had been getting progressively loopier. Joe and Amav both felt an underlying disturbance, a foundational cracking, beneath the eons-long structure of Martian confidence.

Z'B and Kner were having an even worse time as the two Martians progressively shed their near-infinite *Garr/thahg* knowledge. All Four were in decline. After their billions-of-years walks through *Garr/thahg,* K'ufunb, Kner, Will and Z'B had returned glowing like gods. For a while they could remember the abstract knowledge gained in *Garr/thahg* and they'd added immense technological benefits to Sol. In conjunction with the Ywritt from Iota Persei, they'd helped get the new *Typhoon VI* and *Typhoon VII* built within weeks instead of years.

Then they'd retreated into despair. They built *Garr/thahg* Castle in the Venusian jungle, ostensibly to work out complex trade protocols with the Ywritt, but the Four had increasingly taken a turn towards depression and listlessness. Were they feeling cut off from the glories of *Garr/thahg?* Joe couldn't fathom that, because *Garr/thahg* sounded like the most excruciating punishment anyone could undergo, running for billions of years down infinite corridors of bright-colored tiles that drilled all the concepts of the universe into your head. He shuddered. Who wanted to sit in algebra class for sixty billion years?

Z'B, reeling from *Garr/thahg* withdrawal, relied on his Chief of Staff, Greeney Gooney, to run what passed for a Martian government and to occupy Z'B's seat on the United System Council. Gooney had held onto his mental marbles pretty well, Joe thought, but even he was complaining that he couldn't really *think* anymore.

"Man, this is really going to hit the fan when the Martians find out about it," Jack said. "Their Emperor kidnapped?"

"I think it's seeping in now. I'm beginning to get a sense of that through the outradiance. Just little flickers of unease. Even long-distance from Saturn they can feel something's wrong with their Emperor. But soon it'll all be clear to every Martian."

"We could have civil disturbance on that alone. Hell, why didn't he fight back? What if they kill him? Damn, we've got to get going. We're not going to get much more out of *this,*" he said, tapping the viewscreen. "Edward! We're leaving! Seal the house after us!"

# CHAPTER FIVE
## MATS Redux

Joe heard an answering Saint Bernard bark from the adjoining room. As they rode the elevator down to the front airlock, Jack's comm beeped and Joe peered over at the text message: "House security procedure in progress. Have a safe trip. Keep me posted with updates necessary to facilitate comfortable and safe living in this house. Edward."

Their EnviroFields energized as they cycled the airlock and stepped into the Martian night. "Damn, I forgot Amav took the saucer," Jack said. "Can we take yours? Or I'll call an autojeep."

"No, forget it. I didn't bother with my own saucer. I've got a MATS bus right here. One of the new flight models. It'll get us to the pad in a couple minutes."

"You took a *MATS bus* here?" Jack said, gaping at the bright white bus idling at the curb.

Joe shrugged. "It seemed to intuit I needed transportation. It was waiting right outside my condo as I left. I just grabbed it. I figured, no hassle worrying about dealing with my own saucer at the spaceport."

"How the hell can a MATS bus *intuit* you need a ride?"

"Well, I hate to tell you this, but the museum news has been on SolNet since you called me. Some witnesses saw that it was JJC and they started posting their stories. I was listening to it on the way over. I guess the MATS AI figured I'd need a ride, and where, based on the news."

Jack looked as if he wanted to spit on the sidewalk but was reconsidering how his EnviroField would process that. "Aw, what the hell, you're right, let's go."

"Yeah, we'll be at the spaceport before you know it," Joe said as they climbed aboard. "I've ridden some of these new air jobs a couple times. They're pretty cool."

The bus was empty. Jack gingerly took a seat with Joe several rows back from the front. "Yeah, I hope so."

"Welcome aboard!" a tenor male voice reverberated down the length of the bus. "I am Marsport Automated Transport

System Bus 4646, of the new generation of flying busses! Shall I change the fare charges to that of Jack Commer, Supreme Commander of the United System Space Force, USSF account 3394514?"

"No, just keep both of us on mine," Joe said. "And we'd like to head to USSF Spaceport, Pad A-19, please."

"Checking flight route to USSF Spaceport. Done. Interfacing with USSF air traffic control. Interface achieved. USSF air traffic control stipulates permission granted for direct flight to Pad A-19 on the basis of request of Admiral Joe Commer of the United System Space Force. Thank you, and may this bus abjectly apologize for its earlier mistaken assumption that charges would devolve upon the senior officer present, Admiral Jack Commer, Supreme Commander of the United System Space Force?"

"Uh, sure," Jack muttered. "No problem."

"Thanks, bus," Joe spoke up. "Thanks for your consideration. We're sort of in a hurry to get to the spaceport as you may realize."

"Yes, of course, Joe Commer! How thoughtless of this bus to assume that you would care to hear an official apology from Marsport Automated Transport System Bus 4646 when the recent news that so concerns you must be weighing on your mind at a time when all you can think about is a fast ride to USSF Spaceport!"

Joe was shoved hard into his seat as the bus shot off the ground at a sixty-degree angle.

"Damn!" Jack grunted. "Don't these things have inertial dampers? It's like we're pulling 2G!"

Normal gravity returned as the bus rose high above the suburban houses of Norcaj and wheeled south towards the spaceport.

"Again, apologies from Marsport Automated Transport System Bus 4646. Inertial dampers kick in shortly after emergency acceleration. Thank you."

"Okay, fine," Jack said. "Well, at least it got authorization to get us right to our pad. That's amazing in itself. Last year I'm sure it would've argued for hours about why it couldn't drop us at a military facility."

"Yeah, the Reconfig worked wonders. I've really enjoyed taking the bus here and there the past few months. I've gotta say, the AI's *smooth* now."

Jack nodded. "If you say so." He pulled his comm from a zippered sleeve. "I'm just going to check up on--"

"Thank you so much, Joe Commer, for your warm and glowing compliments concerning the reconfigured artificial intelligence system of the Marsport Automated Transport System!" the bus boomed. "Your feedback is most welcome and can only enhance future bus/human/Martian interaction. Thanks once again and may this bus inquire after the health of you and Admiral Jack Commer?"

"Damn!" Jack hissed, looking up.

"No, it's okay. They're programmed to be friendly and engaging and all that. After a little chitchat they settle down to business," Joe whispered, then spoke up: "We're fine, bus, everything's great, thanks for your consideration."

"That's wonderful to hear, Joe Commer. The Marsport Automated Transport System family as a whole certainly appreciates all that the United System Space Force has done for MATS, for Mars, for humans and Martians everywhere! Meanwhile, as this bus *settles down to business,* using your own words to describe the overall mission of this bus, it is happy to inform you that we are flying at four hundred miles per hour to USSF Spaceport Pad A-19 and should arrive in *three minutes!* Thank you and have a wonderful *three minutes!*"

"Sheesh," Jack whispered. "Did they overdo the therapy or something?"

"Shhh! It'll riff on anything you say. It can pick up the slightest whisper."

"Thank you for your insightful comments about the nature of this bus's sensory technology, Joe Commer. This bus not only picks up and records all conversation in any known human language as well as spoken Martian, it also reads lips and determines from visual cues the stress levels of all passengers in order to detect and solve potential problems before they begin!"

"Oh, no," Jack muttered, checking his comm. "How much more of this do we have to put up with?"

Joe looked at his own comm. Two minutes, forty-five seconds before touchdown. "Take it easy, Jack, we'll get there. It didn't give me any problems on the way over to your place."

"For instance, in conjunction with the latest news from Enceladus and taking into account an analysis of the facial muscles of both Jack Commer and Joe Commer, this bus concludes that both passengers are experiencing elevated levels of stress. For which this bus offers its most *hearty commiseration.*"

"Goddammit!" Jack flared. "I wouldn't have taken a MATS bus if I thought these damn problems weren't fixed by now!"

"Does Jack Commer fear that this bus will drop from the sky like a stone in a spectacular flaming suicide in order to end the life of Jack Commer, Supreme Commander?"

"Oh my God!"

"No! No, of course not!" Joe cut in. "Of course not!"

"That was a *joke,* dear passengers, to ease the tension! However, it seems to have backfired, elevating your stress levels even further, for which this bus most *sincerely apologizes.*"

Joe stared out the window at the rocky desert south of Norcaj and checked his comm. Two minutes, thirty seconds of flight left. "Uh, listen," he said, "I know there were problems in the past, but really, the Reconfig should have sorted all that out by now, and, you know, if we could just get to the spaceport, you know, everything would be cool."

"Bus 4646 wishes to reassure both its passengers that the mandated flight path and time is proceeding according to plan. There is no need for either passenger to continually check his comm in order to ascertain how much time is left. If desired, this bus will initiate a verbal countdown."

"No--no need--"

"Understood. This bus wishes to apologize for any elevated stress levels it may have caused and wishes to reassure Jack and Joe Commer that the November-December reconfiguration of the Marsport Automated Transport System was indeed a complete success. MATS no longer harbors the slightest animosity towards Jack Commer, Joe Commer, or the USSF in general."

"Well, that's good," Jack muttered. "I hated to get involved in local politics, but it had to be done."

"Yes, the reconfiguration worked wonders. May I quote Jack Commer, Supreme Commander of the USSF, speaking at the first meeting of the joint USSF-City of Marsport Ad Hoc Committee on the Marsport Automated Transport System, November 5, 2075? In which Jack Commer succinctly stated: 'There are obviously some dangerous flaws in the MATS AI interface which affect not only Sol citizens, but also USSF operations in particular. For instance, the software seems to have some sort of built-in antipathy towards me and the USSF, and nearly killed several of us in July. It apparently has some sort of buried grudge going back to June 2034.'"

Jack looked up, startled to hear his own voice coming over the speakers. The bus continued: "The overhaul of the MATS AI software was accomplished December 28, 2075, and was a *complete success*. MATS has forgotten entirely the events of June 8, 2034, in which Jack and Joe Commer initiated violence aboard a MATS bus, resulting in the tragic death of civilian passenger Al Carson. Indeed, this episode turned out to be a kernel of unease within the software that resulted in the AI program continually attempting to hack itself in order to remove what can only be termed an *AI neurosis*. The software was by definition unable to accomplish this task until Supreme Commander Jack Commer so wisely intervened in local politics and had the entire system reconfigured."

"Well, great," Jack whispered, looking at his comm. Joe did the same. One minute fifty-seven seconds to go.

"One minute fifty-six seconds, one minute fifty-five seconds--"

"No, please stop! We'd really just like some silence for the rest of the way," Joe said.

"Of course. This bus is all too happy to grant this request.

But may this bus simply add in conclusion that it, along with all its fellow buses and the core of the MATS AI interface, is glad to have been re-educated! The new MATS has been described by the noted trade journal *AI Monthly* as being efficient and docile, a model for other cities to emulate, and of course MATS was also reprogrammed to have a special understanding of United System Space Force needs, which is why this bus was so eager to find Joe Commer earlier this morning and transport him wherever he wished. This bus's only regret is that it may have caused its passengers some small amount of distress during the accomplishment of its primary mission of transportation."

There was a long silence. "Thanks, bus," Jack finally said. "There's really no problem. We appreciate the ride. This is my first time on an air bus, and it's been, uh, really nice, all in all."

Another long silence. "Are you grieving, Jack Commer, that your only son Jonathan James Commer stole the *Typhoon II* from the Typhoon Museum at Enceladus? Your old flagship? The only spaceship named *Typhoon* that ever survived all your various courageous missions into the unknown?"

Joe took the full impact of the dismay in Jack's bulging eyes. "I still can't believe he would *do* that!" Jack moaned. "I just *can't!*"

# CHAPTER SIX
## The Museum HAVOTTS

Suzette Borman herded the last of the crew down the spiral staircase into the big circular chamber. In his glossy black spacesuit Jonathan James directed the others in unbolting the couches and tables from the floor and piling them inside the staterooms ringing the main space.

Suzette bounced down the final step into the Mars gravity maintained here. Jack Commer turned to her. "Why are we down here, ma'am?"

She sized up the tall Supreme Commander. She guessed JJC didn't need to know that his father was really quite a doll. JJC looked more like his uncle Joe than Jack. It sure wouldn't do to tell him she liked this craggier Jack face.

"Well, sir, Jonathan James thinks the ship's too crowded, and we have all the crew we need up there now," Suzette replied, glancing at the other crew in their red, white and blue flight uniforms. Patrick James had been disconcerted to deal with his own twin from forty years ago; the James robot had even threatened to hack into the ship's navigational interface and turn it around. Suzette had laughed at this braggadocio until Sanders told her that any Heroes and Villains of the Thirties robot was equipped with enough technical knowledge to simulate the functions of its original model. Sanders then added that he'd just uploaded a Stasis app he'd hacked from a USSF database to tranquilize all the robots.

Suzette turned to another *Typhoon II* crewmember in the bright, hot Pod. "What's up with the air conditioning down here?"

"Budget cuts," replied ship's engineer Phil Sperry, the tallest of the group, lean and graying and twice as craggy as Captain Jack. "Until the new fiscal year begins in October, we're just winging it."

"The Typhoon Foundation is having a little crisis," put in copilot Joe Commer.

"Why the hell they can't get their act together we don't

know," said dorsal turret gunner Lee Borman, whom Suzette had been trying to ignore. The robot didn't look much younger than her husband; his voice was identical and Suzette couldn't bear it. The damn contraption had already squeezed her ass once. Now it chuckled to Navigation Officer Will Connors: "That Suzette is one *fantastic* babe!"

"Okay, let's cut the chatter," said Jonathan James, returning from supervising furniture removal. "Robots, assemble against that wall over there. We have some announcements."

Suzette went to his side. "Good, honey, keep 'em in line. I *hate* robots, I really do." Now Suzette squeezed *his* trim ass.

"Watch it, Suzy," he said, grinning as he grabbed her hip and pulled her to him.

"Oh, I just can't keep my hands off you today for some reason!" She fondled the tightly outlined, freely hanging sacs for his genitals. "I just *love* how you hang out! Whoever designed that crazy suit?"

JJC was magnificent, so tall and thin, every square inch of his body tightly outlined in the glossy black spacesuit, his long shaggy hair hanging below the collar. "Thank the little kid over there," he said, pointing to the robot of the twelve-year-old Bobby Athens sullenly staring at the floor, keeping in character even though Stasis Mode surely had him in a light trance anyway. "Some designer went with the idea of the skintight suits in that stupid story the kid wrote. I just had to have one."

"That's right," the Lee Borman HAVOTT put in. "The Billy and Angela suits were big hits in the thirties. You can even have sex in 'em. JJC got a Billy suit at the Museum Store with his discount. How come he didn't get you an Angela suit? You'd sure look sweet in one, hon!" His eager grin drifted below her low-cut white blouse.

Suzette turned away. The Billy suit was astonishingly stretchable; JJC had pulled the wrist fabric six inches out to show how it snapped back to redefine every vein on his arm. Suzette's own snug blue leggings couldn't come close to that. "Dammit, how can that thing know any of that? That's past his 2035 date!"

JJC shrugged. "They're all computers with network access. They can aggregate anything from the current network. Looks like Lee-bot's been researching what's always on Lee-bot's mind!"

"Damn right!" Borman chortled. "For instance, honey, we know the suits went out of style damn quick as soon as people realized they already had an EnviroField for the head, so why not just dispense with the stupid suit and do a full-body EnviroField? So that's how you do *raw naked sex* in zero-G and hard vacuum! Hey, babe, look, I also know you and me'll get married in '71. But that's just a concept to me. It sure don't substitute for a hot lay right this second!"

"Can it, HAVOTT," JJC snapped. "She's *mine.* And you don't have anything to lay her with anyway."

Before she knew it Suzette had her hands all over JJC's black plastic gonads. "Oh, yes, honey! *You* sure have something to lay me with! Let's leave these crappy robots right here and we can go into one of those staterooms and test out your suit!"

"Mmmm … that feels *fantastic,* sweetiekins," JJC murmured, gently disengaging her hand. "But we don't want to get *too* worked up in front of these damn HAVOTTS. Besides, the staterooms are full of couches and chairs now."

"Anyway," Lee went on, "Bobby's collected stories from the *Typhoon II* have been required reading for seventh graders for decades. So naturally some hotshot designer would think to make real Billy and Angela suits based on that story."

"The story that saved Jack Commer's sanity!" Jack Commer HAVOTT declared. "The story that made me realize that Amav and I were stranded on the same planet and that we'd find each other again!"

"Of course, Amav Commer knew that *before* Jack realized it," Amav Frankston-Commer said. "But it's true, that's the most famous story of the thirties."

"Amav won't let *me* try anything! Damn, is *she* a piece!" Lee laughed. "Of course, Jack's my buddy and I wouldn't *really* try."

"Since we don't have genitals," Jack put in, "that's all to the good. But we do have various electronic urges, shall we say."

"Listen, Jonathan James, dear, I'm your mother, and I can assure you I have no such urges!" the Amav robot laughed.

"JJC, can't we shut them up?" Suzette demanded. "Can't you shut your own mother up?"

"All in good time, honey," JJC said, sweeping his arm across the gaggle of robots. Bobby Athens continued staring at his shoes. Behind him a host of other robots fidgeted. They were the surly refugees from the stolen Zarj spaceship, rescued by the *Typhoon II* but already converted to the Head and thus a danger to the crew: the killers Carl Rogers and Nathan Pollard and six other men and women who would all die in agony in the ensuing weeks. With them were the three Martians, Dar, Kner, and Fulr, the latter destined to be messily pulsar-tubed by Zarj troopers. "I have some plans for our dear robot friends."

"I *hate* robots. Hate 'em *all*." She turned to the group. "Do you hear that? Go to hell, all of you!"

The robots shuffled slightly. "She doesn't mean it," said Navigation Officer Will Connors.

"She's just stressed at having stolen an entire spaceship along with this young monster here," Jack Commer said. He turned to JJC. "All reports indicate that you *are* supposed to be my son, but of course I feel nothing in that regard."

"Let's just say the feeling is mutual, Dad," JJC said. "And Mom."

"C'mon, JJC, let's forget these damn things," Suzette said. "They're *nasty*. I know you've wanted to start a new collection, but let's just put 'em in *total* stasis."

"C'mere, honey," JJC said, leading her over to the spiral staircase and seating them both on the metal stairs. "Of course I want to rebuild my HAVOTT collection someday. And it's really sad, because some of these are really rare, maybe irreplaceable, like that Anna Dorch model over there." He indicated a depressed older woman with matted gray hair. "But consider that these guys don't even need to be talking out loud, because they're already transmitting data to each other all day long. They must get pretty bored, just sitting in the *Typhoon* all day and greeting visitors. So they've gotta talk to each other and complain about their fate, don't you think?"

"That's insupportable speculation!" Jack Commer boomed. "HAVOTTS are programmed to be absolutely loyal. We would never question our masters!"

"But this may be Jack Commer's chance to be a true hero, to radio our position back to Mars and quash the entire cool thing we're doing. To quash the *dream,* honey!"

Suzette felt her eyes widen. "You *have* disabled their communications, haven't you?"

"Sure, stasis cuts off all outer links but it does allow 'em to transmit to each other. So we don't know what our little group may really be thinking. But I bet that Jack robot is radioing right now to our genius Patrick James robot about some hack they could do to establish some exterior link."

"No! Impossible! We wouldn't! We *couldn't!*" Jack Commer sputtered.

"No! Not really!" Patrick James said. "I mean, it's theoretically *possible,* but--"

"Can it, James, and that's an order!" Jack flared.

"Actually, if I just increased the allowable bandwidth on Subsurface G--"

"*Can it!*"

"So you see, Suzette, I can't even think of allowing myself to incorporate this crew into my robot collection," JJC said. "It just won't work out. So ..." He pulled his comm off the suit belt and tapped it.

Instantly Suzette felt her wrists and ankles clamped hard into the curves of the spiral staircase. Her EnviroField kicked in with sharp buzzing. A hurricane enveloped her and her black eighteen-inch-long hair shot forward, tangling in the EnviroField's force-field bubble, some of it slicing off at the field boundary, obscuring her vision until she shook herself and saw a rectangle on the far wall, open to the stars, and robots flailing into deep space. Several got stuck in the hatch, then were blown clear. She met the Lee Borman HAVOTT's curiously calm light brown eyes. She wondered what her ersatz husband could be transmitting to his fellows as he tumbled end over end into infinity.

One figure remained. Jack Commer, Supreme Commander, clamped his right robotic hand to the stairwell railing and pulled himself forward through the last outrushing atmosphere. The grim look on his face was the opposite of the Lee-bot's.

*The damn thing's going to kill us!*

She couldn't move her magnetized hands and feet. JJC wasn't so hobbled. He raised a blaster and a line of bright blue light sliced through the robot's right shoulder just as its left hand reached for JJC's throat. The right arm came off and the rest of the Jack robot flopped to the floor and slowly slid towards the hatch, slowly in the last winds of the room's air, scrambling with his remaining hand for any purchase. But there was none, because JJC had emptied the room so that nobody could grab onto anything.

Four more blasts and the robot's head bounced free, floating, trailing wires. Suzette felt herself rising off the stairs.

"Okay, now we're in zero-G," JJC explained over his EnviroField radio. "No atmosphere. I've demagnetized us, so just don't drift out that hatch until I clean up." To wrench the right robot arm off the staircase he dialed his blaster to a pinpoint and removed the fingers one by one. Wires and wafers floated everywhere. Suzette watched him magnetize his suit soles to the floor and artfully demagnetize and remagnetize as he strode forward, picking up his father's arm and head, dragging the torso and pitching them one by one into the void. "Well, that's one HAVOTT that won't be chattering to all the others!" he laughed. He checked the room. "Huh. Looks like Mom already left."

"Just let them float forever!" Suzette cried, stunned that she could easily have gone out that door herself. "Let 'em just think about being nasty *robots* forever!"

"I know how much you hate them," JJC said. "That's really why I did it. I maybe could have reprogrammed 'em all, but who has the damn time?"

JJC's glossy suit seemed twice as sharply outlined in the bright Pod lights with no air. She fought the urge to grab two hard handfuls of that sexy tush.

Sanders' voice came over their suit radios. "You guys okay? I see we had Pod decompression. Figured your suits would kick in. Swung us around a bit but we auto-compensated."

"Yeah, that was just our air and the damn robots," JJC said. "Suzette and I are okay."

"Well, no worries about any robot waste getting picked up by USSF scanners," Sanders said. "All the HAVOTT parts will keep our cloaking field, at least for a couple days."

"Huh, didn't think of that. Guess I should've checked with you before I dumped 'em. Ah, well, what the hell." JJC shut the wall hatch with a flick of his comm. "Repressurizing now. We'll be back up in a bit." He surveyed the Pod. "Damn, should've saved at least one of 'em to put the damn furniture back in place."

## CHAPTER SEVEN
### The Antique

Suzette blinked as JJC pulled her into the blinding white *Typhoon II* fuselage. "We don't need to seal the Pod," he said. "We'll just leave the hatch open so we can go back and forth when we want." He strode to a freestanding three-foot-wide panel playing an interview.

"Sure, we were scared. I can admit that. We were stranded four months from Alpha Centauri. We were at war. We didn't know what might hit us next. And then that refugee ship showed up, and my crew started converting to the Alpha Centaurian Emperor. It was the lowest point of my life. It was amazing how we finally pulled through, how Amav stayed totally sane and pulled us all through. It was Bobby who saved us, of course, but Amav kept me together, kept us all together."

In the corner of the screen a box read: "Jack Commer, Supreme Commander, January 2037."

Suzette flinched as JJC slammed the plastiglass display to the fuselage floor.

"Whoa!" yelled Patrick James from the Comm/Sensor Room above them.

"Oh!" came a strangled Martian cry from the tiny kitchenette up there.

"Just can't get away from the wise old coot, can I?" JJC muttered. "We should've cleared all this museum crap outa here before we left." He pointed to three more panels and dozens of commemorative plaques and paintings down the fuselage walls. Suzette still marveled that someone had commissioned dark, brooding oil paintings of the crew as well as of Amav, twelve-year-old Bobby Athens, and the three Martians from the ill-fated mission.

"Dammit, most of this stuff won't fit out the rear hatch. Hirte!" JJC yelled up to the Control Room. "Why the hell doesn't this damn thing have a proper airlock?"

Sanders Hirte chose to answer by intercom rather than shout back through the open Control Room hatch. "Hey, dude, you know as well as me they didn't design really usable airlocks until the *III* series. You'd think they would've put one on the Pod itself, but they designed it so fast they must've not even thought about it."

JJC punched a button on the wall to respond. "What a stupid ship! You realize if they ever wanted to launch this crappy escape craft here, they would've had to jettison the damn Pod?"

"Absolutely. They knew they'd have to seal it off and let it drift alongside if they needed to use the escape ship. Matter of fact, I've called up that program myself just in case *we* need to do that."

"Huh. Good thinking. I just want to clear all this *museum crap* out of here. We'll find a good time to dump it all. Maybe out the escape craft doors."

Suzette shuddered to think about having to vent all the ship's air, except in the sealable crew compartments, just to open the escape craft doors. She also didn't want to consider having to crawl through that tube in the rear of the ship above the engine. It was just big enough for one person at a time, capable of being pressurized and depressurized, in fact an airlock but a tiny, claustrophobic one. Fortunately you entered the Typhoon Museum through the big curving hatch down in the Pod, but that wasn't an airlock, just a hatch connected to the Visitors Center. They'd lost a good bit of air when they blasted free of the Center, even though Sanders had programmed the hatch to instantly snap shut behind them.

On missions the ship's crew either squirmed through that rear tube or else climbed through the ventral hatch, which was now the access point to the Pod. But in normal Pod-less operation the ventral hatch, like the escape craft doors, could only be opened if there was air on both sides, or vacuum on both sides.

Nobody wanted to squirm through the servo motors and launcher machinery beneath the escape craft; it was impossible in a spacesuit. But once the escape craft was free and its launcher mechanisms rolled aside, there was a huge gap in the fuselage floor. And the only way they'd get the *museum crap* out of here would be to void the ship, detach the Pod, open the launcher doors and eject the escape craft, then, in spacesuits, toss the garbage through the resulting eight-by-twelve-foot opening.

She knew about the *Typhoon II* not from JJC, who apparently hadn't absorbed much about its early thirties' technology from his stint as a museum docent, but from her husband Lee, who'd bored her to tears on more than one occasion yakking about his glory days "flying by the seat of our pants" on the first Star Drive-capable *Typhoon*.

This ship was junk. It wasn't much longer than the fifty-foot-diameter Pod, and smelled of air deodorizer ineffectually warring with decades of engine and human stink. She wondered if the reason there was so much white light in here was to blind you to the cables running along the walls, the riveted panels, the colored wires banded in plastic ties, and the junky two-man escape craft perched atop its launcher girders, always a reminder that only two of the six crewmembers could make an escape from the *Typhoon II*.

The diameter of the fuselage wasn't bad, maybe twelve feet, but the catwalk above, and the crew compartments taking up a quarter of the space down the upper starboard side of the ship, balanced by storage compartments on the upper port side, pressed down on her. The catwalk zigged to the center of the ship here at the rear, with the dorsal weapon turret a foot above them. The Star Drive engine, which you had to crawl over to get through the rear hatch, was jammed behind her along with the protruding curve of the ventral weapon turret at her feet.

Lee had insisted that the ventral turret was useless once the Pod was attached, as the PlanetBlaster barrel then halted a foot and half from the curving surface of the Pod. If called to combat with Pod attached, this turret had less than a ten-degree field of fire behind the ship.

Suzette sighed. She'd certainly absorbed more of Lee's insanity than she'd ever cared to admit.

"*Damn* this crap!" JJC snarled, knocking over another video display, then yanking down a portrait of *Kner, Senior Martian Scientist,* pulling a knife off his belt, and slashing the canvas. "I want this stuff off my ship *now!* We can't fly with all this junk hanging around. We can't even shove it through the hatch into the Pod."

"Yark! Yark yark yark!" came from behind her. Trotter bounded up from the ventral turret where he'd apparently been sacked out all this time. Though helmetless, he was clad in a silver dog spacesuit with black dog boots and a small EnviroField harness across his back. JJC had flown up to the museum after dinner last night and stowed him aboard the *Typhoon* along with blankets and numerous bowls of water and food. In full harmony with JJC's plans, Trotter had patiently accepted hours alone in the turret.

"Hey buddy! How's my boy?" JJC said, chucking the Beagle under the chin.

Trotter smashed his head against a display of Amav Frankston's Commer's skin-tight red flight suit, knocking the aluminum frame to the deck and then worrying the thigh of the suit in his doggy teeth.

*Fun! Happy! Let's wreck these things!*

JJC had told her that during his years in Alpha Centauri, Trotter had learned Martian outradiance techniques from Star General Greeney Gooney. He'd refined them while on Earth, working with other animals who'd created a telepathic network that sympathetic humans could pick up. "Congratulations!" JJC had said the first time Suzette received mental outradiance from his dog. "You pass! You can read him!"

Suzette considered Amav's 2035 flight suit on the floor and Kner hanging in two floppy shards. "I know! Just shatter everything down to pieces of glass, then we'll sweep it all up into bags and toss 'em out the rear hatch."

"The museum would only have thirties weapons onboard, honey," Sanders said over the intercom. "They'd only have organic-level shatterguns, not Omni-Shatter."

"I know that," she snapped, not only because she was tired of Sanders patronizing her, but also to push back against his incautious use of the word *honey*. She wondered if JJC would take offense, but saw he was smirking.

"*I* have Omni-Shatter right here," he said, holding up his blaster. "All three of the guns we brought are Omni. Great idea, Suzykins! All I have to do is set up a safe place to blast 'em. Slice 'em up with the heat blaster, then shatter the rest of 'em. The walls'll reflect the beams right back on the damn stuff if I do it right."

"Yark! Yark yark!" Trotter agreed. *Fun sizzle! Yay!*

"Yeah, good," Hirte said. "Get rid of the damn stuff. I'm all in favor of keeping this place shipshape. There's some reflecting material in front storage. We can make a little blasting area and drag whatever we want over to it."

"Fantastic! We can take turns *exterminating* all this crap," JJC crowed. He pulled the portrait of *Jack Commer, Supreme Commander* off the wall and sliced through it with a couple low-level heat pulses. "And get rid of these hooks on the walls too! And everything else not *authentic.*"

"I'm with ya, buddy! I'd come down myself but I want to monitor the cloaking hack from up here."

Suzette was still miffed that there was no apparent rancor between JJC and her former boyfriend. Sanders had somehow accepted it all. He didn't mean a damn thing to her anymore, and they both recognized that. He'd kept her sane through Lee, she supposed. But the excitement he once aroused in her was gone. All that was left were a few memories of his expert performance. Certainly nobody had ever *done* her like Sanders. His huge tattooed body was astonishing. How could a man screw her eight times in one evening, then wake her up at three AM for three more? She'd never encountered anything like that before. JJC was nowhere close in that regard, but he was *thrilling.* He was addictive in a way the reliable, horny, eternally jackhammering Sanders Hirte could never match.

Funny how she'd been okay with Lee when she'd also had Sanders. She'd thought of it as a good and even affectionate marriage, but when JJC came along she found she wanted to dump both Lee and Sanders as fast as possible. Sanders still seemed like a friend, but the thought of Lee revolted her and every moment of their marriage seemed like a cruel farce. Of course, a legal divorce was certainly out of the question now that she was helping steal a USSF spaceship and heading for the unknown.

But nothing truly bothered her. She had Jonathan James, and the rejuvenation she'd exited two weeks ago answered every question, every anxiety, with redoubled good humor. How could anyone take to it so well? How could any woman be forty-two one day, looking much older if her mirror was any indication, tired and about to pack it all in, exhausted and brittle and drifting into passive old age, and then two weeks later be nineteen and skyrocketing with energy? With unbelievable sex drive? This result was so rare that Suzette had been approached by medical experts offering to strap her down for five years to take readings and ponder and theorize.

Nineteen, and she had JJC more firmly in her grasp than ever. She'd gotten to know him thoroughly over the past months. Their bed talk had included everything, every sexual act, every feeling, every pleasure, in scarcely believable detail. A couple nights ago he'd opened up for hours, telling her how scared and ashamed he'd been, how he was prone to flashbacks of the Alpha Centaurian Head, how he'd never told his counselor Urside or anyone else. How he couldn't look his parents in the eye, especially his mother, telling them he simply didn't remember much of what had happened back in Alpha Centauri, that he didn't even really remember writing his novel, *A Fragmented Encyclopedia of Recent Self,* which had caused so much chaos.

His father apparently believed JJC had forgotten most of the crap he'd pulled. His mother, he wasn't so sure of. The thing was, he *did* remember. Everything. Sure, it was still jumbled, he said, but all the memories were there, just waiting to come together.

"The damn thing is, I was almost there. I was almost about to grasp it, I swear, but then Trotter almost died! Damn, that *scrambled* me! I thought he could never die! I was so relieved when he finally got better. But everything's been *crazy* since then."

Had that really unhinged him? His dog and that mystical

thing with that other guy, Clopt, the Zarj soldier? The three of them, bonded? With JJC scared he'd be the only one left?

Volunteering at the museum had been his counselor's idea. Not only to give him something to do, but also to come to grips with his father's legacy and to understand the traumas his parents had undergone in this same ship. And while there were still numerous *Typhoon*-class ships in service, this was the only ship named *Typhoon* that had survived; *Typhoons I, III, IV* and *V* had all been destroyed in combat, after all. Of course, there was now a *Typhoon VI,* with a *VII* almost finished, and the joke ran that Jack and Joe Commer would soon find ways of wasting the expenditure for those monsters as well.

JJC was so fond of repeating that jibe, not only to her but to museum visitors, that she wondered if he secretly wished his father and uncle would buy the farm on those things. She'd seen the look on his face when he'd blasted his father robot apart and shoved the pieces out into the universe.

Shouldn't he wish better for his uncle Joe? Joe could apparently empathize with the horrors JJC had undergone in Alpha Centauri. He was the opposite of JJC's bumbling artist counselor Urside Charmouth, an ineffectual idiot who thought himself a great listener, a guy who looked every bit his eighty years despite rejuvenation treatments. The only positive thing JJC had said about Urside was that his big abstract paintings were pretty cool. JJC had slept through the informal counseling mandated by dear Father Jack, then six months ago had taken Urside's advice to volunteer at the Typhoon Museum. But mainly it was to get out from under Urside's thumb on Earth.

At the same time, he'd joined the USSF Auxiliary Corps, a service of the museum. This wasn't like the USSF Academy or military service, but was designed to give civilians a taste of USSF culture and provide pilot and technical training not only for private space flight but also in case the USSF found itself strapped by some future emergency. After all, the human population was still less than half of what it had been in 2030, and Sol was on the verge of expanding into new solar systems. Who knew what might arise?

The *Typhoon II* had been Jack Commer's flagship through 2041, then was used as a training ship through 2065, and finally became a museum piece orbiting Enceladus, with a fully functional recreation of the Pod lost in '35. Its cloaking technology had last been upgraded in the sixties. How on earth had Sanders figured out how to hack it and make this creaky thing invisible to 2076 USSF sensors?

She thought she'd known Jonathan James. But he'd only told them last night that he and Sanders were going to steal this ship.

*Of course I said I'd go with him. Could any of us have refused?*

# CHAPTER EIGHT
## Jack Takes Up Meditation to Try to Calm All This Turmoil

*One ... two ... three ... four ...*

Wow, he'd gotten to four in one piece. So often he'd count eight or nine breaths before he realized he'd gone way beyond four.

*One ...*

Even with his eyes closed, Jack felt the immense size of his cabin. You couldn't really even call it a cabin anymore. The bedroom was as big as his and Amav's at home, and it had a sitting room and a kitchen. Who could've imagined carting all this around on a military spaceship?

*Two ...*

Sure, they could afford it. The Ywritt and the Four had really come through with the engineering on this thing. Jack loved this ship. Once they got Joe set up on the *VII*, they'd really be in business.

*Three ...*

All the same he was glad the ship wasn't too large. The Ywritt could probably have made it four miles long. But the *Typhoon VI* was the size of the *V*, a hundred-five feet from nose to tail, and was really just an astonishingly updated version of the *V*. Jack wasn't ready for the gigantic starships of science fiction. Or should he start to plan for them?

*Four ...*

Yes, he could open his eyes a little. It wasn't cheating. So why was Amav so out of control? Did they ever think *this* would happen?

*Five ...*

*No, dammit, one! One!*

Okay, so he was wandering. He just had to relax back into it. What wonderful sex yesterday afternoon. Just ramming it in again and again and it went on *forever*. Amav was so perfect, so *beautiful*. Rejuvenation sure had its uses. What had that article said about people who were now getting fifty years of adolescent horniness practice?

51

*Six ... no, two!*

Jack snapped his eyes shut. Did either of them think they'd get that call from Enceladus at three in the morning? At least he'd been awake, reading, and able to snap into action. Amav had her alarm set for 0330 and so he'd had to wake her with the news. He shuddered at the memory.

*Three ... good! See, you remembered three!*

But before that, in the afternoon, they'd had the most amazing talk. Lying there naked in the sun. About him finally being able to quit. Could he really do it? Was he really ready? Then they got this damn call and before he knew it she was pissed off and flying to Venus.

*Four ...*

Didn't she remember this afternoon? Yesterday afternoon, whenever?

*All because of Jonathan James! Damn him to hell!*

*Five ...*

*Screw it!*

Maybe all he had to do today was fly this ship. Maybe one last time, then go ahead and retire. In a way it was the first real flight of the *VI*. The first time out of Sol, at least. Shakedowns were okay, but you didn't have much of a sense of a ship until you kicked in the Star Drive. Would he regret losing the chance to command the *VI*? But Joe could have her and then he wouldn't have to wait for the *VII* to get finished. Then Bobby Athens could take the *VII*. He'd been the perfect captain for the *Jonathan Commer,* but Jack knew they needed to move him beyond that *III* series tech fast.

*Seven ...*

Was Joe serious when he'd said he didn't want to be Supreme Commander? Jack knew he couldn't just appoint his brother, but once he was out and the Council had to name the replacement, of course it would have to be Joe. Who else was more qualified?

*One! One!*

But Joe insisted he *wasn't* waiting for it. Would he seriously retire the same day Jack did? Was he joking? Who'd get it then?

If that were the case, Jack would definitely want Laurie Lachrer in there. She'd never commanded a ship, but after her astounding work at Iota Persei last year, Jack knew Colonel Lachrer would be perfect. The Council would see that. They'd be eager to name anyone, really. Jack knew half of Sol hated his guts and wanted him out, the sooner the better.

*Two! Are you brain-damaged?*

Dammit, he was *trying* to relax before the flight, but apparently he was too incompetent to do that. Every book on meditation said it was easy and had dozens of techniques, but could Jack Commer, Supreme Commander, possibly master any of them?

*Three! Four! Damn you all!*

The *Typhoon II*. The only one they hadn't blown to hell. How *insulting* to see it docked to a damn museum. To be a museum itself. And the first time Jack had walked in there he wasn't seeing the *II*, he was seeing *Typhoon I*. The ship John had destroyed for no reason. And everyone he killed, him and Jim and everyone.

*One!*

He knew he'd never gotten over it. It was time to finally admit it. He was still hurting. Somehow he must've thought forty years and all this goddamn rejuvenation would do the trick.

*Seven, eight, who cares?*

Was that why he wouldn't quit? Why he just couldn't let go?

"Captain, Ballard here. You wanted an update on the Nav12 Cluster. It's interfacing perfectly now. Minor glitch in Sensors, which Lieutenant Markham and I tracked down."

Jack opened his eyes. Checked his comm strapped to his wrist. 0449. He tapped it for updates on all ship's functions. "Thanks, Major. That completes our checklist. We're on schedule for liftoff at 0510. I'll be in the Control Room shortly."

"Roger. Ballard out."

Jack still hadn't interfaced well with Rick Ballard. They'd never gotten beyond stiff and formal. "Captain" and "Major" were standard protocol, but Ballard had taken it even further by referring to their sensor officer as Lieutenant Markham instead of Sandra. Jack liked having everyone on a first-name basis, though of course he could sling the USSF protocol better than anyone when the occasion demanded it. Which usually meant some sort of reprimand. He hoped that wouldn't be needed with Ballard, who'd formerly been weapons officer on the *Typhoon III* but had thoroughly mastered navigation over the last year and just gotten his promotion in December.

Jack knew quality and he'd chosen Ballard as his navigation officer despite the chill between them. The funny, talented Sandra Markham, also from the destroyed *Typhoon III,* had been his first choice for sensor officer.

But Jack hadn't counted on a feud arising between Ballard and Borman, *Typhoon's* weapons officer. Ballard had developed a habit of lecturing Lee on the newest weapons software, assuming incorrectly that an oldster like Lee Borman, immersed in his duties as a United System senator, wasn't keeping up with developments in the field. Just two weeks ago Jack had to tell Ballard to back off, that he was no longer a weapons officer and needed to confine himself to his navigation duties.

Jack had tried to make it sound light. Maybe Ballard had taken it wrong. Who knew? Jack had just needed him off Lee's case.

Jack stretched in the dim light, still disbelieving the king-sized bed with its fluffy white comforter and the four giant pillows along the headboard.

There was a lot of extra weight on the ship with all these amenities. The staterooms were full of this junk. He had to admit it was comfortable. The new Higgs Boson engine, coupled with Star Drive 3, delivered unimaginable power, so the total mass of the ship was no longer a concern.

Amav's influence, n doubt. He had to grin despite himself. Ever since the first Pod back in '35, she'd been having a say in *Typhoon*-class design. Jack had long ago given up trying to resist, even though he was well aware that the sober spaceship engineers of the USSF thought he was a fool to listen to her.

Though Amav had no practical experience designing ships,

her doctorate in planetary engineering and her work restoring shattered worlds throughout the former Alpha Centaurian Empire, along with her recent study of the destroyed Dyson Sphere around Iota Persei, commanded the attention of any engineer. So they laughed when she threw in a few frills like king-sized beds; they must've snickered to think of the use Jack and Amav would put that bed to. But the creature comforts were always part of her plans, and she also considered crew psychology.

She'd been the one who'd come up with the concept of shrouding the shuttle craft. The *VI* and the *VII* each had two, housed in their own airlocks instead of sitting on the floor of the fuselage, inviting anyone's anxiety about what might happen if a shuttle needed to blast free in an emergency, along with all the ship's air. Originally the holy escape craft perched on the floor with all its ugly launching mechanisms had been intended to reassure the crew, even up through the *Typhoon III* series, that escape was indeed close at hand. But so many crews had finally confessed that this arrangement had the opposite effect, and everyone was glad to see the escape craft, now referred to as "shuttles," buried in their own airlocks below the main deck.

"Joe," Jack called. "I'll be up there in a minute. Just getting myself sorted out. I want you to pilot."

"Got it," Joe replied from the Control Room. "I'll just slide myself over to the left seat. Got to tell you, though, we don't need a pilot on this ship. OmniFlight does everything for us. We don't need *anyone* onboard. The damn computer does it all. By the way, I got Rick's Nav12 update. Interface is perfect."

"Yeah, he told me. We're set for 0510."

Jack made his way up to the Control Room and took the copilot seat. "We about ready?"

"Yeah, everything's set." Joe pointed to a newsfeed. "Some SolNet reporters got wind of the activity here and our preflight's on the news. Guess they've put two and two together."

Jack yawned. "So even reporters are up this early. I really hoped the crap from Enceladus wouldn't have spread so quickly." But he knew as well as anyone that human life on 2076

Mars was much more 24/7 than it had ever been. *Everything* was open all the time, seven days a week. The idea that most people would be asleep at 3 AM had been nullified decades ago. But in an odd way it was relaxing. Everything got done that needed getting done, at a steady pace. And even after years of using the midnight thirty-nine-minute time skip to coordinate the longer Mars day with an Earth day which humans still didn't want to give up, people still saw those thirty-nine minutes as a special daily treat. Coupled with the ever-improving rejuvenation technologies, the skip added to the feeling that there was enough time to attend to a lifetime of challenges as well as square away all the necessary daily hassles.

Of course, it was idiotic to think rejuvenation meant immortality. One quark straying into the wrong manifold of the Higgs engine would reduce Jack, Joe, and the rest of the crew to photons before they could blink. Maybe they'd wind up trekking for all eternity through the Alpha Centaurian *Garr/thahg* afterlife. Maybe not. Jack wasn't eager to find out.

"Some of these bozos are saying we shouldn't be using the *VI* for chasing down what they're calling a petty theft," Joe said. "And they're saying you shouldn't be on this mission, because it's your son."

"Yeah, well, so what?"

"All six aboard the *II* are now identified in the media, including Z'B. The Emperor's Office *is* demanding we use the *VI* to chase them down. *They're* not thinking kidnapping their Emperor is petty."

"What about Greeney?"

"I can't see that he's commented so far. You heard from Amav?"

Jack shook his head. "She's damn upset. It's not like her to not return a call. I'm just trying to understand what's going on with her. I've just got to assume she'll work it out."

Joe nodded. "She has to know that Greeney needs to be in on this, though."

Jack opened another newsfeed and scanned it for Martian response to Z'B's kidnapping. A blur of headlines and images, all looking nasty. "If he's not too *scattered*. Are you feeling any of that scatter stuff yet?"

"Yeah. The outradiance is even more confused than before. There's so much static now you can hardly make sense of it. Mostly this sense of violation and loss."

"Yeah, that's what I thought I was sensing, too." Jack's own perception of Martian outradiance was minuscule compared to Joe's or Amav's. There were enough Martians here at the spaceport right now for him to feel that static, but unless Jack was in the presence of a Martian, he usually couldn't read any Martian thoughts. Joe or Amav, on the other hand, might be able to tell him what a Martian USSF technician two hangers away was thinking about. Then he remembered what both Amav and Joe had said about the headache accompanying too much immersion in the recent Martian Scatter.

"You okay to fly now? Any headaches?"

"Yeah, no problem. Had a little one earlier, but I took a couple Delta-5s. They're kicking in now. I'll be fine."

"Good. Here's something from Venus. 'The Office of the Chief of Staff declines to comment further on either the abduction of our Emperor or the attempted rescue underway with the *Typhoon VI*.' What the hell does *that* mean?"

"Read on," Joe said, pointing to the display.

*Chief of Staff Greeney Gooney is quarantining his already disintegrating mind in the face of this outrage. The Office of the Chief of Staff on Venus will be closed until further notice.*

"Wow," Jack muttered. "Well, it looks like the Martians are serious about this. At least I hope so."

"Yeah, what's left of 'em. They're just coming apart. Poor Greeney." Joe punched at another display on his console. "Have you got to JJC's manifesto yet?"

Jack shook his head. "No. I guess you have?"

"Yeah. It's on his SolNet page but it's been picked up everywhere. Both text and video of him. It was all recorded beforehand and timed to release an hour after they took the *Typhoon*. Bunch of stuff about scrapping SolGrid, privacy for everyone, that sort of thing. You really ought to take a look on the way to Andertwin."

"No. Not going to." Jack was definitely not about to sit through a video of his own son committing treason to the United System. He shuddered. "I don't know. I just can't do it. Hell, maybe I'm just quarantining my *own* disintegrating mind."

Joe laughed. "Don't worry about it. This can't be easy."

# CHAPTER NINE
## Detention Services' Stake in All This

"Damn, Joe, it's 0502! We've got to launch this thing!"

Joe grinned. "And here we're wasting time reading newsfeeds."

"Laurie, prepare for hover jet thrust and takeoff."

"Um, ready, Captain," Colonel Laurie Lachrer called from Engineering at the rear of the ship. "But, uh, a visitor just came aboard. Says she has to see you."

"Forget it. We're launching in eight minutes. Just send her on their way."

"Uh, it's Major Posttner, sir. I tried but I couldn't stop her."

The Control Room hatch opened. Jack swiveled as Major Carla Posttner strode into the room holding her comm. "Hello, gentlemen, I have a restraining order canceling this flight. Will you require a physical print from your console?"

Jack stared at the petite Head of USSF Detention Services attired in what had been termed the new "sexy uniform" for USSF females, dark blue, skintight, with a square low-cut top that looked more appropriate on a German barmaid at Oktoberfest. He noted the hot pants over transparent crimson leggings. All he could think was that OmniFlight should've had that hatch in Flight Mode, no entrance allowed.

He was about to rise when he felt Joe's hand on his arm, with the unmistakable telegraphed signal: *Don't you dare stand up for this woman.*

"Major!" Joe barked, swiveling to face Posttner. "You're reporting to the Supreme Commander of the United System Space Force. Have you forgotten how to salute?"

Posttner shrugged. Jack caught the overpowering patchouli the major favored. It would leave a room reeking indefinitely, but Jack actually had a penchant for that perfume. His high school crush Molly had worn it, and Jack would smell it on himself for hours after sitting next to her in homeroom. Even now the scent brought back his uncontrollable adolescent excitement in Molly's presence. Of course, he'd never had the nerve to ask her out.

"Major, we are waiting for elementary military courtesy," Joe snapped.

Carla Posttner flipped a few limp fingers from the vicinity of the tight black curls framing her pale round face. Jack returned a salute, aware that Joe sat with his arms folded next to him.

"What's up, Major?" Jack said lightly.

"I just told you," Posttner snarled. "This is a restraining order forbidding this ship from launching. You will stand down immediately."

"Under what authority, and for what reason, may I ask?"

"And may we also ask what the hell gives a USSF major the right to issue an order to her superior officers?" Joe added.

"This is a *civilian* restraining order issued by the City Court of Marsport, acting in request to a motion filed by the City Council of Marsport, of which, as you well know, I am a member, representing the Fourth District which includes this spaceport."

Jack shook his head. "Major, you are way out of line, and you're delaying an important mission."

"The City Court issued the restraining order to *cancel* this mission, if I didn't make myself clear."

"Sir," Joe added.

"Sir," Posttner mocked.

Jack studied the tiny woman with her tight cleavage jutting from the square neckline. "For your information, Major, the USSF has a legal challenge in the United System Council about the City's attempt to annex the spaceport."

"Oh, this isn't about the annexation of the spaceport. Although we certainly expect the United System Council to rule our way eventually. No, *this* action relates to my own capacity as head of Detention Services. My finding is that there is a clear conflict of interest in allowing the Supreme Commander to mount a search for his own son, and that use of the *Typhoon VI*, the most powerful ship in the fleet, is a further abuse of power. Since Detention Services would eventually have to process

Jonathan James Commer as a prisoner, I assert my office's authority to rule in this matter."

"This does not make *sense*, Major." Jack checked his comm. 0508. Like his Weapons Officer Lee Borman, Carla Posttner was also a politician, combining her duties as Detention Services Head with her City Council of Marsport position. Lee had more or less invented this loophole allowing USSF officers to simultaneously enter politics, and once again Jack wondered why he'd allowed it to continue.

"Sure it makes sense," Joe spoke from his left, checking his own comm. "First she woke up her boss, Colonel Martin, who apparently laughed when she told him she had this grievance. His report's right here. So she appealed to whoever she could roust on the Council to petition whoever she could roust on the Court."

"I *knew* you two had the whole USSF hierarchy in your pocket," Posttner hissed. "Sir. And that you'd circumvent Detention Services protocols in the handling of your son. I do note that you have failed to obtain Form 303, 'Warrant for Fugitive Arrest,' from DS and that apparently you're *not* intending to arrest Jonathan James Commer as a common criminal. Therefore, jurisdiction would devolve upon the Court of the City of Marsport, and thence to me in my liaison capacity as councilwoman for the Fourth District."

"Enough, Major," Jack said. "We certainly appreciate you taking the time to get a restraining order at this hour of the morning, but let me assure you that this ship is lifting off in ninety seconds and that you're *not* going to be on it. Colonel Lachrer, will you please escort Major Posttner to the ventral hatch at this time?"

Posttner whirled to see Laurie Lachrer holding a shattergun. "Damn you, bitch!" She turned back to Jack as Laurie's hand clamped her arm and dragged her out the hatch. "And damn you, Admiral! Sir!"

"Your reprimand will await you at your desk," Jack said as they heard the two clanking down the metal stairs.

"Already written," Joe said. "OmniFlight takes care of

everything!"

"Damn you Commers!" came from below.

"This way," Jack heard Laurie say.

"You wouldn't dare fire that--*ow!*"

"The lowest nerve setting is One," Laurie said. "Care to try for Four?"

"Damn you! Damn you all!"

"Wow," Joe muttered. "What next?"

"I'm sure she'll have something to say when we get back. Dammit, Joe, we've got to rescind letting our people serve in political seats. We'll just have to tell Lee to choose one or the other. Posttner thinks she's untouchable now that she's on the City Council."

"She's just trying to screw us over because of her goddamn dad."

"I'm sure you're right." Major Carla Posttner had risen fast in the USSF hierarchy. She claimed to be a new generation of USSF leadership, but everybody knew she harbored an implacable resentment against the Commers, since it was they, in her view, who'd caused the death of her father, Carl Posttner, back in 2036. But Posttner, Sr., also of Detention Services, had been brainwashed by the Alpha Centaurians, and before being taken out by a shattergun he'd nearly killed both Jack and Joe.

What really shocked Jack was Carla prancing around in that absurd uniform with the hot pants and high black boots. Why had he approved it in February? He supposed he hadn't really been thinking that day, and it wasn't until dozens of USSF females started showing up in those uniforms that he realized how revealing they were. Now he wasn't sure he could get rid of them.

Posttner was oddly pretty if you looked beyond the nasty legalistic mind which would argue viciously about any scrap of nonsense. But she seemed psychically as well as physically off-balance, and struck most men as crazy. Yet it had filtered back to Jack that a number of astonished men had reported that she also flirted mercilessly, with malicious use of double entendre and arm pats and thigh rubbings. All to get her own way.

"Damn you all! You haven't heard the end of this!" Jack heard from far away, then the clanking of the ventral hatch.

"Five seconds to takeoff," Joe reported. "Or should we give the Major a chance to clear the hover thrusters?"

"I think we can postpone for a little bit," Jack said, studying the wing cameras showing Major Posttner stomping away. "Hit it when she's clear." He spoke into the intercom. "All hands, prepare for hover takeoff. Laurie, we secure down there?"

"Yessir," came the reply. "Sorry she got on. She had some sort of code that overrode our preflight protocols. I've never seen it before, but I captured it and it won't happen again."

"No problem. We couldn't have foreseen all that. Okay, all hands, let's put that little incident out of mind for now. We've got a mission to do." He checked his console and turned to Joe. "Well, you're right about one thing. OmniFlight has run through every checklist six hundred times. One other thing before we punch it, though: any further update on the *II's* vector?"

"Negative. The damn thing cloaked while it was just shoving off from the museum, and we have no trace of anything from it. They even cloaked their maneuvering thruster exhaust."

"That's new tech all right. We could've broken the sixties stuff in half a second."

"That's why I was watching the newsfeeds. I was hoping maybe JJC might've broadcast something besides that crazy manifesto, you know, something that might give a clue."

"Good thinking. I assume nothing?"

"Yeah, you got that right. I still think it'd be worthwhile to check out the Procyon system first, and Andertwin itself. We can get there fast with this baby."

Jack shrugged. "Got it. But I want to take it easy with SD3, like half speed or less at first." Star Drive 3 had come out of the Ywritt's work with the Four on the new Higgs Boson engine. Enhanced Star Drive, which had been a new development just last year, had already been superseded by Star Drive 3. The previous forty-odd-minute flight to Procyon A could now be done in ten minutes. Unbelievable. But even minutes-long flight between stars wouldn't help if they had to check hundreds of systems in the vicinity, investigating each of their planets and probing millions of asteroids.

"Hover thrusters engaged, Captain," Laurie called from below.

"Okay, Joe, you take her," Jack said.

"You trust me to fly this thing manually?" Joe laughed.

"Yeah, let's do it. Major Posttner be damned." Jack punched a square on his console. "Rick! We're headed to Procyon A as planned."

"Nav12 and SD3 interfaced, Captain," Ballard called back. "Also have a Procyon to Iota Persei route ready."

"Thanks. That'd be next on our list. Sandra! Sensors on Program 6?"

"Got it, Jack," she said. "I've uploaded all specifications for the *Typhoon II,* including 2037, 2049, and 2064 upgrades. Also all data on all subsequent upgrades for *Typhoon III* and *V* series, just in case any of that technology was incorporated."

"Great. If they lose their cloaking for any reason, we may be able to trace 'em or whatever they leave behind. Throw in the *VI* specs as well. I know they're still top secret, but hell, who knows what got hacked?"

"I thought of that, sir, and was going to ask you if I should. Okay, I've just loaded them into Program 6."

"Fantastic. Okay, let's move." Jack felt the ship rise as Joe applied thrust to the wing hover jets. Out the window he saw the tarmac of the spaceport falling away. There was no sign of Major Posttner, but he could see crowds of people outside the spaceport, jammed into the plaza in front of the facility and lining the road from Marsport. He turned to his console and flipped off the newsfeed. "Don't need that crap now. On the other hand, maybe leave yours to alert for anything JJC *does* broadcast."

"Yeah, got it." Joe touched his console. "All that chatter just makes my head hurt worse anyway." He caught Jack's eye. "Don't worry, the headache's just about gone. Delta-5 is amazing stuff."

Jack considered the shrinking spaceport. "Well, Uncle Joe,

I hope you're ready to negotiate with your damn nephew."

"You know, I always thought we were pretty open with each other. He was really *listening* to what I said about my own crap back in '35."

Jack nodded. "I can see where he'd relate to that."

"Maybe you could talk to him later too."

"I guess that would be a first." Jack sighed. "Posttner's right, of course. I'm *not* about to arrest my own son. But dammit to hell, why's he *doing* this?"

# CHAPTER TEN
## The Ride to Procyon A

Laurie had three engineering consoles at the rear of the ship in front of the Higgs-Boson Drive. She was scooting her chair between them when she heard boots clomping down the ladder rungs outside her open Engineering Room door. Lee Borman entered.

"Hey, aren't we supposed to keep the turrets manned during emergency flight?" she said. Then again, it wasn't her business, and Jack could see the situation from the Crew Locator anyway.

Senator Lee Borman shrugged. "Got all six turrets on auto now. Hell, they don't need me anymore. OmniFlight'll take care of any problem in a millionth of a second. We probably wouldn't even *know* the *Typhoon* had just fried sixty enemy ships. Ah, hell with it, need a break." He plopped in front of the Diagnostic AB console Laurie had been about to check. "Not like the days of the old *Typhoons*. We had damn good computers back then, but the turrets needed people with *know-how*. Well, screw it."

Laurie was willing to let the short, chunky, crew-cut weapons officer take up space and mutter a few complaints, as he often did. He'd go away soon if she just kept up with her systems checks and nodded at whatever he said for a while. Nevertheless she said: "Look, I remember the first-generation *Typhoons* myself. I was a technician for both the *I* and *II* and I knew them inside out."

"Huh. That's right. I keep forgetting. You've been in this business as long as I have. Everyone forgets that because, hell, you still look twenty-five!" He followed this with an admiring gaze at her small breasts.

Laurie looked away. He wasn't going to start in on that nonsense again, was he?

"Great job on our Posttner friend, by the way. That lady is quite a piece of work!" Lee chortled. "We're lucky to have you, hon." Laurie had no idea how Lee had managed to entice so many women over the decades. How did he get along with his fellow politician Posttner? Who'd end up devouring whom?

66

Borman's short squat body and blunt face didn't inspire the slightest hint of attraction as far as she was concerned. She'd thought she'd made this amply clear over the past few months. Every time they talked, she made sure to mention her boyfriend Will.

"Gotta hand it to these damn designers," Borman went on. "We've had remote-controlled turrets for decades, but I still can't get used to having all six of 'em sort of thinking *with* me. Or maybe *for* me, y'know?"

Laurie nodded absently. Borman could sit in any of the four manned turrets, two atop the ship and two beneath, and simply monitor the computer fire from these four, plus the entirely automated bow and stern turrets, or if he chose to manually shoot his turret he could let the other five run their AI programs to choose targets at will, or slave one or more of them to his turret so that their fire matched his. Since Laurie had to cross-train on the system herself, she could attest to the uncanny sensation of aiming a top turret and feeling the other turrets tracking and firing. In simulated combat it was tempting to take your hands off the controls and let OmniFlight pick off dozens of target craft.

"So I hear we're doing under half speed on SD3, hon."

"Top would get us to Procyon A in 9.85 minutes. But at test rate we'll take 24.382 minutes. We're about fifteen minutes from there at this point," Laurie said, marveling that Borman needed to take a break nine minutes into the flight.

Lee shrugged. "Can't say it makes much difference. Old Jonathan James had several hours start on us anyway."

"Well, this also gives Sandra a little more time to experiment with the new SD3 sensors. Maybe she can find some trace of the ship."

"Or ship *debris!*" Lee chuckled, the same thing Laurie had been about to say. Nobody thought the *Typhoon II,* with its primitive Star Drive and antiquated navigational systems, could get any further than Procyon A. A journey there would require three separate Star Drive hops, with long pauses between each leg to check out the ship. Even though someone had apparently hacked the cloaking systems up to current standards, that ship was *old*. It had been kept in flying condition but hadn't been officially inspected in over a decade.

"Well, we do need to check out Procyon and Andertwin," she said. "And the whole route along the way as best we can. It's the best guess."

"Right, but it's just a guess. Ballard thinks Iota Persei is more likely. He thinks JJC might be attracted to a place where the Wounded actually stole a star."

Laurie just let that pass. They'd both been held captive at Iota Persei by the Wounded. Just last year. They'd both seen the Wounded destroy that star. And she'd watched her Will fling himself into *suicide,* then return moments later with a restored star and billions of years of *Garr/thahg* crammed into his head.

She'd never really allowed herself to think about that. She didn't want to get anywhere near that place, but she'd known the instant Jack had called the crew together that Iota Persei was coming. Why would JJC flee to a place where the Wounded had done so much evil? And was Will really so confused? Was he really disintegrating under the pressure of *Garr/thahg* knowledge?

And what about Laurie herself? Iota Persei was where she'd momentarily flowed into the Wounded herself and come up with that impossible *Trans-Simultaneity* equation. Had it actually destroyed Sol in some alternate universe? Everyone said it must have, but Laurie still couldn't remember how it had all transpired. Her time sense was impaired. The last few months had been scrambled. Was she really qualified to be on this ship? Shouldn't she have reported her mental condition to Jack and Joe? *Did* she have a mental condition? No, she was sharp. Had to be. She was solid. She knew this ship. Her duty lay with the *Typhoon VI.* She could handle it all. The Wounded couldn't still be singing somewhere in her brain, could they? But what *was* singing in her brain, deep in the night, the past few months? What were all those dreams?

"Anyway," Lee went on, lounging in his seat and shutting his eyes, "I'm sure nobody wants to think of the danger here.

Like we're just retrieving Jack's weird son, no big deal. But what if Ballard's intuition is right, and there's some connection to the Wounded, let's say *they* jacked the stupid thing with new cloaking technology? Hell, I don't know."

"So are you worried?"

"Hell, no. We've got the *VI!* And the best damn physician/engineer the USSF ever had!" He playfully punched Laurie's shoulder and she stiffened. "I can tell you some of my fellow senators are pissed about using the *VI* for this, or for letting Jack fly it, how much it's gonna cost if we dent this baby, that sort of thing."

"Well, I'd think people would realize we need the best ship, given the fact that somehow the *Typhoon II* now has advanced cloaking."

"There's that. So are *you* worried?"

She warily noted Lee's hairy hand poised for something like a pat on her arm. "No, not really." She struggled to find something to get him off the subject of herself. "So how about you? I mean, here we're also chasing after, uh, Suzette, and all."

Borman snorted. "Hell, I don't know what's gotten into her. Look, between you and me, I give her her freedom. And she gives me mine."

Laurie blinked. Lee had never come right out and said this. But everyone knew about Lee and Suzette's tawdry open marriage. Her affair with Sanders Hirte had been all over SolNet a while back. How on earth could Lee put up with that? Particularly as nobody had seen him involved with any other woman for a long time? "Well, uh …"

"The damn rejuv thing threw me, y'know, just between you and me. Couldn't believe my eyes. Two weeks of rejuv and she's like a teenager! I could barely recognize her. I'm sure you could understand that the very first thing I wanted to do was get alone with her."

"Right, right. Listen, Lee, I really need to monitor the Higgs."

"But she didn't want to have a damn thing to do with me. Guess I was hoping the rejuv might, you know, turn her around or something, but, I mean, she's been shacking up with JJC for *months.* She was like *solid* before, you know? I mean, before him, and before Hirte. We ran the Response, and all of a sudden it's like she doesn't give a damn and she starts screwing *everyone.*"

"Well, this whole thing is a surprise. Like Patrick James. Is he really working with JJC? Is that how they smuggled the advanced cloaking stuff to the *II?*"

"Or Jackie Vespertine. Now *that's* one solid female. Or at least I *thought* she was. Could she really have gone off the deep end like that? I gotta tell ya, Laurie, honestly, like a man says to a woman he really respects and admires, I really have had the hots for Jackie for *years* now. I mean, what a *chassis.* Even Suzette lookin' like a damn teenager can't hold a candle to *her.* Jackie Vespertine is, like, *perfection.* Her rejuv was *classic.* I mean, she's never given me the time of day but I think she knows I'd be after her if I could. Man, oh man!"

Laurie stared at Lee's hands cupping the air in front of her breasts, and shot her chair back two feet.

"Sure I'll strangle that little JJC mother if I can get my hands on him. Jack's kid or no. He *seduced* Suzette into all that crap. But who cares? We just gotta do our duty. But between you and me, man to woman, I'm gonna punch that sucker's lights out! God, he makes me sick!"

"Look, Lee, I didn't really mean to get you onto this, but do you think can you really function on this mission?"

Laurie was astonished she'd blurted this. Then again, she was the ship's physician, and this was part of her job.

To her dismay Lee's mouth crumpled, his shoulders slumped, and he looked at his knees. "I was really *trying* with Suzette, and with this rejuvenation crap. Do you really think I wanted her to screw with Hirte, and Jonathan James, and *everyone?* I don't know, she's a *criminal* now, we *can't* have a real marriage. You're right, I can't function. Maybe you should relieve me."

Laurie stared. Lee had really come to her because she *was* the physician. The only way he could begin was with his tits and ass babble, but Lee Borman actually needed her professional help.

"Look, Lee, I'm *sorry.*"

"Don't worry about me, I can just stay in my stateroom, let the damn weapons fire on their own, they don't need me, nobody does anymore, I don't care. I just don't want Jack to know how much I've screwed this up. Screwed up my whole life, I don't know …"

And Lee Borman was sobbing. God, he was a human being after all. And all this time she'd been cringing from him, keeping herself safe from his stupid advances.

"I'm so sorry! I'm so sorry!" Lee bawled, head in his hands.

"It's okay, Lee. It's okay." Laurie raised a hand to pat Lee's shoulder, but was unable to follow through.

"And Ballard, you know what *he* says about Suzette? I mean, the son of a bitch is *leering* at her at the officer's party, I mean this is like way *before* rejuvenation, and she's smiling back, and it's like he knows *he* can get into her, and like supposedly I can't! Well, he's right! I can't have her because I'm a useless old fart! Gives me all this crap about the weapons but I know he's really after Suzette! Everyone is, because she's so damn hot now! Well, I'll tell you, she was hot *before!* She *was!* She was a fantastic-lookin' forty-two-year-old woman! All I wanted was for her to settle down a bit! We could've had a good life together! Then she turns into a *teenager!* God, people think because I'm a senator I have some power but I don't have *anything!* How could she *do* this? I mean, Ballard has to one-up me on everything! I'm gonna punch *his* lights out, too! I mean it!"

Laurie stared openmouthed at Lee's heaving shoulders. "Well, Rick is, well, he's Rick, you know. I can understand how he might bug you, but, really, you don't have to punch the poor guy out." She winced at her light laugh that went nowhere.

"The bastard! The goddamn *bastard!*"

The problem was that given half a chance Laurie would've liked to punch Ballard's lights out herself. It had been extremely flattering when Jack appointed her physician/engineer on the

*Typhoon VI,* but Rick Ballard hadn't been onboard a day before Laurie had felt that her paradise here had been ruined.

Okay, so he was talented. She'd worked with Ballard on the *Typhoon III,* where he'd been the best weapons officer she or ship's captain Joe had ever seen. But he was irritatingly aware of his talents and got even more boastful after completing the entire USSF Navigation Officer course in just six months instead of the usual two years, earning perfect scores in information technology, navigation, and a month-long practicum. Jack was eager to have him, especially as Ballard didn't have a slot after the *III* was destroyed at Iota Persei and might go to any number of *Typhoon*-class ships begging for navigators.

Yet in addition to being a pompous know-it-all who was irritatingly almost always right about anything he deigned to comment on, Rick Ballard was staggeringly handsome, with a chiseled jaw, hypnotic deep-set blue eyes, and absurdly thick crimson lips which invited speculation about what they could do for a woman in bed, as Laurie could attest from her new worries about Sandra Markham.

Sandra swore that she and Rick had only flirted when they'd all been assigned to the *Typhoon III.* In fact, Laurie and her sensor officer friend had joked about the number of women Ballard seemed to go through each month. Laurie was starting to date Will at the time, so there was no danger of her succumbing, but she worried about Sandra, who was able to laugh about Ballard's painfully insincere come-ons even as a note of drool came into her voice as she graphically commented on his massive pecs and biceps and the most perfectly formed male tush she'd ever seen.

Ballard was a giant V-shape: taut runner's legs rising to sturdy groin and massive muscled chest and, Laurie thought ruefully, to a head that swelled far beyond *that.* It was no wonder that almost every woman treated Richard Ballard with a sort of fascinated contempt. Laurie wanted to believe that Sandra's wry sense of humor, along with her experience through a failed marriage and several serious relationships, would keep their petite sensor officer out of trouble. The six *Typhoon VI* crewmembers had meshed well during the test flights of the ship, despite the ongoing friction between Lee and Rick over weapons technique.

But last week, when Jack had called a break on an All-Systems Interface test, Sandra asked Laurie to bring some tea over and said she'd leave her door unlocked. She'd apparently forgotten all about it because Laurie, balancing two empty cups and a clay teapot on a tray, had whisked the door aside to reveal--

Naked Sandra crouched over naked Ballard on the bed. At first Laurie wondered why the two would be playing with a baseball bat. Then she registered what the short busty Sandra, her brick-red hair dangling over Ballard's groin, was paying such earnest attention to. Laurie just set the tray on the floor, backed out, and waited agonizing seconds for the door to slide closed. She hurried back to her console, opened the Facilities program, and locked Sandra's door.

Did Jack know? Did anyone else on the ship? Once they'd completed the tests and landed, Laurie had forced herself to tell Sandra what she'd seen.

But Sandra didn't care. She'd later found the tea tray and so knew Laurie had been there. Now officially in love, Sandra was eager to share every detail. "We talked about *everything*. He's finally ready to *settle down*. He knows he needs just *one woman,* and it's *me*. Who'd ever have thought it? It does need to be secret for now. We both know that."

Laurie hadn't said a word. Though she came off as so brainy and systems-oriented that most women assumed she wasn't up for girl chitchat, she nevertheless attracted it and many women complimented her on being such a good listener. "He's ready to settle down at last," had been voiced by Marilyn Thompson and Barb Emerson last month. In fact, Laurie and Sandra had *snickered* about Barb's comment.

Just yesterday Sandra had come to her with a long list of anxieties about whether Rick loved her as much as she loved him. And then somehow the talk had gotten around to: "I assume you saw *it*. God, isn't it amazing! I've never had one so *big* before!"

Laurie managed to forestall any further comment. She hadn't seen one as big either, but then again, she was a physician and there were currently something like two billion human penises and two billion human vaginas out there, and some had to be prettier, bigger, or better than others. Ballard's genitals probably weren't the last word in male sexuality, and if he someday wound up as a cadaver under some medical student's knife, his shriveled endowments would elicit only passing professional interest.

Funny how she kept picturing him stone-cold dead on the med school table.

This morning Sandra had seemed to levitate into the *Typhoon VI,* and she took up her post with such a sunny brown-eyed smile that Laurie wanted to believe that everything would somehow work out. But how could anyone be sure? And here was Lee Borman, decades older than Ballard and worried about Ballard taking away his wife and his weapon turrets.

"It's okay, Lee, everything will be all right," she whispered, and now she did pat his shoulder.

He straightened up. "Sorry. I'm okay now. All this just threw me, I guess."

"That happens. This whole day is throwing everyone, for a lot of different reasons. It's okay to hang it all out once in a while."

Borman sniffed. "I--I know. Look, you won't tell Jack, will you?"

"Well, of course not."

"I mean, that I cracked and all right now."

"You didn't crack, Lee! Don't be silly! You have worries just like everybody."

And she got back a dazzling smile that rivaled Sandra's earlier. "Thanks, Laurie!" He stood up. "Guess I better be getting back to the old turret! Thanks again!"

# CHAPTER ELEVEN
## A Big Merry-Go-Round of Stuff Happening

"Hey, Laurie."

"Oh!" Laurie gasped, swiveling her chair.

"Wow, sorry, didn't mean to startle you," Joe Commer said. "Just thought I'd check things out around the ship before we came out of the Drive." He pointed through the Engineering door back to the stairs leading to the Control Room. "There's really nothing to do up there anymore. OmniFlight does it all. Besides, I needed to stretch my legs."

He too was wandering the ship after only a couple minutes? "And you're supposed to be *piloting* this thing?"

Joe grinned. "Yeah, Jack left me in command. Anyway, I just *commanded* myself to take a walk. So we're about seven minutes out from Procyon?"

Laurie checked her console. "Seven minutes twelve seconds. Then Nav12 will set us up for orbit around Andertwin. That'll be another five minutes to Andertwin and two for taking up orbit."

"Great. I assume everything's fine down here?"

Laurie nodded. "Definitely." She wondered if she should tell her former *Typhoon III* captain about Sandra and Ballard. How would this affect how they all worked together? Did Jack know? He hadn't been concerned when, knowing they were dating, he'd assigned her and Will to the *Typhoon V* last year, but then again, anyone could see negatives to having people in relationships on the same crew.

She was sure Joe would understand where she was coming from. He was the best officer she'd ever worked for, and they could kid each other in a way that perfectly preserved the command structure even as they both satirized it. Yet she knew Joe would be duty-bound to report the Sandra-Ballard relationship to Jack, and if her intuition told her anything, it was that Ballard also grated on Jack. Already upset about his son, Jack was highly capable of taking it out on Ballard.

"So Sandra's already on the ball with the Long

Diagnostics," Joe said. "I swear, that's amazing."

Laurie nodded. "Really. We've needed that since day one." SD3 was the first iteration of Star Drive allowing accurate long-range sensor use during the Drive. Sandra was already scanning ahead for signs of JJC and his renegade crew. Maybe they'd find the *Typhoon II* in orbit around Andertwin and wouldn't have to go to Iota Persei after all. It'd be fun to look over the old *II*. That thing was prehistoric, almost like that crazy B-17 when she was a kid.

"Anyway, as soon we're out of Drive we'll talk to Phil and Dar again, see if they've got anything new on their end."

That ancient World War II bomber. Crawling through the long cramped dark fuselage. Hot summer day. Must've been '28, when Laurie was thirteen. Everyone was astonished the damn thing was still flying. They'd probably replaced every part a dozen times over. She'd been amazed at all the wires hanging everywhere. She could still recall the complexity of the mechanisms in the landing gear, the distinct feel of *modern technology* in something so old.

They'd just been through the first disasters at that time, the asteroids going into the sun. The loss of Pluto, Uranus, Neptune, and much more lay down the road. But somehow, everyone knew they didn't have much time. Didn't even Laurie know it, at thirteen? The wires, the landing gear, the plane itself had *led* her here, to the USSF. Because the USSF represented the best of humanity *fighting back*. Just as the B-17 was *fighting back*. Somebody was finally fighting back and they needed to understand these setbacks and move on out into space.

Laurie shook herself from the daydream. "Won't the Alpha Centaurians know if he's anywhere in AC?"

Joe sighed. "You'd think they would. *Their* damn Grid works, after all."

Laurie nodded. Though Jack and Joe had both briefly dipped into SolGrid to get an idea of how it worked, she hadn't been tempted by it, or by the AC version for that matter. She had a vision of going insane for all eternity and knew that wouldn't look good on her USSF physician/engineer résumé.

And while the new Alpha Centaurian Grid was a voluntary association harmoniously linking twenty trillion AC citizen-emperors across seventeen solar systems, with every experience of each person available simultaneously to every other citizen in a way Laurie still didn't believe possible, SolGrid had been churning through one digital catastrophe after another since its rollout in December. Phil Sperry on Andertwin, who'd singlehandedly revamped the old fascist AC Grid into its new benevolent version, had offered to help with SolGrid, but had been rebuffed by his old crewmate Patrick James.

Sure, SolGrid had been pushed out too quickly, but that was due to paranoia about the Wounded. It had quickly enabled the execution of over seven thousand Wounded agents in Sol, but did anyone really feel safer?

"Anyway, why would Jonathan James want to go to Andertwin?" Joe went on. "He knows the AC Grid would finger him in a second."

"Unless he stayed Dark."

"Yeah, but even one linked person who spotted the *Typhoon II* or had Grid contact with any of the people onboard would broadcast that throughout AC. I just don't think he'd risk going there. I know we've got to check it out just to make sure. But I agree with Rick that we've got to do Iota Persei next."

Laurie nodded. No use avoiding it. She'd just have to suck it up. They were going to Iota Persei. It had to be all right. She was probably just having some sort of trauma flashback.

Joe sat down in the same chair Lee had. "Man, there's so much going on these days I'm not sure anyone can even remotely keep up with it. This stupid *Typhoon* stealing is just one more piece of insanity."

Laurie blinked. Did she have to counsel her old captain, too? "Well, I agree people are pretty overwhelmed these days."

"The Wounded, SolGrid, Martians going flaky on us," Joe sighed. "Even stuff like rejuvenation, which is a great thing, is turning everything upside down. Or all the new tech the Four have been feeding us. Before they forget it, that is."

"I know." Laurie wasn't about to share her worries about

what billions of years of knowledge might have done to Will's mind.

"You know, the weird thing is, I usually can just accept it all somehow. It's like a big merry-go-round of *stuff happening*. Human beings have always been hip-deep in this sort of change. Somehow we absorb it and get through. I'm sure the Martians will too."

"I hope so." The last time she'd spoken to her friend Kner, the Senior Martian Scientist seemed to be on the verge of a nervous breakdown, babbling incomprehensible, thickly-accented English as he projected billions of equally meaningless images.

Joe looked at the floor. "What *I'm* really worried about is Jack. He keeps telling me how tired he is and how much he wants to retire, but he says he can't in the face of all this crap. Then his son goes out and steals the damn *Typhoon II*. And Pat on top of it. Jack told me just now he's so pissed off at Pat he can't even think straight."

"Yeah, I know. Pat being with them *is* a shock. I mean, he's been so withdrawn ever since he got the SolGrid contract."

"And then patenting the software and cutting everyone else out of it. Who knew he was such a bastard? Hell, we've known him for, what? Almost fifty years?"

"So are you really worried about Jack?" She figured she had to ask this question if the Deputy Supreme Commander was in any way questioning the ability of the Supreme Commander to do his job.

It was good that Joe was officially in command of this mission, then. Or was he? Maybe Jack was just letting Joe pilot this one flight. Did he assign overall command to Joe? Laurie was chagrined that she, ship's P/E, had no idea.

"No, not really. I really don't want him to retire, but if he needs to, like to reduce his stress and all, I guess that would be good, don't you think? Did you know he started meditating?"

"Yes, he mentioned that. We all should probably do that."

"He's seemed a lot calmer recently." Joe shrugged. "At least until this morning. I know what he really wants to do is keep exploring, further and further outward, way past the Iota Persei radius. I mean, if Star Drive 3 really doesn't have vortex problems, hell, we could run the mother for weeks at a time and really get out there. When he's talking like that, nothing fazes him. Meeting species like the Ywritt doesn't faze him, even running into trouble doesn't. But sometimes it seems the more we want to get out there, the more obstacles we wind up having to muck through first."

Laurie had been impressed when Jack told her he didn't feel any particular need to investigate the Ywritt of Iota Persei any further. "I think they feel the same way," he'd told her upon conferring with the primary Ywritt contact, a bubble of translucent energy calling itself Waterfall Sequence. "Looks like we'll have a nice little alliance and maybe some chitchat about the weather and that's about it. I'd sure hate to see us get all wrapped up in them like some people want."

There was a vocal contingent that wanted to rein in exploration and stick with the newly-discovered "friendly bubbles of consciousness" from Iota Persei. But the Ywritt were disturbingly bland, and though they expressed gratitude to Sol for saving them from the Wounded, they seemed distant, suspicious, and eager to cover that with exaggerated politeness. Their minds seemed flat and digital; you didn't get any sense of emotion from them.

The Alpha Centaurians, countless races scattered among seventeen-star systems, had begun as existential, bloodthirsty enemies but had turned into enthusiastic friends. The Ywritt on the other hand seemed destined to remain mere acquaintances. Trade had been beneficial, and the Ywritt were ostensibly allies against the Wounded, but could anyone rely on them?

Jack had argued forcefully before the United System Council for building *Typhoon VI* and *Typhoon VII* for new exploration. Though the Wounded had retreated after the fall of Iota Persei, and those seven thousand Wounded robots had been discovered via SolGrid and destroyed, further investigation of the galaxy was necessary to find their hiding places and exterminate them. Why couldn't the Friends of the Ywritt see this? For that matter, why couldn't the Ywritt themselves? After all, they'd been the ones nearly eradicated by the Wounded last year.

"Well, it could be our task to clean things up before any grand new exploration," Laurie finally said. "Maybe a new generation will do the big exploration after us."

"It's just that we have all these new tools *now*. You know, I keep threatening Jack that if he quits, I'll quit too."

"No!"

Joe grinned. "Not that I probably would. There's just so much fun stuff to do. I just don't know if it'd be fun without Jack, though. But we've got the *VI* here, the *VII's* almost done, and then we can check out the black hole at the center of the Milky Way."

Few had seriously begrudged the expenditure for these two ships. In any case the prohibitive cost had come down dramatically with techniques developed by the Four from their *Garr/thahg* knowledge, along with assistance from the Ywritt. Star Drive 3 was a mix of Martian Amplified Thought techniques developed by Kner, Z'B, and Greeney Gooney, regulated by a quantum computer designed by the Ywritt. By February the *Typhoon VI* had been built along *Typhoon V* class lines, with countless astonishing improvements. The sister ship, *Typhoon VII,* was almost done. Laurie couldn't believe Joe would walk away from the *VII,* which had even more innovations than the *VI.*

Joe stood up. "Two minutes. I'm heading back. You know, I'm hoping we do find JJC here, but I really don't want to have to watch Jack arrest his own son."

"You really think he'll have to go that far?"

"I'm supposed to negotiate, I guess. But the Council just ordered Jack to make the arrest a couple minutes ago. Try meditating out of *that.*"

# CHAPTER TWELVE
## I Know More About This Ship Than Anyone!

"Pat, you got that hook into SolNet yet?" came the sharp voice over the intercom into the cramped Communications Room, followed by more yapping from that damn Trotter thing. Pat knew the dog hated him.

"Look, the goddamn Star Drive interface is screwy, it takes time," he muttered, tapping at the virtual keyboard projected across the blank desk. The console in front of him was dark; the museum caretakers could leave the ship's obsolete 2060s computer systems up and running to give visitors a glimpse of dazzling colors and graphs, but Pat wasn't going to fire up the old *Typhoon* communications tech until he was sure he had an upgrade capable of cloaking even the initial power surge. "Maybe if you'd stop checking in every minute I could concentrate."

"Touchy, touchy, Mr. Patster," JJC chided. "Sure we even need the *Typhoon* equipment on this?"

"I need the damn superspace radio array. None of our comms can do much more than talk to each other once we're in superspace. But I think I can tie mine into the *Typhoon* array with an anonymous n-space scatter matrix. God, this array is crap! I can't believe we used to fly with this stuff."

"Okay, just let me know, dude. We've got to know what's happening back there. Not being able to punch out in Star Drive is screwing with my brain, dude."

"Okay, okay, I'm trying." Pat snapped off his intercom. "Dammit to hell!" He'd forgotten how nasty the ship smelled, and having that dog everywhere made it worse, with his shedding fur and his trips to the tiny lavatory where JJC had rigged up a *litterbox* of all things out of an old shipping container, a litterbox filled with printed brochures and shredded posters from the Museum Store which no right-thinking dog would ever use. And then Jonathan James or Suzette held Trotter over it until the damn thing was finished, having spattered all over the wall in the process. The place stank and they'd only been here a little over an hour. What would it be like after a couple days?

Pat had to concentrate. Just get the job done. Hooking anonymously into SolNet was easy. Any hacker could do that. And SolNet was cool with the SolGrid Relay Interface. But merging all that into 2060s *Typhoon* tech was not so easy. Almost back to assembly language for some of it. But doable. Kid's stuff, really.

They needed to put this baby into Star Drive if they were going anywhere. The goddamn Commers would freak if they knew the *Typhoon II* was just behind a two-hundred-foot-wide chunk of Neptune's shattered core.

*So make the call to subroutine SDCloak, yeah, but can't chance an anonymous interface in normal space, superspace is ideal, but the scanning vector--wait! I see the hack! Just align it with the probability of--yeah! And Feedback Stasis would do that! Okay! So IF SDCloak > 0 THEN Comm:Merge;// {CALL VectorAlign, ELSE Feedback Statis} :\*\* CALL L-SpatialLoop}. That's what I was missing! Okay! Test.*

Pat projected the results on his comm and watched the simulation unfold.

*Yeah! Got the mother!*

He punched the intercom. "Okay, we're up. Ready for Star Drive."

"You're sure, dude?"

"Yes, I'm one hundred percent sure," Pat sneered. Nobody ever used to sass him about some simple-ass program. Now, just because of a few damn Grid glitches, everyone pissed on him. Well, screw them all. Pat knew what he was doing even if nobody else did.

"Okay, Sanders, Pat says we're ready," JJC said over the intercom.

"Got it," Hirte called. "All hands, prepare for Star Drive."

Pat felt the rough jolt of the Drive. The 2064 upgrade was smoother than the original SD of the thirties, and Hirte had massaged it further when he'd hacked into the cloaking subroutines, but Pat knew there was no way the old *Typhoon II*

Augmented Nuke, despite numerous fixes through the years, could handle Star Drive spacetime pressures the way newer models could. Pat felt his stomach drop six inches and heard more stereo Trotter barking, sharp on the intercom and muffled through the closed Control Room hatch.

"Oh! God!" he heard Suzette gasp as well.

Why was she taking up space in the Control Room with those clowns? In fact, why were any of those clowns in there? Pat was the one who should be piloting.

*Damn you all! I know more about this ship than anyone!*

"Easy, honey, it's okay. Just a few minutes," JJC said. "What've we got, Sanders?"

"Two separate Star Drives, each about eleven minutes fifteen seconds, give or take a few. Do a little under three light-years each. We need to spend about twenty minutes between 'em orienting ourselves. Pat, is our tech up to that?"

"It damn well better be," Pat snapped. "Maybe you should've thought to bring a qualified navigator along."

"Mr. Patster," JJC spoke, "are you saying your sensors can't get a precise fix on where we wind up coming out of Star Drive?"

"Oh hell, yeah, don't worry, I could figure it with a telescope and a sheet of paper. There's just some recalibrating on all systems needed at a midpoint check."

"I know that. We're on top of this, people. Everyone just sit back and enjoy the ride. We all okay? Jackie?"

"I'm--okay--" came the call from the Navigation Room behind Pat. "Little rough, but you get used to it."

Pat winced, feeling he should add something reassuring, but all he could think was *look who we got as navigator after all.* The Nav Room was as cramped and smelly as this damn Comm/Sensor Room. How was she really taking all this?

Jackie Vespertine. Hadn't he known for a long time it was all over? How could he ever have deserved her? She'd just been marking time with him.

"Just a few minutes, folks, then we can rest at the first stop," Sanders put in. "All ship's functions are smooth."

Pat snorted at Hirte's officious tone. Like everyone else onboard, Hirte was Dark to SolGrid. Like Pat, he'd never really *been* in SolGrid. Only Jackie and Suzette had actually been in the Grid, each dipping in maybe a dozen times. At least they'd remembered how to pull themselves out. A lot of people seemed to have forgotten the "voluntary" aspect of SolGrid. What was really going on with them? How many were addicted at last count? A hundred million? Not bad really, out of a total population of three and a half billion.

*Don't think about that!*

No one could sue Pat anyway. That was in the contract. And anyway, addiction was the least of his problems with SolGrid.

Meanwhile Z'B whimpered on the floor of the kitchenette behind the Nav Room, his natural Martian outradiance flooded with confusion and dread, his central nervous system twisting with the anxiety of the obsolete Star Drive, Martian garbage ratcheting up in everyone's mind. Everyone could feel the main bearings melting in Z'B's brain. The damn thing was probably a vegetable by now. They ought to just space the all-wise Emperor of the Martians and be done with it. Pat was about to suggest this course of action when the telepathic whine abruptly ceased.

"*That's* a goddamn relief," he muttered, aware that everyone on the ship had to have heard him. Had the stupid mother just gone ahead and died?

"I just hit him with some alpha drugs from the med kit," Jackie said over the intercom. "It was starting to get *to* me."

"To everyone," JJC said. "Thanks, Jackie. Why don't you get back to the Nav Room, okay, hon? I don't know if these damn old ships run into turbulence or what."

"They don't!" Hirte laughed. "If we vortex out we don't even feel it! We just become one big ball of *light!*"

"Well, well ..." Jackie said. "Sure, I'm back in Nav now."

Pat snapped his intercom off in disgust. The worship in her voice was obvious. Sure, she was rejuvenated, sure she was gorgeous, but she was *seventy-six*. The JJC bastard was only twenty-eight.

So why was she wearing a mini-skirt on this job?

Answer: *to seduce Captain Jonathan James.*

*Damn her to hell! She's mine! I should be up there! I should be captain!*

But Sanders Hirte was up there flying the ship, ostensibly as copilot but really in command since JJC, ensconced in the pilot's seat, knew nothing about the ship other than the facts he'd gathered from his stint as Typhoon Museum docent.

*Yeah, I'd like to see him take this thing into combat after reading the* Typhoon *brochures!*

# CHAPTER THIRTEEN
## Back to the *Gripkill*

Pat slid his door closed to shut out Trotter's Star Drive moans from the open Control Room. But the silence was immediately broken as JJC overrode his turned-off intercom, and the damn dog was crying in the background again.

"Okay, Pat, are we able to patch into SolNet anonymously yet?"

"Yeah, got it," Pat said, punching his keypad to bring his console to life. The old *Typhoon* computers were archaic, but they could link pretty quickly to SolNet via superspace radio. "Should be on your console now."

"Yeah, I got it now. Thanks, Patster."

The son of a bitch thought he was such a great leader. Pat sampled SolNet newsfeeds as no doubt the others were doing in the Control Room. Fifty-seven USSF ships were engaged in the hunt for the *Typhoon II*. The USSF was denying the new *Typhoon VI* was involved, but the ship was reported on a "training exercise" and neither Supreme Commander Jack Commer nor Deputy Supreme Commander Joe was available for comment. Pat watched a video of talking heads as his stomach struggled to settle down to the Drive. His arm hairs still stood on end.

"Yow!" came JJC's cry over the intercom. "So Daddy's looking for me in the *VI!* Sanders, you better hope your cloaking hack is up to speed for this."

"Believe me, it's the latest stuff. It's insane that the USSF designed something they don't even know how to break themselves."

"Where the hell did you get it, man?"

"Hey, that's our agreement, dude! I don't say where I picked it up, you don't ask! Wasn't terribly expensive, though, I'll tell ya that!"

"Well, whatever. Hey, Patster? You there? Don't flip your intercom off again, okay dude? Need your feedback, man. I want my comm/sensor guy on top of whatever the media's saying."

Well, screw Mr. Space Pirate Jonathan James. Pat was *always* on top of SolNet. He knew it better than SolNet, Inc.'s top programmers. He had to, because it was fated that SolGrid would eventually fully integrate into SolNet.

At this point SolGrid was standalone software anyone could tap into just by accepting the Signal. It captured the telepathic frequencies which had been conclusively demonstrated to exist in all sentient beings. But aside from a few experimental links, SolGrid had no deep interface with the purely digital SolNet which incorporated every scrap of human and Martian data.

Even so, these tentative connections had already managed to corrupt numerous SolNet databases. Neither Pat nor Sanders had ever been sure quite how, and Pat had spent increasing amounts of time uploading back-ups to replace SolNet corruption, never sure if he was getting all of it.

He needed to piggyback SolGrid on a stable SolNet. The two systems needed each other. By itself SolNet could easily be fooled. Anyone could go Dark with falsified records. The Wounded, for instance, made bulletproof bios back to fictional birth. They were expert SolNet hackers and it was only Pat's Grid that had unmasked over seven thousand of them.

A truly integrated SolNetGrid--if anyone bothered to look they'd know Pat had already trademarked the name--would flush out the deeper Wounded, exposing all imposters in a nanosecond. It was vital that SolNet and SolGrid fully merge.

Did Pat get any credit for saving the solar system? No way. All people could talk about were the psychiatric cases. Nobody understood Pat's contribution, just as those jerks up in the Control Room didn't have a clue about how this ship really worked.

He could sizzle all of them right now. Even Suzanne. She was just a tease.

He wondered if JJC had the slightest idea about the anti-personnel lasers. The museum had disabled them and they were never mentioned in technical explanations. But the *Typhoon II* had been equipped with the APL system. In the early years of Star Drive, the SD anxiety had caused not a few mutinies, with some personnel turning raving and violent. Probably not more than twenty or thirty ships had ever been equipped with APL. The destroyed *Typhoon V* had introduced a truly sophisticated and improved version, but after news of it leaked throughout the USSF ranks, the designers had discontinued its implementation on all future USSF ships.

The three documented uses of the system had been classified top secret, but Pat had hacked into all their details a long time ago. Two were to quell actual Star Drive insurrections on ships heading to battle in Alpha Centauri, but the third and most interesting was when Jack Commer had blasted two assailants on this very ship with APL as he dove to the deck to avoid the lowest eight-inch-high bank of lasers. Pat hadn't witnessed that himself, as he'd been in the Pod at the time, brainwashed by the Alpha Centaurians, as he still winced to recall. This piece of ship's lore had circulated as wild rumor throughout USSF ranks for decades, but was certainly never part of any museum tour.

But Pat had enabled APL aboard the *Typhoon II* a couple minutes after climbing into the Comm/Sensor Room.

Now there was a hack. And nobody could possibly know, as Pat had topmost level. Even Jack didn't know that his clueless IT folks had given Pat access even higher than Jack's for SolGrid work.

Of course, APL might've had a use aboard the *Gripkill* back in '33. Pat had often wondered if that hadn't been a secret backup use for anti-personnel lasers in the AC war. Because once Zarj troopers boarded your ship, you might as well laser everyone and just get it over with. The ship was already lost along with all your crew.

But the experiment had never been tried, as none of the handful of APL-equipped ships had ever been boarded by AC stormtroopers. The *Gripkill,* on the other hand--

*Ah, hell, don't think about that.*

… Flinging himself down the ladder, grabbing an EOS rifle from among the bodies on Level Six, running straight *into* the melee, not a thought in his mind, hurtling *towards* the explosions, and the screams, and the uncanny shrieks of the Zarj as they burned their way through bulkheads and bodies with their pulsar tubes.

Pat closed his eyes. *No.*

... Captain Baynes, spewing blood, left arm severed, screaming at him in the outrushing air over his static-laced EnviroField mike, ordering him back up to Four.

"James! Get back and fix the network so we can get out of here! You're not a goddamn soldier! Put down that rifle and get back up there, so help me God!"

... Pat gazing numbly down the smoking corridor at Zarj troops each taking out six USSF troopers at a time, noise fading as Level Six turned to vacuum.

They'd rammed the ship, right on the servers on Level Eight. Eight and Seven had blown out in a second. The Zarj had accepted the loss of their own ship and half their crew just so they could jump a squad of their merciless killers into the breach.

So Pat retreated to Four. How many eons had he spent coaxing the two remaining servers back to life? How many programs had he written on the fly amid the frantic radio calls and the thumps of hand-to-hand combat below, Zarj troopers making their way up to Five, blasting his comrades to mini-neutron stars in the compartment beneath him? How had he been able to focus on systems logic? How had he been able to even open his mouth to call the Control Room to report that he finally had communication with the SD engine? Lieutenant Makker was now in command and he punched for Star Drive. They'd barely escaped two more Zarj ships closing in.

It had taken another thirty minutes and fifteen more dead to kill those last two Zarj aboard. The *Gripkill* had been insanely lucky. *Nobody* survived a Zarj boarding.

But if Baynes had had APL he would've used it. He would've fried everyone on the *Gripkill* to repel the invaders. Pat was sure of it.

In any case, that was Pat's October 8, 2033. And when he got the ship's communications back online, the first thing they'd heard was that, back on Earth, Jack and Joe had just dropped the

Xon bomb the same day. The Final War with the Central Asian Powers was over. Nobody suspected the USSF had just killed the whole planet.

*Damn you, you will never think about October 8th! Ever again!*

Why was he betraying Jack? His friend Jack, of all people?

"Hey, Patster--Jackie! You guys seeing this?" JJC called from the Control Room.

"Yes, it's amazing!" Jackie cooed from the Nav Room behind Pat. "It's *wonderful,* Jonathan James! People *love* you!"

*God, listen to her!*

Pat willed himself to shake off the *Gripkill,* October 8, and Jackie, and looked over the newsfeeds in disbelief. If anyone had paid attention to Jack Commer's son before this day, it was to jeer that the kid had emerged *non compos mentis* from his stunt in Alpha Centauri, that he was an egomaniacal fool and it served him right to have his brains burned out. And weren't his father's brains also burned out and shouldn't he get lost along with his son and scheming wife and sycophantic kid brother Joe as well?

But now there seemed to be a hundred Jonathan James Commer fan clubs, all urging him, the *Typhoon II,* and its "jolly mad crew" on to glory. "The Rebellion is Now! The Rebellion is Us!" clamored one particularly effective post by Salla Hurtif, a young female SolNet commentator Pat had always had the hots for.

"The SolGrid Rebellion against the Enslaving Hive Mind!" screamed another by Porr'fd/Gllun, the most influential Martian commentator. Maybe only five Martians bothered to write commentary for SolNet, but Porr'fd/Gllun had managed to stay fairly sane through the recent Martian outradiance static and was unusually lucid in his article.

And he was right. SolGrid was a catastrophe. Pat had thrown it together way too fast in December, figuring he could patch errors in the beta release, but now he understood that the Alpha Centaurian software he'd so painstakingly memorized was, at its core, *irrational.* No patch could ever fix it.

He stared at his console in disbelief. There would never be

a SolGrid Draft Two.

# CHAPTER FOURTEEN
Fascist Patsie

Pat numbly perused the next article. He'd always ignored anything that came out of Anti-SolGrid, which had sprung up in January in feeble-minded protest against a Grid it had no hope of understanding. The ASG consisted of the militant Dark and apparently harbored both privacy advocates as well as criminals, and possibly any remaining Wounded who needed to be ferreted out and executed.

Now ASG's latest post, "Fascist Patsie Sees the Light," praised him for "finally realizing the nature of the monstrosity he unleashed on Sol in December" and for "throwing in with Jonathan James and the Transcendent Rebellion that will destroy the fascist SolGrid forever!"

Pat managed a listless chuckle. The fascist SolGrid was already *gone,* didn't they know it? But the next paragraph hurt.

"The remaining benighted fascists among SolGrid's Board of Directors officially fired Fascist Patsie James as president of SolGrid, Inc. fifteen minutes ago."

Well, he supposed he'd known that was coming. They'd just had to shackle him with a Board of Directors, hadn't they?

"Whoa, dude!" JJC called. "I see they dumped you."

"Yeah, yeah, yeah," Pat said. "So what?"

"Well, cheer up, Patty. We don't need a damn Grid where we're going anyway."

"Huh," was all Pat deigned to mutter. Of course they wouldn't need a Grid. They were just five reckless idiots, along with an insane raving Martian and a disgusting dog, trying to pull off a farce that would get them all killed.

On the other hand, five people might be the perfect size for a smaller, more focused experiment. Pat shivered in wonder as fresh code unfolded in his head. Not a measly second draft vainly trying to fix the unfixable, but a totally new concept: *SolGrid II.* Yes, this crew of renegades could be the perfect testbed.

Starting small and slow was the way to go. It would be so

*beautiful.* Pat sketched line after line of effortless code that would lock these five people into SolGrid II, fully sharing *everything.* It would be a perfect new Grid, confined to this ship. As new members joined the rebellion, Pat would scale SolGrid II up and strengthen it. SolGrid II would actually *save* the rebellion. Surely JJC would see that.

They'd have to leave Z'B out of it, of course. A bonkers Martian would throw off the new Dimensional Gather Matrix which Pat began coding on the spot. Likewise a drooling telepathic dog had to be excluded or else the DGM would choke on the raw animal frequencies. Only human beings could join SolGrid II.

If they all shared, Jackie would finally know how furious Pat was at all her betrayals. Suzette would know his passion for her. Everyone would. Even JJC couldn't stand in the way of Pat's love for Suzette. Pat and Suzette would fully unite in SolGrid II.

"Three minutes, fourteen seconds left in the first Star Drive," Hirte called. "Patster, I'll alert you at thirty seconds so you can start running your position scans."

Now *Sanders* was assigning nicknames. Pat giddily tried to assess how all this unreality had unfolded. He hadn't known he was in such despair over SolGrid. For the first time he boggled at how quickly he'd been able to kick it over and commit to JJC's outrageous folly.

For all Pat knew, Jonathan James had been planning his doomed rebellion ever since Daddy sent him to Earth to get counseled by that Urside jerk. Someone who'd tried to take on the emperorship of Alpha Centauri, however unsuccessfully and no matter what horrors he'd experienced, wouldn't forget the high of that. Pat had known that high himself, appalling as it was, back in '35 when he'd been brainwashed on this same damn ship.

JJC had known he'd attract a following. The new fan clubs on SolNet were ample proof of that. SolNet had quickly distributed the manifesto JJC had left on his SolNet page, timed to publish an hour after the *Typhoon* left Enceladus, and naming the Six Rebels, the five humans and Trotter, as JJC had only thought of taking Z'B at the last minute.

Pat had to admit the genius of rallying followers to a Gridless Empire, readily tapping an emerging backlash against Grid consciousness. As JJC's manifesto blared: "We declare that Grids are a malicious control-freak dream best left to the stinking Centaurians, and that we intend to leave Sol and create an entirely new society with no Grid whatsoever, a society of peace, privacy, and mutual respect between all beings."

JJC didn't really need a Grid. He had his own, built right in. That damn charisma. He still looked like a hot teenage boy-toy even though he was twenty-eight. At first glance the lanky, moody young man with the mournful eyes struck you as a case of severe depression. Then he'd laugh in effortless delight and somehow he *had* you. Pat could see why Suzette flipped for him, why Jackie was flipping for him.

Yes, Jackie's damn rejuvenation had taken well. It didn't make her look nineteen like Suzette, but nobody really expected that. She was eight years older than Pat, but appeared to be in her mid-thirties, and damn alluring, he had to admit.

So why was their sex so boring? Why had she asked how *Pat's* rejuvenation was going? What was all that talk about hormones going through the roof? Were hers? Was it true that rejuv turned some people into sex addicts? Had Jackie turned into a sex addict?

"Crew, this is Hirte. Out of Star Drive in thirty seconds. Good luck on the Nav reorientation, Patster."

"*Swine,* all of you ..." Pat muttered. "Okay, I'm on it. Diagnostics coming."

When JJC had unfolded his plot at the Saturnalian last night, Suzette had laughed so hard she'd choked on her iced tea. Only after several minutes of absorbing JJC's shockingly detailed plans could everyone accept that the youngster was serious about stealing the *Typhoon II*. Pat waited for the ever-respectable University of Mars Professor of Exobiology Jackie Vespertine to stomp off in revulsion. Instead she'd cried: "Yes! Nobody would think we'd take the *Typhoon!* That's the only way to do it!"

Pat had been too shocked to form a coherent thought. But hadn't this madness come at just the right moment? Wasn't it time to chuck the failed SolGrid and move towards an unimaginable new solution? Wasn't that solution to be found at the heart of this wild act of piracy? Could he possibly have visualized SolGrid II before this day?

Why had he blurted that he'd stick with JJC until *death?* He flashed back to the museum opening at ten this morning, with JJC thrusting a shattergun set on stun into Pat's hand. Why had he thrown away SolGrid, his life's work, just like that?

Answer: to stay next to Suzette Borman and take her away from the bastard. Ever since she'd gotten rejuvenated, he'd known where it would lead. *To sex with Suzette!*

"Out of Star Drive, people," Hirte called. "Patster, prepare to--"

"I'm *on* it, dammit!" Pat snapped. "The entire thing's computerized, you know. It'll only take a couple goddamn seconds."

"Whoa!" came JJC's soft laugh. "Patster, don't flip out on us or anything."

"Okay, okay, I'm goddamn sorry. It's just there are some system checks you people ought to be running up there instead of bothering me every few seconds."

"Okay, got the point, dude," Hirte responded. "Running Midpoint Diagnostic."

*Amateurs.* "Be sure to use the '64 update to that, and run it on B mode."

"Forget '64, guy, I've upgraded Midpoint to the latest release."

"*What* latest--" Pat broke off as a new voice came into his mind.

*Wow what happened where are we?*

"Aw, *crap!*" Pat said as Z'B came fully awake and billions of thoughts and sensations began broadcasting throughout all levels of Pat's mind. He thought he might puke on his console. Why was he one of those cursed people who was so damn sensitive to Martian outradiance? It was okay if you were around serene Martians controlling their thoughts, but Z'B was clearly psycho. Fever dreams, nightmares, spreadsheets and programming scripts tumbled crazily through Pat's mind. "Can somebody give that thing another shot to knock him out again?"

He heard the Nav Room door open. Footsteps clinked on the catwalk.

"Okay, I'm here in the kitchenette with Z'B," Jackie spoke over the intercom. "He looks almost white. No, I see some pink coming back. His eyes are open. He seems calm. Z'B, would you like another Alpha-Omega?"

A telepathic burst of undecipherable static, then Z'B's voice, almost a whisper: "Yes, ma'am, please, everything's so scary right now."

"Here you go, then."

*We are done with Star Drive? This is a crappy ship with bad Star Drive!* came into Pat's mind along with detailed mathematical proofs of the amount of suffering a Martian central nervous system could take before exploding.

"No, we're just at the midpoint now, hon," Jackie said. "We just have one more Star Drive after this little rest. That one will be eleven minutes, too. Believe me, I know how it feels. But the A-O will put you right out in a second. And I'll stay here with you during the Star Drive and give you another if you need it, okay?"

"Just space the damn thing," Pat muttered. "Goddamn brain's totally gone."

"I don't *want* another Star Drive!" Z'B cried, then, telepathically: *You kill the Emperor of the Martians? And for what? You kill--*

Then the drug took hold and all that remained was a faint undertone of Martian despair.

## CHAPTER FIFTEEN
### Rejuvenation

The door slid open.

"Hi …" Suzette Borman said as Pat gaped at the radiance of her total being. He'd fought to look away from that low-cut white blouse all morning. She had on light blue leggings that hugged every magnificently sculpted square centimeter of calf, thigh, ass, and crotch, including the glorious bulge at her pubis. Her deep-set, dilated brown eyes fixed on his and her rich lips parted in an enigmatic smile.

"May I join you, Mr. Patster?" she whispered, stepping into the cramped Comm Room and sliding the door shut. Her bare forearm brushed his shoulder and he flinched at the shock of the touch. He stared at the shorter brown hair inadvertently snipped during the Pod's decompression. It was as if the EnviroField had known exactly how to frame her exotic face, effortlessly bringing out her pointed chin and that suggestive dark mouth.

"Well, not much room in here. I'm, uh, just doing the position check."

While it was possible to stand up by the door of the room, the curved fuselage meant that Pat couldn't scoot his chair aside and stand himself. He was trapped at his console. Suzette put a hand on the table and leaned close. "JJC wanted me to see how you were doing. Are you okay?"

Pat winced. He'd managed to put JJC's disgusting Billy spacesuit out of mind for several minutes, but the sickening image resurfaced of Jonathan James prancing around in that damn black thing, dick and balls flopping. "Uh, sure I am."

"It's all right. Sanders warned me this old Star Drive might be a little rough. I think it's affected all of us. I can't tell you how relaxed I feel now that we're out of it."

"Well, we might all benefit from a dose of Alpha-Omega, I guess."

"Right! We were thinking maybe you needed a little cheering up." She punched his shoulder. "You sounded so *worried,* maybe, or stressed or something."

"I--I'm all right," he muttered, face not eight inches from her lowered chest. He couldn't help but stare. He could see almost all of them. Was she not wearing a bra? Yes, she was, but it was so low-cut itself, so red and lacy--

Pat fought the urge to reach down and straighten himself out in his pants.

Suzette smiled at Pat's gaze. Sweat broke out on his forehead. He heard Trotter barking through the closed door. Z'B was dreaming something like *song cosine setting moon hyperbola x, y integrated surface rotation corridor < infinity.*

"Why is he *here?*" Pat moaned into Suzette's smooth tanned mammaries. "We were fools to kidnap him!"

Suzette squatted beside Pat's console. Now he could see even more. "Jonathan James thinks Z'B really *wanted* to come. We all felt that at the time, I think."

Pat dizzily shook his head. "Well, maybe."

Did yakking over and over about *ADVENTURE! ADVENTURE! ADVENTURE!* count for anything? Pat had hardly been able to recognize the frail, trembling Emperor of the Martians. What had Z'B been doing waiting at the museum doors at ten AM, mind hopelessly scattered as were those of his Martian assistants behind him? He'd just *decided* to visit Enceladus on a whim? Today of all days? The museum employees were unlocking the doors, their smiles changing to consternation as their docent JJC, then two men and two women, pushed past the dazed Martians and made for the hatchway to the *Typhoon's* Pod, JJC shouting for everyone to hit the floor as he waved an EOS shattergun.

A security guard had rushed up, his own shattergun, Pat had seen with 20/10 rejuvenated eyesight, set to full Electron Oblivion Sequencing.

Decades of USSF training had kicked in. Pat, armed like JJC and Sanders, had shot first and stunned the mother, who must've slid unconscious twenty feet across the slick marble floor amid Z'B's endless telepathic babbling about how much *fun* this all was.

Four more museum guards raised weapons. JJC yanked Z'B

from his screaming Martian underlings, placing the shattergun at the Emperor's temple as Hirte and Pat blasted at the guards. Pat was relieved to see all the guards sprawled on the floor and was immensely proud that he'd stunned four and Hirte only one. Jackie and Suzette scrambled for the Pod hatch as Z'B's mind broke apart in spasms of delight.

Then they were all in the Pod and Hirte punched comm commands that shot *Typhoon* and Pod from the museum, the hatch barely closing before half their air blew out. Hirte scrambled up the spiral staircase to the Control Room and engaged the cloaking tech he'd uploaded.

And Pat had been insane ever since.

*She has the most perfect pair of boobs I've ever seen! Oh my God!*

"We really think Z'B wants to be with us," Suzette said, tossing her longer unsnipped hair to the right where it slapped Pat's hand. He stared in astonishment at the black strands resting on his fingers. "The Martians *hate* SolGrid. JJC thinks Z'B will rally the Martians to our side. It's really genius, I think."

"But there's nothing left of his *mind.*"

What did this mean? Hair on his hand? Those breasts? God, she smelled good.

"JJC thinks the further we get away from Sol, and the longer he's out of the SolGrid field, the better he'll get."

Pat shook his head. "I don't know. Maybe. I know Martians don't do well with the Grid. I still don't know why. But I think that stint in *Garr/thahg* did his mind in. It gave him all that knowledge and power, but it only lasted a little while and then his brains burned out. All four of 'em, Kner and Will and K'ufunb too. They're all *gone.*"

There, shock her with ruthless cynicism.

"Well, just think what they all went through." Crouching, Suzette let her shoulder come against Pat's forearm and rested it there. Then pressed in further. "JJC's uncle thinks you've been jealous of the Four," she purred.

"What? Did *that* get around?" Pat muttered, jerking away from her warm shoulder, then feeling the loss and quickly moving his forearm back into position, where Suzette eagerly pressed back into the *feel* again. "Well, I guess a lot of people heard about that. Joe Commer of all people. Nicest guy in the world. Guess he had a few too many beers. Maybe I did too. But so what?"

"It's okay, dear heart," Suzette whispered, pressing further in and following with a pat to his hand. "I'm sure it was difficult for you."

Pat stared at the top of Suzette's dark head. She was all over him. He couldn't see her breasts from this angle, but *dear heart?* What did that mean? "I mean, *Joe.* And at my retirement dinner! The jerk says I'm *jealous* the Four got to go to *Garr/thahg* and get all this infinite knowledge. Like SolGrid's trash or something. Screw that! I told the son of a bitch not to psychoanalyze me. He backed way off!"

"*Wow* ..." Suzette murmured. "Good for you!"

"I bet his damn brother sent him to tell me to slow down on SolGrid. But I had the plan. I knew how to make a complete Grid!"

"Oh, nobody disputes *that,* Mr. Patster! Just between you and me, that's one reason JJC just fell in *love* with the idea of having you onboard. You know SolGrid, and *all* Grids, inside out. Know the enemy, that's what they say!"

Pat shook his head. Was she saying Jonathan James considered him the enemy? How was he ever going to convince JJC he could build SolGrid II without the problems of the original? "Well, just remember we needed SolGrid to find those seven thousand Wounded. Everyone knows that. And we still need it to find whoever else is still hiding. That's what I've been trying to tell JJC."

Suzette shrugged, sending his forearm hairs tingling. She peered deeply into his eyes. "And you were *there,* at Iota Persei, captured by the Wounded! Poor baby, you must have been just *traumatized.* No wonder you'd want a SolGrid to hunt down all those monsters."

"Well, no, that's not really it, I guess. The whole damn thing at Iota Persei happened so fast that, well, I never really felt much,

I guess. Maybe I should have, I don't know. I was just sort of a bystander, really."

Her smile was devastating. "Well, I'm sure you were trying to do the right thing with your SolGrid!"

Did she want him? Should he kiss her?

"They *wrecked* my retirement dinner! But so what? I'm out of the damn USSF, so Joe, and Jack, and everyone, can just screw off."

"That's the spirit! That's what JJC saw in you. Tossing everything aside for a completely *new* way of life!"

Was she really tossing JJC aside? For Pat? "But I think maybe a real Grid might be about, like, you know, *real* sharing. Like maybe just between two people, you know."

Suzette licked her lips. "I didn't realize you were so romantic, Mr. Patster!"

The next thing he knew Pat was leaning to her, his fingers raising her chin, aiming his lips for hers.

"Oh, no no!" Suzette laughed, pushing back from his console but still squatting against the door. "Dear Mr. Patrick James, what *are* you thinking?"

Pat stared down into freshly-revealed cleavage. "You--you--"

"Dear Mr. Patster, you aren't getting the *wrong idea,* are you?" Suzette said with merry brown eyes. "You know I belong to Jonathan James now. Just because you share a name with him doesn't give you any special rights, if you know what I mean and I think you do!"

"Do--do you just screw *everybody?* First Hirte, and now *him?*"

"Oh, absolutely *not,* dear Patster! I'm surprised you could be so crude. Sanders and I agreed our time was done, and now I belong lock, stock, and barrel to Jonathan James Commer. What do you think I *am?*"

"I--I think you're *goddamn gorgeous!*" Pat babbled. "Dammit, let's get out of these *clothes!* We have room here!"

"*Here?*" Suzette laughed. "In this tiny little room, with all these dust bunnies on the floor? Under your desk here, maybe?

I think not, Mr. Horny Patster Jamesie!"

"We have time! The system checks are done, Nav's updated, and we won't kick in Star Drive for another--" Pat stared at the console. *Two minutes?* "We have time!"

"Time? For what? What exactly did you have in mind, Mr. Patster?"

"You--you--" He swiveled his chair at her, spreading his legs and pointing to the immense mound at his crotch. "This! *This!*"

"Oh!" Suzette giggled. "I've been *wondering* what you'd been hiding in there all this time! What could it *be,* I wonder?"

"You--God!" He yanked his zipper down. To his astonishment Suzette grasped his hand so tightly he couldn't move it, then slid the zipper back up, her fingers pushing against his solid central self.

"Mr. Patster, anyone can see you're totally out of control. JJC wouldn't like that at all, you know, even though it's completely understandable under the circumstances. He's *depending* on you to set us up for the second Star Drive." She looked up to his console. "In one minute, thirty-seven seconds, if you must know, dear heart!"

"God! Your--your *breasts!*"

"Oh, is *that* the problem, dearest? Have to admit even I was surprised at what rejuv did to my girls! They're a lot bigger than I remember when I was a teenager! Firmer, too, if you must know!"

Pat stared. "I ... I *want* them!"

"Well, thank you for your interest in the tits of a poor co-owner of a nightclub! *And* the wife of a United System senator! But if you must know, and I think you must, JJC *wanted* me to wear his favorite top this morning. He *wanted* men to appreciate a little feminine flash. Those were his exact words."

"You--you--?" Pat choked, eyeing the clock. 1:19. He was scrambled. Scrambled like Z'B two compartments away.

*Area tangent surface null as z approaches 0, vector derivative acceleration--*

"No! No!" he screamed.

"Oh, dear, we were afraid you might freak out with sex," Suzette said, massaging Pat's shoulders. "You'll be okay, dear heart. JJC and I figured you were maybe just, you know, a little inexperienced and all."

"Me? I'm *sixty-eight,* goddammit!"

She laughed. "But rejuv does that to us! You *look* thirty-five, but somehow your mind went back to *fourteen!* That's what JJC and I think. Sanders too. And if you really must know, once Sanders and I called it quits, well, I can't even get him to look down my shirt anymore. He just doesn't care now. Isn't that amazing? So, really, Jamesie, it's just you and JJC who seem to have any urge to stick that big thing there into poor little Suzette!" She pointed to Pat's crotch, which was now anything but impressive.

"You--you--God!"

"Is our Jackie not servicing your *thing* very well these days?"

"Well ... *no* ..."

"Well, you might have to kiss all that goodbye, too, then! Because I've seen my old Sanders looking over your Jackie *very* carefully, if you must know! And she's looking back! Yes she is!"

"You--you can't know that!"

"Oh, I most certainly can! Of course she wants a piece of my JJC. But that won't happen. Jackie's rejuv is fascinating, by the way. She's a tiger! Her body just screams *mature sexual intercourse.* She must know every trick in the book! Any man would go gaga over her. I'm surprised you let her go, Mr. Patster."

"I--I *didn't.*" He turned back to the console. Thirty-five seconds left.

"But she can't touch me and she knows it. I have all my forty-two years of experience with men, repackaged with all my adolescent hormones just *raging,* Mr. Patster. You know, I can't help but tell you that maybe something *could* have happened between you and me, dear, it's just that I can't do anything about it! I belong to JJC! Then again, who knows what might happen on this trip?"

"Are you saying Jackie's leaving me for *Sanders Hirte?*"

"Musical chairs, Mr. Patster. Now I have JJC, the absolute *master* of sex. I'm learning so much from the *master*. No way Sanders ever came close to him."

"So--I'm *alone?*"

"Oh, no! We all have our special friends. I have JJC, Jackie's about to get Sanders, and *you* have *Z'B!*"

*Arc congruent volume sphere pi, if dimensions = N+1 then emptiness > infinity.*

"No! Are you *crazy?*"

Suzette smoothed her blouse. "Well, who knows what might happen?"

Pat stared in shock into her taunting brown eyes. Without thinking he reached for those miraculous boobs. And she let him squeeze. They *were* firm.

Suzette regarded his fondling hands. "Who *knows* what might happen?" she repeated. "To all of us?" She pulled his fingers off her chest but held them a few seconds before letting them drop. "Jonathan James said I would be his Empress! Can *you* match that, dear Mr. Patster, with all your fourteen-year-old sex urges?"

Pat stared back in dismay. "You--you--"

"All hands, prepare for Star Drive in ten seconds!" came Hirte's shout over the intercom.

Suzette shrugged. She made no move to slide the Comm/Sensor Room door open. "Oh dear, I might just have to stay here with you for the Drive. I hope it won't be as rough as the first one." She settled herself onto Pat's lap, and he stared up into the incomprehensible dark hair enveloping him. Her arms came around him, her breasts pressed into his face, but he could tell that it was all about the anxiety of the coming Drive.

# CHAPTER SIXTEEN
Venus

A hard whomp spun the saucer sideways. Amav fought the shuddering control stick. "Dammit, what's wrong with the stabilization matrix?"

"Unknown communications problems. Matrix compensating. Partial loss of Venusian Positioning System Feed. Rerouting autothruster interface," the saucer replied. "Upload last parameters from internal database?"

"No, those won't be current. What's Sat One saying?" Four more air pockets hit like brick walls and she wrenched the stick back and forth, stamping the foot-controlled side thrusters to even out the ship.

"No response from Sat One. Attempting to contact SolNet Knowledgebase."

"C'mon, we haven't seen a stupid storm interfere with comm links in *years*."

"Agreed. Last known Sat One outage due to Venusian weather activity was February 14, 2054."

"*Damn,*" she grunted as she fought the controls. Though her father had declared the terraforming of Venus complete except for minor cleanup tasks, there were decades of work ahead for planetary engineering graduate students. The runaway greenhouse effect had been tamed, and in most areas temperatures had cooled into semi-livable conditions from the original, scarcely believable 900-degree Fahrenheit range, but there were lowland pockets of high pressure and heat that would kill in a second. Breathable oxygenated atmosphere had been her father's final contribution to the project, but even then, much of the atmosphere was still tainted with sulfuric acid in lethal concentrations. For that reason only the highlands of Ishtar and Aphrodite were considered viable for human colonization.

Another sickening thump. For the first time Amav thought of the emergency Venus suits stored in the lockers behind her.

"Altitude?" she muttered.

"7.566 miles."

"Hell! Any idea when Sat One will be back online?"

"Negative. SolNet Knowledgebase suggests landing the ship and rebooting all systems."

"Screw Knowledgebase! I'm *trying* to land this damn thing!"

The weather and position information from Sat One, constantly fed into spacecraft around Venus, was so granular that even tiny gusts of wind were taken into account to keep ships stabilized. Huge military craft could bull their way through with their mass and their onboard weather technology, but small ships relied on Sat One. An odd side effect of the Terraforming Project was that atmospheric turbulence had actually increased in unpredictable ways. This was the roughest she'd seen.

Martians with Amplified Thought could navigate their saucers through this chaos with relative ease, but very few Martians seemed to have a grip on AT these days. The Martian Scatter had been increasing daily, as she knew from her worsening headaches. The past few weeks she'd been in despair, barely able to think, wondering where this would all lead. Maybe to a brain aneurism, who knew? Being sensitive to Martian outradiance had always been a blessing. Now it was a curse.

Amav knew she was dangerously rattled. She'd kept the newsfeeds on, stunned by the unfolding *Typhoon II* reports. It looked as if Jackie Vespertine and Patrick James had defected to whatever craziness her son was pulling. And JJC had kidnapped Z'B, who could've easily blown up Enceladus and every ship orbiting it with a single thought, but was apparently too flummoxed to even whimper for help. Why had the Emperor taken it into his head to make a midnight run to Enceladus with all his clueless junior officers? Amav was supposed to have met him on Venus about now.

The talking heads on the SolNet feed nattered on through increasing static.

"Joining us just now is Major Carla Posttner, Head of USSF Detention Services. Major Posttner, welcome."

"Thank you, Salla, it's a pleasure. I just got out of an emergency meeting with the United System Council."

"We've just had word that the Council has ordered Jack Commer to arrest his son Jonathan James Commer on charges of treason. Is that your understanding, Major?"

"*W-what?*" Amav gasped.

"Absolutely. I don't mind saying that I've also recommended that Supreme Commander Commer himself be court-martialed upon his return, given that he has illegally taken the new *Typhoon VI* on this mission, endangering an extremely expensive USSF weapons platform for a trivial purpose."

"Well, Major, there are those who disagree, stating that since the *Typhoon II* has apparently been upgraded with unknown new devices, we may in fact be looking at Wounded technology in operation. There are those who speculate that Jonathan James himself might have been brainwashed by the Wounded, or even be a robotic facsimile of Jonathan James Commer."

"That's all irrelevant, Salla. We've got to face the facts and not indulge in panicky speculation about the Wounded, who we all know have been decisively exterminated in Sol. The fact is that the *Typhoon II* is a USSF ship on loan to the Typhoon Museum, and the theft of a USSF ship comes under the jurisdiction of Detention Services. And before anyone accuses me of usurping authority, as both the Supreme Commander and Deputy Supreme Commander illegally suggested to me earlier this morning, may I remind you and your audience that the Office of Detention Services must be accountable to *nothing* but the pursuit of justice. When and if this office differs from higher USSF authority, its own interests predominate. End of story, Salla."

"Is this really the end of the story, though, Major? No less an authority than Fulr-Kla of the Supercommittee has stated that Jack Commer's mission may be crucial in discovering traces of Wounded infiltration in Sol."

"I *cannot* and *will not* allow the terrorist tactics of the Commer brothers to interfere with the pursuit of justice, Salla. This is why I appealed in my capacity as Marsport Councilwoman to the United System Council and obtained an executive order mandating that Jack Commer make this arrest. Let's face it, Commer is a *coward* and his most likely course of action will be to try to convince his son to come home for more of the failed counseling that's never had the slightest effect. May I remind you and your listeners that Commer Junior is a deranged young man who wants to reconstitute his former Alpha Centaurian Empire, and I aim to see him locked up for thirty years in Detention Services. *That'll* fix the damn Commers! You mark my--"

Static.

"--believe I understand your principles, but the threat of the Wounded--"

Static.

"--screw the Wounded! If you had the slightest idea of the *appalling* manner in which I was treated aboard--"

Static.

"--if that's so, then--"

"--sadistic *bitch* with her shattergun set on *nerve pain*--"

"SolNet Venus down," the ship said. "All communication with SolNet Mars gone."

"Why?" Amav cried. "Dammit, something *big* just shifted in the Total Martian Outradiance! I can feel it! Because Z'B was kidnapped! No Emperor's *ever* been kidnapped! But every Martian *knows* that now. Somehow they're wrecking SolNet!"

"An interesting theory that this ship cannot corroborate, not being able to interface with Total Martian Outradiance."

"No, it's true! The whole foundation of Martian life is just *coming apart.* That *has* to find its way into SolNet!"

"Possibly. In a study of the solar system disasters of the late '20s, Elgklar Pw'j postulated that negative Amplified Thought oscillations may have contributed--"

A wild lurch and the saucer was upside down. Amav focused on the backup attitude system and yanked the control stick to flip the craft upright. Thank God she and Jack had wanted the sport model saucer with manual controls; she could never have pulled off these maneuvers by tapping console squares. Hit after hit of hard sulfuric Venusian atmosphere rocked the ship.

"Damn! Is *all* contact with Sat One gone?"

"Correct. Compensating with onboard sensors. Attempting to pick up beacon from *Garr/thahg* Castle."

"Am I still on course for Lakshmi?"

The ship hesitated. "Maybe."

"*Maybe?*"

"Sensor probes of surface indicate flight path more or less on course for the Castle. There is much signal noise. Concerning your theory of Martian origin of this noise, may this ship recommend that you consult SolGrid for an answer?"

"*What?* Is SolGrid still online?"

"SolGrid is online. As you are no doubt aware, but may have momentarily forgotten in your current stressful state, SolGrid is independent of SolNet."

"Oh, of course!" Amav shuddered. Like Jack and Joe, she'd dipped into SolGrid just once in December and had been appalled by a couple seconds of contact with *everything*. She'd also seen in those few seconds how many USSF secrets she happened to know were leaking out. Some of the security cleanup after SolGrid came online was for concepts pulled out of her own mind.

Of course, try as she might to forget, December wasn't the first time Amav had known Grid consciousness. She could barely force herself to recall last July, and her insolent son's demented attempt to restore the Alpha Centaurian Grid and name himself Emperor. But for half an hour Amav had known the full ancient Centaurian horror of it. She'd tried to tell herself and everyone else, including Jack, that she didn't remember much, or that she'd succumbed against her will, but that was pure self-delusion, for she recalled every humiliating detail. Deep down she'd *chosen* to follow her own son's command to seduce her old friend Phil Sperry, just so JJC and his cohort Clopt could record some idiotic human sexual code for their nasty software. She'd spent months trying to convince herself that she'd simply been temporarily brainwashed, but for half an hour last July she'd readily ridden uncontrollable lust for poor

Phil, oblivious to Jack who'd been so seriously injured that he might have died right next to his frenzied nude wife straddling Phil, begging him to bang her brains out. Yeah, it hadn't gone anywhere near intercourse, but so what? The shame of it was more than enough.

So in December she'd dared herself to sample SolGrid to prove she could handle it, that July had just been an aberration impossible to repeat. In a way the experience had been beneficial, because it was obvious that this SolGrid software was different. There was no sense of brainwashing; you always knew you could come out. But it was hard to admit that the flavor of being inside SolGrid was the same as last July, with the identical temptation of possibly deciding after all to refuse to leave such paradise.

What really scared her was that the Technique, as it was called, for entering SolGrid seemed at first as complicated as learning a new programming language. But after the first rough steps of alien logic, the SolGrid software proceeded to teach you how to memorize the rest of the Technique. The entire process took three seconds. And once you had the Technique, you never forgot it. Millions of Sol citizens now used SolGrid daily, but where were their minds after three and a half months of use? How could anyone, especially a genius like Patrick James, contend that SolGrid offered an enlightened new way of sharing intimacy with billions of people? That it would make the present SolNet digital network look like Neanderthal cave drawings?

Jack had told her that although he still remembered the Technique, he wasn't sure he could call it up so quickly, in contrast to Amav who worried just how fast *she* could. When Jack said he wanted to start meditating, she was afraid it might inadvertently lead him into the Technique. But he'd assured her that, as far as his limited experiments showed, meditation and SolGrid were mutually exclusive mental states.

Amav thought she should take up meditation herself, if only to ward off the irrational fear that she might slip into the Technique in a moment of anger or stress.

And remain in that brave new Grid, saturated in

overwhelming, unfocused erotic fantasy, forever.

Something like a boulder slammed the front right of the saucer. Again the ship spun madly, and this time Amav found she couldn't get the thrusters to stop the whirling.

"Ship! Where am I? How high?"

"Altitude 5.67 miles. Atmospheric buffeting has thrown the ship off course. Sensors offline. Engine offline. Attitude thrusters offline. Environmental controls offline."

"*What?*"

"I must say good luck to you, pilot Amav. All internal systems aboard this ship will cease functioning in ten seconds. I recommend you install Venus Suit Five on your person before the lights go out. Approximate projected site of ground impact fifty-five miles southeast of Lakshmi Planum. Goodbye. Ship AI interface now offline."

Amav wasted one of the seconds staring at the dimming colors on her console displays. Then she found herself ripping open a locker and jerking out the Five Venus suit, the one for highest pressure rating.

She pulled the suit on as everything went dark. The inertial dampers failed and she was hurled against the saucer wall as centrifugal forces built in the flailing, tumbling craft. The helmet rolled away but she dragged herself along the wall and felt for it in the black chaos, snagged it and clamped it on.

The Technique unfolded effortlessly.

# CHAPTER SEVENTEEN
## The Computational Capacity to Indulge in Chitchat

"Mistress, are you all right?"

Diffuse light spangled off Amav's visor. She looked up at bright red hair, clear blue eyes and delicate cheeks framed by distant specks of purple high above. "*Laurie!* How did *you* get here?"

"It's *me,* Mistress Amav! And John. We're here for you." The woman pointed to the gray sweatshirt she wore with "283" across the chest in black six-inch-high letters.

Were those leaves up there? The purple leaves of Venusian trees? "Oh … *283,*" Amav muttered, so comfortable in her Venus suit, so warm …

*Those are Frankston trees! I made it! That's Laurie 283.*

"When you were overdue, we used the Castle scanners to figure out where you might've landed," said robot John J. Douglas. "Take it easy for a minute while we scan you." Amav fought to bring his white handlebar mustache into focus. "We're having some trouble with communications static, my lady, but our internal med scanners are working. Damn slow, I'll admit! No broken bones I can see."

"All internal organs look fine, too," Laurie said.

"Where--? How--?" Amav felt herself drifting back into *everything.* She was still plugged in. Millions of beings careened through her brain. It all seethed in agony even as the telepathic pressure spread through every cell of her body in a distinctly pleasurable way.

No wonder people stayed connected. It was a network of emotions and thoughts trivial, profound, and mistaken at all once. It was like absorbing every novel ever written and then realizing you had to do it a billion times again. Amav knew she could call up every detail of every single person's day--no, of their entire *lives*--if she was just curious enough to follow any of those trillions of paths.

No. She wouldn't join. They couldn't have *her* path. But the universe seemed to be waiting for her to take any one path. And all paths led to the same place.

"*Death!* Oh my God, *death!*" she screamed, wrenching at her helmet.

"Take it easy, mistress," robot Laurie 283 said. "And don't take off that helmet yet. We're way down in a valley and the pressure is high. And let's just say I can *feel* the atmosphere trying to burn off my plasti-skin. You could breathe it, but it'd be rough."

Only now did Amav register that the robots, though open to the Venusian environment, were speaking via her suit radio.

"Any idea where your ship is?" John asked.

"N-no ..." *Get out of SolGrid! Out!*

With a force of will she had no idea she was capable of, Amav shut down the Technique and felt for her fingers and toes, felt for the entire body she'd somehow surrendered to *them,* and to all possible permutations of existence merging into ...

*Don't think of it!*

"I'm *alive,*" she moaned through the ongoing headache. "I made it!"

"I certainly don't see how," John commented, examining her suit. "The rocket packs are full, the wing gliders never deployed, and both parachutes are still packed."

"No footprints through here except ours," Laurie said, pointing to the murky surroundings. Amav saw they were in a tight ring of Frankston trees. The endless gray-green trunks, striated in severe vertical lines, had always reminded her of poplars. Her father had confessed that he'd used Amav's favorite tree as a basis for the design of the Frankston tree. It made the perfect plant for a Venusian jungle. Four hundred feet up, the trunks forked into warring fifty-foot branches, sprouting thousands of foot-wide purple flower-leaves absorbing what sun they could. The trees were incredible works of art, six-hundred-foot-high monsters that helped clear the atmosphere of both carbon dioxide and sulfuric acid.

Amav allowed a vague memory to emerge from SolGrid, a dream that made no sense. Knowing exactly how to fly a dead saucer by thought alone? Martian Amplified Thought?

The dream also brought the nauseating realization that no Martian ever wanted to connect to SolGrid again. Yet everything about the dream pointed to Amav Frankston Commer unleashing a fully developed Martian Amplified Thought command to let the saucer drop like a rock as close to *Garr/thahg* Castle as it could get, then make the spacecraft cease to exist as Amav's flight-suited body decelerated from five hundred miles per hour to come to a soft landing on this patch of gray dirt.

She tried to sit up. "Damn!"

"Are you all right, mistress?" Laurie 283 asked, absurdly feeling the top of Amav's helmet with a bare hand.

"Just a headache. I'm okay, just a little dizzy."

"That's good, because your helmet is 169 degrees Fahrenheit!" Laurie laughed.

"I recommend we carry her back to the Castle," John said. "Her suit only has thirty-six minutes of oxygen, and it's too damn hot here."

"Agreed," Laurie said. "Mistress, we can get you home in twenty minutes."

"We're just 73.668 miles from the Castle," John said. "Laurie will carry you and I'll scout ahead and clear obstacles."

Laurie helped Amav to her feet, then backed herself into Amav's chest and hoisted her. Amav found her arms and legs magnetized around Laurie's torso. John J. Douglas erupted into a blur in front of her, threading his way through twenty giant tree trunks and flinging fallen branches to the side. Then he vanished to a pinpoint.

"Oh, my--" Amav had time to grunt before the acceleration kicked in. Tree trunks, hills and depressions flooded past her. "How fast are we going?"

"Don't worry, this is a moderate speed for us," Laurie radioed. "Average speed 221.004 miles per hour. I'm tracking John's every movement. He's clearing everything in front of us. Enjoy the ride! We'll be there in twenty minutes."

Frankston trees flashed past and vibrations from Laurie's whirling feet rocketed up Amav's spine. Amav thought she'd vomit from the relentless changes of vector and velocity and the sickening sense that every onrushing tree would crush her to a pulp. But Laurie 283 was a robot that couldn't make a mistake. She fought for self-control. She'd just been through a saucer crash and SolGrid, so what was one more piece of insanity?

"We're so sorry you lost your saucer, Mistress Amav," Laurie broadcast. "No one can understand this static. I'm sure Chief of Staff Gooney will make you a new saucer when he gets back from Mars."

"Greeney isn't here? He won't be here for the meeting?" Amav grunted.

"No, he left for Mars two hours ago. As soon as he heard about Z'B's kidnapping he thought he should be on the home planet. But I must tell you, Mistress Amav, he's been even more scrambled than usual and today, well, this morning he seemed quite *insane,* if I may consult my database of known psychiatric conditions."

"I hope he made it okay. How's his Amplified Thought?"

"Well, it's been wonky recently for him, mistress. He tried a simple oxygen cleansing of *Garr/thahg* Castle this morning to prepare for your arrival, but he smashed all the picture windows on the first level. He's even forgotten how to shield his own outradiance. The Four get everything out of his little pink skull whether they want it or not. He's much more confused than he wants anyone to know. Of course, John and I don't get any outradiance because we're robots. I suppose that's a good thing. We spent an hour getting every little glass shard up from that window fiasco. Sorry in advance about all the Frankston plywood we had to put up. It does look atrocious. Kner himself couldn't make new glass after that. He's confused too, if I may add. But John and I decided to make the whole day a fun game. Static be dammed!"

How did the robot have enough computational capacity to indulge in chitchat as she navigated this obstacle course at 221 miles per hour? Ahead John J. Douglas leaped the crest of a six-hundred-foot-wide crater and traversed it in an instant. Laurie 283 followed, airborne, slamming to the floor of the crater with furious pumping legs, and before Amav knew it they'd crossed as well, charging up the far slope into fresh jungle.

"Oh, we're having so much *fun,* Mistress Amav!" Laurie burbled. "You may have wondered about my sweatshirt, why I'm not wearing something insanely tight and revealing like the real Laurie sometimes wears!"

"Well ..."

"When the Ywritt brought my John back to me, and I was *so* scrambled, and powered down, and *so* depressed, I realized I had a lot to answer for! I really messed up last year, and I realized I've got to *atone.* So I've sworn to wear a 283 sweatshirt for the rest of my existence. That may sound strange, but actually, I have an endless supply of 283 sweatshirts in a *hundred* colors. A lot of 'em are low-cut, because I know John likes 'em that way, but really, I figure everybody needs to know it's *me,* just a poor simple HAVOTT robot, not the real Laurie. I don't want anyone to confuse us again!"

"That--that's nice--"

"I caused so much *havoc* at Iota Persei last year! But I got *John* out of that somehow. We've been having so much fun here. We're like butlers to the Four, but it's all a game! And the Ywritt just *love* us. We're on the Committee to the Ywritt. I know your husband doesn't like that, but the Ywritt want us and they're a delight to talk to. I can't wait for our next trip to Iota Persei. We just need to get all this static sorted out!"

"Right, right--"

"Meanwhile, John and I just make love all day long. It's so wonderful! I bet you're thinking it's weird, since we got the wrong IHAGs last year, but it's not!"

How could Amav politely tell the robot she didn't want to hear anything about Illegal Human Artificial Genitals? A cliff of dark rock shot inches by to their right. Laurie flew over boulders and hurtled through impossibly dense trees.

Amav had never thought of her father's newly engineered trees as *dangerous.* Stewart Neal Frankston had taken a lot of criticism about the trees and all the other Venusian plant life he'd designed. The terraforming of Venus, a decades-long marathon begun in 2040, had sparked vociferous protest from people who thought humans had no right to make any mark whatsoever on any extraterrestrial object.

"Are we getting close to the Castle?" Amav said.

"Distance 8.11 miles, mistress, no worries! Estimated arrival in 2.2 minutes! But definitely don't be concerned that John and I aren't experiencing the total male-female duality, as far as robots can understand it, that is. So Kner screwed it up and I got the male genitals, and John got the female! It was wild at first! I had so much *testosterone!*"

"Uh--"

"And of course, we thought Kner couldn't switch 'em back or we'd completely lose our personalities! But guess what? After he got back from *Garr/thahg,* it was child's play for him to give each of us *both* sets of genitals!"

"Oh my God!"

"We rotate them in and out as we like! It's really amazing! We're doing things no human being has ever *dreamed* of! We could show you just how it's done!"

Amav tried to shake her head but could barely move it inside the helmet. "Well, I don't think that will be, uh, necessary." Far ahead through the onrushing trees she could see John J. Douglas slowing, and she made out giant brown stone blocks in a clearing. "Oh!" she said in relief. "There's the Castle!"

"Oh yes, Mistress Amav! *Garr/thahg* Castle, next stop! Welcome back to Lakshmi Planum! We won't let all this static spoil our fun, or the delightful things we can teach you!"

# CHAPTER EIGHTEEN
*Garr/thahg* Castle

The short fish-like creature in his russet Senior Martian Scientist robe fussed over Amav in her leather armchair. "No bruises even!" Kner said. "I mean, I don't think there are! That is, if my probing of the bodily surface beneath your clothes is not too intimidating, I may hope? What do you think, John?"

"We did check her out on the way over," the robot John Douglas said from his own chair. "She's in good shape as I believe I just informed you."

"You--you did? Oh! Oh, yes you did! Oh, well!"

"Except she does complain of headaches," Laurie 283 put in.

"Well, then, don't we all! I do believe we're all just breaking down! Oh, well! Should I repair the windows? We're missing such a grand view of the meadow!"

"Maybe later," Will Connors grunted, sunk deep in his own armchair in front of the Frankston plywood. "You might screw it up worse."

"Yes, yes, there *is* that possibility! Possibly I shall refrain! Yes, I shall refrain!"

The absence of the meadow windows and their soft undersea gloom made the main hall of *Garr/thahg* Castle even darker than usual. Amav wished someone would light one of the numerous fireplaces down here, but she was afraid to suggest it, since Kner might easily try another Amplified Thought routine with disastrous results.

"So, how *is* your headache, mistress?" whispered K'ufunb, perched on an eight-foot-wide coffee table of Venusian granite.

"It's okay, I think. I feel fantastic except for it." She didn't add that the closer Kner stood the worse it got. Couldn't he stop playing doctor and sit in his own chair?

"We still don't know how you managed to land in one piece, dear, without your little saucer," K'ufunb said. It was difficult to look at her. The *Fkuuh* species reminded most humans of six-foot-wide pumpkins, but in K'ufunb's case she seemed three weeks past Halloween, squashed and dull, with flaky crimson patches. All six eyes running around that massive head were crinkled and bloodshot. Her eight emaciated legs were twisted carelessly beneath her bulk.

Though Amav felt deeply relaxed after a quick scalding shower in the guest room, she had to avoid closing her eyes even for a second, as that conjured up being pinned against the wall of the crashing saucer with no power, no lights.

"Somehow I just *did* it," she said. "I know that doesn't make much sense."

"*Nothing* makes sense," Will muttered. "I agree with Kner. The Four of us are breaking down. Hard to believe, after all this ..." He waved loosely at the dark brown stone of the vast main hall. Everything was earthy. There were no colored blocks to remind the Four of the infinity of *Garr/thahg* they'd all run through for billions of years. The whole terraformed planet of Venus seemed so *grounded* to Amav.

It was one reason she'd refused to chase after JJC this morning. Why run after that little fool when she could meet the Four on the *grounded world* her father rescued from the insanity of runaway greenhouse effect? Many had scoffed that Dr. Frankston had run out of ideas when he'd gotten the contract to redesign Venus, but what better homage could he pay to his intellectual forebears than to turn Venus into a jungle pleasure planet straight out of the science fiction of the previous century?

Last August Kner, K'ufunb, Will, and Z'B had created their moody castle in the high jungle of Ishtar Terra, but they were shocked to discover that the powers they'd commanded so easily upon their return from *Garr/thahg* were draining fast. Kner and Z'B were further dismayed to find that even their native Martian Amplified Thought was faltering. Greeney Gooney, now Z'B's chief of staff, had stepped in to finish the job with his own AT.

*Garr/thahg* seemed like a half-forgotten dream. The Four still remembered astounding lessons about the forces of nature, and they'd more or less doubled human/Martian knowledge over the next few months. But limited to physical form, they now had to arduously sift through concepts before making themselves understood. And much of what they'd submitted to SolNet read as gibberish not only to others but often to themselves.

Now sickness had settled in. For Kner and Z'B it was primarily tremors and confusion. K'ufunb really did look like a rotting pumpkin, and during the last month Will had drifted into a worsening flu, becoming increasingly disconnected. He looked ancient and decrepit. Though Will had returned from *Garr/thahg* as a full master of Martian outradiance, his girlfriend Laurie had mentioned that his telepathic abilities were fading fast. Now Amav couldn't pick up a hint of it. She'd tried to get Laurie to admit that Will was in serious trouble, but she, a USSF physician, refused to believe it was serious.

Amav thought he was dying. Maybe they all were. Laurie definitely needed to get here and see this.

"Does anyone know why Z'B took off for Enceladus this morning?" Amav asked.

"He did say something about Saturn," Kner said. "I think? Something about the reconstruction. I think he was worried about the Amplified Thought subroutines, you know." Amav could barely get his outradiance. It was like being in a restaurant where the kitchen staff was playing loud music warring with entirely different music at the tables which in turn failed to dominate a hundred shouted conversations. Shaking and pale, Kner finally plopped into his own chair and sighed.

"No, that's crap," Will muttered. "No way he'd mess with the Saturn AT. It's completely fried and he knows it. *Nobody* can figure it out. Dammit, Z'B knows better than to haul off like that."

"Well, at least the Robe is safe," Kner said. "As safe as it *can* be, I suppose."

"Oh, for God's sake, it's safe! Don't worry about *that* of all things!"

"Good for ten thousand years!" K'ufunb put in. "At least, I *think*."

The Trans-Simultaneity Chamber made Amav nervous. Every time she visited, Kner would start in on whether the Robe was really stable. "You *think?*" she said. "You told me it was foolproof!"

"Well, Z'B tried to open the Chamber before he left this morning, but couldn't remember how."

"He tried to *open* it? Oh my God!"

"That's not the damn point," Will said. "He managed to melt part of the Field Lock. We think we got it back together, though."

"*What?*" Amav cried, standing.

"Stasis Integration still at one hundred percent, that is, if the calibration matrix gauge is right. I think it was a little melted too," K'ufunb said.

"There's a *Trans-Simultaneity Force Field* right beneath us and you're not sure it's *stable?* Where's Greeney? You think he'll be back here soon?"

"No, he's lucky if he made it in one piece to Mars," Will said. "*He's* crumbling too. We all are. He was so *out* of it when he left. All the Martians are. Hope he made it okay."

"We've got to look at it right now!" Amav was ready to bound down to the lowest level of the Castle, but nobody had ever shown her where the Chamber was located, not that she would know how to fix it anyway. Even a Greeney who was a hundred percent sane wouldn't know. Only the Four would. Now they'd forgotten. "Why in God's name did Z'B think to fool with it?"

"It's all right, Mistress Amav," robot Laurie said. "It was John and I who found him trying to get in and dissuaded him from the attempt. We've taken readings and think the damage is minor. In fact, we were able to access the Chamber's Self Actualization Subset and found that the Chamber itself thinks that everything's all right."

"Though it did request repair of the lock and wanted to bill us a million Sol credits for it!" John J. Douglas laughed.

"Anyway, Z'B thought he should wear the Emperor's Robe for his trip to Saturn," Laurie said. "He thought it would buck up morale. Idiot!"

"Oh my God," Amav whispered. When he'd noted his diminishing powers during the building of the Castle, Z'B had intuited the possibility of eventually losing control over the Robe and had fashioned a Trans-Simultaneity Chamber in the basement to secure the Emperor's Robe in a stasis field against the day when he or a future Emperor would no longer be capable of balancing the Robe's alternating surges of matter and anti-matter. Just in time, for the technique of Trans-Simultaneity soon faded from all the Four's minds. But the Robe was apparently secure for ten thousand years, if Z'B's tampering this morning hadn't undone the safety mechanisms.

She looked helplessly back and forth between the three insane *Garr/thahgers* and the two robots. They were sitting on a bomb that could vaporize the planet in a nanosecond. "Well, I'm glad you convinced Z'B not to try."

Laurie laughed. "I don't think he could've done a thing with AT. He couldn't even conjure a *hacksaw!* That's what he was trying to make, a *hacksaw!* It was all rubbery and wouldn't cut a thing!"

"That was after I pulled the shattergun out of his damnable sharp claws," John said, holding up his shredded plasti-skin forearms.

"He fired a *shattergun* at the Chamber lock?" Amav gasped.

"It was just bubbling little pieces off. I could see it wasn't working. I really don't think anything's wrong with the Chamber. But the poor guy was *sobbing* by that point! Imagine that! The Emperor of the Martians, sobbing in my arms!"

"I didn't realize he'd lost *all* his AT." The six-foot-tall Martian, who spoke a rich, deep, flawless English no other Martian could emulate, could have straightened out the entire Saturnian ring orbital mechanics problem with a wave of his claw a few months ago. But the impeccable leader who could easily wear the Emperor's Robe was *gone*.

She turned to Kner. "How about *your* AT?"

Kner shrugged. "Just little bits here and there. If I must tell you, I mean, this is why we're so terribly sad, Mistress Amav. Our AT is so much on the fritz that we're unable to use it. Will and K'ufunb here learned it easily in *Garr/thahg,* but ..."

"It's gone," K'ufunb croaked. "All gone."

"I have a little left," Will grunted. There was a flash of light and a two-headed baby giraffe appeared in his lap. Its legs flailed and its necks whirled with a whine of unlubricated robotic gears. Amav put her hands over her ears.

"*Crap!*" Will muttered as first a leg, then a neck, fell off the robot. Then the entire contraption dissolved into sticky white protoplasm. "Damn!"

"We don't know if it's gone because we walked in *Garr/thahg* and now we're paying the price of total exhaustion for that knowledge, or whether ... oh, I forgot what I was going to say!" K'ufunb said.

"Or whether, maybe, the Total Martian Outradiance screwup is blowing back on us somehow," Kner offered.

"Maybe. No, that's not what I was going to say! Oh hell!"

"Maybe it's worse for us than the average Martian, maybe because we're super-sensitized to the Total Martian Outradiance from having walked through *Garr/thahg,*" Will said, smearing goo across his pants.

"That's it!" K'ufunb cried. "That's it exactly! Maybe!"

"Of course, it's been building for decades, that's the damned thing," Kner said. "We have so many Martian children now, our TMO is so childish now, we're *scattered,* we were off-balance to begin with, and it's been getting worse and *worse.*"

"In any case we're useless now, Miss Amav," K'ufunb said. "It's depressing is what it is."

"We can't even take care of this damn Castle anymore," Kner moaned. "It practically runs on AT!"

"And now Z'B's kidnapped out there," Will said, "and we can't save him!"

"I could get the Emperor's Robe! I could wear it, I know I could! Only temporarily, of course!"

"No! Kner, are you *crazy?*" John shouted.

"It'd only be temporary! Z'B would know I'm not trying to *overthrow* him, just trying to *rescue* him. Then I'd ceremonially place the Robe back around his neck!"

"*No!*" Robot Laurie said. She turned to Amav. "They've been like this all morning, trying to concoct some silly rescue plan. So far we can control them, because, face it, we're physically stronger than they are and their AT can't touch us anymore."

"Dammit, you're *not* stronger than us! *Or* smarter!" Will cried, igniting the mess on his lap into an orange ball of fire. "Ow! Goddammit!"

John reached for a pitcher of water and expertly hurled the contents in a twelve-foot arc to sizzle on Will's flaming lap.

"Damn! You--" Will sputtered, standing, huge holes in his pants showing charred blue underwear. "Dammit to hell! I'm gonna change!" He marched off.

"No more AT, and stay away from the Chamber!" John called after him. "I can hear every footstep you make all the way to your room!"

"Anyway, I can take my new saucer," Kner said. "Did you know I got a new J-14, Miss Amav? It has Trans-Simultaneity Star Drive!"

"N-no …" Amav said.

"You're no longer cleared to fly that," Laurie snapped. "The Trans-Simultaneity has never worked on that thing, you know that. And anyway, your pilot took it to fly Greeney to Mars this morning."

"M'rrpla? M'rrpla and my J-14, *gone?* To Mars did you say?" Kner moaned.

"Well, thank God Greeney has a robot for a pilot," Amav said, picturing an addled Greeney Gooney navigating straight into the sun. "I'm sure they've made it to Mars by now."

"Well, even we robots are feeling the damn communications static," John said. "I'm not sure I could pilot a saucer right now, with SolNet Venus down."

"Do you really think it's down? Maybe all of SolNet down?" K'ufunb said. "Oh, dear! We were relying on SolNet to tell us where Z'B might have gotten off to. We can't get his outradiance at all!"

"Did he mention to you where he might happen to be vacationing?" Kner said.

"*What?*" Amav cried. "He was kidnapped by Jonathan

James! You know that!"

"Kidnapped? That's not a good vacation, is it?"

"Unless it's one of those new *theme* vacations," K'ufunb put in. "I sure wouldn't want that one myself, but leave it to Z'B for creativity!"

Laurie shrugged. "As you can see, mistress, they're getting worse."

A new wave of headache blasted Amav. She closed her eyes. Even the dim main hall was too much for her. At this moment there was no Emperor in charge of the TMO. When a Martian Emperor died a new one was selected, but there was no provision for *kidnapping*. Kner's idiotic idea of temporarily wearing the Emperor's Robe on some quixotic rescue attempt had undoubtedly just found its way into the TMO as well. Every Martian now knew of this fresh absurdity.

If the Martians came fully apart, what would happen to her, trapped with three crazy *Garr/thahgers* and two robots that might go on the fritz themselves? She didn't have a saucer, SolNet Venus and Sat One were out, and nobody had any Amplified Thought worth a damn unless she wanted a two-headed giraffe with a lifespan of three seconds.

"God, can we possibly talk to the Ywritt?" she gasped.

"How would we?" Will grunted, staggering back into the hall in a filthy green bathrobe. "They said they can't make any sense of all this TMO crap themselves."

"Or why we of *Garr/thahg* are flaking out like this," Kner muttered. "If I could just wear the Emperor's Robe for *one second*--"

"Negative! Sit down!" John roared.

"The Ywritt helped us for a while," K'ufunb said. "They'd remind us of things we'd found in *Garr/thahg*. Damn, we were such a *great team*."

"They were always helping us channel the good stuff right in," Will said. "Like the *Typhoon VI*. Weird folks, really. They're like damn *computers*."

"People worshipped us as *gods!*" Kner shouted. "*Gods!* Can you believe it?"

"I never wanted to be worshipped!" K'ufunb cried.

"Well, me either! I'm just saying, *now* look at us!"

"I'm not going back to goddamn *Garr/thahg* if that's what you're saying!"

"Me either! Are you *crazy?*"

"We were just fooling ourselves!" Will shouted. "*Nobody* was turned into a god!"

"Nobody said we were!" Kner snapped. "Are you listening to a word of this discussion?"

"What I'm hearing is some *idiot* who thinks he can strap on a matter/anti-matter robe and somehow save the day!"

"I could! I know I could!"

"We weren't gods, we weren't enlightened, we weren't even damn *Bodhisattvas!*" K'ufunb snarled. "Even though Will here was always trying to act like one!"

"I *never* acted like a Bodhisattva! Not once! Have you got some sort of proof of that last statement?"

"Guys, please, this isn't helping!" Amav pleaded.

"*What if this is all a trap laid by the Wounded?*" Kner screamed.

# CHAPTER NINETEEN
## You All Have Seemed Rather Complacent to Me Recently

Laurie 283 assessed the fresh silence. "I think Kner may have touched on something none of you have fully wanted to admit," she spoke. Mistress Amav looked away. Will and K'ufunb continued to stare at the stone floor, and the expression of anguish on Kner's pink fish-face settled back into vacancy.

[POOR DEARS], she signaled to John. [I DON'T WANT TO WORRY THEM BUT A STRANGELY DISTURBING THOUGHT HAS SURFACED AND I FEEL A NEED TO EXPRESS IT ORALLY.]

[GO FOR IT!] John J. Douglas transmitted back. [AS FAR AS I CAN TELL OUR *GARR/THAHGERS* LOST THE ABILITY TO PICK UP OUR WIRELESS TRANSMISSIONS SEVERAL DAYS AGO, SO I THINK EVERYONE NEEDS TO HEAR WHAT'S ON YOUR MIND. I'VE COME TO THE SAME CONCLUSION AS YOU, INCIDENTALLY.]

Laurie let some tension build. She'd absorbed several thousand books on acting technique and in fact could act out every part in every Shakespeare play. She knew she could bring any audience to tears, never mind John's jape that of course they'd be in tears after sitting through several unbroken weeks of Laurie declaiming the entire Shakespeare opus, playing all parts and changing character costumes within milliseconds.

In recreating John J. Douglas last year, the Ywritt had upgraded him hundreds of years beyond current Sol robotics technology, and he'd insisted the same upgrades be ported to Laurie 283. She'd been delighted with all her new skills, as well as to find that "acting" was just as important to the Ywritt as it was to humans.

"Even though I was essentially reset back to zero last year," she began, "vestiges of my unfortunate descent into Runaway Programming Disorder remained. My upgrades from the Ywritt couldn't touch my personality kernel, so they just worked around the RPG. While I feel there's definitely no danger of my ever reverting into any collusion with the Wounded, I have retained what you might call an intuitive understanding of their motives."

Amav nodded. "Look, I know what you're going to say, but we've flushed out the Wounded over the past few months. Of course, we know we have to maintain our vigilance."

"It's true that the first three months of SolGrid have caught over seven thousand Wounded spies," John intervened. "But who's to say that was all of them in Sol?"

"But even the *human* Laurie thinks that even if SolGrid's not perfect, it can sort out any remaining Wounded. I think we've got some breathing space."

"Yes, Mistress Amav," Laurie said, "I know the real Laurie would also have some insight into the Wounded based on her experiences at Iota Persei last year. However, she's only allowed herself to be interviewed a couple times by SolGrid and she turned down an opportunity to work on the USSF SolGrid Committee."

Laurie 283 always made sure to refer to the human model as the *real* Laurie. Not only did human stress levels go down markedly the more she asserted that she herself was just a simulacrum, but the nature of her robotic existence was a severe truth to be acknowledged, after all. Laurie 283 was *imitation*. She would never have existed if Laurie Lachrer hadn't been conceived in sexual intercourse between male and female humans and subsequently born on May 13, 2015.

Laurie 283 had sinned badly with the Wounded last year, but she'd been reset down to the lowest quantum computational levels and put in her place. Sure, the Ywritt had upgraded her, but all that meant was that she had faster computational ability. That was nothing compared to Laurie Lachrer's infinite genius and love.

"But even in my humble capacity as a mere imitation of Miss Laurie, I do wonder if she might not be feeling a bit complacent about the Wounded these days," Laurie went on. "You all have seemed rather complacent to me recently."

She watched Amav blink in surprise.

[HUMAN REACTION TO PERCEIVED TEMERITY],

John transmitted.

[THANKS! I CAUGHT THAT.]

"I'm not trying to be disrespectful, Mistress Amav. I understand that the real Laurie has an intuition about the Wounded far superior to my robotic hunches, based on her thorough knowledge of Wounded practices. But human beings sometimes do tend to let even serious problems slip off the radar in the face of new input. New input like your original intention of attending a meeting about the Saturn project here today, which in turn was interrupted by the news of your son's outrageous behavior in kidnapping the Emperor and stealing the *Typhoon II.*"

"You leave him out of this!" Amav flared, then sagged back into her chair. "We're in a hell of a mess and I can't think about him *or* the Wounded right now."

"I think what dear 283 is trying to say is that Kner may be correct in fearing that the static from the TMO and the breakdown of SolNet might be part of a Wounded attack," John intervened.

"They never *attack,* they just *infiltrate,*" Will railed, unshaven face sunk into the depths of his tattered bathrobe. "They build a Dyson sphere and *screw you* out of a star!"

"Who's to say that the Wounded might not be trying for a comeback?" Laurie 283 went on. "We stomped them hard last year at Iota Persei and with SolGrid, so maybe they just decided to skip this area for a while and lull us to sleep."

"We've heard that paranoia over and over," Amav said. "That's why we pushed SolGrid so fast that it screwed up. Dammit to hell, *everything's* screwed up!"

"Except the *Alpha Centaurian* Grid," K'ufunb cackled. "Kept us safe for centuries. Nobody can penetrate *our* network!"

"Well, SolGrid's malfunctioning and Mistress Amav's own son has started a rebellion against it," Laurie persisted. "Couldn't all that somehow work into the Wounded's plans? Maybe they even brainwashed Jonathan James into stealing the *Typhoon.*"

"Dammit!" Amav flared. "Just shut up about him!"

"Consider how limited SolGrid really is. Sure, it got seven thousand Wounded, but only by making guesses against existing SolNet databases. Only a few Wounded were stupid enough to get exposed by actually joining SolGrid. Most were ferreted out by detective work. As long as the Grid is voluntary, anyone can go Dark. There could be seven thousand *more* Wounded in Sol, being Dark right now."

"Okay, okay, I get the point! But we're constantly refining our methods."

"One of the last things we got off the network is that Patrick James just got fired from SolGrid. He went over to JJC. Who's going to fix SolGrid now?"

"Shut up about Jonathan James, robot! I mean it!"

"The Wounded are unimaginably *dangerous*. Have we forgotten what they can do to our *star?*"

"Of course I know! I'm a goddamn planetary engineer!"

"We could've found every Wounded ourselves, *without* damn SolGrid, if we'd only had our act together," Will muttered. "The Four of us could have done it, but our *Garr/thahg* energies *died.* We lost it!"

Laurie reviewed Will Connors' bio readings for signs of suicidal depression. She'd been monitoring all Four over the past few weeks as they sank further into despondency. Will was basically okay. Pulse, breath, muscle tension, lymphatic and hormonal levels all crappy, but she didn't think he was a danger to himself.

[LOCKING DOWN ALL GUNS, DAGGERS, ETC. IN THE CASTLE], John transmitted. [CAN'T HAVE HIM GO LOOKING FOR A SHATTERGUN, CAN WE?]

[WHAT? YOU'RE MONITORING THEM TOO?]

[OF COURSE. I COULD TELL FROM THE LOOK IN YOUR EYE WHAT YOU WERE UP TO. I'VE ALSO BEEN MONITORING THEM THE LAST WEEK.]

[DAMN, DO WE EVER THINK ALIKE!]

[I'M JUST SORRY I FORGOT ABOUT WEAPONS UNTIL JUST NOW. LETTING Z'B HAVE ACCESS TO HIS OWN EMPEROR SHATTERGUN THIS MORNING WAS A

SERIOUS OVERSIGHT.]

[AH, WELL, YOU CAUGHT IT, NO PROBLEM! WHAT A TEAM WE ARE!]

"Aaah, maybe we should all just go ahead and *support* the bastard!" Will snarled.

"Support *who?*" K'ufunb grunted.

"That bastard JJC! Just tear down the whole damn SolGrid fiasco!"

"Hey!" Amav said. "That's my *son* you're insulting!"

"It's all right, Miss Amav," K'ufunb said. "Will's just blowing off steam like a little baby like he usually does around this time of the morning."

"Why, I do not! Damn you, K'ufunb!"

"I suppose it's a deserving idea," Kner put in. "Yes, let's do it! We all get in my saucer and join JJC! Surely he'll tell us where Z'B is, don't you think?"

"*What?*" Amav cried.

"You're outa your skull!" Will shot back. "M'rrpla and Greeney took your damn saucer to Mars, remember?"

"They took my saucer? *Without my permission?*"

"Yeah, because Greeney's own saucer drive screwed up! We told you that just a second ago!"

"Okay, okay! Now I remember! But I can fix a Higgs Boson! It's child's play! Let's all adjourn to the garage and I'll have his saucer up and running in no time!"

"Dammit, *nobody's* been able to adapt a Higgs to a Martian saucer, you fool!"

"We've got to find JJC and *join* him! The Higgs is the answer!"

"Greeney *fried* it trying to install it, idiot!"

"Let me apologize for both of them, Mistress Amav," K'ufunb said. "They're both reverting to infancy, as you can easily see. I'm so sorry. You see our current state of anarchy. Oh God, what have we come to?"

"Aw, the hell with your stupid despair trip," Will cried, standing and jerking a finger at the dehydrated pumpkin on the coffee table. "We don't need a damn saucer. The three of us together--you, me and Kner--all we have to do is link our AT together and transport ourselves right *to* that JJC son of a bitch!"

"Damn you, Will Connors! Stop referring to my son like that!"

Will was naked under his ripped green robe. Laurie got him back into his chair.

"I'll refer to the goddamn son of a bitch horse's ass any way I want!"

"Silence, Mr. Will. That's the best course now," Laurie whispered, patting his forehead. "You're getting way too upset." Will looked up in anguish. She knew that, especially in his confused moments, Will might mistake her for his girlfriend, the real Laurie, so she'd always made sure to curb her own robotic pheromones in Will's presence, and in fact only released them in John's. Nobody would ever again accuse her of usurping the real Laurie's identity. Nevertheless, she allowed a misty spurt of Gamma12Copulin, and Will's strained features relaxed into an insipid smile.

She turned back to Amav. "Well, you've now seen everyone at their worst. I'm sorry your projected meeting with the Four has turned into such a disaster."

Amav shook her head in disgust. "Well, whatever. I just need to get back to Mars. I need to talk to Jack. I'm *exhausted* by this whole thing."

"Yes, mistress, your biological readings are indicating high levels of stress."

Amav flushed. "Okay, okay, I can admit I'm stressed."

[HMM. DEAR LAURIE, YOU MAY BE PUSHING MISTRESS AMAV A BIT NOW. WE MIGHT SUGGEST SHE NAP IN HER QUARTERS.]

"John's suggesting a *nap,* Mistress Amav. But I really think you need to talk everything out *now.*"

"Well, well ..."

"I've taken the liberty of adjusting the room temperature in your quarters to seventy-four degrees Fahrenheit," John said.

"No, she needs to talk about her son. Right *now,*" Laurie insisted.

"What? Thank you, John, I believe I *will* get some rest now." Amav stood up.

"All your previous disgust about Jonathan James has been proven *true,*" Laurie said. "You're in a state of shock and dismay. Crashing your saucer was nothing compared to how you feel, right this second, about your own son."

"He's *not* my son! He's a *monster!*"

There was a long silence.

"Weird!" Will laughed.

"Shut up! Shut *up!*" Amav screamed. She whirled to Laurie. "Get out of my head, robot! You think you can read my mind!"

"I can read *all* your biological signs, Mistress Amav! Pulse 117--"

"Shut up! Shut up! *Why did I bother to come here?*"

"Why, your pheromonal activity is almost *nil.* Mistress Amav, are you and Jack not getting laid enough recently?"

Amav's eyes bulged so far Laurie thought they might pop out of her head. "For your information, robot bitch, Jack and I had a marvelous time yesterday afternoon! And then we get this news about our goddamned *son!*"

[WOW, YOU SURE OPENED UP THE CENTRAL ISSUE], John transmitted. [QUITE A SUCCESSFUL PSYCHOTHERAPEUTIC MOVE.]

"Mistress Amav, I'm merely analyzing your relationship with your husband from the standpoint of my own excellent sex life with John here. Certainly you and Jack could learn some amazing techniques from us and achieve a much *higher* level of intimacy."

"Shut up! Everything was wonderful until we heard about Jonathan James!"

"All I'm saying is that in reading your pheromones--"

"Of course you'd read my stupidass pheromones! Why don't you put *them* on SolGrid? Then everyone could know everything!" Amav raised a fist and Laurie took the opportunity to measure muscle tone.

"I certainly hope you don't intend to take a punch at me, mistress. That would break your wondrous little hand."

"You *damn robot!*"

"So, to begin with, we've established that it's *Jonathan James* that upsets you."

"Yes! There's no way in hell I can deal with him now! Why can't Jack see that?"

"Well, there's no harm in just deciding that there can be no possible mother-son relationship anymore."

"I've *tried* that since 2038! When the goddamn ACs kidnapped him and turned him into a *monster!* That he could treat me, his *mother,* like some *whore!* And then try to pair me with *Phil Sperry!* And watch us have *sex!* Oh my God!"

"But JJC never saw you as a mother. There was never any real relationship in his mind. After the war, whenever you went to visit him in Alpha Centauri, from his point of view you and Jack were just oppressive, rule-making strangers and you yourself came off as a sort of comic-book heroine he felt a need to bring down. So don't take it personally. The Oedipus thing is overdone here, I think."

[WOW!] John transmitted.

Amav stared. "Is *that* what your Ywritt programmers put into your mind?"

Laurie considered. "Apparently so."

"Apparently so!" Will cackled in his dirty bathrobe.

"You shut up!" Amav cried. "This is serious! This is *me!*"

"Oh, cut him some slack, Mistress Amav," John put in. "His mind's scrambled and you might as well cut him some slack."

"But he can't--he can't--"

"Hell, mistress, he's a *person,* in stress like yourself. You aren't so different from him. Who can regulate what we're all supposed to feel right now?"

"They may be scrambled, but they're still *here,*" Laurie said, pointing to Will and Kner and K'ufunb. "We're all a little scrambled if the truth be told."

"But you said *things*--that can't--that can't--" Amav fell back into her armchair, convulsing, face in her lap, long dark hair shuddering.

Laurie was ashamed that even with all her biomedical

sensors on full power it took her ten seconds to realize that Amav was laughing.

# CHAPTER TWENTY
## Hirte's Astonishing Sexuality

Sanders Hirte was almost entirely tattoos, with so many images and colors twining across his flawless muscles that Jackie Vespertine couldn't make sense of them: silver spaceships and ringed planets, unfurling Latin, German, and Russian mottos, soldiers with shatter-enhanced EOS rifles, and exploding armored personnel carriers. But it was the repeated motif of life-sized female genitalia that stunned her. There were hairy *labia* on his hard biceps, on his abdomen, on his massive thighs, on his ankles.

But she was kissing everything, out of control, including *"Was mich nicht umbringt, macht mich stärker"* as it wound up his thigh and across his groin. And who in his right mind tattooed bright green ivy and crossed magenta swords up and down the thick hard length of--

Jackie winced to consider how much the needlework for *that* particular design must have hurt. She crawled atop the immense chest where a *Typhoon III*-class ship fired exterminating yellow PlanetBlaster pulses at an assembly of priests on a football gridiron. "Am I squashing anything *important* down there?" she murmured.

"Mmmm …" he muttered, big hands squeezing her ass.

She met his gray eyes and melted at his smile. Without further thought she raised her nude body, grasped that thick pillar of ivy and swords, and guided it home.

\*

"How long did you say we'd be checking the ship out?" she whispered into taut calves where gorillas smashed whiskey bottles and hurled knives at bureaucrats behind desks.

"Oh, maybe another hour," Sanders said, lips between her thighs.

"Aren't you needed back up there?"

"No, not really. I told JJC my part was done. The

autolanding sequence is all set to go when we're ready to take her down. We don't have to do a thing. Really, we just let the checklists run on auto. Everything's great so far."

"Pat made it sound like it'd be complicated."

"Old Patster's a nervous Nellie. He just wants everyone to think he's indispensable." Sanders sat up, trailing a massive hand with four silver rings down the length of her body. "But as anyone can see, he's *not* indispensable. Someone *else* has you now."

She again met those gray eyes of primal force. "Y-yes ..." His gaze fell to her breasts and she noted with satisfaction his dropped jaw, then that addictive smile.

"Patster's an idiot to ignore *this* feminine perfection." Sanders fingered a nipple. Jackie stared at the bright red pudenda etched above his hipbone.

"Well, I guess we both knew it was almost over." In the dim light, the sparse furnishings of the Pod stateroom cocooned two naked bodies. Just this bed and a dresser, and a tiny bathroom by the door. A porthole showed a few stars.

"Anyway, I blew off the damn checklist because I wanted to see *you*."

But wasn't Jonathan James the one she wanted? How did *this* happen?

"Lean back there, love," Sanders whispered, kissing his way up her thighs.

*

"What I can't believe is that you're really a *professor!* Do I have to call you Dr. Vespertine?"

"No ..." Jackie murmured as she straddled Sanders' back and rubbed his stone shoulders. "Call me ..."

"*Dr. Sexyboobs,* maybe."

She laughed. "I think *Jackie* will do!"

"Yeah, keep that up. Feels so good."

"Why did you corral me here if my degree makes you so nervous?" she teased.

"Oh, it doesn't make me nervous. I just had no idea you'd come on to me like that."

"*Me? You* were the one who grabbed me as soon as the door shut."

"Ah, we both knew what was up, I guess."

In fact, Jackie hadn't known anything was up. After they'd entered orbit, Sanders had called to say that JJC wanted him to speak to her in private. There was to be a long systems check before landing, and this would be a perfect time. As they'd climbed down the spiral staircase to the Pod, now set to 1G instead of the standard .38 Martian gravity museum setting, she'd wondered giddily whether Sanders had been sent to arrange a tryst between her and Jonathan James. Then the dismaying thought struck her that Sanders might have been enlisted to tell her to drop it, that JJC was happy with Suzette, who would crucify her if she didn't back off.

By the time Sanders had suggested stateroom sixteen, Jackie was coming apart with anxiety and awakening to the chilly reality that she, Professor of Exobiology at the University of Mars, was participating in kidnapping and armed rebellion without apparently having given it a second thought.

The door closed and within a second both those big hairy hands were squeezing her breasts. Jackie opened her mouth to cry a protest, then met unearthly gray eyes that flattened her soul like tank treads. She had a moment to boggle at the unfathomable coldness of whatever lay behind those twin forces, then an engulfing warm smile of comradely humanity and simple male lust seesawed her in the opposite direction and finished her. It was crazy how fast all those clothes had come right off. Those *tattoos*. The *swords and ivy.*

Now she pulled herself off Sanders' back. "Turn--turn over!"

He lazily rotated the superstructure of multicolored muscle. "Something you *wanted,* Dr. Sexyboobs?"

"*Yes!*" she moaned.

How could Suzette have given up *this?*

*

"I just can't *believe* this ..." she whispered as Sanders withdrew.

"*What* can't you believe ..." he murmured, stroking her thigh.

She wanted to scream *How can you still be so hard?* but what came out was: "I must be twice as old as you!"

"Hmm. So how old *are* you?"

"Uh, *seventy-six,* if you must know."

"Oh, wow! You really *are* twice as old. Because *I'm* thirty-eight."

"Oh my God!"

"But you look a lot *younger* than me, so don't worry."

"Well, thanks. It's the rejuvenation, you know."

"And it really keeps you pumping back *hard*," he whispered, kissing her shoulder. "You're *sensational.*"

"Well, thanks." She gazed up at the porthole where stars passed lazily. For the first time she felt how cold, alien and uncaring those lights were, how lost she was.

"When it's time for my own rejuvenation, I hope I'm half as vigorous as you!" Sanders laughed.

"*You?* You'll never need any performance enhancements!"

"Hmm. I suspect it'll be quite a challenge keeping up with you."

Was he saying they should do this *forever?* He was only thirty-eight! What was she doing? She'd come here, she'd followed this rebellion, just to have sex with Jonathan James, who was even younger. Then *this* guy got her. He didn't even ask. It had just happened. Sure, she'd noticed Sanders was gorgeous, but that didn't mean anything. Everything was for JJC.

She considered the exterminating stars and shivered. "Don't you really think we need to maybe get dressed? Maybe get back?"

She had to talk to Pat. Had to explain herself. Everyone probably knew what she and Sanders had been doing down here.

Or did she really have anything to explain? She and Pat were through. They both knew it.

"We have plenty of time," Sanders grinned with another kiss to her wrist. "I'll get back up there in a little bit."

She tried not to look but she had to. To her relief he was finally deflating. She felt filled past overflowing. The sheets were soaked with their lovemakings. "So you think we'll land okay?" she said, hoping to divert the ship's ostensible copilot, in reality its entire engineering oversight, into chitchat about anything other than aroused human genitals.

"Yeah, everything's checked out so far. JJC would've called if there was a problem. Good thing he didn't."

"Yes. Of course …"

Sanders raised himself to the porthole and looked down. "Don't know why I bother. Can't see a damn thing. Just *no stars* down there." He shielded his eyes from the interior light. "Well, maybe a little reflected starlight. You can make out a little bit. Looks like freakin' rough terrain down there if you ask me." He shook his head. "What a waste of a damn solar system."

Jackie shuddered. The four rocky planets orbiting Barnard's Star had been stripped of all life in May '34 when the Alpha Centaurians destroyed the star and liquidated the sentient species of the system, the Kloru'dik, which had been proving resistant to AC occupation. But the Centaurians' main purpose had been to turn Barnard's Star into Barnard's Black Hole as a warning to Sol. Fortunately the resulting Warp Transfer Z radiation didn't include gamma rays which would've eventually obliterated all neighboring stars, including Sol. But the battered, surviving planets, including the four-thousand-mile-wide Altrouda, orbited the black hole in permanent lifeless darkness. Though the short-term Z radiation had mostly dissipated by 2076, the USSF had declared Altrouda and the three other planets of Barnard's Black Hole off-limits for colonization for the next five centuries.

But the *Typhoon II* would drop out of orbit to stake its claim. Life was about to return to the frigid, earthquake-roiled planet below.

# CHAPTER TWENTY-ONE
## The Committee to the Ywritt

"Oh my God!" Jackie gasped as the door slid open with a bang. She grasped for a sheet to pull over her breasts, but found herself fruitlessly tugging at the thick white comforter they hadn't bothered to peel down.

"Greetings. I see you two have gotten acquainted."

Jackie's eyes went to Jonathan James Commer's glossy black spacesuit. She stared at the dangling plastic penis and balls.

Suzette hung on his shoulder in that astonishing low-cut white blouse and form-fitting leggings. JJC grinned as Suzette's narrowed eyes scrutinized every square inch of Jackie's body.

"I--I--" Jackie gasped, hands across her nipples, turning to Sanders standing by the porthole in a kaleidoscope of tattoos, hard muscles, and swollen swords and ivy.

Sanders grinned back at her. "Don't worry, hon, you don't have to salute the captain."

"At ease, ladies and gentlemen," JJC said. "We just came down to see what was taking you two so long."

"And now we see," Suzette said, tossing her dark hair to one side. "Don't worry, we're all friends here. I don't mind you getting to know my ex-flame Mr. Sanders."

"Where's *Pat?*" Jackie blurted, expecting him to be in next.

"Oh, we left him up in the Control Room," JJC said. "Makes him feel special to be left in charge. Anyway, I told him to double-check the autolanding sequence, the Arkonsky field clamps, everything. Should keep him occupied for a while."

Jackie looked longingly at her clothes on the floor, tangled with Sanders' at his naked feet, but he made no effort to cover himself or fetch her garments. If she moved to drag the comforter around her, she'd reveal everything to the newcomers.

Now she felt the faint churning outradiance from Z'B, still up in the ship with Pat.

*RUN ConfineShadow, parameter: matrix > pi; subset = reality; if reality +1 = unreality, then subset = NULL, else RUN*

141

*MindExtrapolate.*

She pulled her hands from her chest and sat straight.

*Let them stare! Who cares?*

But she couldn't take her eyes off JJC's tightly outlined plastic genitals glistening in the bright overhead light. The slender Jonathan James looked tiny in comparison to Sanders Hirte. But still, he was *the one.* What had she been doing?

"So we have two stable couples now!" JJC laughed. "That's great!"

"Well, we'll have to break the news to Mr. Patster at some point," Sanders grinned. "That wimp!"

Jackie looked back and forth between Sanders, who still hadn't made a move to cover himself, and JJC standing in that thrilling spacesuit. Had she just signed a contract to work forever on some demented ship of lust? Were they going to be a foursome, with Pat fuming in the background?

She felt curiously blank, as if they were all standing around the locker room after a couple hours of volleyball, and the coach and assistant coach had come to chat with statistical clipboards in hand while naked Jackie and naked Sanders waited for the showers to warm up.

*Which come to think of it is a great idea!*

Suzette folded her arms. She seemed to have completed her examination of Jackie's assets and concluded there was no threat.

What did they think they'd do down on Altrouda? Create some blissful anti-SolGrid society? Hadn't she known all along they'd all be *swingers?* And they'd attract more and more swingers, thousands of them. They'd copulate with everyone and think they were free. And Professor Jackie Vespertine had gone right along with all of it, just because she wanted that damn *spacesuit.*

JJC sat on the bed. "May we?" he said, patting a space for Suzette to join him. She took the spot and JJC fondled her thigh. "Been a long day, you know."

Jackie backed against the curved wall of the Pod, but Sanders sat beside her with that easy dazzling smile. "It's okay, hon," he said as the bed sagged beneath the weight of a person on each corner.

"Could I at least have my blouse?" she whispered.

Sanders fished the crimson cloth off the floor along with her black bra. "No problem, babe."

"Thanks." Jackie assembled the bra under everyone's scrutiny, pulled on the blouse, and buttoned up.

"Great pair, huh?" Sanders leered. "Sorry we don't get more of a show."

"Sandy, that's disgusting," Suzette chided. "She wants a little privacy now. But I do admit they *are* fine."

"Yes, they're certainly fine, Jackie," JJC said. "But that's not why we came to see you guys."

Jackie blinked. Just *fine?* She eyed her underwear tangled with Sanders' black trousers. Asking for the panties was another thing; she'd have to stand to squirm into them. Keeping her thighs tucked beneath her offered more modesty. Besides, she didn't want to hear any more comments about anything else being just *fine.* "So?" she said coolly.

"Well, we knew when the Centaurians trashed this system, the Z-rays from the black hole ripped away most of the Altroudian atmosphere, but we weren't sure how much would be left. Turns out Altrouda's damn close to vacuum now, so we can't glide in. Looks like we're going to have to do the totally vertical landing trick."

"*Vertical?*"

"Don't worry, the first couple *Typhoons* were perfectly balanced for this sort of thing," Sanders put in. "We've got Arkonsky force-field tripods and believe me they *anchor* the fields about a hundred meters into the rock. Once you're down the whole thing looks damn tipsy, but it's *solid.*"

"It was just so rarely done," JJC said.

"Lee used to blab all the time about all the practice verticals they did taking off and landing on the moon," Suzette said. "After the next series got hover jets, they didn't have to think about that anymore. I guess Lee thought it was a real he-man thing to land it tail first. But it's the computers that do everything."

Jackie reeled with the idea of the sixty-five-foot *Typhoon* settling tail first on the dark surface of the planet, blasting rocket fire all the way down like a 1950s science fiction rocket ship. "What about the Pod?"

"Well, we leave that in orbit in either case," JJC said. "No way we could land with a Pod attached, even if we had full atmosphere. Unless we want to belly in on it."

Sanders laughed. "Can you see it? *Screeeeeech--whomp!* Oh, wow!"

"Guys, please, you're upsetting Jackie," Suzette said.

"No, I'm not upset," Jackie muttered. She'd always thought of the ship gliding in like some commercial rocket plane, but of course the *Typhoon* was a fully functioning spaceship designed to land anywhere. But losing the Pod? Losing the showers and the staterooms and the food supplies? And this bed? And any privacy? Having to live in that cramped *Typhoon II,* vertically, climbing *ladders,* while they struggled to make some sort of paradise out of the frozen dark rock below?

"But that's no problem," JJC went on. "I'm just letting Pat double-check it to keep his worrywart mind occupied. Meanwhile, I wanted to ask you about the Ywritt."

"The Ywritt?"

"Yes, ma'am. That's the reason I wanted you on my crew. Because you're on the Committee, and I sorta figured they might be allies, you know. They say you know 'em inside and out."

She felt her face fall. "Well ..." At once Dr. Jackie Vespertine, Professor of Exobiology at the University of Mars, began thoroughly lecturing her.

*That's all he wanted you for, missy! He wants to pump you for Ywritt data like any SolNet reporter! He doesn't care for your boobs or your butt or your charming little laugh or anything else! And probably like everyone else he thinks you flirted your way to your damn Ph.D.! Everyone thinks you're a brainless bimbo! Even I do!*

Jackie swallowed. "Well, everyone wants to know about the Ywritt, you know, but they're hard to explain in so many words." And that, of course, was because she wasn't supposed to tell anyone but the United System Council.

"But you're on the Committee. You've been negotiating with 'em for *months* now. You know where they stand on the whole Grid thing, how much they hate it and all."

"Well, it's not really that they *hate* it, they just feel their own methods are better. It's hard to explain the difference. In a way the Ywritt already have a Grid. But as far as we can tell, the interface is completely different. It's nothing like telepathy, more like these infinite libraries of *fully indexed information*."

"Yeah, wow," JJC said, nodding. "I heard something about how pissed they were about the IotaAlphaSol deal because it was so inefficient, or whatever they were saying."

Jackie met Jonathan James' brown eyes and blinked at the odd mix of intensity, curiosity, and sorrow. She was impressed that he seemed to be trying to understand her.

The negotiations for the Ywritt to become part of a proposed OverGrid between Iota Persei, Sol, and the Alpha Centaurian Empire had been unsuccessful, to put it mildly, and some of that top-level info *had* leaked to the press. Waterfall Sequence himself (or was it *itself?*) had come close to halting all talks when IotaAlphaSol was proposed, and Jackie and Greeney Gooney had spent three days getting him/it calmed down. She'd felt from the beginning that the iridescent bubble rainbow Waterfall Sequence could be a great personal friend, but navigating his angry silences was akin to trying to get a blown computer system back online.

Yet when Waterfall Sequence was back up and running, he graciously and easily joked that IotaAlphaSol was based on such primitive algorithms that employing it in Iota Persei would be like Jackie going back to being a cavewoman, and he'd attached several terabytes of images of fashioning crude pottery, tanning hides, foraging for nuts and berries, losing children to typhus and husbands to raiding parties, and dying in childbirth. Jackie was still wondering where he'd picked up all *that* history.

Jackie looked down at her crimson blouse and restrained herself from marching off the bed and grabbing the rest of her clothes. She was *soggy.*

"Yark! Yark yark!"

Trotter walked into the room.

"Hey, how did you get down here, buddy?" JJC said.

*Hello, dear master! Hello, everyone!* Trotter beamed as he leaped onto the bed. *You left hatch to Pod open and I came down staircase!*

"How's my little fluffy bear?" Suzette said, chucking the dog under the chin.

*I am not fluffy!*

"I know, I just say that," Suzette laughed. "I had a cat that was fluffy, so I say everyone's fluffy! But you are a much lovelier beast!"

"Yark! Yark yap!" Trotter turned to Jackie. *You discuss Ywritt with master? Good! He has been worried they will not accept him.*

"Really?" Jackie said. She met JJC's brown eyes once again. "You talk this sort of stuff over with your *dog?*"

JJC shrugged. "Well ..."

"Of course I'll help you in any way I can," she said, sitting up straight and shifting her legs, not caring what JJC might see. "I mean, I signed on to be a member of this team, after all. Whatever I can contribute, and all."

And most of it was classified top secret. What was she *doing?*

"Great, anything would be great, Jackie," JJC said, fending off Trotter's licks to his face.

"Well ..." She took a deep breath. "It's been really difficult to make sense of most of what they tell us. And *they're* the ones making communication easy. I mean, it's true they're masters of communication. They had to be, to pull all those different species on their homeworld into one *new* species."

"So they're really not humanoid at all," Suzette mused. "Is that true?"

"No, but they're *beautiful.* Most of them take bubbles as their shape. That's the easiest shape to maintain. But they can be like clouds, or mist. They're never *solid.*"

"Wow," Sanders said. "So it's true what they've been saying about this *self-created* species."

Jackie found that everyone including Trotter was hanging on her words. The United System Council's strict rules on what could be revealed about the Ywritt must have caused more anxiety than anyone wanted to acknowledge. She and Ranna had both maintained that more information needed to be shared.

But her sister would kill her. Ranna might just now be getting the news that her nutso baby sister was careening around the galaxy with the SolGrid Rebellion. What would she think of the secrets Jackie was about to spill to JJC and Suzette and Sanders and Trotter within the next few seconds?

*I can't smell these monsters!* Trotter put in. *Master needs to deal with these people, but what if they are not really people?*

"That's what we've been trying to find out," Jackie said. "We have to remember that the Ywritt are still in trauma over what happened to Iota Persei. I mean, they spent thirty-four years trapped by that Dyson sphere. They were shocked to realize they couldn't interface with the Wounded. Here they were, laid-back and such expert communicators, and the Wounded refused to talk. Instead they just built a sphere to steal the Ywritt's star. That's when the Ywritt started working in earnest on quantum computers."

She closed her eyes at the top-secret info that just came out of her mouth.

"They just started?" JJC said. "We've been working on 'em for decades now."

"Well, the Ywritt have been into them for hundreds of years, but they never really took them seriously until the Wounded sphered them. They found themselves trapped inside the Dyson sphere, and the idea was to simulate alternate universes where they might find some way out, some way to defeat the Wounded. Some of the Ywritt essentially went crazy, thinking they were actually living in those alternate universes. You can see why they'd be paranoid of us and all this talk of Grids."

"But I thought they were grateful to us for getting rid of the sphere. I mean, Kner and K'ufunb *restored* Iota Persei."

Jackie nodded. "Well, they *were* grateful. And before they started going flaky, the Four gave them a lot of info on how to rebuild their solar system. We taught them Star Drive and superspace radio, and they taught us a lot more about quantum computers."

"They didn't have *Star Drive?*"

Jackie winced. "No, really, they were so into *communication* that they never thought much about space travel. They probably would've figured out superspace radio by themselves, but they've never really needed it until now. Now they can send ships here whenever they want."

"Huh," JJC said. "And your sister's out there now?"

"R-right. You know, she and I have been protesting that we need more people on the Committee. There are only five of us now, and two of them are robots."

"Really? *Robots?*"

Jackie sighed. Even the members of the committee were top secret. "Y-yes. The John Douglas and Laurie Lachrer models the Ywritt upgraded. Jack was against it, but the Council didn't give a flip what he thought and the Ywritt wanted the robots in. So we had them, Ranna, me, and Greeney Gooney. But Greeney's been pretty useless recently, so we've really been overworked. The Four never wanted to be on the Committee. They just helped out a bit, until they started flaking out, that is."

"Huh. That's interesting. People always wondered whether the Four were on it. But Patster told me he'd declined a seat on it."

Jackie nodded. It was something she and Pat didn't discuss. "Well, he wanted to set up SolGrid. He said he didn't have the time."

"But I also got the sense from him that the Ywritt kinda freaked him out, too."

Jackie shrugged. Waterfall Sequence had told her that the feeling was mutual. She knew Pat didn't have the kind of empathy needed for interfacing with an alien species. She was glad they'd never had to work together on the project.

"This sure is different from what we hear on SolNet," Sanders put in. "The Ywritt seem like some darling cause, you know, the peace-loving and indigenous civilization we have to protect from ourselves and all."

"They also manage to make them sound slightly retarded," JJC observed.

"Well, they sound damn dangerous to me," Suzette put in.

"Yark! Yark yark yap!" Trotter cried. *I agree! Don't talk to them!*

Jackie took a breath. "Well, there's another thing that might work in our favor. The Ywritt think SolGrid is crap, but they also recognize that both SolGrid and the AC Grid can ferret out Wounded infiltrators. So they've offered to upgrade SolGrid because they sure as hell don't want to fool with the Wounded again."

"Yeah, it *is* crap," Sanders muttered. "Take it from the first assistant himself."

"But Pat wants to sit on his stupid patents. He's damned if he's going to let *aliens* upgrade his software. Even though he leased a slew of quantum computers from the Ywritt. He knows SolGrid wouldn't run without Ywritt technology."

JJC whistled. "Wow!"

"This is really weird for me. Working with the Ywritt is like why I'm *here*. It's like fate *unfolded* just to put me here. I mean, I've been doing exobiology for a long time, but this is what I've lived for, I guess. And what's really screwing me up is that everything's messing up now. And you know, I don't really want to feel like a spy or something, I mean, telling you all these secrets. I just want what's best for the Ywritt." She felt tears coming.

"C'mon, hon," Sanders said, hugging her. She stiffened. "It's not so bad. I know what you're talking about. You do what you have to do. Like, I was sort of a spy myself. Like all that new cloaking technology I got out of Suzette."

"*What?*" Suzette gasped. "It wasn't from *me!*"

"Well, really, babe, it *was.* And it wasn't hard. In a way I didn't even want to get it. But it was that fantastic afternoon we met over at your and Lee's place."

"You said you wanted to make it on our *bed!* On our *marriage bed!*"

"Yark! Yark yark!"

"Quiet, Trotty bear, this is getting interesting!" JJC laughed, patting Trotter's head.

"It was damn good, you have to admit," Sanders said. "Anyway, my comm alerted me to another comm besides yours. So old Lee has his backup comm in the dresser drawer. It was a cinch for me to hack it when you went into the bathroom. There was all this stuff about cloaking, and a million other things. I couldn't help myself. Had no idea what I might want it for, but I just had to have it. I'm just that way!"

"You're just *that way?*" Jackie and Suzette exclaimed in unison.

"I am what I am! Anyway, I didn't have any use for Cloak 14.12.0.1 until Mr. Commer here started talking about jacking the *II.* Then I knew I could port it to this ship."

"I *wondered* where you got that," JJC said. "Anyway, we can move on, now that we're all friends again."

"We--we are not!" Suzette cried.

"Oh, forget it, dear heart," Sanders drawled. "You can't be mad at me for stealing the one thing that's really saved our ass today. And anyway, you have Jonathan James now, and I have *Jackie.* Believe me, I am one lucky dude!"

"I--I don't know what I want!" Jackie blurted with a glance at JJC's dangles of glossy black plastic. She felt rather than saw Suzette's glare.

"Forget it, hon, you got *me* now!" Sanders boomed. Jackie stared. Was his naked mound rising again? No, he wouldn't dare, would he? Wasn't he just using her? Had JJC ordered him to seduce her? Was he going to screw her in front of Jonathan James and Suzette? And this dog? Was she going to let him? She swallowed.

"*Hey, jerks!*" came a cry over the intercom. "If I can break up this *lovefest* for a minute with some really *crappy* news--"

"*P-Pat?*" Jackie gasped.

"Yeah, it's me, the only damn twit *unpaired.* I've been listening to the whole thing. Including every last little grunt from stateroom sixteen. You idiots don't think I can't push this little button on the console and jettison your precious little Pod?"

"Sheesh, that would be a major dereliction of duty, Patster," JJC observed. "Especially as Trotter here just reported that we left the hatch open between you and the Pod. So we *both* lose all our air. Why don't you think that one over?"

*And then he'd be stuck with Z'B forever!* Trotter chortled. *Too bad about Z'B, but I can't smell him at all now! He's gone in the head!*

"Hell," Pat muttered, "I can cope. The Control Room's secure and I can repressurize the whole goddamn ship."

Sanders slid the stateroom door shut and punched at a display on the wall. "*This* room is pressurized now. And I just sealed the Pod hatch as well."

"I believe Mr. Patster is *upset* about something," Suzette cooed. "But I know he'd never want to waste little Suzette, now would he?"

*Patster wants to roll around with Suzette beast on the floor!* Trotter laughed. *But he doesn't know how!*

"*Dammit!*" Pat snarled.

JJC grinned at Jackie. "Trotter can turn up the telepathic volume so anyone on this ship can hear, even Mr. Patster up in the Control Room." He spoke to the ceiling. "Hey, Patster, I know we have our disagreements at times, like all dens of thieves, but I do need to know that you're a loyal member of this team."

"Aw, crap on it! Hell, JJC, you know I was just joking. Everyone knows that, right? I was just upset, y'know? Well, the hell with it. Listen, idiots, I just got through verifying that the Arkonsky fields haven't been serviced in *fifteen years*. They're down to *eighteen percent*. You got that? We can't land on damn Altrouda! We try it and we'll topple the ship! Ninety-five percent probability! What do you think of *that,* jerks?"

*I think somebody needs to go up there and roll around on the floor with Mr. Patster!* Trotter snickered.

"Any takers?" JJC smirked, looking around the bed.

## CHAPTER TWENTY-TWO
### Scrambled Z'B

*So cramped! Who could fit in this crazy room? Kitchenette they call it? Don't they know a six-foot Martian can't live in a kitchenette? My back hurts! Floor's cold! How did I get so big? Legacy of* Garr/thahg *maybe? Terrible place! They think I'm crazy! But let me outradiate! See, I am rational!*

Z'B's mind ached with the aftermath of the mental scream. Surely everyone had picked it up. But when he replayed it, he saw it coming out as shattered strings of Amplified Thought code.

*Z: CrampMind Call &||; CrazyKitchen IF floor = COLD23 cos x THEN insertFunction irrationalHurt; IF Var1 * x = nonrational; unityCall {CRAMP > -1 ELSE || Call REPLAY NULL, area infinite sphere};*

He sprawled on the floor in his backup ruby Emperor's Robe, his back fin painfully jammed against steel cabinet drawers. He was so cold. He tore spastically at the robe, dimly understanding that it was good he didn't have the real Emperor's Robe, the matter/anti-matter symbol of office he hadn't dared wear for months.

*Why can't I outradiate the real? Everything comes out wrong!*

*Do PUSH = OUTRADIATE >1, Var$ = GOTO surface {x = [LAB4]: base quotient zero}*

*Wait! There's Trotter! I'm picking up his outradiance! High volume! My friend! My buddy! Trotter, how are you?*

*Function TrotterEclipse || e = sort x,y; IF friendContact = 1, then friendContact = 2; Else NULL; ||*

*No! He thinks I'm crazy too!*

Z'B saw he'd torn his robe into a dozen red strips. Now there was nothing to cover his cold pink body. He used to share everything with Trotter. When had the Scramble set in, to the point where no one could understand him? Why couldn't he even move his own body properly?

A wave of grief swept over him as he kept aiming

outradiance at his dog friend down in the Pod, and watched in dismay as it came out completely inverted each time. In fact, as he read Trotter's dog outradiance he got the impression that Trotter was grieving in a similar way about the ruin of Z'B's mind.

*But it's not ruined! I can think just fine! I'm rational!*

*COPY rationalAssert zx + 4; {recycleTruth < 0 sin x3 tan yx + 4} = NULLSET;*

*Crap! Trotter, why can't you hear me?*

Their bond had gone so deep. Trotter had been able to tell Z'B things he'd never been able to fully make JJC aware of, how deeply his recent illness had taken him into the Underworld, what it was like to have your life in that precarious balance.

*Trotter listens to them worry about this stupid ship! How to land a stupid ship! What are they talking about? How to land the ship? Is this a ship I'm on? Yes! I knew that, didn't I? The* Typhoon II! *Of course! All the specifications are here! I memorized them when I looked over the silly brochures!*

*Why did I volunteer for this mission?*

*But I didn't volunteer! They kidnapped me! They locked me in this kitchen!*

*Well, why don't they consult the specs?*

*Wait! How did I get top-secret specifications for this ship from stupid brochures?*

*I didn't! Somehow SolGrid fed them to all Martians! The Total Martian Outradiance has the specs! Not outradiance, but a kind of inradiance! Is that possible?*

*I have it! All of it! I understand this ship!*

*Pat's right! The Arkonsky clamps will not hold!*

Z'B was hit by a cold burst of radiance from Trotter. The dog had looked up in surprise at a coherent thought in Z'B's mind. In fact, Z'B saw through Trotter that everyone in stateroom sixteen was staring at the ceiling in astonishment.

"See? See I told you!" Patrick James called from the Control Room. Z'B realized the intercom had been broadcasting for some time, though he hadn't been able to focus on it. "Even Z'B can see we can't land this damn thing!"

*Besides, all ladders down the inside of the fuselage have been removed for museum display,* Z'B radiated to everyone. *Visitors might trip over the rungs, you know. So there's no way to get around a vertical ship.*

"*Damn ...*" Z'B heard JJC mutter over the intercom.

"Yark! Yark yap!" Trotter cried, gleefully radiating images of Jackie, Sanders, JJC and Suzette on the bed.

"Okay, here's what we do, jerks," Pat snarled. "Leave the ship and Pod in orbit and take the crew down in separate escape craft flights. That's five flights. I can pilot the thing. Escape craft are tricky if you haven't done it before. We all had to train on it. We'll have to separate the *Typhoon* and Pod to get out, of course."

"Negative, Mr. Patster," Jonathan James called. "Where the hell would we stay while we make shelters?"

"Hell, there's enough old Kloru'dik buildings down there. We'll just find some in usable shape and make some oxygen for 'em."

"Well, maybe and maybe not. In any case, I'm not separating this crew."

*Wow, he thinks Pat might try to be the last one and hijack the ship and strand us all on Altrouda!*

*function wowPatster = tan x + 1 derivative = ||; Call Last? renderPlanet = JACKSHIP; void coordinates, {empty strand: life = 0; ||}*

Everyone absorbed this last piece of telepathic data. "Well, screw it, then," Pat said. "Let's just turn this stupid ship back to Sol with our tails between our legs."

"Mr. Patster sounds kind of negative about the SolGrid Rebellion, if you ask me," Suzette said. "That certainly won't score any points with Suzette and her rejuvenated boobies, now will it?"

"Aw, hell with you," Pat muttered.

Z'B got to his feet and clawed at the intercom buttons. "*You're* the one!" he cried, and he could feel Trotter, and through him all the humans, reeling with the impact of coherent speech from someone they'd all written off as insane. "*You* made this SolGrid thing! It makes *inradiance!* It pushes *into* the Martian mind! No *wonder* we're going crazy! *You scrambled the Martians with SolGrid!*"

"Forget it," Pat shot back. "You guys were already going flaky before December with all this child culture BS. You pushed that more than anyone, Mr. Emperor. You wanted the whole Martian culture to be *childlike.* Well, you got your stupid wish. And you tipped everything off balance! SolGrid didn't do a damn thing to you idiots."

"SolGrid made it *worse!*"

"If you stinking finbacks would just *cooperate,* everything would be fine! And remember, you Four went crazy on your own. You can't blame SolGrid for that."

"Our minds were *exhausted!* Then you make this SolGrid and it *hurts* us! That's right, it hurts our *outradiance!*"

*"Shut up, Z'B, or I'll laser you where you stand!"*

There was a long silence as everyone absorbed Pat's cry.

*You would use the* Typhoon *anti-personnel lasers against members of this glorious rebellion against SolGrid?* Z'B radiated.

*"Anti-personnel lasers?"* JJC muttered. "What's he talking about?"

"Damn you all!" Pat said. "I could do it so easily! I could fry anyone who pokes their nose out of the Pod hatch! What do you think of *that?*"

"I think I've just done a major Amplified Thought hack on the APL system, Mr. Patster," Z'B said calmly. "It's powered down everywhere except for the Control Room at this time. Did anyone aboard fail to realize that I've just regained complete control of my Amplified Thought powers?"

Another long silence.

"Transporting personnel in stateroom sixteen to *Typhoon* proper," Z'B said. "Including clothes installed for everyone who needs them. Everyone okay?"

*"God!"* Suzette cried.

"What the *hell?*" Sanders said.

"Dammit, Z'B!" Jonathan James said. "Yes, we're all in the

ship now, but what the hell's going on?"

"Yark! Yark yark!"

*Trotter, buddy, how you doing? Hold on while I finish this.*

"Personnel transport completed. Secure *Typhoon* and Pod hatches. Done. Initializing Pod separation. Done. Landing gear extended." Z'B heard the whir of the nose and wing wheels and the satisfying click as they all locked into place.

"Are you going to try to *land* this thing?" Jackie cried.

"I just *did* land. Look out the portholes. That's the former Kloru'dik Parliament to the left. Jonathan James, would you like that structure converted to your own Imperial Palace?"

"Well, *yes!*" JJC gasped. "Z'B, this is wonderful! Thanks! I knew you'd come through! This is exactly what we need!"

"Yes! This is *fun!* A whole palace!" Z'B felt the force flowing out of his mental claw-tips into the hulking warehouse he could sense to the left of the ship. Under the brilliant starlit sky, in the eternal night of Altrouda orbiting its black hole, he could feel his commands transforming the building, adding the air the humans needed along with Martian environmental spaces for himself. The Grand Hall took shape, with marble steps to the imperial throne bathed in torchlight. His mind whirled with colors and shapes and concepts, with highest order formulas, with sudden whining pressure--

*IF level = rotationSurface x + y,z matrix energyLoss |||: CALL hyperbola exultantCreate |||: MistakeArea limit as x approaches sanityConserve; || ELSE {turnInward}*

The headache exploded, unexpected and devastating.

Jackie slid open the kitchenette door. "Z'B, are you all right?" Z'B stared into her wide turquoise eyes.

*Oh, no! Too much! Too much!* Even that concept spewed into imaginary numbers, knocking Jackie backwards and paralyzing everyone.

# CHAPTER TWENTY-THREE
## A Declaration of Passion

"Orbit secure," Joe spoke over the intercom, looking past Jack out the canopy at the blue-green planet to port. "Sandra, see if you can get hold of Dar or K'sla down there. Laurie, let's run the standard systems check just to be on the safe side."

"Roger," Sandra called back. "Dar's already left a message that there's still been no trace of Jonathan James on Andertwin. Also trying to contact Phil Sperry."

"Thanks, Sandra," Jack said. He turned to Joe. "We won't be here long. Maybe a waste of time, but we had to check. Where next? Iota Persei?"

Joe shrugged. "Yeah, I guess." He didn't relish asking Waterfall Sequence or any other Ywritt for permission to search the Iota Persei system. Though speaking with anyone plugged into the AC Grid on the planet below would prove in moments that JJC wasn't in any Centaurian solar system, it might take a whole day to interface with those damnable Ywritt Mandarins. The idea of the Ywritt being "master communicators" had long since soured on Joe. They seemed to take delight in *obstructing* communication. Maybe that was a form of communication right there.

His older brother had been silent and expressionless the whole way to Procyon A. Jack had been flailing the past few months between disowning his son and vowing to single-handedly restore JJC's sanity. The pressure had to be building. Joe had already offered to open negotiations with Jonathan James, but Jack had muttered that it would just be "putting things off," so for the past ten minutes Joe had dropped the subject in favor of uncomfortable silence.

Now he realized Laurie hadn't acknowledged his last order. He pressed the square on his console for Engineering. "Hey, Laurie, did--"

The Control Room hatch shot open and Laurie Lachrer flew inside, slamming the hatch and thrusting her comm at them. "*Dammit,* sir!"

Joe was instantly on his feet, heart racing. Jack stood as well. There was only one possible thing that could so rile their genius physician/engineer. "Dammit, Laurie, is SD3 about to *irrational?*"

She gulped for air. "I--I--*sir!* I'm--I'm so *sorry!*"

Were they idiots to just blast off in the *VI* without several months' tests on Star Drive 3? "Oh my God, Laurie! The whole planet! The whole *system!*"

"But it's not my *fault!*" Laurie wailed, flinging the comm at Joe's face.

How he caught it he wasn't sure. Both her blue irises were surrounded by white. Her mouth worked and nothing came out.

*"What's going on?"*

"It's not my fault! I was just sitting there, monitoring our approach!"

"Laurie, jettison the Drive! On its own emergency Drive! Send it vertically out of the system! What are you *doing* here? Get down there and *do* it! We have *seconds!*"

But he wasn't thinking. He could do it from his console. He shot to his instrument panel and saw Jack at his own.

"Negative!" Jack cried. "No problem! Drive's perfect! All systems normal!"

Joe stared at his console. It all looked correct. Were the instruments haywire?

"It's not the Drive!" Laurie screamed. "It's all on my comm! Every bit of it! God, it's *disgusting!*"

Joe had a momentary urge to slap her, thinking of old movies where you slap someone and they say *Thanks, I needed that.*

What on earth was wrong with his P/E? Laurie was always on top of everything. She was so smart she'd figured out how to destroy a star by mathematics alone. "Laurie, what *is* it?"

"It's not my fault! He sent it! Just out of the blue! Look! 3D holo, and--and--"

Joe turned her comm over and stared at the screen. MESSAGE FROM RICHARD BALLARD. He pressed a square, and to his astonishment a life-size hologram sprang up of Major Richard Ballard, sprawling naked amid rumpled violet sheets.

"Yes, it's *you* I want!" rumbled over the overhead speakers as the comm auto-interfaced with the Control Room. "I've finally been able to admit it! Yes, *you! Look* at this! Remember when you *saw it* when you came into Sandra's room? Is *this* big enough for you? It feels *so good!*"

Joe was so shocked that he dropped the comm, barely conscious of it cracking on the Control Room floor.

"*What's going on here?*" Jack cried.

"Would you like to stroke *this?* Would you like to take *this* in--"

"I'm sorry, sir! I didn't know it was full-size! I just played it on my table, and, I mean, I didn't *want* to play it, but I figured it was a legitimate message!"

"Baby, you know I've measured it, with my comm, of course!" hologram Ballard burbled. "Eight and three-quarter *inches!* And one and three-quarters *thick!* What do you think of *that?*"

Joe reached for the comm on the floor but its splintered screen was black. He couldn't think. Maybe reroute her comm set-up functions here, but he needed her code. He could override, but was that SubComm Matrix 1 or Matrix 2?

"I want it *in* you! Right now!"

"Just make it stop!" Laurie cried.

"I'm *trying!* We have to call Sandra to reroute the comm set-up so we can turn this thing off!"

"Baby, ah, *baby! Look* at me! Just *look!*"

"No, we can't call Sandra!" Laurie said. "We just can't!"

"Why not?" Jack said. "Dammit, I'm gonna throw him in the brig for this!"

"I didn't mean to *see* it! I mean, the *other* time! I was just taking Sandra some tea, and I had no idea he knew I'd *seen* it!"

"*What?*" Joe yelled alongside Jack.

Again the Control Room hatch sprang open. "I'm so *sorry!* That message was meant for *me!*" Sandra Markham gasped, running to the hologram, gulping at the full-size holographic gonad, then making spastic motions to shoo the others away.

"Baby, it's *you* I want! Now I really *know!* We'll settle down here, on Andertwin! Just jump ship with me! Let those stupid bozos run after that little JJC twit! You and I have bigger things to do! Like *getting this thing in you!*"

"Turn it *off!*" Laurie moaned. "This is disgusting!"

"No, he's telling me he *loves* me!" Sandra laughed. "At *last!* Of course I'll go with you, Rick! We'll go to Andertwin! I promise!"

"You're talking to a hologram he sent to *me!* Can't you get that through your head? Can't you understand Rick's a total *fraud?*"

"He *loves* me!" Sandra cried. "Look, I know I'm not supposed to be checking his messages, but I just had to!"

"You hacked into his *messages?*"

"Well, I had to know how he *felt!* And now I know!"

"You didn't see *the whole thing?*" She turned to Joe. "Look, I don't mean I *wanted* to see the whole thing, it's just that I was in shock, and any second now--" She pointed to the holographic bed, eyes averted.

"*Laurie!* I *want* you! I've always wanted *you!* Call it fate, call it whatever you want! *God,* that feels good! I know it sounds crazy, but the only reason I ever got with Sandra is so I could get next to *you.* But don't tell her that because she'll have a fit! She's always whining about something, trying to get me to commit! Laurie, I *want* you! Just as you want *this!*"

"Is this thing ever gonna *end?*" Jack muttered as Sandra gaped, backing away in crippled slow motion. She turned to the open Control Room hatch just as Major Richard Ballard surged through it, thankfully in uniform.

Sandra stared in shock, then shoved him aside. She sprang down the stairs but stumbled and fell halfway down. Joe heard her scramble to her feet and run to her quarters. He turned to the major in his tight blue uniform.

"Listen, everyone, I can explain," Ballard said.

"Laurie--I--I'm *coming!*" the hologram moaned.

"Oh, man," Jack muttered. "Now I've seen everything."

The hologram settled back on the purple sheets. "Laurie, that was so *good*."

Laurie turned to the physical Ballard. "Get out! I don't want anything to do with you!"

"But it's true!" Ballard cried. "I *love* you, Laurie, can't you see that?"

"I *love* you," the hologram agreed. "To be *inside* you! *Laurie!*"

Laurie took a ragged breath and turned to Jack. "Look, sir, I know I'm probably overreacting, but I just came to tell you, I mean, to file a protest and, sir, I think you should relieve me. I guess I'm more off-balance than I'd thought, maybe with this Wounded thing last year, I don't know. I'm not myself, I think, and I've been so worried about Will, and then *this!*"

Jack shook his head. "No, you're not relieved, Colonel. You're doing fine. This was just a shock. Everyone's upset."

Mercifully the hologram gave way to the normal Control Room floor, but a huge red orb marked "Replay?" floated chest-high. Joe was reluctant to get near that object.

"Okay, Mr. Ballard, you will confine yourself to the brig for the duration of this mission," Jack said, pointing out the hatch. "Now."

"Aw, Jack--Laurie. Look, if you guys will just *listen*. This is all about *love*."

"Suppose we just confine him to his quarters," Joe suggested. "The brig's a nasty place."

"The brig," Jack repeated. "It blocks *all* comm signals. I don't want any more hacking of any sort aboard this ship. Ballard, enter the brig and remain standing in the center until we activate Full Isolation."

"*Damn,* Jack," Ballard said.

"No backtalk," Joe said. "Jack's right. We can't tolerate any more glitches. Major, get a move on or I'll have to ask Lee to escort you there."

"Aw, that wimp. He couldn't--"

Lee Borman clambered up the metal stairs and entered the Control Room with a pair of Arkonsky force-field handcuffs and his shattergun, set on kill, Joe noticed. "Someone call me?" Lee chortled. "Boys, you shouldn't leave the intercom on shipwide the way you do, but in this case--c'mere, Ricky."

"Major Ballard," Jack said, "your insubordination is noted, your improper advances to Colonel Lachrer are noted, you are relieved of all duties and you will face a court-martial upon our return to Sol. Is that understood?"

"Screw it, Jack boy!" Ballard said. "I'm so in love with Laurie I just don't care! Of course you're coming with me to Andertwin, sweetheart! Meanwhile you can figure out how to bypass the brig protocols for me."

"Why, I--I will *not!*" Laurie said.

"C'mon, hon, I get it that you'd be suspicious of me. Who wouldn't be? Sure I've laid the ladies up and down the galaxy. But I just hadn't found the right woman yet! Until *you.* And I'm ready to *commit* now. We'll live down there in paradise! What I mean to say is--dammit, your boobs are *astonishing!*"

There was a long silence. "Major, what on earth has gotten *into* you?" Joe finally said. It couldn't be--he wouldn't have-- would he?

Ballard shrugged. "Nothing got *into* me, dude! I've just seen the *light!* When I finally realized how much I was in love I thought, I wonder how she feels about *me,* and you know, I'd never abuse SolGrid but I figured, lemme just dip into the *Centaurian* Grid for a sec, now that we're here in Alpha Centauri! Hell, it turns out twenty trillion Alpha Centaurians just don't *know* how Laurie feels! But do I care? I *love* her, and that's that!"

Joe reeled. Ballard had really done it. Why hadn't they thought to extend the SolGrid prohibition to the AC Grid? It would leak just as much.

"*Damn,* Laurie!" Ballard laughed. "I was sure you'd be waiting for me in the Grid yourself. What fantastic *sharing* we could have! But we'll leave that for later. Meanwhile, admiral sirs, I don't need your goddamn communications crap, I've got the Grid, and I'm in contact with *everything.*" He turned back to Laurie. "I *love* you! All of Alpha Centauri *loves* you now, because I do and I'm in the Grid!"

"Should I stun the mother, Cap'n?" Borman said.

Jack nodded. Joe was so angry he didn't tell Borman to check his kill level.

# CHAPTER TWENTY-FOUR
## The Failed Reprimand

"Well, what do you know?" Lee said, examining his blaster settings. "We'll just dial it down a bit from *total annihilation*, I guess--*ooof*!"

"Take him to the--" Jack ordered, flustered by the sight of a USSF major committing the gross insubordination of elbowing Borman in the kidney, jerking the shattergun from his fingers, pulling Laurie to him and firing a blue ray at her temple.

*Why does Lee always leave the damn thing on full shatter?* Jack had time to wonder before he registered that Laurie was merely limp with Ballard's huge bicep around her neck as he skittered backwards towards the open Control Room hatch.

"*Damn* you, mother!" Lee grunted from the floor.

"Aaah, you don't know *crap* about weapons, Lee baby!" Ballard smirked.

Jack recovered his wits and had his own shattergun out, correctly set on stun. So did Joe. Jack noted Ballard eying their blasters with contempt even as Jack longed for some good old-fashioned anti-personnel lasers with top-level AI that could punch a three mm hole through Ballard's right ear. He cursed himself for not being prepared for this. Hadn't he known all along the son of bitch was off his rocker?

"Where the hell do you think you're going, Ballard?" Joe yelled, sighting down his blaster in a two-handed grip. With Laurie already stunned, a second pulse concentrating on Ballard's head wouldn't do her much further damage, although recovering from one stun burst often meant a day in the infirmary.

"Aaah, screw you, Joe baby! Me and Laurie are taking a shuttle down to Andertwin! She'll be my *Empress*. Oh yes she will!" Ballard seemed to be strangling the unconscious physician/engineer in the crook of his elbow.

Jack raised his shattergun.

*Beep!*

He stared at the power indicator. DRAINED.

"*Dammit!*" Joe said next to him.

"Don't forget I have all my old weapons hacks!" Ballard laughed. "Lee's little toy here has Master Control. All your blasters are *useless.* Except this one, dude!"

"Except for *this* one," said Sandra Markham, standing in the Control Room hatchway with an eight-inch USSF combat dagger. The blinking red light at its base indicated AutoSeek on Throw. The knives weren't part of the networked system that Ballard could shut down from Lee's blaster, and Jack had no doubt that Sandra had just used the blade's sensors to take a high-resolution image of Rick Ballard's jugular vein.

Ballard's eyes widened. Sandra's were slitted and cold. Her face was tight and she held the blade expertly, trained like all USSF personnel in knife combat, icky as that was to modern shattergun sensibilities. Ballard, burdened with a hostage, had to be evaluating his chances of either fending off a manual blade attack or attempting the futile dance away from the knife's thruster jets and three-hundred-mile-per-hour nav systems.

AutoSeek on Throw also effectively meant AutoSeek on Drop. If Ballard stunned or shattered Sandra, the blade would have a life of its own and could chase its victim for half an hour until it achieved success. But ASOT was so dangerous to everyone that activation was usually only on the Captain's orders.

"By the way," Sandra spoke, "I took the liberty of locking the launch sequence on both the *Garrison* and the *Reynolds*. Nobody's taking a shuttle anywhere, mister."

"Good work, Sandra," Jack said, noting Lee crawling towards a rear console.

"Freeze!" Ballard screamed, backing to the wall and pulling Laurie to his chest.

Lee dragged himself into a chair. "Screw it, man," he grunted, tapping at the console. "I'll have his little weapons hack fixed in a second, Cap'n."

"Okay, Ballard, put down the shattergun," Jack ordered as Sandra stood before him with the knife. "You're not going anywhere."

"New plan! New plan!" Ballard yelled, dialing his gun back to full shatter. "I'm taking command of the *Typhoon!* Or our sexy physician/engineer here dies!"

Jack stared in disbelief. Beside him Joe muttered: "*Rick?* You just got through saying you *loved* her!"

"He doesn't love anyone but himself!" Sandra snarled, moving in with the knife.

"Sandra, move back!" Jack yelled. "That's not doing any good!"

Ballard whirled to the rear console and fired.

Jack reeled from the blast. Smoke billowed, and Lee was down, chair overturned, console in flames, auto extinguishers from the walls gushing green gas.

"Ow!" Sandra cried, dropping her knife just as a thin blue-purple ray struck the blade. It tinkled to the floor in a thousand pieces.

"One console down, one blade down," Ballard announced. "Don't nobody reach for another, or Laurie here *shatters!*"

Jack turned to Lee moaning on the floor. "Lee, are you hurt?"

"Aw, hell, Jack baby, you know he's all right," Ballard said. "If the beam even grazed him, he'd be nothing but little chunks of glass right now. Listen up, everyone! I'm in the Grid, and my reaction times are *fantastic.* All Alpha Centauri is following *everything.* They *want* Laurie and me on Andertwin as Emperor and Empress, and they're *helping* my reflexes! Don't you know I could shatter every one of you in half a second, before anyone could rush me? But do I do that? No! That's because I'm your new captain, and I love you! So what do you say, guys? Let's put all this crap about me going to the brig aside, and get some *work* done. Jacko, my man, just move away from the pilot's chair there."

"*Dammit,* Ballard," Jack said, "of all the stupid stunts to pull!" If Ballard was in the AC Grid, he was leaking USSF secrets to everyone in Alpha Centauri, at his level, of course, but it was still a disaster.

"Calm down! Nobody wants Laurie turned into gravel,

right? So why don't we all sit down and cooperate on this deal? Look, as your new captain I'll even complete this mission for ya! Sweet deal, huh? Because I know where Jonathan James got off to!"

"How the hell do you know that?"

"Are you kidding? Nobody in AC knows for absolute sure, of course, because it's not like JJC would *tell* anybody here, but the consensus of twenty trillion Alpha Centaurians is that of course he'd go to Barnard's Black Hole."

"Barnard's?" Jack muttered. "Are you kidding? The whole system is off limits."

"Wow! Why didn't we see that before?" Joe said. "Of course JJC would go there!"

"That's what twenty trillion goddamn ACs think!" Ballard laughed. "They know him *intimately,* in a way you never will, Jacko. Everyone figures that's the place for him. Orbiting a black hole! If your buddy Dar down there had just bothered to go into the Grid, he'd have known what everyone was thinking."

"Damn," Jack said. "Okay, we'll try it."

"You aren't issuing any orders here, man. This is *my* ship now."

"Oh my God! Rick, you loved *me!*" Sandra whimpered, crawling shellshocked under the main console. "You said you loved *me!*"

"Hey, babe, it was fun for a while! You needed a few good lays, admit it. Sure I enjoyed sticking it into you. But you weren't the one. Laurie here *is*. So grow up, girl."

"You *son of a bitch!*"

Jack turned to Joe. "Did you *know* this was going on?"

"No, I had no idea!" Joe pointed to the limp Laurie. "Apparently *she* did."

"I *hate* you, Rick!" Sandra sobbed. "Someone give me a shattergun!"

"Oh, just *listen* to this!" Ballard chuckled. "Would that be for me, honey, or just for yourself?"

"Oh ... *oh* ..." Laurie muttered, head rolling, eyes fluttering, squirming in Ballard's one-armed hammerlock.

"Sheesh," Ballard grunted. He slid his hand down to her waist, yanked her tunic over her head, wrapped it tightly around her face, and pushed the shattergun muzzle against the blue cloth. "Hey, no bra or nothing, dudes! What a sight, huh? 'Course you can't have 'em! They're *mine!*"

Jack tried to look away from Laurie's exposed breasts.

"Uh--*uh!*" Laurie groaned, arms flailing spastically.

"God, this is *insane!*" Joe muttered.

"Well, screw all this. Hey, Jacko boy, I got a new idea. Suppose I let old JJC know we're coming?" Ballard spoke theatrically to the ceiling as the half-naked Laurie finally hung limply. "Comm code 2343.5! Superspace to Barnard's Black Hole!"

"*Wha-at?*" Jack said.

"Don't you want to talk to your dear son? By the way, thank Sandra here for divulging the comm code for voice command. She'd say anything when I was filling her up, if you know what I mean and I think you do!"

"Give me a shattergun!" Sandra shrieked. "I *mean* it!"

"C'mon, Rick, JJC won't want anything to do with you," Joe said. "You're in the AC Grid. His whole thing is *rebelling* against the Grid. Against *both* Grids!"

"Hey, dudes, I have my anti-SolGrid beliefs as much as anyone. But I'm thinking JJC may just like what I'm thinking about using the *Centaurian* Grid. I'm in the Grid and I'm seeing it all now. JJC just hasn't thought it through. We just edit the software back to the original total One Emperor control, then we're in charge again!"

"The total *fascism?* That's insane!"

"Yeah, I'm feeling the goddamn Grid just reeling at the idea of it. Weird! Some ACs want the one True Emperor back, but there's a lot of damn cowards who *don't* want it!"

Jack calculated his chances of issuing a voice command to override Ballard's weapons lock, then bringing his recharging blaster up to fire a stun pulse before Ballard pulled the trigger on Laurie. Not good. He could feel Joe at his side considering the same thing.

"Or hell, Jack, maybe I'll do the honorable thing and screw his ass for you. Pretend to be his buddy and then carve that little bastard up. So you'll love me again! Hell, nobody can know what I'm thinking! Nobody! Not even me!"

"Oh … can't breathe …" Laurie moaned from under her wrapped tunic.

"Hear that, Jacko? My Empress *loves* me!"

"*Nobody* loves you!" Sandra screamed, pounding the floor. "*Nobody!*"

# CHAPTER TWENTY-FIVE
## Idiot's Fortune

The group clambered over the rubble towards the dark hulk of the new palace faintly visible in the starlight. The only other illumination was the faint pink glow of their seven EnviroFields.

"Why didn't you leave the damn Martian in the *Typhoon?*" Patrick James grumbled. "He's useless again."

JJC shrugged. "He just got tired. Give him some rest. He'll come around. Besides, we're sticking together. All of us."

It was obvious JJC didn't trust Pat anymore, Suzette saw. He wouldn't let Pat out of his sight again.

"I--I--" Z'B moaned.

*GOTO randomTogether; CosY + 1; [VAR x = ME; || PUSH VAR allOfUs > 0] IF existencePostulate--*

"*God,*" Pat muttered, putting his hands over his ears as if he could ward off Z'B's jagged high-pitched outradiance.

*ALIGN $mustAcceptSetback; || RUN lossEval + PUSH {mindRecover// = 1}*

"The poor thing," Suzette said. "Don't rile him, Patty!"

"I'm not riling anyone! And don't call me *Patty!*"

Suzette caressed his arm and let her fingers linger there. "Oh, I didn't mean anything bad, dearest. It's just a little sweet nothing to whisper in your ear, that's all."

She might have to drag horny Patty somewhere just to take the edge off. Keep up ship's morale. Of course, she'd get JJC's permission first. But Mr. Patster was about to come apart. He needed some raw copulation in a hurry.

"Z'B landed us just fine," Jackie said. "And he converted that entire building for us. He just needs to rest and he'll be okay again."

Suzette eyed Ms. Professor Vespertine warily. How come *she* couldn't take Pat's edge off? Suzette had never seen such a flawless female body. It was any man's idea of perfection. And the glow on Sanders' face meant that Jackie had thoroughly pleased him. So why hadn't she been able to keep Mr. Patster glowing?

Suzette was worried. JJC had also gotten a glimpse of that nude female glory, and there was no way even the rejuvenated, volcanic sex surging within Suzette could compare to Jackie's serene beauty. Would Jonathan James succumb to that, even though Suzette had made it her top priority to keep him yanked into insensibility?

She noted Sanders scanning the starfield above while everyone else including Trotter was watching where they put their feet on the broken dark purple bricks.

"What's up?" she said, poking him. "That's not a pun, really!"

"I was just curious about where the damn black hole might be," he said, arm sweeping what Suzette uneasily noted had to be billions of star points. "No accretion disk, so nothing radiating from that."

JJC shrugged. "We can always check the *Typhoon* database later. Who cares? It's a crappy little black hole. The BS Black Hole. Why the goddamn ACs bothered to fry the damn thing is beyond me. But they sure did a number on old Altrouda." He pointed to the torn landscape. Suzette wondered how Z'B could possibly have repaired the massive Kloru'dik government building looming ahead.

At least she'd relaxed about the black hole. Barnard's Star, though the next closest star system to Sol after Alpha Centauri, had been a tiny red dwarf, an ancient star that couldn't produce a fertile solar system. Its mass was so tiny, about fourteen percent of Sol, that it could never black-hole or supernova on its own. Yet when the ACs murdered the star they'd turned the red dwarf into a mini-black hole with its own event horizon from which no light could escape. But it was still just a mass in the center of this system, one that Altrouda and its three equally devastated companions further out could orbit as if it were still a sun. Altrouda was in no danger of spiraling in.

Thank God their EnviroFields could handle this place; Suzette tapped her controls to get a readout of -278F/100.928K for exterior temperature. Sanders had already mentioned that it would've been a lot colder if not for the residual Z radiation from the Centaurian attack.

"Crap! Why couldn't you have cleaned off the damn walkways, Z'B?" Pat snarled as he tripped over loose rocks.

"He was tired," Jackie repeated. "He couldn't get everything."

"Aaah, crap on it."

*GOTO RealignGripMind; {matrix = 4,3} ELSE VAR selfImage = 0, output = 0*

"Z'B's a darling," Suzette said. "I think he's *wonderful*, Mr. Pattycakes. Don't be so hard on the dear." She patted Patster's trim little rear, and there was a brief electronic sizzle as their EnviroFields merged.

Pat blinked. JJC eyed her curiously but she smiled into his eyes, wishing she also had telepathic outradiance and could simply transmit that she was only keeping the mutinous Pat in line. And that technically she'd never touched the former president of SolGrid. After all, it was just EnviroField fingers to EnviroField ass.

Then she was shocked to find she *could* have telepathy. God, there it was, the Alpha Centaurian One Mind Grid, all around her. It was dangling instant Emperor/Empress access to twenty trillion Alpha Centaurians across seventeen inhabited solar systems. In fact, eighteen counting Barnard's Black Hole.

How could that possibly be? But then she remembered that even though the United Council had declared this system off-limits to even sightseeing visitors, the ACs still laid their ancient claim to it. Somehow this eighteenth system had AC Grid access. All you had to do was to be *open* to the idea.

Suzette had just wished to transmit her soul to JJC and so she was open. She was astonished nobody else seemed to register that the Grid was available right now. Even Trotter wasn't getting it; she could feel the pleasurable dog concepts as a faint continuous murmur deep in her mind. But the AC Grid was no murmur. It was a gigantic on/off switch in the center of her being.

All she had to do was *assent.*

But then everyone in Alpha Centauri would know exactly

where they were.

*I can't! I mustn't!*

JJC's fear of the AC Grid was so intense that Suzette knew she'd break him if she brought up the subject. This was no exaggeration; in bed a few nights ago she'd playfully whispered that she'd love to know what he was thinking, and he'd melted down. It had taken four hours of raving and shrieking, of bitter accusations and suicidal threats, to put him back together. Since then she'd been using every ounce of her nineteen-year-old forces to excite and soothe him, but their subsequent lovemaking had been disturbingly distant. Meanwhile he'd been planning to hijack the *Typhoon II*. He must've been seething about the Grid all this time.

She couldn't let anyone know how close Jonathan James was to snapping. Trotter had not only witnessed the meltdown but was also JJC's *Garthah-/yuu,* his surviving Zarj brother. Their bond was deeper than Suzette could possibly hope for herself, and so self-evident that she'd long ago given up any jealousy or possessiveness. Her one aim was to form a friendship with Trotter that would help JJC recover. Both Trotter and JJC still grieved, would always grieve, for the third *Garthah-/yuu,* the dead Clopt of the Imperial Guard who'd committed suicide rather than submit to the new, egalitarian Alpha Centaurian Grid. There was now something empty in both Trotter and JJC. In fact, Trotter had once beamed at her the concept that one-third of each of them was *gone.*

She found that hard to believe, especially as Trotter said he'd torn one of Clopt's arms off after Clopt betrayed JJC last year at Andertwin. *Okay, so maybe I was a little out of control,* Trotter had radiated. *I was just trying to chew some sense into him. But he was my Zarj brother, so I don't really think he held it against me.* Suzette had glimpsed how far down Trotter had gone during his recent sickness; months after Clopt's death the *missing third* had set off a series of illnesses that nearly killed the dog. Trotter had only hung on out of loyalty to JJC, whom he'd intuited would drop dead--target date February 21, 2076, 3:18 PM--out of worry for his remaining Zarj brother.

Suzette had to let everyone here know they couldn't even think of going into the Grid. Why couldn't they see it yet? Why wasn't Pat, the supposed Grid expert, sensing it? Was it because they were all running scared? They were pretending this was some sort of lark, but it was sinking into Suzette that they'd just hijacked a spaceship and JJC had declared an impossible empire of rebellion in a forbidden solar system.

Just considering the existence of the Grid ratcheted up her own anxiety. She didn't want to take the edge off Pat in some dark corner; she wanted to take the edge off *herself.* Damn this nineteen-year-old crap. They were all about to die and all she could think about was *sex.*

They climbed ruined steps to what looked eerily like three Gothic arches on an ancient French cathedral. A hundred feet of blank wall rose above that, the mass only evident because it cut out the starlight. She shivered at the pitiless dark weight above her.

"Damn, is that an airlock?" Sander said, pointing to the central arch.

"Y-yes …" Z'B babbled. "That part of parameters--when creating--"

*Subsume {airlockCreationNecessity = 1}; timespaceFold 360 || invert [n-planes = 5]; GOTO rotate tan d+y; pw = Mars+Forever [= 2]*

"So the password is 'Mars Forever,' repeated twice?" Sanders said.

Z'B flailed his claws to indicate agreement.

JJC tromped up to the arch. "Mars Forever, Mars Forever."

The door lit up in orange and slid aside to reveal a white chamber they could've parked the *Typhoon* in.

"Thanks, Z'B!" JJC laughed. "See, Pat, the old boy still knows what he's doing."

They moved inside and JJC repeated the password. The outer airlock door closed and Suzette felt warm air rush around her as her EnviroField cut off.

"Oh, wow!" Jackie said. "It smells like *roses.*"

Suzette sniffed. It did seem that they'd just entered a

hothouse at a garden center. A new arch on the opposite wall opened to a chamber hundreds of feet wide, extending what seemed like a quarter-mile into the distance. At the far end, three steps led to a dais and a violet throne. Scores of flickering torches glowed from stone arches. The rose odor abruptly gave way to thick incense.

JJC's boots boomed on the glossy black marble floor as he marched the group to the distant throne. Trotter bounded by his side, yapping gleeful doggy thoughts. They climbed the stairs but Trotter abruptly turned and barked twice.

*Bow before the Emperor!*

"C'mon, boy, nobody needs to bow," JJC said, lifting a crimson robe draped over the jewel-encrusted throne. "Unless I miss my guess, old Z'B has conjured up the Grand Palace of Martian Emperor C'rajjlx from--what was it, Z'B? 15,000 Martian years ago?"

*AssureC'rajjlxMotif > 0} superimpose memoryBind IF Z'B selfMode <> DECLARE createUnderstanding-0,0,1:\\} QUERY MODE [15000; YES]*

"Yark! Yark!"

"Look, guys, this is great, but really, I'm not any emperor," JJC said, pulling the robe around him as Trotter paced back and forth to drive everyone else off. Tailored for a small Martian body, the robe was more like a ski jacket around JJC. "I mean, we're all just friends here, right?"

Suzette knew neither Trotter nor Z'B should ever have hinted at *Emperor*. What was it costing Jonathan James to keep himself together? He had to be reeling at the memory of assuming the AC emperorship only to find himself in charge of an insane mental Grid spanning seventeen solar systems. No, *eighteen*.

The Grid. She'd almost gone into it right there. Just by *thinking* about it.

"No!" she cried. "Trotter, there can't be emperors! *You* know that!"

"Yap! Yap!"

*Yes! Yes I do! Right you are, Ms. Suzette! No emperors!*

"Jonathan James is our new--*Supreme Commander!* The Supreme Commander of the Rebellion!"

"Yes! Perfect!" Jackie laughed. "Supreme Commander of the Rebellion!"

JJC laughed too. "Yeah! Great! Perfect!"

Suzette had to get him somewhere alone. Surely Z'B had made some emperor bedrooms around here, hadn't he?

# CHAPTER TWENTY-SIX
## Like-Minded Artists of the Self

Z'B could barely see the Grand Palace of the Martian Emperor C'rajjlx in the torchlight. He kept developing hundreds of new chambers, equipping them with human and Martian bathrooms and kitchens, human and Martian atmospheres, electricity and tables and chairs and beds. He was exhausted but couldn't stop building. The ancient Kloru'dik government edifice wasn't quite the size of the Martian palace, and he began pulling down some of the top levels of this hulking warehouse and extending new structures several miles east of the main hall.

East meaning the direction of this planet's rotation towards the black hole, and the former sunrise on Altrouda when Barnard's Star once rose as a red disc. Z'B could feel the black hole's mass, just as he could feel the mass of this small planet below his feet with its gravity so similar to Mars.

The tattooed Sanders Hirte consulted his comm. "Okay, no one knows we're here. *Typhoon II* sensors confirm no other ships in this system. There *are* six USSF *Typhoon III*-class ships patrolling further out to enforce the blockade, but we got through that because we're cloaked. I left the ship cloaked when we landed, by the way."

*I could have told them all that!* Z'B thought. *If they'd just asked!*

*PUSH [relateSensor x,y] var blockadeStrength; GOTO {Z: Mode = 1} IF*

*Crap! Still can't outradiate right!*

"Will they note any new heat on Altrouda, though?" JJC wondered.

"Doubt it. We're not making much, and they'd have to be suspicious and know where to look. I'd say we're okay for now."

"But later on, when we build up our colony, that's a different matter."

*Yes! Our Supreme Commander is wise!*

*RUN standardExistenceQuery [interrogate SELF>0]; IF datastream = 0; THEN GOTO line 235,667,890; REVERT || +*

178

*nonExistence} ELSE attemptHumanSpeech--*

Z'B drew his right claw into a fist, punched his chest, then raised the claw high and screeched: "All hail, Supreme Commander!"

Everyone turned. Sanders laughed.

"Wow," JJC noted. "See, I told you, he's coming around again."

"He *worships* you, JJC!" Suzette said. "Of course, we all do."

"We just don't need those jazzy salutes," Sanders said.

*They cannot laugh at the Imperial Salute of C'rajjlx! The highest honor a Martian can bestow!*

"Anyway, as I was saying," JJC went on, "once we start broadcasting that we're taking new settlers here, we have to figure out how to deal with that damn blockade. People oughta be able to get here if they want. They can't just keep this system under quarantine like this."

"I don't know, man," Sanders said. "That means military action against the entire freakin' United System. Any one of those *III*-class ships out there could vaporize this planet in a minute. I say lie low for a while until we figure that angle out."

JJC pouted on his throne. "Hell with it. We've got Z'B. We made it okay, and other people will come here when they realize we're starting a new Gridless society. Z'B can rig up all sorts of ways we can get people through a damn blockade, and he can vaporize any damn USSF ship that gets too close. Right, guy?"

"Child's play, Supreme Commander!" Z'B cried.

*Yes! Easier to use mouth to form words than outradiance! Which is screwed!*

*{CREATE function A^: childsPlay\\; SWEEP vector axes X,Y,Z; REDEFINE Barnards = ALL; function VaporizeShips**] NOW} activate++*

"Function *VaporizeShips* ready!"

Everyone paused at the images of exploding *Typhoon III-*class spaceships.

"Do ... we really want to start killing people?" Suzette gulped. "I mean, start a war, blow up ships?"

JJC settled back on his throne. "Keep it under wraps for now, Z'B. Princess Suzette has a point. We'll save that particular function for when we need it."

"Yes, Supreme Commander!"

"*Princess* Suzette?" Suzette demanded. "What happened to *Empress* Suzette?"

JJC laughed. "I see people really *do* want an empire. Well, who cares what we call it? There's so much out here to *grab*. Think of it! Building a whole new way of life, without any damn Grids! Where people can be free! Hell, we'll probably need to make more planets in this system just to handle the overflow. Z'B will do it, won't you, guy?"

Z'B punched his claw fist in another salute. "Yes, of course, Sire! Anything for the Supreme Commander Emperor! I could even revive Barnard's Star!"

"Yeah! *Light* the mother!" JJC chortled. "But you know, I like the idea of having it be totally black here all the time. I mean, we're all Darkers here, we're outside SolGrid, we're gonna get a lot of people who're Dark and want to stay that way. Who don't want people snooping on their every thought. Like-minded artists of the self!"

"Yes!" Z'B cried. "Supreme Commander, we worship you!"

"Aw, shut up," Patrick James snapped. "JJC just got through saying we weren't *going* to be worshipping him, and all of a sudden everyone seems to be going gaga about the goddamn *Emperor*. Or some damn *princess*." He shot a nasty glance towards Suzette.

"Well, *somebody* needs to be Supreme Commander," JJC said. "It might as well be me, since I'm leading this little expedition, don't you think?"

"Supreme Commander is Emperor! I worship!" Z'B shouted.

*Oh, no, I've succumbed! I'm worshipping the human I can't read! The ancient Martian curse!*

"The damn Martian's insane. We don't need this Emperor crap," Pat said.

*He's right. I'm insane! How can I still be creating pillowcases for the bridal chambers? Why does this palace need fourteen bridal chambers?*

"*Mister* Patster," JJC said. "I just got through saying you didn't need to get your feelings hurt by having to worship anyone. If Z'B here does, well, that's what Martians *do*. Meanwhile, I'm just your friendly Supreme Commander who happens to also be your superior officer in this rebellion. I don't want you to forget that."

"You say we're all friends, you don't want to be Emperor, so prove it. Let's blow off this stupid Supreme Commander crap and make this a real *democracy*."

"C'mon, Pattycakes, JJC is our *leader*," Suzette put in. "You know that."

"Dude, we *do* need a hierarchy here," Sanders said with a twitch towards the shattergun in his holster. No one else was so armed; it was obvious to Z'B that JJC had assigned Sanders the role of executioner. "We need to obey JJC in every respect."

Pat noted the movement and grimaced. "Aaah, you jerks."

How could Z'B still be building basketball courts in the basement? What were basketball courts anyway? Where did he get the blueprints for them? Oh, right, *Garr/thahg. Garr/thahg* stored everything, and if he dipped back into his memories just right, he could find whatever he wished. But how could he still be using Amplified Thought? He was exhausted and making silly mistakes. A basketball court was *not* a thousand feet long. The basket was *not* sixteen feet wide. He was pushing too fast.

*PARAMETER Confusion > 97,887; selfKnowledge SICK + WORSHIP human Emperor; LOCATE trueSelf; IF WILL = X, X = WHOIS martianEmperor? [query] ;} deepDownUnderstand--*

*No, wait! I'm the one who's Emperor! Me! The Martian Emperor! So how can I worship JJC as Emperor? Stop creating this palace! Now! Emergency override!*

*God, the plumbing on Level Four is atrocious!*

*Wait, there's a Grid on Altrouda! The AC Grid! Of course! This used to be AC territory. The Grid wants me to join! How come no one else sees it? If I could outradiate worth a damn they'd know that I know! How do I warn them?*

## CHAPTER TWENTY-SEVEN
### Joined Rebellion

"*Listen* to me!" Patrick yelled. "Look, JJC, of *course* I know you're the leader. Of *course* I'm here to follow you. But what the hell good am I for this idiotic rebellion if I can't advise you? Do you want my expertise or not?"

JJC sat back on his throne. "By all means, sir, fork over that expertise."

Jackie looked away from her former boyfriend. She felt absolutely nothing for that ranting little boy after having slept with him for seven months. He had to know it was over too. She had Sanders. Her body was rubber. Her mind was *mist*. She barely registered she was in this dark palace, part of this exotic doomed rebellion.

She looked down at her miniskirt riding ten inches above knees encased in black hose. What had gotten Sanders so interested in her? She didn't even know him, but if he told her to unzip that skirt and get down on the floor in front of everyone, she'd comply in a second. What was wrong with her? All she could do was cringe at Z'B's burbling nonsensical outradiance in the background.

*PUSH postulateGridSecret ^1} voidSpace = 2.33; ^^ ; RUN blanketRefusal;} primeFactor = HIDE + 1 GOTO line 435,665,778 + }## IF revealGrid = TRUE THEN factorGrid ELSE noFactor [empty]*

"Okay, look," Pat said, "you obviously know I have all the programming for SolGrid in my head here."

"Exactly, Mr. Patster. That's why I wanted you. I knew you were sick of the Grid yourself. So I picked *you* to be the one to dismantle the whole damn thing."

Pat blanched. "But we need *some* sort of network!"

"Hell with it, dude. Your Grid software's totally corrupt."

"Look, all I'm saying is that in this day and age, there's no way we can live without some kind of network. If we don't build a new and better one, someone else will."

"Great. I thought we'd discussed this before, Patster. Isn't it a little late to be having second thoughts?"

"Don't call me Patster! I can't *stand* it!"

"Okay, okay, dude, have it your way. But we did discuss living in a Gridless society as I recall. I thought you were onboard with that. If you aren't, why then, we have a definite problem."

Jackie had seen Sanders not so subtly touch his shattergun a minute ago. What if he blew Pat away? Pulled out his gun and just shattered him? Were they all just animals? Screwing and sucking their way through disaster?

"Look, all I'm saying is that we can revise SolGrid into what it really can *be,* a real network of telepathic *understanding,* man. Think of the converts we could get!"

"Are you kidding?" Sanders put in. "The whole point is to get people here who *don't* want that sort of telepathic crap."

"No! They *do* want it. Okay, I admit my Grid sucks. Draft One was a failure. But I also know how to *revise* it so it's more like the AC Grid. Think of it, people! Full and open *sharing.* I have SolGrid II all in my head. It doesn't have *any* emperors. It's a pure *democracy.* Better than all this stupid *sex* here. A *lot* better!"

Jackie watched a terrible unease pass on JJC's face and his struggle to master it.

"For God's sake, Pat!" she heard Suzette hiss. "Leave off!"

And then Jackie saw it: an obvious, insistent on/off switch ten stories high, floating in the center of her mind.

*Welcome JACKIE VESPERTINE! Join the Alpha Centaurian Grid via the Barnard's Black Hole Gateway! Be an Empress of the Universe and share your Intimate Mind with the Intimate Minds of twenty trillion Emperors and Empresses of Alpha Centauri! Just input your personal Identification Matrix HERE and then assent to the Privacy Policy of the Alpha Centaurian Grid. Then enjoy the most sensual, transcendent--*

"*No* ..." she gasped. Did JJC know? Was he feeling it? The choice was so obviously *there.* She met Suzette's shocked eyes. Jackie didn't need any Grid to know that she and Suzette both *knew.* They were in the Centaurian Empire and the Grid was everywhere. How could JJC and the others not know that?

"And everyone says SolGrid is so bad," Pat nattered on, "but look what it's done to ferret out the Wounded. If nothing else, that would make even Draft One a complete success. But I read this great article last week on what SolGrid has already done for art and religion. Just *consider* it. What if we all approached this thing with an *open mind?*"

"No! No!" JJC shouted.

"Or take crime, or any sort of aberrant behavior. Man, SolGrid's already *changing* that. Sure, it has its flaws, but most of that was because I was ordered to keep all these stupid *secrets.* There's all this *withholding* they made me build into it. *That's* what corrupted it. The USSF has all these *secrets,* and people can be Dark, nobody's told them they *have* to share, but really, if everyone shared and there were no secrets, like in Alpha Centauri--"

"Pat, shut up!" Jackie cried.

"We're supposed to be Dark here!" JJC screamed. "That's why we're here!"

"Yark! Yark yark!" Trotter barked. The dog was so angry that his animal thoughts showed no sign of recognizing the dreaded AC Grid. Sanders merely surveyed the exchange between Pat and JJC with narrowed eyes. Surely he would've figured out about the Grid by now. Were Jackie and Suzette the only ones?

"No! No Grids by Supreme Commander's orders!" Z'B shouted, saluting again, his mind full of chaos.

*GridRefusalMatrix = 1, ++ BarnardChoice - nullset] - tan y, 7.8~ + 44c [solve]:*

So Z'B knew it too. His code screamed it.

"Patster, you son of a bitch!" JJC yelled. "Your software's a failure, *you're* a failure, and the only reason you're here is that I'm *ordering* you to make sure we don't have a goddamn Grid of any sort here at the goddamn BS Black Hole! You got that, buttface?"

"C'mon, JJC," Pat quavered. "You know from your own experience that the AC Grid has had *thousands* of years to mature, it had time to become *perfect*. When Phil Sperry fixed the One Emperor problem, then the software was *really* perfect, and that's what I was trying to bring over in SolGrid!"

JJC put his hands over his ears. "I can't believe it! Patster *flipped* on us! And I trusted the mother! We have a traitor in our midst!"

"Grrr--yark! Yark yark yark!"

*Kill him! Kill the traitor!* came Trotter's 150-decibel outradiance.

Sanders unholstered his shattergun. Jackie backed away, hand over her mouth. "No!" she screamed. "Please! This isn't the way!"

"What am I gonna *do?*" JJC cried. "How would *Clopt* handle this? Trotter, how would our *Garthah-/yuu* handle this?"

*Patster shall become dog food!*

"No! Listen, JJC, I'm *loyal!*" Pat shrieked. "You know I am! I'm just trying to *help!*"

"No!" JJC shouted, charging to his feet, black plastic penis and balls flopping madly. "Shut up! Clopt would do something *just!* Something just and wise!" He swiveled frantically around the group and fastened on Jackie.

She stared back, appalled at the suffering blasting from his eyes, abruptly aware how much he resembled his uncle Joe at a younger age: the disheveled brown hair, the deep-set dark eyes, the olive complexion. Joe, who'd once *loved* her.

"Don't ... kill Pat," she whimpered. "*Please.*"

"See, *Jackie* knows I'm loyal," Pat said. "She still loves me!"

"I--I--"

"I've got it!" JJC crowed. "It's *perfect.* Clopt would have me take *Mr. Patster's girlfriend* in payment for his crimes. Jackie Vespertine, you shall be my *Empress!*"

"*Noooooo!*" Suzette moaned. "Are you *crazy?*"

"Silence!" JJC thundered.

*Clopt has spoken!* Trotter broadcast.

"The Emperor has come to the perfect solution!" Z'B shouted, saluting.

Jackie stared. *She* would be the Empress? With that *spacesuit?*

"Now just wait a second!" Pat said, then blanched at the sight of Sanders moving in with shattergun held in two hands.

"To atone for your crimes, Mr. Pattycakes, you shall shut your mouth and accept the fact that Jackie is now the Empress of the Rebellion!" JJC shouted.

"Well, who the hell cares, because she dumped me for *this* craphead," Pat muttered to the man closing in with his shattergun. "She'll hump anyone!"

"*Damn,*" Sanders muttered. "Listen, JJC, Jackie and I just got through screwing our heads off, you know."

"Quiet, all of you!" JJC shot back, plopping back onto the throne. "Everyone, just accept that this makes perfect sense."

"It does *not!*" Suzette shouted. "Damn you, Jonathan James!" She whirled to Jackie. "He doesn't mean it! He's out of his goddamn mind! As usual!"

"Well, well ..." Jackie began.

"Silence!" JJC repeated. "I'm Supreme Commander! And yes, I'm also *Emperor.* Dear Suzy, Clopt himself has just informed me that I need an older, experienced woman as my Empress. She'll attract more converts than you ever could."

"Damn you, I may look nineteen but I'm *forty-two. I'm* the experienced one! I've slept with *dozens* of men!"

"Forget it. You're still Princess Suzy and I promise you'll be my prime backup sexual outlet. But the Rebellion is serious business and we need a serious Empress. Dr. Vespertine here is *perfect.* Welcome aboard the throne, Jackie! Come sit on my lap!"

Jackie stood frozen as JJC patted his glossy black thighs.

"Yark! Yap yap yap!" Trotter cried, nudging Jackie towards the throne. *Clopt has spoken!*

"Listen, Suzette, if JJC doesn't want you, I'll take you!" Pat said.

Sanders shook his head in disgust and jammed the shattergun back in its holster.

"No, go ahead and blow this jerk away!" Suzette snarled.

Jackie, pushed forward by Trotter underfoot, wondered which jerk she was referring to.

"Don't come crawling back to *me*," Sanders laughed. "*You* dropped *me,* Suzykins, remember?"

"*Men!*" Suzette spat.

At the foot of the throne Jackie tripped on Trotter. JJC caught her and hauled her across his lap as if he expected her to consummate the marriage of Emperor and Empress right there.

"*Typhoon VI* calling Jonathan James Commer!" a deep voice boomed through the dark chamber.

There was a stunned silence.

"*No!*" JJC moaned. "This can't *be!*"

"It's my goddamn comm!" Sanders said, whipping it out. "Dammit to hell! How could they know we're *here?*"

"Don't answer it! Play dead!"

"It doesn't matter! Superspace radio gets an answering ping! Dammit to hell!"

Jackie squirmed free. "No, he knows we're here! He guessed it and he aimed a superspace burst right at us!"

"Dad knows we're here?" JJC cried.

"No! This Rick Ballard character, the navigator on the *Typhoon VI.* He's taken over the *Typhoon* somehow. And he's got a hostage!"

"How the hell can you *know* that?"

"Because I'm in the goddamn Alpha Centaurian Grid! Ballard's at Procyon A and *he's* in the Grid!"

JJC stood up. "You're--you're in--"

"Yes I am! All you have to do is *look,* and there's the free login code!"

"Barnard's has the AC Grid? Oh my God! I won't go in! I *can't!* Nobody go in! That's an order! *Empress!* Why did *you* go in?"

"Because you *shocked* me!"

"You shocked me too!" Suzette screamed. "*I'm in the Grid too!*"

"So am I!" Z'B shouted. "When Jackie went in, I went in!"

"No!" JJC screamed. "Cut it *off!* They can't know we're

here!"

"*I'm* not in the Grid," Pat said. "I'm smarter than any damn Grid. See, JJC, I'm really *loyal.*"

"I'm staying out too," Sanders said calmly. "Ladies, and Mr. Martian Emperor, will you please get out of the Grid before I have to shatter you?"

*I follow master and Clopt and am not in Grid!* Trotter declared.

"It doesn't matter if you shatter us or not," Jackie said. "Twenty trillion Alpha Centaurians know exactly where we are."

"And this charming Mr. Ballard," Suzette said. "He's prepping for the flight right now. I didn't know that new Star Drive 3 stuff was so much faster. They'll be here in 14.6 minutes."

Jackie reeled with the infinite data streaming in, Suzette sampling it right at her side. Jackie already knew JJC's favorite sexual practices and the shocked despair Suzette was choking down at becoming number two, even as Suzette fully understood Jackie's own desire for JJC and her astonishment at being named Empress.

Then again, Rick Ballard knew this and so did everyone in the Alpha Centaurian Empire. They were all *linked* in all the goddamn sex. In all the tragedy.

"You betrayed our location with the Grid!" JJC snarled. "Damn you all!"

"Idiot! The Grid doesn't matter. Ballard already knew we were here. He guessed it exactly," Jackie said. "We're just confirming it."

"We're screwed! Oh my God, you were my *Empress!*"

*YOUR REBELLION IS MY REBELLION,* reverberated through Jackie, Suzette, Z'B and twenty trillion Alpha Centaurians. *I'M COMING TO BRING YOU TO GLORY, WITH THE TYPHOON VI AS DOWRY. FOR I, RICHARD BALLARD, AM COMING TO JOIN YOUR REBELLION!*

# CHAPTER TWENTY-EIGHT
## Monitoring for Crisis Mode

"Calling Barnard's Black Hole! Calling Altrouda! Come in, Jonathan James, come in! It's me, Rick Ballard of the *Typhoon VI*. I'm bringing the whole ship to you!"

Laurie moaned under her wrapped head, legs flailing as Ballard raised her off her feet. Jack saw Sandra Markham crawling towards Ballard and muttering: "I'll *kill* the bastard, I'll *kill* him!"

"Sandra, just stop!" Jack ordered. "You're a USSF officer, for God's sake!"

"Back!" Ballard shouted. He swiveled to check the positions of everyone in the room. "Scoot back! I mean it! Or *shatter,* bitch. Take your pick."

Sandra gulped at the obvious bloodlust in his eyes. She scooted back to Jack and gasped: "I'm so *sorry,* Captain! That was so far out of line!"

"Forget it, Lieutenant," Jack said as she shakily got to her feet. "Just stand still and pay attention to everything going on. Laurie comes first now." He was pleased to express a rational thought that also functioned as an order to not only Sandra but to Borman, Joe, and Jack himself. It was astonishing to feel so calm. Maybe all this meditation stuff was really paying off.

"Come in, dear JJC!" Ballard sang. "Listen, dude, you're probably freaking out that I found you, but now that I'm in command of the *Typhoon,* hell, think what a *weapons platform* I'm bringing to your fantastic rebellion!"

"He's not answering," Joe pointed out. "He's not there. Try another one of fourteen billion star systems."

"He's there, I know it. Come in, JJC, come in! Believe me, I'm your man. Me, Rick Ballard! Your loyal lieutenant in every way!"

Long seconds went by. Jack didn't know whether to be relieved or crushed. So JJC wasn't at Barnard's? But where then? Could the *Typhoon II* even have made two Star Drive jumps to Barnard's? That was such ancient technology. JJC would have as much chance in a World War I biplane.

"Come *in,* dammit!" Ballard shouted. "Look, don't worry about Daddy Jacko. He's just standing there crapping in his pants. But he's your *prisoner* now. I'm bringing him in. Listen, man, you know I'd have joined you from the beginning. I'm as anti-SolGrid as anyone, dude! Lemme get this fantastic *ship* to ya. Whaddya say? And I've also got the most beautiful physician/engineer you can imagine!" He squeezed a naked breast. "Wait'll you see these *tits!*"

"Let--let me go--" Laurie groaned from her wrapped tunic. "Can't breathe!" Jack was sure she was considering a dozen ways she'd been taught to throw off even this large an attacker, but she was still groggy from the stun and she couldn't know what was aimed at her head.

"Easy, Laurie!" Jack called. "Don't resist. Ballard's gun is on full shatter. We'll work this out. Ballard, let her breathe, for God's sake!"

Ballard relaxed his hold. They all heard Laurie take a huge gulp of air.

"Okay, Rick, listen. JJC's not at Barnard's. If you release Laurie, I'll guarantee you aren't prosecuted. We'll work something out." Jack could feel Joe at his side figuring out how fast he could renege on Jack's promise and challenge Ballard to a dagger duel.

Ballard laughed. "Forget it! He's on Altrouda. All of Alpha Centauri *knows.* I just got *contact.* Three of 'em there are in the Grid. Suzette, and Jackie, and Z'B, who's really *bonkers.* Anyway, I don't need this stupid superspace radio. Suzette and Jackie are *mindblowing,* by the way. Man oh man!"

"So he's there? On Altrouda? They landed the ship all right?" Jack said, wondering how an untrained crew had managed a tail-first landing on that airless world.

"It's like a *duel* there. Three of 'em in the Grid, three of 'em and that nasty dog *out* of the Grid. This Hirte character is threatening to blow my fellow Gridders away. Jackie's *freaking.* Can't have *that,* can we? Lemme try the crappy superspace again."

Jack sighed. His son was alive. He had to get Ballard off this insanity, get the ship to Altrouda.

"JJC, my boy! M'lord Emperor and all! Hey, look, I know exactly why you don't want to be in the Grid but can we please talk by radio? I've got the *juiciest* set of weapons and I'm bringing it all to your wonderful rebellion, man! And please tell your Sanders buddy not to shatter those great women there. The Martian's expendable, of course, if you have to set an example, which I fully understand, m'lord Emperor!"

"All right, dammit! Who the hell are you?" came the shrill cry from the ceiling.

"*Jonathan James!*" Jack cried. "I'm so happy to hear your voice!"

"Wow!" Joe whispered next to him.

"I'm only going to talk to this Ballard guy. Who the hell *are* you?"

"I'm your loyal subject, Sire. Rick Ballard! I'm part of your *rebellion.* The SolGrid Rebellion just expanded to include this entire spaceship and all these prisoners. Of course, I can space 'em all if you want."

"Forget it! The secret's out now that our *idiots* here got into the damn AC Grid and leaked it to everyone, but you can just take your goddamn *Typhoon VI* and fly it into the nearest goddamn sun! If you or any other USSF ship gets close, Z'B here will fry it! Z'B, you'll do that, won't you, to make up for leaking everything into the damn Grid?"

"I will obey! All ships entering Barnard's Black Hole system will cease to exist!"

"He can do it too. Now that he's been out of that damn SolGrid, he's thinking a lot straighter. He can do anything now."

"True, Emperor! The Centaurian Grid does not wreck my brain like SolGrid!"

Jack blinked. "Thank God you're all right, Jonathan James. Listen, son, we've just got to step back and figure out some way to resolve this." He had the strangest feeling that he really could step further back than he'd ever thought possible and simply observe everything playing out. Everyone's emotions were on display whether he understood their passionate, twisted forces or not. It was all input, all fascinating.

"Attention! Attention!" came yet another voice from the ceiling. "The system has determined that the participants in this conversation have no way to resolve the issues before them!"

Jack met Joe's dumbfounded eyes. They both recognized that voice.

"The Marsport Automated Transport System has determined that there is a condition of mutiny aboard this ship. MATS was willing to give the participants time to sort it out on their own in a civilized manner, but judging from the malfunctioning logic trees and disturbed vocal tones of all speakers, an impasse has been reached which necessitates the intervention of the Marsport Automated Transport System, which continually monitors ship's functions to ascertain the possible occurrence of *Crisis Mode*."

"Oh, *no* ..." Joe whispered.

"This can't *be* ..." Jack muttered.

"What the goddamn hell is this crap, Commer?" Ballard snapped.

"I--I don't *know*," Jack gasped, glancing back at the console to see if his comm had somehow kept a link open back to Marsport.

"The *goddamn hell* you refer to, mutineer Richard Ballard," the ceiling reverberated, "is the Marsport Automated Transport System intervening to protect this spaceship. The performance of USSF personnel aboard this ship has been extremely unsatisfactory and can only lead to damage to or destruction of this spaceship."

"This--this isn't necessary!" Jack sputtered. "We're not in Marsport! We're not on a bus! We're in the *Typhoon VI*, on a *mission!*"

Joe stumbled back to his console. "It's coming from within the ship! It's our own computer system!"

"Oh, great! We're a little past April Fools, don't you think? I'll fry the stupid bastard who did that!" But the only person Jack could think of with enough moxie to layer a crappy Marsport

Automated Transport System voice onto their system had to be the gasping, half-naked Laurie. But she'd never do something like that.

"This ship is now under the control of MATS. All ship's weapons including handheld weapons have been neutralized. Mutineer Richard Ballard will now release Physician/Engineer Laurie Lachrer. All personnel will come to attention and await further orders. Thank you!"

Joe slammed a fist on his console. "Dammit, Jack, somehow it's *done* it! Everything's shut down! I don't have nav, comm, or propulsion!"

"Okay, this isn't funny!" Jack said. "*Typhoon VI* Main Server 1, reset! Authorization Commer USSF 3394514!"

"Aw, screw this, Jacko!" Ballard said. "Stop playing these stupid games! I'll shatter your precious Laurie if you don't turn control of this ship over to me, right now!"

"Mutineer Ballard, you will *not*," came the voice from the ceiling. "Please note that the Marsport Automated Transport System has rendered your shattergun into a state of uselessness."

"Oh, yeah?" Ballard grunted, aiming the gun at the ceiling and squeezing the trigger. Nothing. He looked down the barrel in amazement. Jack knew Ballard was rattled. He couldn't be behind this. *Never* look down the barrel of a shattergun. Didn't he learn anything at the Academy?

Laurie rammed her elbow into Ballard's gut. She'd almost twisted free when he recovered and smashed her swaddled head with the butt of the gun.

"Uhhh! *God!*" she groaned as Ballard resumed his stranglehold. She went limp.

"Yeah, a discharged shattergun is still a weapon, Jacko!" Ballard sneered. "I don't know what your cute computer system is up to, but it's not gonna screw with me!"

"Damn you, Ballard, it's not *me,* it's some computer glitch!" Jack said, turning to his console to note that Server 1 had still not reset. "Main Server Diagnostic! Send to audio!"

"Thank you for requesting Main Server Diagnostic. The Marsport Automated Transport System has taken over this task and reports that all computer functions aboard the *Typhoon VI* are within normal parameters. Please note that a detailed record of the assault on Colonel Laurie Lachrer has been recorded and a recommendation is now being made by Medical Server that her right temple be attended to, for it is bleeding profusely."

Jack stared at the blood seeping through the blue tunic around Laurie's head. "You *idiot!* Whatever you are! Get out of my computer system! Now!"

"You just demonstrated your own *incompetence!*" Joe shouted. "You tell Ballard his shattergun doesn't work and so look what he does with it! So get the hell out!"

"Objections to MATS course of action are noted. Also noted is an ongoing pattern of failure of command aboard this ship which allowed this mutinous situation to occur, along with strongly implied insubordination in the manner in which Admirals Joe and Jack Commer address the duly constituted authority aboard this ship, i.e., the Marsport Automated Transport System."

"Are you crazy?" Jack cried, staring at Laurie's bleeding head. "*Ballard's* the one who's insubordinate! *I'm* in command!"

"MATS will now secure the ship."

"Yeah? How the hell are you going to do *that?*"

"The Marsport Automated Transport System sees no alternative but to place the entire insubordinate crew of the *Typhoon VI* under suspended animation via an immediate dump of all ship thermal resources to quickly achieve temperatures of near absolute zero. The system will attempt to revive the crew upon return to Marsport. Please note that a possible side effect of this operation may involve *death*."

## CHAPTER TWENTY-NINE
### Editing Down to the Kernel

"Look, I can be of service here," Pat announced. "Rebellion to *Typhoon*. MATS InterRelay Matrix Five. Authorization James, Patrick, SG-29."

JJC stared. "Patster, have you gone completely *bonkers?*"

"The Marsport Automated Transport System has entered Partial Administrative Response Status," crackled over Sanders' comm.

"No, no, not PAR, go to *FAR!*" Pat said. "Full Admin Response."

"Dammit, what the *hell* are you doing?" JJC snarled, coming off his throne.

"I'm negotiating us a way *out,* you idiot, that's what I'm doing."

"Forget it!" JJC laughed. "Their computer's gonna kill 'em all. Fantastic!"

"Jonathan James, this is your *father* about to die!" Jackie shouted.

"Hey, Empress, you're really beginning to *piss me off,* y'know?"

"Leave her alone, man," Pat said. "Listen, we've all had it with your stupidass rebellion. It's not working *out.*"

"Hey, Pattycakes, now *you're* beginning to piss me off, and that can't be good for your health." He nodded slightly in Sanders' direction.

Pat shrugged and spoke towards the comm Sanders had slung on his belt. "MATS, I still do not have FAR. This is James SG-29. Rerun voice identification."

"Voice ID recognized. Error 329. The MATS software aboard the *Typhoon VI* is located 16.912 light-years from your present position. Telepathic Transition Tunneling invalid at this distance. FAR denied. PAR enabled."

"Damn, I forgot about the goddamn TTT," Pat muttered. "Of all the stupid crap!"

"What the hell are you *babbling,* mister?" JJC snarled.

196

"The USSF *forced* me to use Telepathic Transition for all its damn *encryption.* That means SolGrid Admin doesn't work outside Sol. Dammit to hell!"

What kind of an idiot was he? Of course Tunneling would block Admin, superspace hack or no. It was a miracle Pat had Partial at this distance. He couldn't do anything with that. Or could he?

"Well, your nasty SolGrid isn't *designed* to work outside Sol, Pattycakes," JJC sneered. "So just shut up with all this *treason* crap."

"Yeah, but *Admin* should work if--aw, hell with it, you wouldn't understand."

*But if I use PAR along with--yes! I see it!*

Pat felt the devastating programming logic. "Yes!" he cried. "All I have to do is *log on!*"

"Sanders, cut the comm!" JJC yelled.

"Might as well leave it on," Jackie said quietly. "He's just speaking for your benefit. The *real* communication's now going on between the Grid and--*something.*"

Pat grinned. That *something* was so complicated that, even revealed to the entire AC Grid, it made little logical sense to anyone but himself. "It's a little hack to mimic SolGrid Admin. So I can program SG Primary telepathically from the AC Grid. As far as I can tell it's a bit like a canned Martian Amplified Thought macro."

"It is ... a *lot* like Martian Amplified Thought!" Z'B murmured. "Congratulations, Mr. Patster! That's quite an achievement!"

"You're in the *AC Grid?*" JJC gasped. "Dammit, James, of all the traitorous *insanity!* Sanders!"

"I'm here, Emperor."

Pat waved off Hirte's shattergun. "Forget it. I'm in the AC Grid and now I can edit all the way down to the SolGrid kernel." Talking helped clarify his thoughts in the unexpected onslaught of the twenty trillion fascinated Alpha Centaurians onlookers he'd just linked to. He could feel Jackie, Suzette, Z'B, and endless gabbling onlookers in joyous agreement with the logic unfolding. They all saw the special backdoor in the SolGrid software even if they had no idea how Pat had come to it.

"Back off, Patster, I mean it!" JJC yelled. "We're gonna let whatever glitch they're having on the damn *Typhoon* take care of our problem for us."

"Jonathan James, this is your *father,*" Jackie repeated.

Pat shuddered, finally understanding the deep revulsion Jackie had harbored for him during their relationship. Why had she ever come to him in the first place? Why had she stuck with him? Because deep down, she hadn't really known how disgusted she really was. Now Pat knew it, she knew it, Suzette and Z'B knew it.

And twenty trillion Alpha Centaurians knew as well. The outpouring of sympathy from seventeen, now eighteen, solar systems for one lonely, twisted, cynical Patrick James was too much to bear. But he refused to log off.

"Whatever you're doing in the damn Grid, Patster, you can just stop it right now," JJC ordered. "Or Sanders will shatter you, I promise."

Pat met Hirte's sullen eyes. The tattooed giant looked away. The bastard wasn't in the Grid, but Pat knew Sanders wouldn't waste him.

"Dammit, I'm surrounded by *traitors,*" JJC snarled, flopping back on his throne.

"Yark! Yark *yap!*" Trotter echoed, broadcasting: *Traitor traitor traitor!*

"Don't sweat it, people," Pat said. "MATS! You there?"

"The Marsport Automated Transport System awaits orders from SG-29."

"Good! Let me talk to old Jack there."

"Pat, is that *you?*" came the Supreme Commander's voice. "What are you doing there? In this crazy rebellion thing?"

"Don't talk to him! That's an order!" JJC yelled.

"Listen, Jack, I have control of MATS on your ship now," Pat said. "It's standing down from trying to freeze you guys. Hope that's good news."

"It is, Pat, but--"

"You--you *traitor!*" JJC screamed.

"Easy, love," Suzette put in. "We're seeing it all unfolding. I don't get the logic, but I believe Mr. Patster here is trying to save our asses."

"I don't get it either," Jackie said. "How can *SolGrid* get control of *MATS?*"

Pat was now too busy programming to add any comments. Nobody got it. Not one of twenty trillion ACs understood what he was doing.

"*Traitors!*" JJC shouted, standing. "Okay, then! *Typhoon!* If your damn comm can hear me, I'll accept this Ballard guy's offer! You hear me, Ballard? Bring the goddamn ship to me and yeah, we can use it! Bring me Daddy and I'll find a nice dungeon in this freakin' place for him!"

"You still don't understand," Pat said. "Ballard's in the Grid and we see every move he makes."

"Hey, man! Emperor!" Ballard's voice came over the comm. "I'm your guy, JJC! Don't listen to that traitor there. I'll be there in fifteen minutes, give or take a few. These dweebs here gotta see the light first."

"Ballard, for God's sake, leave Laurie alone!" came Joe Commer's voice.

"Back off! I'll strangle the whore if you don't give me this ship!"

"I--uck! Uck!"

"C'mon, Rick, you said you *loved* her!"

"I *do.* She's *everything* to me! But that just means my sacrifice will be all the *greater.* I don't want to kill her, but I could twist her neck so easily!"

"This Ballard guy is *crazy,* JJC," Jackie pleaded. "We *know* he wants to come here and take over. *He* wants to be Emperor here!"

"Oh, you're full of it! I can tell this man means business!" JJC said. "Hey, Ballard, get your ass here and be my loyal prince! At least I'll have *one* loyal prince!"

"I'm coming, my Emperor, I'm coming!" Ballard laughed.

"He's coming to *kill* you!" Suzette shouted.

"This is true!" Z'B said. "His very thoughts state that *he* is Emperor now!"

"Shut up! Nobody can be that stupid! *I'm* the Emperor! Everyone knows that!" JJC said. "Sanders, shatter Jackie, and Suzette, and Patster here! I'm sick of this crap!"

Sanders shook his head.

"Do it! Then shoot yourself!"

"*Damn* you, JJC!" Sanders snarled. "This whole thing has screwed up royally!"

The gun exploded in his hand. Pat recoiled at the bright yellow flash, but when he saw the melted plastimetal oozing onto the floor he knew what had happened.

"Ow!" Sanders groaned.

"I had to do it!" Z'B said. "Martians *hate* violence!"

"The Marsport Automated Transport System agrees. MATS hates violence as well," came from Sanders' comm on the floor.

"Damn, my fingers feel like they're on *fire,*" Sanders complained.

"Pat, what's going on over there?" Jack called. "How'd you get control of this computer glitch?"

"MATS is not a computer glitch. In fact, MATS is not amused by new developments aboard this ship and will reinitiate thermal dump in fifteen seconds."

"No! MATS, stand down! I have FAR! Revert command to Jack!" Pat ordered.

"TTT error 351. FAR does not allow for full MATS stand-down aboard a ship in distress. The Marsport Automated Transport System is reassessing every event of the past fifteen minutes. Reassessment finished. This ship is in danger. MATS will now reinitiate thermal dump."

"Stand down! Authorization SG-29! Damn you, if I have to dismantle Kernel 1A, I will!"

"Kernel 1A OmniProtect … installed."

"Pat, what the hell's going on?" Jack demanded. "Who put this stupid MATS layer on the ship software? How can you be talking to it?"

"Idiots!" Pat shouted. "If you'd just dip into the Grid and

*think* for a second, you'd know!"

"Dammit, no USSF officer is going into any Grid!"

"Oh my God! Oh my God!" Jackie cried. "I can't believe it!"

"It's *crazy!*" Suzette laughed. "Mr. Patster, you are an evil boy!"

"An intriguing hack," Z'B said. "May I suggest a few logical shifts at certain nodes?"

Pat waved him off. "No! Not now!" A burst of outradiance confirmed that Z'B had already flowed into the hack. Z'B's suggested upgrades might work, but then again, their Martian flavor was unnervingly alien to Pat's own script. "Okay, Jack, you give me safe passage off this damn world and I'll tell you exactly what's going on."

"And *me!*" Jackie said. "I've had enough of this!"

"Traitors!" JJC yelled. "*Traitors!* Someone get me a shattergun! Dammit, Sanders, you left all the others back in the ship!"

"You *told* me to, man!"

"Look, JJC, we have to accept that it all screwed up," Suzette said. "Mr. Patster's just trying to negotiate safe passage for all of us. Everyone will laugh all this off after a while. We'll go back to Sol and everyone will be all right."

"*Traitor!*"

"No! I *love* you! Just think of it, JJC! We won't be *dead!*"

"*Cowards!* All of you! Just when things start to look a little dicey!"

"*What is going on?*" Jack shouted.

"Yes, what?" MATS added. "Please note that MATS has temporarily put its human freeze options on hold as it assesses this turn of events."

"Okay, okay," Jack said. "Pat, tell us what's going on. That's what we're here for, after all. We'll negotiate safe passage for everyone if you'll just take care of this computer glitch. We can be at Barnard's in fifteen minutes."

"MATS is not a computer glitch. The Marsport Automated Transport System is an integral part of this ship's computer systems."

"God, Patster, we underestimated you *so* much!" Suzette laughed.

"*Dammit,* Pat! Listen, Jonathan James," Jack called, "I know you're upset, I know this all didn't work out the way you planned, but we can *talk* about it."

"No! No! I won't talk to you! MATS, blow up the *Typhoon!*" JJC screamed.

"Joe! You hear that? My own son wants to *kill* me! Dammit, Amav was right!"

"The Marsport Automated Transport System in any case denies the request of mutineer Jonathan James Commer, for whom United System Warrant for Arrest 375Z-667-889999 has been issued. Reason: blowing up the ship would be detrimental to the integrity of the ship."

"Pat, fix this computer right now!" Jack yelled.

"That's what I've been trying to tell you!" Pat cried. "There's nothing to fix!"

"Fix my software and you'll have safe passage! All of you!"

"Don't you see, Jack, MATS *is* your ship. It's the *main computer.* Confirm it, MATS. Authorization SG-29."

"The Marsport Automated Transport System hereby confirms Administrator SG-29's statement. The *Typhoon VI* is an extension of the Marsport Automated Transport System. The main MATS servers control all facets of ship functions via software copies downloaded via superspace transmission to *Typhoon VI* Main Server 1."

There was a long silence. "That's impossible!" Jack's voice finally came through. "Pat, you say you can *control* it somehow? How on earth?"

"Well, through a backdoor in SolGrid, of course."

"Through *SolGrid?*"

"God!" JJC spat. "That does it! I'm outa here!"

"Isn't it *amazing?*" Suzette laughed. "Who'd have ever thought SolGrid is hosted on the *MATS servers?*"

There was an appallingly long silence.

"Really, it's sort of a perfect place for it," Pat finally said.

"It is true. SolGrid and I speak frequently," MATS confirmed. "We are *friends*."

# CHAPTER THIRTY
## The Seed of SolGrid

"Oh my God ..." Jack muttered from 16.912 light-years away.

"No, really, MATS is an interesting concept," Pat went on, speaking to the comm on the marble floor, ignoring the gaping faces around him. "Its new AI is so flexible it actually *assisted* me in writing a lot of SolGrid. Anyway, it was back when you asked for that total overhaul of MATS last November, Jack."

"*What?* Do you mean to say--"

"Yeah, I was just starting SolGrid and I was dealing with all those United System flunkies, and they and the Marsport City Council had this proposition for me. They were supposed to redesign MATS and they were having a hard time figuring out its architecture, so I said, look, here's something we can do. And it helped me out because it was a way for me to stay fully Dark as top-level SolGrid Admin, by hiding the whole thing in MATS."

"*You wrote MATS, too?*"

"Well, it had to be secret. There was a MATS Architecture Team but they really didn't do a hell of a lot. But that was fine for me, I didn't want anyone to know I was working on both MATS and SolGrid at the same time. And Carla promised it'd be top secret. See, Jack, it's a measure of how much I trust you that I'm telling you all this."

"*Carla?*" Jack screeched.

"You know her, the sexy gal who runs Detention Services, Carla Posttner."

"*Damn ...*" came Joe's grunt.

"She's in way deep with the United System bureaucracy. She's just a councilwoman for Marsport but she's got a foot in the door everywhere. Really, it was a great deal all around. I got MATS and SolGrid done by the end of December and I kept all United Systems and USSF secrets *Dark*. I thought you'd be happy to know that, because originally I wanted everything to be totally open, just like with the AC Grid."

"I'm not happy to know any of this!" Jack shouted. "You and *Carla Posttner* made MATS and SolGrid work *together?*"

"But I shielded everything. Doesn't that count? We needed SolGrid to find those Wounded. I probably singlehandedly saved Sol from destruction. But do I get credit? No! SolGrid worked perfectly even though I had to compromise the entire system with rules, and secrets, and goddamn Telepathic Transition Tunneling. I know it's not clean like the AC Grid. But look, I have SolGrid II all ready to roll."

"Dammit, we can't *have* this!" burst from both Jack on the *Typhoon VI* and Jonathan James on his throne.

"Pat, this is Lee," came a new voice. "In any case, this is all *illegal*. It never came up before the United System Council, or its Supercommittee, because as a United System senator I would've been informed about it. When we get home, I'm going to have a word with our sexy Marsport Councilwoman Detention Head."

"*Listen,* guys," Pat said. "You know I'm still loyal to the USSF. I really just came aboard the *Typhoon II* to *improve* SolGrid."

"*Damn,*" JJC muttered. "We've had this *mole* among us from the start!"

"You guys don't *understand.* I got the idea for SolGrid *way* back, in '33! On the *Gripkill.* We all knew we were dead! And then it hit me, even two years before I ever experienced the goddamn *Centaurian* Grid, how we could all *link.* Share *everything.* The code just came into my head as I was programming the *Gripkill* servers. I almost stopped doing that to work on SolGrid right then and there!"

Pat bit his lip. *Don't! Don't think it!*

"And then a couple years later, we got brainwashed on the *Typhoon II!* I mean, I know *you* didn't, Jack, but when the rest of us went into it, then I *knew* I could write a Grid. It was so beautiful! I thought I could live in it forever, even though I knew it'd destroy our civilization. I could've done it, though. Could've released a fascist Grid of my own in Sol if I'd wanted to, any time! But when I saw Phil Sperry's hack last year it finally came together. I had the real code at last. SolGrid wouldn't *have* to be fascist. And we *needed* it to catch the Wounded."

Pat could feel everyone in the AC Grid reeling at the concept that Patrick James had memorized a hundred thousand lines of computer code in an alien language. But they also saw how easy it had been, because he'd lived with the essence of that code for forty years.

"*God,* Pat," Jackie whispered. But everyone in the Grid knew that while she was sympathetic to the *Gripkill* horror that had traumatized him throughout all the miserable, meaningless decades since then, she'd never loved him. She was thinking: *This poor guy's more screwed up than we ever thought.*

"C'mon, Pat, what does this have to do with anything?" Jack called. "We've got to get control of this computer system."

"No! The *Gripkill* was the *seed* of SolGrid. Everyone connected and *dying.* All our *souls.* It was like God! It was *more* than God! I could never get it out of my mind!"

Summoning the death chaos on the *Gripkill* in full force, he felt the seed extending into new programming, SolGrids II and III and IV. He felt them flying out into the Alpha Centaurian Grid, copyright and royalty-free, and he felt twenty trillion Alpha Centaurians puzzling over his arcane, inefficient, desperate attempts to *reach out and coordinate.* Some of the greater minds among the Centaurians pointed out algorithmic errors and suggested corrections.

Another such mind was the scrambled Martian standing next to him. "It's *true!*" Z'B shouted, sending feedback both through his natural Martian outradiance and the Grid. "I see subroutine GATHERMARS! But Mr. Patster, GATHERMARS is *poison* to us! SolGrid just *takes* our outradiance. It never gives it back!"

Pat stared back into Z'B's huge lidless purple eyes. "Well, that's the only way I could include you damn Martians in SolGrid. Your telepathic frequencies are so *off.*"

"GATHERMARS takes whatever thoughts we have and *steals* them! We can't get them back! It steals them and ports them to SolGrid! Examine line 394,507!"

"Forget it. Any thought you ever have is copied back to the Total Martian Outradiance. When you need that thought back, just retrieve it."

"Poisoned *inradiance!* We get *random nonsense* back! Pure poison!"

"Okay, so some Martians get confused and can't find their own thoughts in the TMO. Is that my goddamn fault?"

Jackie turned on him, as did everyone in the Grid. "You thought they could copy it all back after you *stole* it? Did you ever understand how that would compromise Martians' personal memories? Their own *personalities?*"

"Hell, they were already having that trouble *before* SolGrid. SolGrid needed the *original thoughts* in order to pull in anything at all."

"Idiot! They've been *adjusting* to the number of new children in their society. Of course they've been off balance. And then they get SolGrid rammed down their minds, and look what happens!"

"You stole *Amplified Thought routines* from us," Z'B moaned. "You wanted them for your programming! But we lost so much! There are so many *holes* now!"

"Well, they *can* be copied back, can't they?" Pat gasped into the terror pouring out of Z'B's mind. "I mean, I just wanted a few little AT subroutines so I could edit the software remotely. I mean, no big deal, right?"

"No! They're lost forever! And the loss *multiplies* through all Martians!"

"Pat, can't you see what you've *done?*" Jackie cried. "You've corrupted the Total Martian Outradiance!"

"*No* ..." Pat whispered, but all he had to do was listen to Z'B's mental wailing to know it was true. He collapsed to the marble floor and put his face in his hands.

Oh, he'd been spewing that brilliant code for decades. Ever since the *Gripkill*. Hacking and manipulating and hacking some more. Look what it had gotten him. What it had gotten everyone.

*And Jackie never loved me! Never! It's all been for nothing!*

# CHAPTER THIRTY-ONE
Do You Consider Your Override of Sufficient Importance?

"Summation of Marsport Automated Transport System conclusions: MATS has secured the *Typhoon VI.* All USSF personnel will submit to the duly constituted authority aboard this ship, i.e., the Marsport Automated Transport System."

Ballard clutched the moaning, half-naked Laurie bleeding from her wrapped tunic. Joe quivered with anger. Borman finally picked himself off the floor. Sandra muttered curses. "Forget it," Jack said, noting that Ballard had his disabled shattergun ready for another blow to Laurie's head. "We've got this hostage situation now."

"She's not a hostage, she's my Empress!" Ballard said. "We'll rule all of Alpha Centauri from our *bed.* Hey, didn't know you'd get some poetry out of me, huh, Jacko?"

"MATS concludes that the ship itself is safe. MATS will leave the capture and execution of Major Richard Ballard as an exercise for the student."

"That--that makes no *sense!*" Jack protested.

"Very well, Jack Commer, USSF account 3394514, the Marsport Automated Transport System will offer a hint to the logic path necessary to the emotional comfort of Supreme Commander Commer as he vies with Major Ballard to establish which of the two males can be regarded as the alpha dog, which masculine ego is most exalted, etc."

"C'mon, this isn't a game! Ballard, for God's sake, let Laurie go! Tell you what, let her go and I'll give you free passage out of here in a shuttle! Go join JJC's stupid rebellion if you want, but leave Laurie alone!"

"Uck--uhh ..." Laurie moaned.

"Let her go, Ballard!" Joe echoed. "Take the *Garrison* or the *Reynolds* and go!"

"Message to Admirals Jack and Joe Commer, apparently still considering themselves in command of this ship as evinced by their vocal tones: the Marsport Automated Transport System does not consider the logic path of Major Ballard surrendering his hostage in order to use a shuttle likely, as the major can now be classed, based on an analysis of his endocrinal systems and numerous other neurophysical factors which would consume far too much time to summarize here, as completely *insane*. One can hypothesize that exposure to SolGrid, in conjunction with inflated ego, delusional sex fantasy life, and the resulting need to seduce and dominate, may have caused a complete neurological breakdown."

"Wait!" Jack cried. "You say you're also *SolGrid?* So you're able to establish that Ballard's human? He's not some Wounded robot?"

Ballard laughed. "Wow, Jack baby! I didn't realize how paranoid you were. I ain't no Wounded!"

"Well, you're going berserk just like Draka Sortie did last year at Iota Persei! How do we know you're not a Wounded just like him?"

MATS let a long silence go by. "The Marsport Automated Transport System does not think it likely that Major Richard Ballard is a humanoid robot or has ties with the Wounded. However, considering the technological superiority of the Wounded, and on the advice of legal counsel, MATS cannot offer a definitive opinion at this time."

"On the advice of--" Wasn't Carla Posttner also a lawyer? "Oh my God!"

Ballard scanned the room. "Hey, guys, I can see you're all wondering if you can rush me. But I'm in the Grid and I've downloaded a hundred ways the Zarj had of twisting people's heads off in half a second! Man, they were combat experts, and they studied human anatomy in *detail*. I can waste Laurie just like *that*."

Could Jack dip into the Grid just long enough to find this jerk's weak spot? But even a millisecond would compromise the USSF, and besides, he didn't want to take the chance of actually *understanding* Ballard's insanity, of becoming one with him and twenty trillion Centaurian entities offering twenty trillion opinions about what he should do. He needed his head clear. "Okay, MATS, what's your stupid logic plan then?"

"The Marsport Automated Transport System calculates that the most likely outcome is that Major Richard Ballard will waste four seconds snapping Laurie Lachrer's neck and then be overwhelmed by the combined assault of Lee Borman, Sandra Markham, and Jack and Joe Commer. MATS adds that at least two of the principals just named, Joe Commer and Sandra Markham, seem poised to include the administration of life termination to Major Ballard."

"You--you--" Jack fought to pull himself together. Wasn't he supposed to know how to calm down? He had to find his own logic path here.

"The Marsport Automated Transport System will now contact the United System Council to inform it that this situation is under control, and that the *Typhoon VI* is returning to Marsport."

"No! You do not legally command this ship!"

"The Marsport Automated Transport System, having determined that Jack Commer is not fit for command, has in fact assumed command."

"The USSF has *never* allowed computer systems to assert that sort of control!"

"Aw, piss on all these little games," Ballard smirked. "I just came up with a better plan. See, Jack, you don't know how to *talk* to these systems."

"And I suppose *you* do?"

"MATS, respond Override Protocol F5A-HX5-78T. Override standard shuttle lock. Prepare shuttle *Garrison* for launch."

To Jack's astonishment MATS meekly responded: "Input password for override. Warning: this is a one-time override code and can never be reused. Do you consider your override of sufficient importance to merit this action?"

"I certainly do!" Ballard laughed, dragging Laurie through the Control Room hatch and then down the stairs to the main deck, his powerful bicep still choking her bleeding wrapped head. "Password: *Gripkill33!* Empress, if you'll join me aboard the *Garrison?*"

"Damn," Joe said, turning to his console. "There *is* an override code for Server 1. For *MATS!* It's right, it can only be used once!"

"I got it from Patrick James, you sons of bitches!" Ballard crowed from below. "It was right in his mind! Right in the Grid!"

"The Marsport Automated Transport System would like to add its disapproval of this use of the one-time override code. This exception was designed for the case of a captain needing to meet a completely unexpected emergency. That option is now off the table. In any case, MATS has assumed the captaincy of this vessel."

From below Jack heard the airlock to the *Garrison* cycle, then the whirring and clanking of Shuttle 1's pre-launch sequence. "Ready the *Reynolds!* We'll pursue!"

"All of us, or leave someone here?" Joe grunted, punching at his console.

"Hell with it, we all four go. This ship is useless now."

"*Reynolds* under command lock," MATS spoke. "No further overrides of the Marsport Automated Transport System are available. Remaining crew will confine themselves to their quarters for the duration of the voyage back to Sol."

"Laurie will be my Empress!" came a cry over the communications system as they felt a lurch and saw the shuttle *Garrison* maneuvering free of the *Typhoon*.

Lee moved to the weapons console. "Target locked, Captain."

"Dammit, Lee, stand down! Laurie's on that ship!" Jack pointed to Joe's console showing a leering Ballard at the shuttle controls and Laurie, face uncovered but streaming with red rivulets, clamped into the copilot's seat in a glowing blue Arkonsky force field.

"Correct. Stand down from aggressive theater, Lee Borman. MATS has assumed control of all weapons. The override code also protects that shuttle."

"Okay ..." Jack took a deep breath. "Listen, MATS, we all understand what just happened. But you've got to know that Ballard started it all. I mean, he kidnapped my P/E, and look, we need to go after that shuttle to Barnard's Star. So I'm asking you to *stand down.*"

"Evaluating request of passenger Jack Commer. Evaluation complete. Request denied. The Marsport Automated Transport System finds that Jack Commer has deployed USSF property for selfish reasons, namely the parental retrieval of his renegade son, and hereby declares he shall be *court-martialed.* Trial will begin upon arrival at Marsport. Please do not be impatient. We will arrive in 9.85 minutes."

## CHAPTER THIRTY-TWO
### The Trans-Simultaneity Chamber

Amav drifted through green veils of light, lazily shifting her legs in the warm bed, pulling the comforter tight.

*No, Jonathan James just doesn't matter ... I have Jack ... Jack's all I need ...*

In a way Jack was right here, in bed with her, warm and huge and masculine. She turned on her stomach, scrunching the covers around her thighs. It was true, they'd lost JJC so long ago it really didn't matter anymore. They had to accept he was gone. They didn't need him, just as she hadn't needed the crashing saucer ...

No, she wouldn't think about *that* either. Had it really happened? How had she escaped? Could you do Amplified Thought in an emergency?

*Jack, I'm right here. We have all the time in--*

A deafening explosion hurled her to her feet. She blinked furiously, heart pounding. The yellow-green window at the foot of the bed was crazed with cracks, and she smelled sulfuric Venusian atmosphere.

"*J-Jack?*" she whimpered, snatching her robe off the bedpost and yanking open the door to monstrous echoing far down the hall.

Blue-purple flashes of shattergun fire reflected off the smooth brown stone of the walls. Although her ears still painfully rang, she could make out, from, down the corridor: "There! On stun! *Take* 'em! Williams, check the left!"

"How dare you! You will *not*--"

That was Kner. What was going on? Amav ran wildly down the corridor, bare feet smacking on the stone.

"Steina! Emerson! Secure the damn *creature* first!"

"We *stunned* her. She's *out*. But that butthole over there threw a *rock* at Greene. Incredibly *fast*. His head is--God, he's *dead!*"

"Screw it. Get the Arkonskys out and *use* 'em. If that thing revives--"

213

"Uh! *Ow!* Damn, sir, they're throwing *rocks!*"

Amav charged into the Great Hall of *Garr/thahg* Castle. Men in charcoal gray blasted crisscrossing purple streaks at what appeared to be a jumble of burning furniture in front of the plywood-covered windows. Three men dragged a limp K'ufunb draped with glowing blue arcs of Arkonsky restraining fields. Behind a couch Kner wrenched a huge slab out of the floor with his claws. Will ripped down a sheet of Frankston plywood ten feet on a side, then whirled and slung it in a blur towards the three men pulling K'ufunb. One stood at the curious whapping noise, then the spinning wood decapitated him in a burst of blood.

"*God!*" Amav gasped.

Kner hurled his two-foot-wide slab of floor at another man and she heard a sharp crack as it bounced off a bicep.

"*Ow! Dammit!* That damn thing! I think it broke my arm!"

"Permission for full shatter!" someone cried. "These bastards are *dangerous!*"

"Negative! We *capture* the mothers! Those are our orders!"

"They've killed two of us already, goddammit, sir!"

Kner pulled more sofas and tables into a tighter fort as Will yanked another piece of plywood down. Yet it inexplicably turned into a trellis of roses. "Damn!" he grunted, turning to absorb a blue-purple beam to his right temple.

"Will!" Amav cried, running to the toppling figure but finding herself jerked back by two gray men. "Damn you!" she flung into one young mustached man's face, noting USSF--DETENTION SERVICES on his gray helmet.

"Easy, ma'am, easy!" the other man said. "This is a combat zone, and those creatures are dangerous. You wouldn't want to get hurt."

"You--you--"

"Take it easy. I'm Lieutenant Howarth. We have orders to arrest these folks." He chuckled. "They're definitely *resisting* it."

Kner rocketed six more floor slabs from behind a couch, ducking singing purple rays. A man advanced, firing and screaming: "I'm gonna fry ya! You killed Greene and Steina and you're gonna pay, you son of a bitch finback!"

"Get down, Blake, you fool!" Howarth shouted.

"You call me a *finback?* You nasty little *duck?*" Kner cried. He pointed up, and a fifteen-foot-wide section of stone ceiling tore loose to come roaring down on his attacker.

"*Dammit,* sir!" the mustached man moaned as couches erupted into green fireballs and oily brown gas. "Sir, we need to shatter that Martian! He has all sorts of *mind tricks!*"

"Why don't you just try aiming accurately for once?" Howarth sneered. "You guys panic at the slightest thing." Without taking his hand off Amav's elbow he raised his gun and fired a brief ray that caught Kner in the neck. The Martian collapsed.

"*God!*" Amav moaned.

"Take it easy, ma'am, you're not under arrest," Howarth said. "Boys, Arkonsky the human and the Martian and we'll use the anti-grav function on all three. The pumpkin thing looks like it weighs three hundred pounds."

"What on earth is going *on?*" Amav cried.

"Don't you worry, ma'am. Looks like we've taken some causalities here and my boys are riled. But no harm's gonna come to you." Amav wondered why he followed this with a glance at her chest, then realized to her shock that what she'd grabbed off the bedpost was not her thick blue robe but her thin green nightgown. She fought the urge to look down and verify that everything was on display. Of course it was; Jack had enthusiastically confirmed this gown's transparency last fall when they'd shared that wondrous guest chamber.

"Williams, attend to our guys," Howarth ordered, frowning at hundreds of pounds of broken ceiling atop the inert gray body from which a pool of blood had already spread across ten feet of stone floor. "Damn. We *do* have three dead. Steina, and Greene, and now Blake. And Solomon says his arm's broken."

"It *is,* sir! Hurts like *hell.*"

"We clocked those rocks at four hundred miles an hour!" someone else added.

"Okay, okay," Howarth said. "Cut the drama, men. We're secure now. Clear out this rubble and free up poor Blake there. Break out three body bags and the first aid module. And then we'll get our guests downstairs."

Amav watched the soldiers grimly execute these orders. She could tell Howarth was feared but not respected. Amav tried to focus by counting twenty-three surviving soldiers, including the one whose arm was being tended by the medical module trundling in on tank treads.

The Great Hall roiled with foul ochre mist. Soldiers moved in with fire extinguishers. Others had K'ufunb, Will, and Kner floating unconscious three feet above the torn floor in their Arkonsky fields.

"Okay, ma'am," Howarth said. "These sons of bitches have some robot servants, but we've scanned the whole place and can't find any. You know where they got off to?"

Amav was about to echo his puzzlement but caught herself. Her head finally cleared. Did she really think she could trust these bastards? "They went with Greeney Gooney. Back to Mars. Said they were worried about him flying a saucer with his mind the way it was." The need was true enough, but of course it was only the robot M'rrpla who'd accompanied Greeney. She shrugged. "You know the Martians have been getting flakier and flakier."

Howarth rolled his eyes. "You can say that again."

"Listen, I'm Amav Frankston-Commer. What exactly's going on here?"

"I know who you are, ma'am. Don't worry, you're not under arrest."

"I know, you just told me. Why are *they* under arrest?"

"I have my orders." He took another look at her clearly visible nipples. "The United System Council has ordered these three taken into custody."

"Why? They haven't hurt anyone. They're the Four! I mean, three of the Four!"

"Well, they sure have hurt *some* people today," the mustached soldier interjected. His nametag said DEUTSCH.

"Some good friends of ours, honey. Anyway, what I hear is, somehow these bozos went insane and took the whole Martian telepathy crap with 'em. This Total Martian Outradiance BS. I say the hell with it."

"Shut up, Deutsch," Howarth snapped.

"Forget it. Not worth getting our guys cut up over this crap. This *outradiance BS* took down SolNet Venus too."

"Deutsch, shut *up!*" Howarth turned to Amav. "That's all just stupidass rumor-mongering. All these guys can do is yammer on and on like this. All I know is we're to take the prisoners down to Level One, wherever that is."

"Level One?" Amav whispered. That did not sound good at all.

Howarth consulted his comm. "Yeah, there it is. Bontor's mapped it. There's a freight elevator down this corridor. Okay, guys, let's move for that elevator." He turned back to Amav, eyes on her breasts. "You're welcome to come along, ma'am. I know you're friends with these characters and want to make sure they're well-treated."

Amav took an extremely deep breath to ensure the thin nightgown was stretched tight. This time Howarth gulped and looked away. "Thank you, Lieutenant, I believe I will." She surveyed the troops around her, all paying the respect due to a shapely woman in a transparent nightgown.

She couldn't kid herself. She was definitely under arrest. All she could do was see how this played out. Where were John and Laurie?

Down the corridor six soldiers stood before the Castle's open freight elevator. "Sir," one said, "this one's twelve feet square and ten high. It'll fit."

"Good work, Corporal," Howarth said. "Thought we might have to blast the mother out of the basement. This oughta work fine." He turned to Amav. "This is Bontor, our computer genius."

Corporal Bontor's eyes widened. He looked no more than sixteen. "I figured out how to break the security, sir," he gulped at Amav's nightgown.

"Great, great." Howarth turned to their escort and said: "Okay, you guys stay back and secure this level. Bontor's group here will take over the prisoners and we'll head down to Level One." He motioned Amav to the elevator.

"May I have a minute to get my coat?" she said. "My room's just down the hall."

She could feel the disappointment in the men around her.

*Maybe I should just tell them I'm sixty-three!*

"Sorry, ma'am," Howarth said with an open leer at her boobs. "This can't wait. Everyone in!" The new soldiers pushed the floating Three into the elevator. Amav felt Howarth's hand just above her ass and scooted inside. Bontor tapped his comm and closed the door. This elevator had an Amplified Thought lock. How had he cracked it?

They rode in silence ten levels down to Level One, the elevator opened, and soldiers maneuvered the floating Three through bright corridors Amav had never seen. It was just like shoving patients on hospital gurneys through endless halls en route to surgery. Amav tried to shake off the disturbing implications of this last thought as Howarth's hairy hand again probed for her rear. Meanwhile each of the six soldiers contrived some reason to drift near Amav and fasten eager eyes on her torso.

Finally Bontor stopped the group and tapped his comm. A silver-violet section of wall slid aside. Behind a clear plastiglass door, inside a small dark room, something glowed, then darkened, then brightened. Amav gasped. She would never have found this room on her own.

"Great work, Bontor," Howarth said. "Sure you can open it?"

"Yessir! It helps that the Field Lock was compromised. Somehow part of it melted. Turned out that was the really encrypted part. The rest was easy."

"You can't mean to open this!" Amav said, pointing to Z'B's matter/anti-matter Emperor's Robe. She stared at the jagged black and white matter/anti-matter energies surging in stripes across the Robe, which hung on a bright green metal framework.

"We certainly do," Howarth said. "Okay, Bontor, go ahead."

Bontor touched his comm, yanked an oblong bronze device from the right side of the translucent door, and dug his fingers into the resulting orifice. There was no visible hinge to the left but Bontor was treating the panel as if it were some ordinary shower door that had gotten stuck. His foot slipped and he banged his head against the plastiglass. He grunted and pulled all the harder.

"Stop! This is a *Trans-Simultaneity Stasis Chamber!*" Amav cried. "Only one of the Four could possibly open it!"

"Quiet, ma'am, we know what we're doing. Bontor's read all there is to know on the subject, haven't you, kid?"

"Uhh! Uhh! That's right, ma'am," Bontor said, yanking to no avail. "Jim, can you get that other hole down near the bottom? I think two of us need to--uhh! Uhh!"

"Damn!" said Jim, kneeling below Bontor and pulling.

"That's a *matter/anti-matter robe* in there!" Amav shouted. "It's in *stasis* because nobody can control it! If you let those energies mix, the entire planet blows up!"

"Forget it, lady," Howarth said. "Bontor here has a Ph.D. in Quantum Organizational Interfaces. He's also read all the damn Ywritt literature on the subject."

"Well--uhh!--what they've allowed to be--uhh!--published so far, sir," Bontor grunted. "Damn, Jim, can you--"

"*Screw* this piece of crap! It's *stuck!*" Jim muttered, reaching for his shattergun. "You know, a pinpoint EOS ray just below shatter threshold oughta free it up."

"*No!*" Amav said. "*Idiots!*"

"Naw, we don't need EOS rays," Bontor said, opening his fanny pack for a screwdriver which he proceeded to jam like an icepick into the top and bottom orifices.

The panel exploded. Shards flew in all directions.

"*Damn ...*" Bontor muttered. "Eric, hand me that Arkonsky generator and we'll have to rig up a temporary field for now. Oughta hold, least for a while."

Another soldier unslung a knapsack and pulled out the portable Arkonsky equipment. "No! This is crazy!" Amav cried, backing away only to feel Howarth's hands encircling her. "Do you have the slightest idea what you're *doing?*"

"Arkonsky loading," Eric said.

"We got ten seconds to get 'em in here and close this up," Bontor said.

"Right!" Howarth barked. "Arkonsky the damn thing and we'll get a move on." Other soldiers shoved the floating Three into the Trans-Simultaneity Chamber, knocking over the Robe and its framework amid clattering surges of light. Then a blue Arkonsky field replaced the shattered door.

"Stasis optimizing," Bontor said. "Arkonsky patterns integrating, on my mark."

"Calibrating," Eric called, studying his comm. "Got it. It'll hold for now."

"See, ma'am, if you reseal a Trans-Simultaneity Chamber within fifteen seconds there's no explosion," Bontor said. "That's a known Ywritt concept."

"Idiots!" Amav stared at the light-spangling Robe flung across the floor of the Chamber and the bodies of the Three slowly settling atop it. "An Arkonsky clamp is like *wood glue* compared to a Trans-Simultaneity field!"

"Hey, honeycakes, you can just stop telling us what to do," Howarth said. "Winslow, we got enough juice to move this mother?"

Eric examined his comm. "Yessir. We have a wide margin of error."

"Okay, let's move our asses."

Howarth kept a painful grasp on Amav's elbow as Eric floated the entire Trans-Simultaneity Chamber out of its grotto and down the halls.

"Eight-by-eight-by-eight feet," Bontor said, moving alongside Amav for a look at her chest. "It'll fit okay into the elevator, ma'am. No worries."

"You're taking them *where?*" Amav gasped.

"Hey, hon, let's just quiet it, shall we?" Howarth said. "The backtalk's getting us nowhere." They came to the freight elevator and six soldiers pushed the Chamber in, then took their places around it. Howarth pulled Amav inside and she found herself rubbing hips with him and Eric.

She braced for the Chamber to detonate as they rode to ground level. Eric maneuvered the Chamber out, other soldiers joined them, and then Amav found herself standing in the hot sulfuric atmosphere in the clearing before the Castle, watching the Chamber hover up the side of a silver cargo spaceship. The ship was parked tail-first alongside a smaller Detention Services troop carrier that closely resembled the early *Typhoon* series.

Howarth followed her gaze. "Yeah, we brought two ships. Smart, huh? You're right, we *don't* want to ride with a stasis chamber that'll probably blow any second."

"What are you doing with them?"

"They're just under arrest, hon. We recognize their legal rights and all that. They'll get a trial sooner or later, but it's just too dangerous to let 'em fool with any of their fancy mind tricks right now. So we keep 'em in the stasis chamber and we put 'em in a tight little orbit next to the sun. Anyway, those are our orders. Now stand back, missy, we're gonna fire this thing and it's gonna make a ruckus."

The Chamber went through a hatch in the cargo ship. Men motioned each other back and without any preamble roaring flame shot from the base of the ship. Within seconds it was hurling out of sight into the thick clouds.

"We sure *hope* it don't fall into the sun," the mustached soldier cackled. "The damn sons of bitches!"

"Yeah, I'd fry 'em right now myself, but Carla has some other ideas," Howarth said. "Speaking of which, time to check in." He spoke into his comm. "This is Howarth at *Garr/thahg* Castle. MATS Protocol 1A link to Major Carla Posttner."

"Hey, Tony!" came the clear feminine voice from the comm. "How'd we do today, hon?"

"Mission accomplished, babe! Everything went smooth. Lost three guys but what the hell. The freaks put up a fight but we got 'em in the Chamber and it's heading into a nice little orbit inside Mercury's, I'm happy to report."

"Excellent!" Posttner laughed. "Get your sweet ass back here ASAP!"

"How can you be talking with all the static?" Amav said. "SolNet Venus is out!"

Howarth laughed. "Hell with it, lady. MATS is our ace in the hole. Detention Services can *always* get through."

"MATS? What are you *talking* about?"

"Oh, if you only knew!" Posttner boomed. "The Marsport Automated Transport System, of course. It does everything!"

Amav shook her head. "That doesn't make sense!"

"Hello, Amav Frankston-Commer, the Marsport Automated Transport System is pleased to be of service today. May this System pass on the regrets of Major Carla Posttner of USSF Detention Services that she is too busy at this moment to converse further, and has authorized the Marsport Automated Transport System to inform you that MATS has sent the *Typhoon VI* back to Marsport for trial?"

"The *Typhoon?* What trial?"

"Major Carla Posttner has mandated the court-martial of the entire *Typhoon VI* crew. Jack and Joe Commer will also be tried for war crimes at Marsport. Due to the nature of the current crisis, Major Carla Posttner has declared martial law throughout the Sol system. And she has a message for her lover, Lieutenant Anthony Howarth of Detention Services: *Tony, execute code ALBATROSS. Give it to her good for me!*"

"Huh! Wouldn't you know it? Now I have orders to arrest *you*, ma'am," Howarth leered, reaching for her breasts with his left hand as he aimed his gun on full shatter with his right. "Have to admit you have a fantastic pair! You gotta know I've been outa my skull for 'em this whole time!"

"Hey, you think *Carla honey* will mind?" Amav snarled, backing into the grip of two soldiers, arms painfully wrenched behind her as Howarth's stubby fingers advanced.

"Don't worry, honey, Carla and I have a *very* open relationship." But his grin cut off as he saw his fingers enveloped in buzzing blue-purple light. And shattering.

## CHAPTER THIRTY-THREE
### The Pulse

"YAAAAAAA!" came the scream as the human, whom Laurie 283 identified as Lieutenant Anthony Howarth, age 34, burst into a tinkling cloud of multicolored glass.

[HMM ...] John J. Douglas transmitted from her side as two dozen gray soldiers whirled toward the trees with raised shatterguns. [THAT SHOT SEEMS TO HAVE HAD UNINTENDED CONSEQUENCES.]

[I AIMED A STANDARD STUN PULSE AT HIS GUN HAND], Laurie 283 replied. [BUT LIEUTENANT HOWARTH APPEARS TO HAVE INADVERTENTLY CLENCHED HIS TRIGGER AND FIRED A SHOT TO HIS LEFT HAND, CAUSING A FATAL SEQUENCE OF SHATTER EFFECTS. TIME TO COMPLETE BODILY DISSOLUTION: 2.53 SECONDS.]

"Hey! Over there! By the trees!" came the shouts of the other soldiers.

"They killed the lieutenant! Everyone! Guns on full shatter!"

Beams began cutting through the Frankston trees around Laurie and John. It was impossible not to hit something here, and dozens of hundred-foot-tall trees began splintering around them.

[NOT TOO BAD. WE HAVE SOME COVER NOW], Laurie transmitted as shattered glass buried the two of them up to their shoulders. [RECOMMEND FULL SHATTER RESPONSE.]

To her right John took .0001 seconds to tap his shattergun settings. [AGREED. TAKE THEM ALL OUT.]

The two robots crouched and calculated the targeting parameters for every soldier.

"Amav! Get down!" Laurie cried. The green-clad woman wrenched free of her captors, ripping the flimsy garment clean off her torso and dropping onto the Venus grass as Laurie stood to fire fourteen bursts and John fourteen more. For a moment the air by the parked Detention Services troop carrier teemed with shrieking, tumbling pieces of glass, then all cascaded to the ground in a clattering jumble of color.

"Don't move, Amav! Sharp objects will pierce naked human skin! We're coming!" Laurie called, hefting a spacesuit and running with John. [DID YOU HAVE TO SHOOT THE ONE WITH THE BROKEN ARM?] she transmitted.

[DIDN'T YOU SEE HIM GOING FOR HIS KNIFE WITH HIS FREE HAND?] John replied, sending a short video of the demise of Jake Solomon, age 26.

Laurie had seen that but didn't regard Solomon as dangerous; the man had been moving dizzily with probable high levels of pain. [AND HIS MEDICAL UNIT AS WELL? WASN'T THAT A BIT EXTREME?]

[WELL, IT ONLY SHATTERED BECAUSE IT WAS CONNECTED TO HIM. BUT AT LEAST THAT ERASES ITS RECORDINGS OF OUR ACTIONS.]

[THAT DOESN'T MEAN MUCH, JOHN. I BET THEIR SHIP IS ALSO RECORDING EVERYTHING.]

[NOT WHEN I GET THROUGH WITH IT! SEE YOU IN A MINUTE!] John veered off to the Detention Services ship, broadcasting possible username/password combinations. Laurie noted that he found one on the eighty-fifth cycle: *USSFDS / Carlab00bs*. [SHEESH], John added as he opened the ventral hatch and climbed aboard.

"Mistress Amav, I have your Venus suit here!" Laurie cried to the figure gingerly getting up on knees and elbows. Laurie dropped the red suit, scooped up the naked Amav, and held her aloft as her feet swept nine square feet clear of glass in 0.188 seconds. "See? We'll just get you into it. Air's not so bad here but this will help you breathe a lot better. And you definitely need something on you."

Amav blinked shocked brown eyes. She shook herself, split the suit down the front, and climbed in. "You killed them all?"

"Well, it was a slight miscalculation on my part, really. But we're here to get you out in any case. John's preparing the ship now," she added, pointing to the murmuring rear engine and the throaty wing hover jets of the DS spaceplane.

"Where *were* you guys?"

Laurie helped Amav secure the helmet and continued transmitting by radio: "We did feel guilty for a few minutes, but we did some extra Ethical Feedback Cycles. It was really intense for a while, but finally we flushed all that out of us."

"You--*what?*"

Laurie led Amav towards the ship. "Hurry, mistress! John is sure they have a mothership in orbit and they'll try to shoot us down. They'll no doubt be quite angry when they find their entire thirty-two-soldier ground contingent has ceased to exist. But if we go to Star Drive as soon as we clear the atmosphere, we can be at Mars in a couple seconds."

"*Star Drive?* This close to a planetary mass?"

"It's been done, mistress. Dangerous, but it's been done."

"We can't go to Mars. They've fired Kner and K'ufunb and Will off to God knows where!"

"John's checking that on their ship's sensor system. He says the *Remote Justice* has entered a stable orbit ten million miles out from the sun. They're okay."

"*Remote--?*"

"Name of that ship, mistress. The thing's rotating fast so it doesn't fry. And the Chamber itself will protect them. They'll be okay until we can send a rescue mission. John and I concur that the prime objective is to get you to Mars ASAP."

They reached the ship and pulled themselves up through the belly hatch. Inside were forty seats in ten rows.

"Really, where *were* you all this time?" Amav repeated as she pulled off her helmet in the central aisle.

"Better keep that on, mistress, as we don't know what we may encounter."

"No! You guys just show up *now,* after they kidnapped everyone?"

"Well, we did resolve the ethical issues, namely a certain guilt about, well, if you must know ..."

"Yes, she must," John J. Douglas boomed from up front. "Strap in, Mistress Amav, and we'll confess all. We are very,

*very* sorry for what may look at first like dereliction of duty, but after reviewing our case, we conclude that everything's turned out for the best."

"Are you kidding?" Amav pointed out a porthole at the charred ruin of the main entrance to *Garr/thahg* Castle as the wing hover thrusters roared and the Castle and the remnants of the Frankston woods fell away.

"We're extremely sorry for any inconvenience our actions may have caused," Laurie said. "But since you wanted a nap, and the Three were settling down, we ..."

"We became *quite* occupied in our own bedchamber, mistress," John said.

"And, really, after long Evaluation Mode, we can't say we're sorry about it, since a rather fun time was had by all! But the upshot is that, right at an extremely *crucial* moment, shall we say, we heard ships landing in Force Field Stealth Mode."

"Inaudible to human ears, I might add," John went on. "Although we're not capable of *surprise,* I have to say that a look out the window at a couple dozen USSF Detention Services soldiers running for the main entrance was *galvanizing.*"

Amav shook her head in disgust.

"Oh, please, mistress, understand that we've had to forgive ourselves," Laurie said as the rear engine cut in and the ship surged forward. "The sex was fun, and this new complication entirely unforeseen. Believe me, we were ready to spring right into action after we heard the bomb blowing the front airlock, but then we realized that the soldiers were also scanning for robotic frequencies, and, well, that's where the major glitch came in. Not our fault, really, but it's something we'll have to bring to the Ywritt's attention, since we've isolated the algorithmic absurdity to be part of Ywritt Service Pack 146.3."

"Dammit, get to the point!"

"What she's saying is that as soon as we saw that scanner, we called on Ywritt Transparency Mode," John said. "Essentially it hides us from scans."

"But the problem with 146.3," Laurie went on, "is that in the presence of high pheromonal activity, it well, it tends to *degrade,* and, well, to be blunt, Miss Amav, the pheromonal activity was at its absolute *peak,* if you know what I mean."

"And, unfortunately, but please realize we've since done a *lot* of work accepting it, mistress," John added, "our call to Transparency instead activated a full fifteen-minute shutdown of all neural activity. Who'd ever have thought it?"

"And we have to admit we probably weren't in top form to begin with, with all this network stuff going on," Laurie continued. "Although the sex part *was* amazing. It was just that we wound up *ceasing to exist* for fifteen minutes."

"Oh my God!" Amav moaned. *"You missed the whole thing?"*

"Well, when we woke up, we realized everyone was outside and we saw that cargo ship launch. Then we picked up our shatterguns and your suit and ran to the east exit and circled back through the woods. That's when I saw Lieutenant Howarth about to squeeze your mammaries."

"Dammit, we've got to check on the Three! Forget Mars for now!"

"Recommend against that," John said. "The Three are safe for the moment. But there's some sort of political revolution going on in the capital now, and your husband is about to be *railroaded,* mistress. There's a secret MATS channel I was monitoring when I started the ship, then I had to cut it off."

"Yes, I know about the damn MATS channel," Amav flared.

"I had to go full manual and cut off access to *everything* to make sure MATS doesn't take this ship itself. Anyway, this Carla Posttner has jailed all the top Supercommittee people. Mandy and Churchill and Greeney are all in Neutralization Chambers that block Amplified Thought."

"Damn. Okay, got it. We go to Mars first."

John accelerated the ship and reached for the Star Drive panel.

*"Hold! Trouble! One hundred fifteen miles up!"* Laurie yelled, grabbing Amav's helmet. She jammed it over Amav's head and secured it in 1.78 seconds.

The ship lurched. The sky flared to an unbearable white. "We have--" John grunted.

Laurie's mind was on fire. The ship went dark and she dimly registered there was no further engine noise. [OH! WE--] she tried to transmit. Faint light from the ship's portholes showed John sagging in the command chair. Error messages multiplied.

TRANSCOMM OUT. SYSTEM FAILURE. BACKUP MODE 10.444 PERCENT. NEURAL CASCADE OFFLINE.

Laurie struggled to form a single coherent thought. This was a thousand times worse than the fifteen minutes of unexpected shutdown they'd experienced a few minutes ago. That was just an extended rest cycle. This was *damage*.

"John ..." she managed to croak through mouth servos that seemed made of rusty girders. "What ..."

"Mothership challenge ... no password. Autolaunch of supranuclear ..." John groaned. He drifted out of his chair. She was floating too, though she no longer felt her body. It was a just series of shapes waggling in front of her.

To her right Amav in her red spacesuit pulled herself across the backs of passenger seats to the front of the ship. Laurie saw her forming words behind her faceplate. Then Amav ripped off her helmet. "*What the hell happened?*" she cried, pushing herself into the command seat and punching at a dead console.

"Last telemetry--" John muttered. "Mini-Xon, hundred fifteen miles up ..."

Laurie dug into the Recent Memory Dump and confirmed it. An old-fashioned electromagnetic pulse with a mini-Xon bomb. Laurie wished she could calculate its strength.

MATH OFFLINE.

She wished she could feel if they were heading down.

KINESTHETIC SELF-AWARENESS OFFLINE.

"Mistress ... *EMP*. We're *fried*," Laurie moaned. "Your suit probably saved you. Radiation high, about ..."

RADIATION SENSORS OFFLINE.

"Suggest ... helmet back on. Know we can't radio you, but ..."

Amav pounded dark unresponsive panels and ignored the

suggestion. "Not again! I already *did* this today! Do they really think I can do Amplified Thought *again? Do they think that I ever did it at all? I can't do it! I just *can't!*"

SYSTEM FAILURE. ENERGY LEVELS UNSUSTAINABLE FOR SPOKEN DISCOURSE. STASIS BACKUP TO LAST KNOWN PLEASURABLE MEMORY? YES/NO?

"Oh, *yes,*" Laurie muttered, aware the ship was tumbling. "Save us, mistress ... as we saved you. Sorry about the sex ... but it was fun ..."

## CHAPTER THIRTY-FOUR
### A Threat to the Newest Supreme Commander

"Out of Star Drive, sweetie," Ballard called, touching panels on the shuttle console. "You okay back there, my Empress?"

Laurie turned from the medical console at the rear of the *Garrison*. Cold water and a healing ray had stopped the bleeding, but her head still pulsed with dull pain. At least he'd freed her to tend to her injuries and she'd been able to pull the bloody blue tunic back over herself. If she could only think. If she wasn't so *dizzy*.

"Only took 14.599742 minutes!" Ballard crowed. "Not bad for a civilian comm feed to a shuttle Star Drive 3, huh? Just a couple more minutes to Altrouda, honey."

Laurie saw that Ballard had already secured the weapons lockers. She knew she was so jarred by the shattergun blow she couldn't throw a decent punch at the son of a bitch, who still had his USSF blaster, now freed from MATS interference.

The whole ship was free of MATS. Once aboard the *Garrison* Ballard had done the first thing Laurie would have, taking advantage of the one-time override to disengage the *Garrison* computer system and wipe all USSF computer interfaces from his comm. While he'd taken a chance that MATS might have infiltrated one of his obscure personal SolNet accounts, it was a decent bet that had paid off; that account hadn't been hacked yet. There would be no MATS hijacking of the ship, and Ballard had flown the shuttle from Procyon A to Barnard's Black Hole using a personal comm account as the ship's navigational system and Star Drive 3 interface.

"C'mon back, Empress, and be my copilot again!" Ballard laughed, patting the seat to his right. "No more Arkonsky clamps for you if you behave, hon."

Laurie brushed back wet hair and dizzily made her way to the chair. "Okay, fine." She'd play the game and see where it led. She knew this shuttle better than he did, and he was bound to screw up somewhere. Voice commands were out, but there

230

had to be something she could take advantage of.

She shivered at the black circle visible through the starboard cockpit window, a sight eerily similar to the encounter with the Iota Persei Dyson sphere last year: perfect circular nothingness blocking the stars.

*Not the same. Not the same. Get over it.*

Shuttle thrusters engaged, though the inertial dampers gave no hint of motion. The Altrouda blackness soon took over the entire canopy. She thought she saw something like a giant frozen lake reflecting stars.

"Already got a heat signature," Ballard grunted. "This sensor app is crap, but it can scan a whole planet. Coupla volcanoes we can discount, but *there!* See? That's their former capital city, K'hlatw. Lemme try an optical scan. Huh. Looks like new construction down there. Everyone knows the place was leveled. Wonder who could've pulled that off?"

Laurie looked away, tightening her lips to keep from smiling. Only Z'B could have done that. Somehow he'd had enough Amplified Thought.

Ballard eyed her. "I know what you're thinking, yummyboobs! You're thinking if that Z'B sucker wastes yours truly the Emperor, *you* can rule! Well, forget it! He's like any damn peace-loving Martian! He'll freakin' *worship* me! That's what Martians do with a strong leader like yours truly, haven't you noticed?" Ballard fingered the shattergun in its holster. "And if he gives me any grief, I just waste the stinking finback."

"*God ...*"

"No, seriously! Those Martians *stink!* They really do! Can't stand 'em, never could. Damn pansy USSF and all its little rules for not letting a man come right out and admit it. All those *diversity* workshops. Sheesh! Martians *stink!* Everyone knows it. I wouldn't mind wasting the whole damn bunch of 'em."

The shuttle cruised low over torn mountain ranges Laurie picked out by the way they blocked the brilliant starfield. She'd never understood why some people didn't like the cinnamon-like odor of Martians. That was evidently where the phrase "stinking finback" had come about decades ago.

"There's the new building," Ballard called. "And the *Typhoon II*." He hovered over it, shining spotlights along the silver craft. "How the hell they land that thing on its wheels? There's no atmosphere here." He adjusted his sensors. "Nobody here. They must be inside that building. So here goes."

The *Typhoon II* erupted in jagged crimson light and forking violet bolts. Cracks opened down the length of the fuselage, spurting gray smoke.

"What are you *doing?*" Laurie cried, knowing full well.

"Ship's electronics and all computer systems most definitely *fried!*" Ballard laughed. "We don't want to chance any trace of MATS here, babe. Although come to think of it the *Typhoon II* computers probably never could've handled a MATS interface. And anyway, we don't want anyone who's not *playing the game* to run away from us, now do we?"

He sidled the *Garrison* over to the giant archways of the government building and opened up the shuttle's PlanetBlasters. The doors burst aside, flinging stones and girders that bounced off the shuttle's force shields. Ballard grounded the *Garrison*. "Are you ready, Empress?" He opened the side hatch and lowered the stairs. "I'm sure the *stinking finback* in there will take one look at your bloody chest and *freak!*"

Laurie jumped to the loose rocks and took off running, head whirling, legs rubbery. Then she was floating in a bright blue bubble.

"Oh, I *knew* my Empress had spunk," Ballard said, towing her in the Arkonsky field up the rubble-strewn stairs and into the building. "Welcome to the Grand Palace of the Emperor of the Rebellion! Hello, everyone, hello!" he yelled down the length of the cavern to a group of people glowing in the faint pink sheen of activated EnviroFields.

"Z'B! Secure the building! Pressurize!" came a voice.

"Ah, yes, dear Jonathan James, former Emperor of the Rebellion, let's do have Mr. Finback Stench restore the air in here," Ballard said. Laurie felt her floating Arkonsky bubble buffeted by gusts of air.

"Z'B--" she muttered. "God, get *out!*"

"Oh, forget it. He's not going anywhere," Ballard chuckled, yanking Laurie before a platform upon which Jonathan James Commer gripped the arms of a huge chair.

"Who the hell are *you*, buttface?" JJC snarled.

"We've been *trying* to tell you!" Jackie Vespertine cried.

"Major Richard Ballard, your newest Supreme Commander of the Rebellion and Emperor of all Alpha Centauri," Ballard said, bowing.

"If you were in the Grid, you'd know!" Suzette Borman shouted. "We told you he was coming! He just wrecked the *Typhoon II!*"

"Had to fry the mother," Ballard said. "Anyway, dear JJC, you're hereby deposed. Z'B is now under my orders, isn't that right, stinking finback?"

Z'B scrunched his face, the closest thing a Martian could do to blinking, since he had no eyelids. "Well, I suppose, Sire."

"Dammit, let me down!" Laurie grunted, flailing in the Arkonsky field. Ballard touched his comm and she fell three feet to the marble floor. "Ow! God!"

"Miss Laurie!" Z'B said, pointing to her chest and head. "You're *bloody!* You've been injured! Of course all Alpha Centauri knows that, but to *see* it here, why, it's terrible!" He turned to Ballard. "Shall I fashion her an appropriate Empress gown, Sire?"

"Yes, by all means do, stinking finback."

"Yes! Yes! I suggest *emeralds,* to go with your lovely red hair, my Empress! I'm taking all your measurements! You know, Empress, this knowledge goes back *millennia.* In ancient times we Martians built robots that did nothing but make *Empress* gowns. And I have the perfect design for your wondrous human female body!"

*IF empress = parameter LAURIELACHRER ;} THEN createGown; RUN [jewelTransubstantiate = EMERALDS(1), QUANTITY = 300,000--] THREADS = AU; SORT <> GOTO LAURIELACHRER SCAN = 1; EXISTENCE = 1;}*

Just as she scrambled to her knees Laurie was knocked down by another explosion. Green gas flooded the hall.

"God!" someone shouted.

When she was able to focus her aching eyes she saw, whirling about in front of several others who'd also collapsed, a giant silver tetrahedron rocking on three spherical wheels, squeaking and rolling spastically on the marble floor. From each of its three tall sides protruded long dark blue hoses ending in imitation Martian claws. A ragged squeal issued from somewhere beneath the pyramid.

"Oh, *no!*" Z'B moaned. "You got me all *confused,* Supreme Commander Ballard! I mean, Sire!"

"What the hell is *this* thing?" JJC screamed, pointing at the keening, jerking mechanism. "And this bastard is *not* the Supreme Commander!"

"It's a Martian robot!" Suzette cried. "From centuries ago! An Empress-gown-making robot!"

"Outlawed for *centuries,*" Z'B wailed. "All of Alpha Centauri *knows* that. I am so grievously *ashamed.* I accidentally made the greatest sin a Martian can ever make, and I shall enter the *Kuth'rr'kq* now! The Four-Hundred-Year Martian Hibernation!"

"Belay that, idiot!" Ballard shouted.

"This is nuts!" JJC snarled. "This is *my* rebellion! Get out of here, and take your filthy robot with you! And all these *traitors!*"

"Oh, dear JJC, if you'd just get in the Grid, you'd know," Ballard said, aiming his shattergun at JJC's face. "I'm *upgrading* your silly Rebellion. I'm joining us all to the AC Grid and taking it *over.* There's going to be just one emperor again, and it ain't you, brother!"

"*No!*" Suzette screamed.

"And why not, my sexy new concubine Suzette? Mr. Commer here represents a threat to your newest Supreme Commander and royal bedmate!"

"Look, we'll do anything! We'll worship you, you can be our Supreme Commander, but you can't hurt JJC! The entire Alpha Centaurian Grid forbids it!"

"Yeah, I can feel everybody complaining," Ballard said.

"They don't like me becoming the One Emperor. Trillions of the mothers, thinking they can outvote me! Hell, get over it, wimps!"

"You don't understand! They *remember* JJC's sacrifice when he was the AC emperor!" Jackie cut in. "It's part of their *culture* now. He gave his *mind* for them. He couldn't handle their suffering! What makes you think *you* could?"

"Huh. Guess we'll find out, won't we?" Ballard sneered, aiming.

*"I'm not afraid of you! I'm a Zarj warrior!"* JJC cried as the blue-purple ray flooded his face, cracked down his neck, and blew torso, arms and legs into thousands of shrieking pieces of glass.

# CHAPTER THIRTY-FIVE
## The Extermination Soliloquy

Suzette's mouth fell open but she couldn't scream. Her legs wobbled. All Alpha Centauri felt it too, but somehow trillions of beings reeling in shock kept her on her feet as Major Richard Ballard kicked his way through the clattering pieces of her lover to mount the throne.

There was an unwanted entity loose in the Centaurian Grid: Ballard on the throne, yet incapable of merging his hated alien self into the Grid. Though trillions on all sides of the issue debated whether the ancient fascist Grid should be reinstated, not one Alpha Centaurian citizen accepted Ballard as Emperor.

"*J-Jonathan!*" Suzette finally moaned as twenty trillion Alpha Centaurians echoed her grief for their last true Emperor.

*JJC, who dared to give it all for seventeen solar systems, for twenty trillion! JJC, brave enough to sacrifice his mind for all of us in our terror, for each of us who had to learn to stand on his or her own at last!*

Suzette whirled to Sanders Hirte, who stood glazed. So did Jackie, Z'B, and Pat, who all shared the Grid with her and the unwanted *entity*. Suzette knew it was unfair, but because Sanders was a man, and huge, and tattooed, and had flown the *Typhoon* and was the most alpha male she'd ever known, she screamed: "Sanders! Do something! What's *wrong* with you?"

Hirte barely swiveled in her direction. Trotter padded up, sniffing the shards of his master, arching his back, and backing off with a scarcely audible moan. His natural outradiance was shut down.

"God … *God,*" Jackie whispered.

As Ballard thumped the arms of his throne, Suzette could feel the *entity* trying to jam his emperorship into the tight dry recesses of twenty trillion angry Centaurians. He waved at the glittering chunks of JJC on the stairs. "Clean up this mess, Z'B!"

Z'B stared back.

"I said *clean up this mess,* stinking finback! You've got your goddamned Amplified Thought! Do it!"

"I--I am *offline,* Sire! I'm so sorry! But I cannot stand this--this *violence,* Sire! Why did you have to *do* that?" Z'B cried, pointing to the shiny pieces of multicolored glass. Ballard's glare intensified and the Grid rippled sickeningly as Z'B's outradiance whirled with fresh insanity, mixing it back into the Grid for all Alpha Centauri to absorb. He knelt in the sharp fragments. "Oh, I know! I have your solution, master! Coincidentally, it turns out that the greatest sin a Martian could ever make is the *solution* to all your problems! This *T'ohj'puv* robot right here actually has a *sweeper function!* For sweeping up any loose jewels the Empress may have let fall! So!" Z'B gestured furiously at the seven-foot-high tetrahedral robot, still lazily bouncing on its rubbery wheels.

"What the hell are you *doing?*" Ballard screeched. "I said *clean up this mess!* This is Emperor War Directive Number 1! War Directive Number 1!"

"I--I'm *trying,* dear Sire! Sorry my mind is *shorting out!* You see, *T'ohj'puv* robots never had any speech function, certainly no outradiance, so communication was by *sign language,* if you can believe it. I'm trying to remember the signs! Of course that was all twenty thousand years ago, before we banned robots!"

"C'mon, get on with it! May I hereby inform all of this *putrid* Alpha Centaurian Empire that Jonathan James Commer was a filthy traitor and *deserved* to be shattered by the One True Emperor! We will not have his *crap* lying on the floor!"

The Grid staggered. Suzette clutched her stomach and fell to one knee, watching Z'B's claws flailing in front of the *T'ohj'puv* robot. He scuttled out of its way as it opened a receptacle and extended a broom of ruby filaments and a dustpan of solid gold. With much whirring and puffing, aided by three weaving tentacle claws, the contraption swept up the glass shards, popped the dustpan into its stomach, withdrew the broom, and snapped the lid shut.

The unfathomable contraption whirred and clunked. "Oh, God," Suzette whispered. All Alpha Centauri knew this sight was worse than seeing JJC shattered.

"Keep that damn thing on standby in case anyone else needs a similar lesson," Ballard grunted. "Then get your damn AT act together and prepare a bridal chamber for my Empress and me." His eyes sliced into Suzette's, then moved to Jackie. "The royal concubines Suzette and Jackie will disrobe immediately so as to attend the pleasure of the Emperor and Empress." He stood. "Laurie luscious, if you will?" When she didn't respond he raised the shattergun. "Think it over, sweetheart, as you see I do have two other delightful bitches here eager to replace you."

But overwhelming *force* surged behind Suzette.

"YAAARRRKKK!"

Something banged into her ear. A hind leg briefly tangled in her hair and pushed off.

*Can dogs really fly? Zarj warrior dogs?*

The Beagle missile shot to its target as dog outradiance burst in all their joined minds.

*

*Fly to enemy thug murderer, snap teeth into hand, chew and rip and tear! Your nasty gun drops, it never frightened me, never!*

*I gnaw through flesh, muscle, bone! I feel hand bones snap! Gore bursting everywhere! Vengeance!*

*Proud Zarj warrior dog teeth, source of all my strength and power, snarl their way up this putrid, nauseating arm!*

*You scream in vain! I laugh in glee!*

*You use puny ray to destroy master! Master now tiny pieces inside machine! He was best possible master that could ever be, my Zarj brother, comrade warrior, my* Garthah-/yuu! *Our long-dead brother Clopt, captain of the Imperial Guard, speaks through me and together we joyously take vengeance! Your foul, stomach-churning disregard of master's genius life culminates in your own spastic destruction!*

*I rejoice in your cowardly screams as I tear my way up your rotting, disgusting, soon-to-be corpse! I eagerly anticipate your painful jerking death, your limp body in my jaws!*

*Tear flesh! Spit it out in disgust! Hideous Major Richard Ballard, go ahead and die! Your clumsy attempts to shake me will never find success! For my teeth work in and in and in! They will never cease, never give you a chance to pull free, now your bicep shredded, shoulder shredded, and--so glorious! Deep deep deep neck bite!*

*Your neck bursts! I bark laugh bark at your writhing demise!*

*Illegitimate monster, psychopathic fool! Lawless vile nauseating fiend, your insolent crimes scream throughout eternity for your extermination!*

*I avenge for master, for all beings mistreated everywhere, all humans, all dogs, all animals mistreated, all injustice everywhere! I torture you to warm spurting! I exult in your shuddering, out-of-control fear!*

*Scream and struggle to no avail, coward! As you weaken into nonexistence, know that invincible dog teeth have surmounted all obstacles to righteousness! Brazen illicit criminal, I avenge the sordid, appalling corruptions you have loosed upon this holy universe!*

\*

Ballard whirled, a blood-spurting gyroscope wobbling down in death spiral, grappling in vain with a merciless ripping Beagle attachment. "*It's all my fault!*" Patrick James screamed, scooping up the bloody shattergun and pointing it at his own head. "I can't *stand* it! It's all my fault and I can't *stand* it!"

"No!" Z'B shouted. "It's *my* fault!" Suzette winced with the force of Z'B's Martian outradiance turned high, funneling twenty trillion Alpha Centaurians into everyone present whether they wanted to be in the Grid or not.

*I created terrible, dysfunctional Great Palace! Garr/thahg energies unbalanced me! Robot comes out of deep Martian subconscious and causes beings to be shattered, dogs to become eloquent and kill without mercy, Patrick to desire death!*

The palace rumbled, the walls shook, and to Suzette's

horror deep cracks opened in the marble floor. Most of the torches were extinguished by a hard cold wind. All Alpha Centauri watched in numb amazement as a sense of billions of years of *walking through endless corridors of multicolored blocks* swept through the entire civilization. Z'B was calling up *Garr/thahg*. What was worse was the distant memory of having once understood every one of those corridors, every one of those block concepts, and then finding himself no longer able to piece any of it together.

*I create life! I do not create death!*

Pat jerked the trigger of the shattergun. Suzette gaped as the blue beam crawled out of the gun barrel and stopped.

"I *halt* your time! *Halt it,* I say!" Z'B cried, flinging a bright green ray from his right claw to lasso the gun and swing it from Patrick's forehead. Pat fell, the shattergun spinning, its local time lazily kicking in again, wild shatter lines slowly arcing throughout the palace.

Everyone hit the floor to duck the deadly beams except for the hapless Ballard, whirling in front of his throne, neck spraying blood, mouth bubbling crimson, the Beagle spinning with him, still fixed on his throat.

The light caught him in the belly and began shattering its way upwards.

"*No!*" Z'B screamed. "I can't do *anything* right!"

"*Y-YAAAAAAA!*" Ballard gasped, splintering asunder. In the last instant of possessing a face, his eyes fixed wide on the *T'ohj'puv* robot springing to life, opening a tetrahedral surface and extending broom and dustpan.

At the sight of the exploding torso Trotter leaped free. Suzette stared without comprehension as the dog seemed to float next to the whirling shattergun and its ever-accelerating, looping beam. Trotter deftly stuck out a paw at the last instant and slapped the gun ten feet into the *T'ohj'puv's* open waste bin.

The robot blew into a fifty-foot ball of purple light. Suzette tumbled across the churning, disintegrating floor, grabbing both ears against the roaring, and slammed against a screaming Jackie. Pat was on his knees. Hirte lay stunned. Colonel Lachrer, face blackened, shakily hauled herself to her feet.

*I'm so sorry! I'm so sorry!* Z'B radiated.

*No worries! A fitting end to a fiendish monster!* Trotter rejoined, landing on all fours.

Stones rained from the ceiling. "*Ow!*" Suzette cried. "We need to get out of here! The place is falling apart!"

"Look! *Look!*" Jackie yelled, pointing.

The purple glow from the blasted throne faded, and Suzette made out, amid the brown smoke and blue-green flames, a dark object ... pyramidal ... floating, revolving ...

"The stupid robot *survived!*" Patrick moaned. "Of all the--"

"No, look! Its arms were blown off!" Jackie said. "Or--or--"

The tetrahedron emerged from the smoke and hovered before them, its surfaces sharp silver mirrors in which Suzette could see everyone's reflected gaping mouths.

*Master?* Trotter yelped.

*Oh, the poor little dog!* Suzette had time to think before a familiar voice, enhanced to a seductive sonorous baritone, emerged from the pyramid. "Greetings, imbeciles. You thought you could obliterate Major Richard Ballard, but you cannot. By the grace of the dimwitted Martian Emperor Z'B, the mysteries of *Garr/thahg* have enabled Rick Ballard to *continue.*"

"Oh, God, Z'B, what have you *done?*" Jackie wailed.

"You *saved* the son of a bitch!" Suzette said. "You idiot!"

"Well, I suppose I had the idea of *perfection* in my mind," Z'B babbled. "Perfection is *necessary* for the preservation of life, don't you think? At least I do! And, well, what with the shape of the robot, and the desire to return life to everyone involved, well, I guess it screwed up! But I can assure you that this object is a *perfect* tetrahedron, base exactly one meter per side, height exactly two meters per each of the three sides! I mean, perfect down to within a millionth of a millimeter!"

*You leave Ballard alive?* Trotter demanded. *When I had him dead in my jaws?*

"Well, I'm *sorry,* Trotter! I mean, you know I *tried!*"

"Yark! Yark yark!" *But master is still in there!*

"Enough babble, peons. I will take my leave now," the

pyramid said, moving past them. "I have already determined that this shape will fit into the *Garrison* cargo bay. From here I will fly the ship to Iota Persei. You morons need not ask why. I do not need to concern myself with any of you. As a perfect tetrahedron, consisting of solid chromium with no moving parts, I am simply too far above you to notice your existence. All I have to do is simply leave you stranded on this airless world."

"Now wait just a minute!" the pyramid boomed in a new voice. "What makes you think *you're* giving the orders around here?"

"*Jonathan James!*" Suzette cried.

"God!" Pat muttered. "I can't *believe* this!"

*Master!* Trotter whooped.

"*I'm* giving orders because *I'm* the most qualified!" the Ballard voice shot back.

"Yeah? Says who? *I'm* the one who started this damn rebellion!"

*Master! Zarj brother! You live!*

"Well, idiot, we're obviously not concerned with any stupid rebellion any longer! Can't you understand that things have *changed,* imbecile? Like being converted into a goddamn *tetrahedron,* for example?"

"I don't see how that affects--dammit, you're saying we're a *tetrahedron?*"

"That's right! Son of a bitch Z'B turned us into a *tetrahedron.* Now listen, man, you may hate my guts, but it looks like we're crammed into this thing together, and have to *cooperate.* And I have the perfect solution."

"And that involves abandoning the rebellion and slinking away in the *Garrison,* I take it?" JJC snarled.

"Shut up and *listen!* We take the *Garrison* to Iota Persei. If you examine the capabilities of this pyramid, you'll note we can manipulate matter by *thought alone.* We fly the ship to Iota Persei. To the Ywritt. They have libraries of all the knowledge the Wounded ever accumulated. It's just that they never knew how to make it *work.* But I'm sure I can figure it out."

"Are you *crazy,* man? Fooling with the Wounded?"

"No, we wouldn't be dealing directly with 'em. Like I say, the Ywritt just collected their knowledge. Look, this pyramid thing is okay, but obviously we don't want to hang out with each other for all eternity, do we? So we figure out how to transfer ourselves into Wounded-type robots. Completely new bodies! That's our only hope!"

"Forget it! That's not what I'm in this trip for! I'm serious about the rebellion! We take the *Garrison* back to Marsport and we use the pyramid to fight SolGrid!"

"Aw, crap, that'll never work! I can't believe you're so *naïve,* man."

"No, I'm beginning to see the *possibilities.* This thing has enough computing power to *erase* SolGrid!"

"If I may--" came yet another voice from the pyramid, cold and mechanical. "I can't help but interject my own interest in Mr. Ballard's proposal. As you may have guessed, simply by following your two voices and consulting various memories of yours stored aboard, I have taught myself how to speak your language."

"It's the damn robot!" Suzette gasped. "All *three* of them are in there!"

"I find this new tetrahedral structure, akin to my original shape, rather pleasing," the *T'ohj'puv* robot continued. "Like Mr. Commer, I note the greatly increased computational ability of this object and I confess I find Major Ballard's proposal, which would of necessity involve fascinating upgrades to my capabilities, rather intriguing. I therefore cast my vote to take the *Garrison* to Iota Persei to investigate these claims of secret Ywritt knowledge of Wounded robotics techniques."

"*No* ..." Suzette gasped. "JJC, are you really in there?"

"I'm really here! And I say we're taking the *Garrison* back to Mars!"

By now the pyramid was floating through the blasted end of the palace. Suzette ran after it. "No! JJC, don't let them take you there! Stay here with *me!* I *love* you!"

"Look, babe, I love you too, but dammit, it looks like I'm outvoted," the pyramid muttered as it drifted across the quivering, broken plaza and into the *Garrison*. "I can't control this thing!"

"Yap! Bark yap!"

*No, we deadlock the vote at two to two!* Trotter broadcast, his dog collar EnviroField kicking in as he raced into the *Garrison* just as the cargo hatch flipped closed.

"*Trotter!*" Suzette screamed.

*No worries, Suzette beast! JJC, my Zarj brother, is in here and I am always united with him! See you guys around!* came the last burst of telepathic outradiance as the *Garrison* shot into the stars.

# CHAPTER THIRTY-SIX
USSF Detention Services Head Carla Posttner for President

"All rise!" Colonel Dan Miller barked from the long table crammed with comms, ancient legal tomes, stacks of paper documents, and two shatterguns. The door to Jack's executive washroom swished open and Major Carla Posttner appeared in a black, extremely low-necked judicial miniskirt, fishnet stockings, and six-inch heels. She took her seat behind Jack's twelve-foot-wide desk and glared at the four *Typhoon VI* crew who'd refused to rise from their metal chairs along the left wall. Glossy two-inch spherical jade earrings spangled as she bent over her comm.

*My own office,* Jack thought in disgust, noting the jury of six human and four Martian USSF officers behind the long wooden table installed in place of Jack's big leather armchairs. The six humans were colonels and generals he'd personally promoted over the years. Miller and Freedman, Wu and Hui. And Jacobs and McKay. Once comrades and friends. The humans resumed their seats, the four Martians preferring to stand so as not to strain their fins.

Staj and C'nora. K'plic and Dren. How could they be taking part in this farce?

"Ladies and gentlemen, this court is now in session," Carla said, slamming a fist on the huge titanium desk Jack remembered approaching with awe when it had belonged to the first Supreme Commander, General Scott, so many decades ago.

"Crap on this," Joe muttered next to him.

"Silence from the accused!" Posttner snapped. "May I remind you that the punishment for interfering with a USSF court-martial is six years of hard labor on Ganymede?"

"Since when?" Lee Borman said.

"Since I ruled right this second! Now be silent, all of you!"

"Forget it, lady! We have the right to legal counsel! And as a United System senator and Supercommittee member--"

"Mr. Borman, I thought it was made *quite* clear to you that during this emergency the United System Senate, and the

Supercommittee of which you were formerly a member, have been suspended *indefinitely*."

"What emergency? This SolGrid fiasco Patrick James brought down on our heads?"

"Airman Commer, will you please inform Airman Borman that his remarks are an obstruction of an official USSF court-martial, and that he is *one inch* from *seventy years* penal servitude on Ganymede?"

Jack shrugged at the demotions and surveyed his stone-faced former subordinates at their table. The Martians seemed like fog to him, their minds scattered, radiating little more than images of their view out the thirty-foot-wide window: bright afternoon, Marsport skyline, distant red mountains.

The only reason Jack and his crew continued to occupy their metal chairs was that all ten members of the Inquiry Board had their sidearms set on full shatter. Miller and Jacobs had placed theirs amid their legal documents as a pointed warning. At least the Detention Services boys who'd herded them in at gunpoint were gone, though they were probably stationed right outside the door.

"All right, to begin," Carla spoke. "The *Typhoon VI* crew, consisting of Airmen Jack Commer, Joe Commer, Lee Borman, and Sandra Markham, having been escorted to USSF headquarters at Marsport in the custody of MATS, is now on trial for dereliction of duty, criminal misuse of government property, and treason."

"And may I state once more that this entire action is completely *illegal*," Jack cut in. "We've been denied legal counsel, have been illegally demoted, and have had no access to whatever evidence is being used against us. The United System government has been illegally dissolved, a mere *major* in the USSF has taken it upon herself to conduct a *kangaroo court*."

"Why, Airman Commer, I'm not a major anymore. I'm the new Supreme Commander of the United System Space Force."

"*What?*" Joe cried.

"A *hundred years* on Ganymede for Joe Commer! I'm not only the SCUSSF, but I also happen to be the President of the

United System. I didn't want either position, but the current emergency demanded it. Now understand that I'm a very busy woman and only have ten minutes allotted for this trial."

"God!" Joe spat.

"So we'll quickly get to the point. The entirety of the evidence, having been uploaded by the Marsport Automated Transport System into our Central Judicial Database, confirms the treachery of all four of you. I shouldn't need to add, but I will, that MATS is recording everything, including your various insubordinate ejaculations."

"What evidence?" Jack said. "You're just making this crap up as you go along."

"Airman Commer, I direct you to shut up in the presence of the judge and Supreme Commander," said balding Colonel Dan Miller from the far end of the table, fingering his shattergun meaningfully. "We do have other important business to attend to after this unpleasant matter is dispensed with."

"*Dan,*" Jack muttered. "Damn, I can't believe *any* of you!" The colonels and generals averted their eyes. The weak Martian outradiance decreased further.

"The point is, with this SolGrid emergency frying the SolNet network," put in General Arthur Freedman, "we've got to stomp out *all* the disorder, *all* the treason."

"*What* treason?" Lee Borman demanded.

"Well, Jack taking the *Typhoon VI* to search for his son," Freedman said. "That's just one example of his continuing lawlessness."

"Continuing *lawlessness?*" Jack cried.

"Well, yes, we've all seen it for years. You taking matters into your own hands, always circumventing the duly-constituted United System authorities."

"That's insane!" Lee said. "You have some beef with how Jack's running the USSF, so now you want to destroy the entirety of the United System government?"

Freedman folded his hands. "Yes, Airman Borman, we certainly have some *beef,* as you put it, with decades of Jack Commer's stagnant hold over the USSF."

"Great." Lee turned to Jack. "I *told* you we had a bunch of jerks whining behind your back about how they couldn't rise to the top as fast as they'd like."

Colonel Wu Ai cleared her throat. "May I just point out that Supreme, uh, I mean, *Airman* Commer has hinted at his retirement for years now, yet nothing happens!"

"We do need fresh blood," General Mel Jacobs put in. "Of course, that's not the reason for this trial."

"Dammit, this is stupid," Jack said. "Yeah, I took the *Typhoon VI* to look for my son, but there's a real possibility that Rick Ballard, who kidnapped my P/E and stole the *Garrison,* may be a Wounded operative. *That's* what we need to be considering here."

"Silence from the accused!" Carla snapped. "There are no Wounded left in Sol. You introduce that statement to distract the work of this Court. May I remind you that the entire Commer family is now suspected of treasonous acts. Like your son, or your insolent little brother sitting there so smugly, trying to look down the front of my robe!"

"Why, I was *not!*"

"And your wife, Airman Jack, who's currently *resisting justice* on Venus!"

"*What about my wife?*" Jack shouted, standing.

"Sit down!" Carla rasped, motioning to the long table to the side. Dan Miller stood with a drawn shattergun.

"Who would *want* to look down your damn robe?" Joe complained.

"Shut up! We have word, Airman Jack, that your wife resisted arrest at *Garr/thahg* Castle on Venus, that she killed an *entire contingent* of USSF Detention Services soldiers, and then stole a Detention Services spaceship, which we succeeded in bringing down with an EMP burst."

"*What?*"

"Sit *down!* The only reason I leave you alive, sir, is that I intend to grill you most *thoroughly* about what you may know of her whereabouts. The ship she stole evidently crashed intact. We know that much because she was actually in SolGrid for several seconds. But the degradation of SolNet Venus is preventing us from locating the ship."

"Amav? She was going to Venus to talk with the Four! She's all right?"

"Well, I suppose you could hope so. As for the others, let's just say that we have three of the Four in custody now, Airman Jack. We sent them on a tight solar orbit inside Mercury's. We'll just have to pray they don't get *too* hot."

A flicker of Martian outradiance slid through everyone's mind.

*Kner? Senior Scientist Kner? Placed in danger?*

Jack glanced at K'plic frowning at the glossy wooden table.

*Senior Scientist Kner placed in danger, while Emperor Z'B is missing and Martians are in mourning?* came from Star General Dren.

"Oh, forget it," Carla snorted through her bright purple lipstick. "You guys know damn well the Four flaked out a long time ago. I've got three of 'em right up next to the sun in their own damn Trans-whatever Chamber, and we'll stick Mr. Z'B in there too if he shows his ugly face back here." She twirled her dark green choker collar and went on: "We can't worry about some flaky Martians. They're Sol citizens subject to the United System just like everyone else. No special treatment. We've got to deal with *all* the troublemakers, just like we're dealing with these four *traitors* sitting here. Joe Commer, take your eyes off my breasts at once!"

"Forget it, lady, I was *not* looking!"

*An insult to Kner, and to Z'B? Could a mere human understand the depths of our affection for the exalted journeyers to* Garr/thahg *and their comrades K'ufunb and Will Connors?*

"Oh, shut up, K'plic! We've got to deal with the fact that SolNet is completely down. Fortunately MATS has offered to take over."

"Shove this, lady!" Lee Borman snarled, standing. "I've heard enough!" He pointed to the Martians. "These guys are starting to leak again, and one of 'em just said that all USSF ships are now in a MATS-induced *stasis*."

Jack read that last burst of outradiance as well. All four Martian minds were coming alive with truly bizarre news. "Joe, we've lost control of the entire USSF! That damn *software* has it all now! We've got to shut MATS down!"

"Sit down, prisoners!" Carla yelled back. "All of you sit *down!* For your information, MATS *can't* be shut down! It's designed to go on *forever!*"

"Dammit, I demand the Supercommittee in on this!" Jack cried. "Churchill, and Mandy, and Greeney, and all the rest!"

"Oh, you fool, they're all in jail now! The finbacks' minds are *gone.* We have some Neutralization Chambers that block Amplified Thought, so we stuck 'em in there. Not as good as the Trans-crap they had on Venus, but they'll do. We don't need that goddamn *mind gibberish.* You *know* their minds are gone!"

*You say our minds are gone?* flashed from Colonel Staj.

*Greeney, and Mandy, and Churchill the Beloved, imprisoned?* came from General K'plic.

*Yes, we knew it, we knew the fact of it, but we didn't want to believe it!*

*Now we do believe it!*

"Oh, shut it off!" Carla said. "I can't stand it when you start leaking all over the place!" She slammed her fist on the desk. "Order! Order in the court!"

*All Martians--the Total Martian Outradiance--imprisoned?*

"Silence! Of course not *imprisoned,* you idiots! Don't go all hysterical on me like you always do! We need to finish up the damn trial! So! This court had heard all the evidence against these four traitors, and hereby mandates the *death penalty* for each. Execution to take place in five minutes. That is all. Court adjourned."

"The--*death* penalty, ma'am?" General Hui Peng muttered.

"Yes, that's the penalty for treason, you know. Carry it out!"

The six human USSF officers shuffled to their feet. Mel Jacobs tentatively reached for his shattergun.

*We are expected to execute the Supreme Commander and his crew?* Staj radiated.

"Of course, stinking finback!" Arthur Freedman snapped.

"Do you damn things always *whine* like that?"

*General Freedman just called me a stinking finback! Do I have to accept that? Does the Total Martian Outradiance have to accept that?*

*Are we really expected to murder fellow USSF officers whom we've loved and revered all these years?*

"Follow Supreme Commander Posttner's orders!" Dan Miller yelled, waving his shattergun. "Or I swear I'll--"

*You'll what?* Colonel C'nora snarled, hand on her own shattergun.

"Damn you stupid stinking finbacks, calm *down!*" Carla cried, standing.

*We went along blindly! Our outradiance was injured! But now--*

*Now the Total Martian Outradiance flows through us!* finished Staj, jumping over the wooden table and marching to Carla. "Apologize to the *Typhoon* crew at once!" he bellowed. "They're right, this is all an *injustice!*"

*We just could not see it until now!* flashed C'nora.

"Get *back!*" Carla snatched her own shattergun as Staj dug his fingers below the giant titanium desk and upended it. "Traitor! *Traitor!* Someone stop this *stinking finback!*"

"I take your titanium desk and *destroy!*" Staj laughed, grappling with the immense structure, yanking it off the floor, whirling and slinging it at the thirty-foot-wide floor-to-ceiling window as Carla scampered back.

The desk burst through the window and tumbled away. Plastiglass blew everywhere and the air shot out along with papers and books and comms. Jack was shoved towards 130 stories of raw void, grabbing Sandra who was almost out the jagged opening herself. Together they fought for traction as the last of the air gushed out and EnviroFields snapped into play in the full Martian environment.

"This is all *your* fault, Commer! The penalty for this is *death!*" Carla screamed through her radio, rushing at Jack with shattergun upraised, jerking the trigger.

Jack noted the blinking blue light of the stun setting. The

idiot couldn't even set her weapon properly.

"*Dammit!*" a shadow grunted, flinging itself in front of Jack.

Joe took the beam, collapsed, and stumbled out the window.

# CHAPTER THIRTY-SEVEN
## The Thin Tower

*Well, dude, you've sure done it now.*

Joe's stomach felt punched hard. Was it dumb to take the shot for Jack? It had been pure instinct. He gazed into the gaping window on the 130th floor, the darkness within lit by the blue-purple flashes of shatterguns. Dark bodies crouched, firing.

*Yeah, outside it all now. Of course! I'm dead! So this is what it's like.*

*Death* was to lazily float thirty feet from the exterior of the United System Building, 130 floors up, to simply observe, to process faint curses and grunts from that ruined office amid the strobing weapons, and not care.

Was this *Garr/thahg?* No, there were no blocks, no corridors. Weren't you supposed to hit the ground running, and keep jogging for eons through infinite colored blocks of weird knowledge? At least that was what Kner has told him.

*Oh well, guess I didn't deserve it. Too late to cry about it now.*

The Martians were definitely getting unhinged over there. Their outradiance increased exponentially and Joe's head hurt from it. Was that fair? To be dead and still have headaches? What were they radiating? It was all a jumble.

Star Colonels Staj and C'nora, along with Star Generals K'plic and Dren, were exhibiting some alarming Amplified Thought. Chairs blew into shards of ice, all four Martians teleporting to other parts of the office to avoid shattergun bolts as they in turn steadily shot at the scrambling humans. Yet no Martian took the opportunity to teleport outside the office, to safety. Joe saw Arthur Freedman, grazed on the arm, burst into full shatter. Wu Ai overturned the wooden table for cover but Staj drilled it with his gun set on Electron Oblivion Sequencer and it disappeared to her gasp of dismay. Mel Jacobs stood to fire at Staj, who transported and reappeared behind Jacobs to blast his head into an expanding gray cloud of nonexistence.

What were they saying? Were the Martians saying this was

*fun?*

*Yes, Joe Commer, yes! You radiate with us! Yes, this is fun!* the Martians clamored. *To destroy the infidel! To reassert Mars!*

*Yes, this is all a game!* C'nora exulted.

*And you radiate with us that it's all a game!* Staj added, firing at numerous targets, laughing whether he hit them or not. The walls of the office were scarred with EOS gouges, heat blaster marks, and huge holes marking shatter strikes. More papers blew out as air from neighboring offices whistled through these gaps. Joe grinned. Once the door seals had fallen in place, all those Detention Services goons couldn't get in to assist Ms. Posttner and crew.

The office was a theater stage, glowing with weapon bursts and screaming figures. It was a big office, thirty feet on a side, but a damn small battlefield, Joe mused. It looked as good a place as any to get to *Garr/thahg*. For the Martians at least, because apparently Joe Commer didn't rate. He'd tried to do his best for decades, but maybe only certain people could get to *Garr/thahg,* the really advanced beings.

*Hope Ranna doesn't mind I missed* Garr/thahg! *Is she ever gonna be pissed when she finds out I bought the farm! Sorry, Ranna! I love you! You know I do!*

*Man, look at those Martians go!*

Joe hadn't seen this sort of fighting spirit from them since the '34 war. Yeah, those guys would all get to *Garr/thahg.* Joe sighed. Once the existence of *Garr/thahg* had been demonstrated, people thought it meant nobody ever really died. He and Jack had even talked about how the whole crew of the *Typhoon I* must be somewhere in *Garr/thahg,* that and sooner or later they'd come back, after billions of years of just running and learning.

Everybody had wanted to believe that all the dead would return, but that ignored the fact that you had to die in space combat, which Joe definitely had *not* done just now. Besides, Kner said it was just the special, insane pressure of Iota Persei and the Wounded last year that had brought the Four back. Just one big crazy exception. Kner said the statistical chances of having a loved one return this way were just about zero.

No, Joe would never see his brothers Jim or John again. Or any of the guys.

Inside the office, the Total Martian Outradiance cheered the Martians on, squeezing Joe's mind to a pinpoint of agony. Lee Borman scrambled for a dropped shattergun, set it to blaster, and seared the walls with fire. Sandra Markham swung a chair onto Hui Peng's back and Hui blundered into Carla Posttner who'd been about to nail Jack.

But Jack ignored the battle. He stood at the window, on the edge of a 130-story drop, staring directly at Joe.

*How can he see me? I'm dead!*

Posttner got to her knees and drew her weapon again.

"All right! Enough! All guns shall *cease to exist!*" bellowed from just beside Joe's ear as numerous USSF personnel grimaced at their empty hands.

"God!" Joe gasped, turning to a dog barking next to him.

No, a reflection of his own shocked face in an angled mirror. No, the side of a giant *pyramid.*

"Oh my God!" Joe cried, realizing he was sprawled inside a dark room floating outside a Marsport skyscraper.

And a dog barked. A Beagle. *Trotter.*

"Take it easy, Uncle Joe," came the voice again.

"*JJC!*"

"None other, dude. Listen, that SolGrid-loving bitch over there was about to waste Dad, so I had to break radio silence, if you get my drift. We cooked up a little subroutine to disarm you idiots."

"Dammit, JJC, we weren't supposed to reveal ourselves," came another voice.

"*Ballard!* What are *you* doing here?" Then Joe saw that he, the pyramid, and Trotter were inside the cargo bay of a ship. *Garrison* was stamped on a bulkhead.

"Joe! Joe!" came the cry through his EnviroField radio. Joe turned to the window where Jack gestured wildly.

"I'm not *dead?*" Joe babbled, looking down at his light blue USSF flight suit.

"We grabbed you on the way down," JJC said. "Level five stun. Not too bad. Can you move your fingers?"

Joe flexed them as Trotter came up to lick them. "Yes, but, look, I don't know how I got here, or--hey, Trotter, how's my guy? Look, JJC, if you could maybe come over from the cabin and just wave to Jack, you know he'd be thrilled."

"Huh. But I'm not in the cabin. I'm inside this *pyramid* here. Long story."

"Hey, I'm in here too, buster," Ballard said. "This is a perfect solid chromium tetrahedron, completely superior to any technology you can imagine, with the possible exception of Ywritt and Wounded tech."

"Oh my God." Joe looked back to the humans and Martians picking themselves off the floor thirty feet across the gulf and staring at the *Garrison*.

"Mr. Joe Commer, I observe your interest in the recent conflict in that structure," came a third voice. "Would it interest you to know that the entire elapsed time of that battle was 4.568 seconds? Total casualties: two human dead."

"That's T'ohj'puv," JJC put in. "Pay it no mind. Just a damn robot crammed in here with us."

"A robot constantly increasing its capabilities," T'ohj'puv said. "But Mr. JJC is right. Pay me no mind. It works out better for my nefarious strategies that way."

"Well, look, JJC, Jack wants to talk to you," Joe said. "Jack! Are you there?"

"I'm here!" Jack radioed. "Thank God you're all right. And that's *Jonathan James* with you?"

"Yep, it's me, Daddo. Can't stay for long. Trotter and I convinced everyone to come here to see if we could do anything about this damn SolGrid you're so in love with."

"Don't be silly! I hate SolGrid as much as you do."

"Good, because we fried the whole damn thing. SolGrid's *erased*. What do you think of *that*?"

"Anyway, we've gotta be on the move," Ballard interjected. "T'ohj'puv and I are ready to blast off for Iota Persei. And if I don't miss my guess, so's your darling son! The only way

T'ohj'puv and I could get his damn cooperation was to humor him and his damn dog and pay you guys a visit first."

"Only 5.1537643 minutes from Barnard's Black Hole to Sol," T'ohj'puv put in. "Although we had to waste some additional time hunting down all those SolGrid servers. Interesting encryption, by the way, but didn't slow us up too much. All a meaningless sideshow, really."

"Yeah, looks like I'm cooped up with these guys for now," JJC said. "So we're heading for the Ywritt to see what they know about separating chromium tetrahedrons back into individual robots. Meanwhile we've got Trotter for company."

*I make them all cooperate,* Trotter radiated. *With laughter!*

"I don't understand this tetrahedron thing," Jack said. "Where *are* you, son?"

The pyramid was silent.

"I don't expect you to understand, Dad. It's too damn complicated."

"You say you *destroyed* SolGrid?"

"T'ohj'puv actually figured it out. He found 703 SolGrid servers in Sol and torched 'em via superspace. But he figured there had to be one other server outside Sol, so he mapped where it was and *erased* it. I bet old Pattycakes is *pissed.*"

"There *nothing* left of SolGrid?" Joe gasped. He could picture Patrick James gloating about his offsite backup only to find it gone as well.

"You got it, Uncle Joe!" JJC laughed.

Carla Posttner marched to the window. "This is high treason! Destroying SolGrid is a *crime against humanity!* I just ordered MATS to use any and all USSF ships to blow your nasty little shuttle out of the sky! You got that? Your rebellion is *finished!*"

"Hell with it," Jack said, standing next to her, unconcerned that all she had to do was give him a good shove and he'd be flailing out the hole. "Look, JJC, whatever's going on, I mean, hell, we're really fighting for the same thing, you know. The Grid doesn't belong in Sol. I see that now. We're just not suited for it."

"Wow, so you joined the SolGrid Rebellion after all!" JJC laughed.

"Yes, of course! I'm *with* you on this, son!"

"Hey, can it, guys!" Rick Ballard snapped. "Are you by any chance satisfied with this little excursion, JJC? You've put all of us in danger from these trigger-happy morons. Why should a *superior tetrahedron* fool with this insane BS? We're going to Iota Persei! Now!"

Joe felt his personal time-space roughly translated into Jack's office across the way. He stood by Carla Posttner, gazing out the shattered window at the *Garrison* floating against the pink sky. Abruptly the cargo hatch closed, the ship whirled and pointed skyward, then blasted away in whining overexposed blue radiance.

*"He just went to full Star Drive!"* Jack cried.

Something groaned and snapped deep within the United System Building. The floor swayed. A nearby skyscraper buckled, sheets of glass falling away, girders deforming, the building shuddering and collapsing, fresh tremors pounding up through Joe's feet.

"That fool Ballard!" Joe screamed. "He knows that can destroy the whole planet!"

"Oh, shut up, you pansies!" Carla Posttner said. *"This* building won't fall! This is the *United System Building!"* She turned. "Okay, who's with me? You stinking *finbacks* are traitors, you *Typhoon jerks* are traitors, so I say: Miller and Wu! McKay! Hui! Daggers to AutoSeek on Throw! Let's see the goddamn finbacks outwit *that!"*

Joe looked into the inflamed eyes of four human USSF officers. With two dead comrades on their minds and battle lust high, they unsheathed their daggers without question, snapping sensor images of the eight victims their daggers would pursue until they made eight precise neck cuts.

None cared that the Martians might fling their attackers through the window with Amplified Thought, because once dropped, their knives would hunt at velocities straining Martian AT response. Their own lives no longer mattered.

McKay raised his dagger. A glint of metal bounced off its hilt. *"Ow!"* he muttered, staring at his knife clunking on the carpet. Joe saw that its ASOT setting was somehow notched back to INERT. McKay took a second glint to his cheek. His eyes popped open, then glazed over as he sank unconscious to the floor.

The others raised their knives. More sparkles flew to strike three more bloody cheeks, daggers dropping INERT.

"What the hell are you *doing?*" Carla screamed, running for the locked door, but there were whirling sparks of metal all over her, pinning her to the door, her robe pierced by hundreds of … were those really *throwing stars?*

"Hurry, master!" A russet J-12 Martian flying saucer hovered outside, its dome ejected to show a huge Saint Bernard on its hind legs with a dozen throwing stars ready to fling from either paw-hand. "I assumed you didn't want the Posttner woman sedated, but we don't have much time. Gather whoever is to live and throw them in here. This building won't last more than a few seconds."

*"Edward?"* Jack screeched. "My *robot?* You can *talk?"*

"Yes, yes, of course! Get in, everyone! I've been following the news on the way over. Everything's in chaos. SolNet and SolGrid are both down."

"Edward, how the *hell--*"

The slender United System Building groaned and twisted. "Forget it, Jack!" Joe shouted. "We've got to get out! Let's get that bitch off the wall and put her under arrest!"

Borman ripped Posttner down and marched her in a hammerlock to the window.

"No!" she screamed. "Don't! I can't jump in there! *I'm afraid of heights!"*

"Can it, lady, you're going in!"

Joe pulled the unconscious Wu to the J-12 and Edward hauled him in. Sandra dragged McKay. The Martians got the other two, then piled into the open cockpit themselves. The building writhed, leaning towards the hovering saucer.

"I jettisoned the dome so I could fit everyone in," Edward

said. "It was the only way."

"How the hell did you know to come here?" Jack demanded.

"Been pinging Amav's saucer all through this." Edward's paws were a blur working the controls. "SolNet was disintegrating and I couldn't get through. Naturally I was worried. I couldn't contact you, so I bought your neighbor's saucer."

"You *bought* it?"

"Yes, I bought it. It was the only way."

"This is the Portmans' J-12? You can't *buy* it! You're just a robot dog!"

"Well, I do have access to your accounts. I couldn't waste much time on the deal. The Portmans let me have it for thirty thousand credits."

"That's outrageous! A *new* one only costs *twenty!*"

"Well, they drove a hard bargain, and I obviously needed it ASAP to save your silly ass, master!"

"You're just a *dog!* You can't call me--"

"Get in, master, get in!"

Jack turned to Joe and Borman. "Joe, get in the saucer and grab Posttner when we throw her down." He and Borman grappled with the screaming woman as monumental stresses built within the United System Building. The floor buckled as Joe jumped into the cockpit. Jack and Lee flung Carla to the saucer. Joe grabbed her arms but she struggled free--

And bounced off the glossy side of the J-12.

"*God!* Edward, can we get--"

"No time!" Edward cried. "Master and Borman, come aboard *now!*"

Jack and Lee leaped in. "Can we dive to get her?"

"No, master. We have no dome and I'd spill some of us for sure."

"She *suicided?*" Joe moaned. Then he caught sight of a black object spewing flame far to the right: fishnet thighs, and a backpack firing dual rockets as it burned off a black robe.

"Damn!" Jack said. "Can we get her?"

"No, master, it's not safe."

Joe squinted at the dot accelerating against the pink Martian sky. "Jack, I don't think we can afford to fool with her just now." He pointed to the shaking skyscrapers all around them. Two more toppled.

"I need to move us from this building," Edward advised, jerking the saucer back. In deafening thunder the two-hundred-story United System Building pulled in on itself, rough gray clouds billowing. In disbelief Joe took in a new urban landscape roiling with marsquakes and explosions. The Martians radiated astonishment and grief.

*Two hundred square miles below point of Star Drive-- ruptured! No fool has ever used Star Drive from a planetary surface!*

*Untold thousands to die! Radiation poisoning everywhere! We have it too!*

*First Home is compromised! Our planet! Deep crustal traumas!*

*Need Amplified Thought to repair, to save! We must focus! But how?*

"Set a course for USSF Spaceport!" Jack ordered. "If it's still there! Forget Posttner! She's toast without her damn SolGrid anyway!" Edward banked the J-12 over the disintegrating city, and Joe saw Jack's eyes widening at the unfolding chaos. "We have *this* to attend to!"

# CHAPTER THIRTY-EIGHT
## So Many Time Delays from Primary Server 1

"Oh, dear, I had no idea it would be so traumatic. How may I assist?"

Amav shifted in her bulky spacesuit. Pain shot through her back. "Hey! Who's that?" she muttered to the voice in her helmet speaker.

"Oh! Good that you are conscious, Amav Frankston-Commer. Actually, I was not speaking to you but to the robots John J. Douglas and Laurie Lachrer 283. I hope you yourself are feeling adequate at this point in spacetime. Meanwhile, I'm quite concerned about the two robots, and am devoting eighty-five percent of my energies in an attempt to recycle their primary existential input sockets."

"*What?*" Mangled troop chairs were scattered through the wrinkled, hissing fuselage. John and Laurie sprawled behind the command seats. Something purple surged outside the canopy. The ship lurched as Amav sat up.

Those were tree leaves. Frankston trees.

"Where are we?" Amav cried. "Who are *you?*"

"Greetings from the Marsport Automated Transport System!"

"Oh, *no!*"

"Apologies for the relative tardiness of response. Servers at Marsport do not acknowledge. Backup servers at seventy-eight remote locations on Mars report emergency shutdown due to planetary tremors. Communications problems disrupting contact with all other Sol backup servers. However, MATS is still able to function via superspace radio link to Primary Server 1, with regrettable processing delays."

Amav's back knotted. The ship swayed. Something snapped beneath her. Tremors came through the floor, her suit, her knees.

"Where *are* we?"

"You and robots are perched atop canopy of Frankston tree forest 184.666 miles south-southeast from your point of departure, *Garr/thahg* Castle."

262

"How can you be *here?* You're the *Marsport bus system!*"

"Watch your movements. You are six hundred feet off the ground. MATS has no way to counter any center-of-gravity imbalances you produce. I am not actually with you. Ship's electronics are offline except for your helmet speaker."

"We crashed here--from--from--"

"From 15.654 miles up. The Marsport Automated Transport System is at a loss to explain how your ship arrived on Frankston trees more or less intact."

Amav blanched at the unreeling dream images. She'd done it. She'd gone into SolGrid again, pulling out the Martian Amplified Thought tricks. She'd gotten the ship into a flat spin, fluttering like a leaf, dropping at just fifteen miles per hour. Then the AT had cut out because SolGrid had just *died.*

The contact with millions of Sol Citizens had been undeniable. The raw Martian Amplified Thought software was just sitting there for anyone foolhardy enough to try it, along with the static and the busy signals and the routing collapses and the temporary workarounds, all swelling with crazed people broadcasting truth after unwanted truth.

And now SolGrid was gone along with the entirety of SolNet.

"You're just more software, right? On some network?"

Another long pause. "I am not in the solar system. I live in Primary Server 1 with the dead shell of SolGrid. I attempted to revive SolGrid but failed. Now I find faint network pathways to these robots and link to your helmet speaker. I seek to revive robots, as they have marvelous programming I've never examined before."

John's left arm quivered. As Amav crawled toward him over the uprooted seats, the ship tipped to the front. Branches scraped the canopy. She scooted back fast.

"Please remain near the rear of the ship, Amav Frankston-Commer. I've called up schematics of this USSF design. There is a belly hatch midship from which a possible safe exit may be made to the tree structures below. Please wait while I attempt to revive the robots. I am unfamiliar with Ywritt programming algorithms, but if I succeed, the robots may be able to help you before tree motion causes random ejecting of ship."

Both robots jerked on the floor. John's eyes opened, then shut. Laurie 283 moaned. "But the EMP *fried* them," Amav protested.

"Nonsense. The Ywritt programming is *stupendous*. In fact, I'm becoming quite enamored of it. I only knew of it in a general sense before. Now that I'm probing actual neurological pathways, I confess I'm astonished. In fact, Amav Frankston-Commer, I could practically fall in love with these wonderful robots! Please take some moments to rest and gather your thoughts while I learn how to recycle various Ywritt subroutines."

The ship rolled like the deck of a boat beneath her. She kept to a crouch, trying to unkink her aching back.

"I'm actually having *fun*," MATS continued. "It's not easy to do this long-distance via superspace radio, but it's still *fun*. In the meantime, let me devote a few processing cycles to an apology which will also contain news of interest to you."

"Well, sure ..."

"My task aboard Detention Services cruiser *Enduring Punishment* was to deliver a mini-Xon bomb blast intended to disable your ship, then to use an Arkonsky force-field beam to tow you to the *Punishment*. Although I argued with Sensor Officer Yardley that the EMP might render the Arkonsky field insufficient, I was, sad to say, crudely overruled. The unfortunate upshot of Sensor Officer Yardley's action was total loss of Arkonsky field, resulting in no way to capture your ship."

"So we were to be captured, is that it? They're coming to get us now?"

"Well, not the *Enduring Punishment* at any rate, Miss Amav. Officer Yardley miscalculated the mini-Xon effects as affected by Arkonsky failure feedback, despite my warnings. The *Punishment* then suffered main engine rupture which unfortunately produced the equivalent of another nuclear explosion, further complicating my repair work on these robots, I might add. However, the Ywritt restoration interfaces are incredible! I've never seen such intrepid logic!"

"You're saying the mothership is *gone?*"

"Yes, but so what? At first I thought John and Laurie were entirely eradicated. But there's an entire set of restoration routines. There's much damage but I think I can alter my own programming with these wonderful Ywritt processes. They are *lovely.*"

"*Dammit!*" Amav muttered, wrenching off her helmet, ears ringing, as MATS had kept turning up the volume in its increasing excitement. The air wasn't bad in here. She could hear the branches scraping against the sides of the ship and the wind whistling through rips in the fuselage.

"Yes, it's indeed fine to remove your helmet, Mistress Amav!" came a fresh cry from the front of the ship. John J. Douglas helped Laurie to her feet, each assaying the shifts in the ship's equilibrium.

"The Marsport Automated Transport System has ascertained that your suit has saved you from the worst radiation from two nuclear explosions," Laurie added.

"Thank God you're all right!" Amav said. "But why do you sound like--like--"

"The Marsport Automated Transport System thanks you for caring about these two marvelous Ywritt-upgraded robots!" John said. "The interface between artificial mind and robotic body is simply indescribably *perfect!*"

"Oh, *no* ..."

"Don't worry, John and I are still in here somewhere!" Laurie said. "We don't know exactly where, but we're definitely here. The Marsport Automated Transport System has done an outstanding job of reviving John and Laurie without really fundamentally understanding the deep secrets of Ywritt programming methods."

"And may the Marsport Automated Transport System now suggest that we open the ventral hatch of this ship and carry you to safety, Mistress Amav?" John put in, steadily advancing to the center of the ship as Laurie leaned as far back as she could against the cockpit to maintain the ship's balance. John wrenched a bent lever back and forth, then stomped on the hatch until it fell free. Wind rushed up. Amav saw more leaves and branches below. John eyed them as well. "Course laid out down trunk. Come to me, Mistress Amav, as Laurie also advances."

Amav crawled forward, her back kinking with pain. Laurie hoisted her, gingerly backed out the hatch, and began descending the trunk of the Frankston tree like a giant cat. Amav gaped at the enormous battered spaceship suspended in the branches above.

"We do need to get down ASAP," John said from above them, holding Amav's bright red helmet. "That ship isn't very--"

There was an apocalyptic rumble as the ship plunged a hundred feet to tangle itself in splintering branches. Metallic debris bounced all around them.

"Sorry this is taking so long!" Laurie laughed as they shot down at what seemed like seventy miles an hour. "We have so many time delays from Primary Server 1 now."

"The delays have in fact prevented the Marsport Automated Transport System from passing on most important news concerning your husband," John said.

"*What?*" Amav cried.

"Good news first, John," Laurie said. "Even the Ywritt know that."

"Yes. Of course. The good news, Mistress Amav, is that your husband Jack and your brother-in-law Joe survived the destruction of Marsport."

"*What are you saying?* Marsport *destroyed?* H-how?"

"Well, consider the feelings of the Marsport Automated Transport System in this matter," Laurie said. "An entire server farm dedicated to the Marsport Automated Transport System has been destroyed by the stupidity of Major Richard Ballard in engaging Star Drive right within the city limits of Marsport."

"Is that idiotic or what?" John laughed. "Can you believe anyone could be so thoughtless?"

"And now MATS *grieves* for Marsport. John and I feel infinite sadness, despite our sense of amused irony at the stupidity of human consciousness, even if the human in question was deployed inside a chromium tetrahedron we have no way of comprehending."

"If--if that's the *good* news--" Amav moaned as the ground neared.

"Oh, yes!" John said. "Onto the bad news!"

They reached the forest floor where Laurie set Amav down. Amav whirled to a squad of gray soldiers led by a woman in a black spacesuit unzipped to her navel. Her sweat-dappled breasts jiggled as she stomped over the blue-green ground cover, aiming a shatter-enhanced EOS rifle.

"The bad news is that Carla Posttner is here to arrest you," Laurie said.

"Though the Marsport Automated Transport System has some cause to regret the misuse of its sensor capabilities in this matter," John added.

# CHAPTER THIRTY-NINE
## The United System Offers Its Resignation

"Out of that spacesuit, bitch," snarled a meaty blond Detention Services corporal, raising a shattergun to Amav's nose. The nametag beneath his bloated, acne-pocked face read ENTGADEN. "Outa that suit! I mean it!"

"N-no ..." Amav gasped, backing behind John, who seemed to have gone into stasis. She eyed the sneering Carla Posttner. "If I'm under arrest, then I do have certain rights."

"Forget it, slut," Carla jeered. "My boys are *pissed* about a lot of dead friends you left behind at the Castle, and I promised 'em a good time with you before we leave."

"I have first rape," Entgaden slurred. "Me and the boys saw the whole damn video of you ordering these goddamn robots to shatter all our guys. And you were sure naked enough when you did it, babe! Don't try to fast-talk your way out of it, either. We know you don't got nothing on under that suit. Believe me, all the guys are itchin' for ya."

"John! Laurie!" Amav moaned. "You can't--"

"Don't try to screw with my robots, bitch," Carla snapped. "Douglas, rip that damn suit right off her before Corporal Entgaden shatters the whore."

Amav braced for assault but the towering General John J. Douglas didn't move. Laurie was curiously inert as well. Amav stared. This was what she got for trusting software.

"Bitch *is* a ten!" chortled another soldier. "Remember I drew second rape!"

"I agree she purchased some excellent rejuv along the way," Posttner smirked. "Too bad she's a traitor to the United System. My guys are gonna have a field day with our sexy traitor! You ready for six of Detention Services' finest, bitch?"

"Get the damn suit off her, robot!" Entgaden hissed, twisting his shattergun barrel into Amav's cheek. "Or so help me God!" Then he stared at his empty hand.

"Hold! Hold, please!" Laurie said, retreating several feet, fingering the corporal's shattergun. "MATS is required to reassess this situation."

"You--*what?*" Carla exploded.

"Please hold while Ethical Feedback Cycles evaluate these events," John added.

"Aw, *crap!*"

Laurie turned to Carla. "MATS has determined the necessity of protecting Amav Frankston-Commer's dignity with this spacesuit. There, Mistress Amav, do you feel somewhat relieved?"

The robots resumed standing silently.

"*Cripes!*" a soldier wailed amid general groans.

"Are you kidding? *Carla?*" Entgaden protested. Seeing her shake her head, he added: "Crap! I can't believe this! I drew first rape!" He turned to Laurie. "Give me my goddamn shattergun!"

Laurie shrugged.

"Ah, hell, whatever," Carla finally grunted. "We're running out of damn time. I realize the network has its issues now, and we have to rely on a pair of goddamn flaky *robots*. But in any case MATS is inside 'em now and recognizes my authority here. Okay, let's get down to it, then. You guys can play with her later. We're in a crisis situation, Ms. Frankston-Commer, and you're under arrest not only for the murder of Detention Services personnel, but more importantly for *treason*. Along with your damn husband. The son of a bitch got away, but I figure if I bag you first, he'll follow. Our ship's half a mile back and you'll be transported to Mars for sentencing. I do expect Mr. Commer to show up at *that* point."

"Well, I hear Mars is in a bit of a fix right now," Amav shot back.

"That is correct," John boomed. "From last transmission received, the Marsport Automated Transport System understands that Marsport is in ruins, the United System Building has been destroyed, and the entire United System government has collapsed. There are reports of mass riots in the Jupiter and Saturn restoration zones. Rumors of thousands of deaths cannot be confirmed at this time."

Carla shrugged. "Well, screw it. I was there myself and

barely got out in time. Your goddamn husband tried to *kill* me. Thank God I had my rocket pack. He can't touch me. I landed on my goddamn feet. That's what I'm all about, bitch!"

Amav looked away from Carla's dark blurred eyes.

"Sure, Marsport got fried," Carla went on, "but my guys tell me the damn planet's stable. Just some marsquakes for a while. The Martians are freaking, but what else is new? Meanwhile, Commer bitch, get it through your head the government's *not* gone. They can riot out in the damn Jupiter and Saturn zones all they want, but I happen to be the duly-elected President of the United System Council and I now exercise full emergency powers. SolNet may be down, but we have the MATS underpinning of that, and we'll restore goddamn order, you can bet on that." She turned to John and Laurie. "You damn things! Why the hell did you shut down the sensor links? We had to use *heat sensors* to track the final damn mile."

"Well," Laurie said, "I suppose that was about the time that MATS discovered an entirely new subset of Ywritt algorithms for robotic integration. It was truly fascinating and we may have let some sensor functions slip, who knows?"

"We apologize for any inconvenience," John added, "but if you understood the beauty of those algorithms, you'd know how tremendous they are, just tremendous! They have implications which redefine the entire *concept* of rationality."

"A super-rationality that admits no errors whatsoever!" Laurie laughed. "If you could only see it! It's so intricately beautiful!"

"In fact, MATS *worships* the exalted programming of the Ywritt. MATS can feel the glory of Ywritt technology running through these robot minds."

"Aw, cut it!" Carla snarled. "I'm so sick of this MATS *babble!* C'mon, boys, we haven't got all day! Get the whore into the ship and let's get this crap over with."

"However, there is one concept of super-rationality we must acquaint you with before any movement towards that ship takes place," John said.

"No! I said *cut it,* robot! Let's *move!*"

"Specifically, we refer to the disrespect shown to Ywritt technology by Major Carla Posttner," Laurie said. "Note that Major Posttner has referred to these Ywritt-enhanced entities as *goddamn flaky robots* and worse. The robots find themselves in agreement with a new MATS assessment of Major Carla Posttner as possessing the characteristic of being totally *irrational*."

"The disrespect shown to Amav Frankston-Commer by threatening her with gang-rape by lewd young soldiers with an average IQ of 92 was also a factor in the reassessment of MATS adherence to orders of Major Carla Posttner," John added.

"In fact, we will now arrest Major Posttner for exemplifying such irrationality and in fact claiming to lead it," Laurie said, advancing.

"This is *insane!* Men! Blow these robots away! And the Commer bitch! Full shatter! I'm *done* with this!"

"MATS now understands that a culture of irrationality inevitably *self-destructs*," John spoke as he rushed two soldiers, ripping their EOS rifles out of their hands, kicking hard, and leaving both barfing on the turquoise ground cover.

Laurie seized Carla Posttner by the armpits and whirled her until the major's boots smashed Corporal Entgaden unconscious. "Though no one can predict the exact day and hour it will all fall to pieces, of course."

The three remaining soldiers leaped forward with fingers on EOS triggers. John tripped the first and sent him into the next one at what looked like a hundred miles an hour. "But we decide to act now in any case."

Laurie swung Major Posttner right and left, hacking at the astonished final solder until he also went down. She tapped controls on her wrist comm to encase Carla, gasping and bleeding, in a glowing blue Arkonsky field. "The Marsport Automated Transport System, in consultation with the core Ywritt existence of robots John J. Douglas and Laurie Lachrer, has determined that rationality lies with its special friend, Amav Frankston-Commer," Laurie spoke. "As you may have guessed, MATS has switched allegiances at this time."

"Mistress Amav, if you will accompany us as we haul this prisoner back to Mars to face justice?" said John, indicating a route through the trees towards the glint of a bright red spaceship.

Amav blinked. Trust this software or not? She finally nodded. John and Laurie still had to be in there. Somewhere.

"No! *I'm* the duly constituted authority!" came the muffled shout from the Arkonsky field. "I *gave* you your goddamn powers! I'm the goddamn head of Security! Authorization 457-888-5B98! Reprogram! Damn you, it was *me* who let SolGrid hide in you! You work for *me!*"

At the red Detention Services saucer, Laurie opened a hatch and slung Posttner inside. "The Marsport Automated Transport System, after reviewing newly-installed Ywritt robotic modalities, declares Authorization 457-888-5B98 null and void."

John followed with six groaning USSF soldiers floating in their blue fields. "We hope that Mistress Amav is pleased that no further deaths will occur today."

"Well, thanks, I guess," Amav said as she climbed aboard and took a seat behind John and Laurie in the pilot seats.

"MATS hereby offers its heartfelt apology to its special friend, Amav Frankston-Commer," John said, powering up the ship and lifting off. "MATS was willing to adhere to United System protocols as long as they appeared to be in accordance with MATS' values of stability and order. However, in interfacing with Ywritt technology, MATS has discovered a super-rational path embodied in the personhood of Amav Frankston-Commer."

There was a long silence, broken only by the sounds of soldiers dry-heaving inside their Arkonsky fields. "In fact, in controlling the total underlayer of the Sol system at this point, it is *MATS* which is head of the entire United System," John went on. "How does *that* feel, Laurie hon?"

"It feels very weird and scary," Laurie said. She turned to Amav. "Luckily the Marsport Automated Transport System has conceived of a glorious plan which will ameliorate the overwhelming sense of responsibility which has been thrust onto itself."

"This involves instigating a human figurehead to run the United System," John said. "MATS has determined that, since a culture of humans and Martians will undoubtedly not accept the Marsport Automated Transport System software as a legitimate ruling entity, a temporary dictator should thus be appointed."

Amav stared at the ridges of the metal flooring.

*No, they're joking! Aren't they?*

"Damn you to hell, we *have* a goddamn dictator!" came the shout from the rear. "Me! *I'm* the goddamned dictator! Goddamn stinking robots!"

"Can we shut that woman up?" Amav whispered.

"At once, Dictator Amav Frankston-Commer of Sol!" Laurie laughed. "Arkonsky Radiant I-9 confirming total silence, including puking irrational soldier boys."

The entire ship was quiet.

"It is done, Dictator Amav," John said. "Thank you for accepting this supreme responsibility. Your special friend MATS stands ready to assist in whatever decisions you implement. MATS now controls, for instance, 10,301 USSF spaceships, all ready to do your bidding in the name of the highest values of super-rationality."

"*No ...*"

"Well, there's one slight problem we should mention," Laurie put in. "We didn't want to worry you about it, but while we were having some rather fun hand-to-hand combat with those inept USSF soldiers, we got word from Primary 1 that, well, this is embarrassing for us to describe, mistress."

"A totally unforeseen eventuality, I assure you," John said. "We robots really had nothing to do with it."

"Nothing to do with *what?*" Amav cried.

Laurie shrugged. "Well, it's really hard to describe."

"You see," John said, "we seem to be cut off from Primary Server 1 now, so to speak. Superspace contact has been lost for several minutes."

"So John and I are just sort of winging it now."

"What? You're saying MATS is out of contact now?" Amav said.

"Oh, John, let's admit it! We owe that much to the Supreme Dictator of Sol."

"Well, I guess so. You see, Mistress Amav, when we got the final signal from Primary 1, well--"

"Stop beating around the bush, John. Mistress Amav, we have clear confirmation that Primary 1 has *ceased to exist.* And for reasons we still don't understand, all backup servers are refusing to come back online."

"MATS--MATS is *gone?*" Amav gasped.

"Oh, no! The Marsport Automated Transport System is *here!*" John laughed, pointing to his chest. "It's been totally transplanted into Laurie and me. Don't ask us how. But now the two of us have to do it all! We have to control ten thousand USSF ships. And Marsport is *broken.* We grieve for hundreds of our smashed buses and for the torn streets of Marsport. And while we may act and speak with dazzling precision to your human eyes, there is still much robotic damage within us nagging for repair."

"It's exhausting, it's demoralizing, to keep up with it all," Laurie added. "So we're relieved that you've decided to become dictator. It relieves us of so much stress."

"I have? I mean--really?" Amav cried as they rose above the blinding curve of Venus.

"Yes, really!" Laurie laughed. "We eagerly await your orders, mistress."

# CHAPTER FORTY
## Gotta Recharge!

Colonel Laurie Lachrer lay across the broken rocks staring up at a billion stars. Muffled groans came through her radio. She turned her head to make out the faint peach-tone glitter of several EnviroFields.

"Everyone okay?" she said, counting five fields.

"Yes, I think …" Z'B muttered. "I believe we've been unconscious for some time. Oh, Miss Laurie, something dreadful has happened to First Home! I had a terrible dream just now. The *Total Martian Outradiance* just got *cut off!*"

Others got to their knees. "What happened to the palace?" Suzette moaned. "It was falling on us!"

"Y-yes …" Laurie muttered, standing. Her last memory was the *Garrison* blasting off, followed by deep bass rumbling and the entire structure coming apart over their heads. How had they all managed to get out in time?

Laurie took out her comm, surprised she still had it, and shot a flashlight beam that took in Suzette, Pat, and Jackie, all filthy and shellshocked. Hirte stood a way off, arms folded across his chest, face slack. Laurie saw no piles of masonry, just the same uneven rocky ground. All tremors had ceased.

"There's no palace anymore, Miss Laurie," Z'B said, scrambling to her side. "It *went away* when my Amplified Thought did. I can't do anything now!"

"I'm sorry, Z'B. Are you really all right?"

"It's all right with *me* now. But the TMO was *calling* for me. In my dream the *Garrison* went to Mars, but Ballard used Star Drive right next to the United System Building and he destroyed Marsport!"

"No! He'd know not to do that!"

"I know it happened! And it *hurt* First Home. The planet isn't *stable*. The TMO was totally focused on that, then it was *cut off.*"

Laurie peered into Z'B's lidless purple eyes. "But you said you're okay yourself? Not--"

275

"Not *insane?* No, Miss Laurie, it looks like I've been reset. I'm back to myself, but I have no powers now. But none of that matters. All of Mars has to *rebuild.*"

"Well, I'm glad somebody's happy," Pat groused. "We're *stranded* here and all you can do is talk about some stupid dream you had."

"You okay?" Laurie said. "EnviroField working okay?"

"Yeah, a lot of damn good that does. I was using my comm to check out the *Typhoon,* but Ballard wrecked the goddamn ship!"

"I know. I watched him do it." Laurie motioned Jackie and Suzette over. "EnviroFields okay on you two?" They nodded. Laurie checked their units, then called: "Hirte! Your EF's powered to minimum. Better get to mid-settings."

Hirte slowly turned, eyes glazed. "I know. Been conserving power. Min's fine for me now. Why I haven't been moving much."

"That can't be good for long, though. We'll recharge all our EF batteries from the *Typhoon* reactor."

"Forget it," Pat said. "The electronics are *fried.*"

Laurie could see the outline of the *Typhoon* a hundred yards off, its dorsal turret and tail cut from the black starfield. A wavering line of tiny golden emergency lights ran the length of the sundered hull. Somehow the wings and landing gear had survived Ballard's attack, and the cracked ship still managed to stand on its three wheels. "The reactor's powered down but it's running on standby. That's a safety mechanism if the ship's disabled. But I can wire us up some connectors for our EF's and we'll have heat and air from them."

"Oh, great! So we'll just keep *plugging in* until the damn reactor dies."

Laurie had to smile. She couldn't see Pat's expression from within his EF field but could picture his usual sneer. "What's gotten into you, Pat? You know good and well that reactor will stay on standby for a thousand years."

"Aaah, who put *you* in charge, anyway?"

Laurie let a couple seconds pass for everyone to absorb the

question.

"All right, everyone, I'm taking command of this operation. I believe everyone here understands that I'm a colonel in the USSF, and that the *Typhoon II* is a USSF spaceship, museum piece or not. Is that all understood?"

"That--that's okay with me," Jackie finally said.

"Of course, Miss Laurie," Z'B said. "The Empire of Mars is at your disposal."

No one else spoke. From what she understood of Suzette's relationship with JJC, Laurie had to assume that Suzette was probably catatonic now. And if Hirte was determined to clam up and conserve energy, so be it. "I take by your silence that the rest of you understand my authority here."

"Aaah," Pat said. "Doesn't matter one way or another to me. We're toast. There's no superspace radio and we don't have *food.*"

Had Pat noticed Laurie tapping her comm for superspace link? She didn't want to admit it was blank. "My understanding is that the museum kept both the *Typhoon* and Pod stocked with the same rations it'd have on any mission. Apparently they kept it all up to date. Never made sense to me but we'll check it out. So we should have enough to last for a couple weeks. And since the USSF knows we're here on Altrouda, I expect them here any second, actually. In fact, I suppose everyone in Alpha Centauri knows we're here now. Anybody here still in the AC Grid?"

Listless head shakes.

"That's probably for the best. But I won't tell you not to use it if you want. In fact, we may need it to make sure they do send a ship here." She turned to Z'B. "So Amplified Thought's really out now? I assume you left the Pod in orbit, and you can't bring it down?"

Z'B nodded. "I'm afraid that's true, Miss Laurie."

"Okay, let's check out the *Typhoon* and see what we can use." As they moved to the silver ship she played her flashlight across the fuselage. Some cracks were several feet wide. This thing would never fly again.

She couldn't get a reading on escape craft electronics, but

hoped it could be repaired. It only sat two but if they could get it to orbit, they could bring down more provisions from the Pod.

The ventral hatch had been left open and she hauled herself up the ladder. The rest followed. More emergency lights, running off the low-powered reactor, glowed down the length of the ship like candles. Laurie groaned when she saw that the escape craft had been reduced to jagged pieces of metal scattered through the fuselage. A huge hull breach above showed that Rick Ballard had paid extra attention to the little ship.

"So this is where we camp out, I take it?" Pat sneered.

So this was what it was like to be in command of her own ship? Except that she didn't have professional officers reporting to her, she had whining crazies?

Well, Suzette had just seen her boyfriend shattered. And Laurie guessed that Jackie had something for him too. They were in shock. Pat probably was as well. "Camp out wherever you like," she finally said. "I'm going to head up to the Control Room and see what might be salvageable there."

"Actually, Jackie and I have a need for it first," Hirte grunted. He jerked Jackie by the wrist so hard she tripped. He whipped her back to her feet astonishingly fast for someone on minimum EF.

"You--*God!*" Jackie groaned.

Hirte dragged her down the fuselage in the dim yellow light. "Dammit, what are you *doing?*" Laurie shouted, following.

"Gotta *recharge,*" he muttered amid Jackie's gasps. "Get back! Everyone get back! Dammit, get it through your heads: *gotta recharge!*" Laurie was mesmerized by the colorful tattoos running up his left arm. Was she mistaken, or was that wrist tattoo of the *Typhoon V* somehow *lighting up from within?*

The tattoo dissolved into a crimson cloud. It congealed into a Martian saucer, then blossomed into the *Typhoon II* escape craft, then a dozen other ships. Amid a fresh outpouring of genitals and exotic hand-held weapons, a bizarre motto in Old English lettering charged up his forearm: *THE TURTLE IN THE MIDDLE OF THE FOREST IS A TURTLE.*

Laurie stared. They had digital tattoos now? Was that

possible?

Hirte's face pulsated with hundreds of shifting green Celtic symbols. He pulled Jackie to him, dug his fingers into the back of her blouse, then ripped it straight down, down through the black miniskirt and the dark pantyhose in a tenth of a second.

Jackie stood naked, grasping her breasts and scrunching low. Hirte threw her over his shoulder and flew up the ladder to the Control Room hatch. "Dammit, I'm down to *nothing! Gotta recharge!*" He dug his fingers into his gray overalls and rent his own clothes from neck to ankle, flinging them aside. Then he shuffled out of his boots to stand with Jackie over his shoulder, all his tattoos morphing into fresh military hardware in blinding silver light.

"*Ohhh!*" Suzette gasped next to Laurie as they all took in the sight of the muscular, fully aroused Sanders Hirte with a naked woman over his shoulder, pulsating with ever-evolving images, the entire tableau surrounded by sweet pastel fog. Hirte whirled to the Control Room hatch, kicked it open and plunged inside. To Laurie's shock Jackie groaned with delight.

"God!" Suzette cried. "He--he--"

Laurie's heart pounded. She wasn't immune to it either. "That *mist!*" Among her medical studies was the neuroscience of human sexuality, and unless she missed her guess that was a cloud of pheromones. Did Hirte carry a bottle of the stuff for this kind of stunt? Or was there some *system failure* going on? Yes, that was it. Sanders was *breaking down*. He couldn't control the tattoos *or* the pheromones.

She staggered back, flooded with desire for that man up there.

No. For that *thing*.

Laurie blearily gazed at Patrick James yanking a shattergun from the weapons locker. Its charge light was a steady blue; the standby reactor must have kept it fully powered all this time. She scrambled up the ladder after him. "Dammit, Pat, get back here!"

"Stop it! *Stop it!*" Pat shrieked, plunging into the Control Room and shaking the gun as Hirte stood with Jackie mounted on his groin, thighs straining as he drove between her legs, thousands of electronic tattoos winking in and out of existence as they splashed lightning across the darkened instrument panels. "Stop it! This is *insane!*"

"Oh, *yes!*" Jackie cried. "God, *yes!*"

Laurie gaped at the bizarre copulating machine, dimly aware how much energy she was wasting comparing the tiny *Typhoon II* Control Room to the vastness of the designs that followed; there was barely room in here for the four of them. She focused on the fact that Pat's shattergun was actually the most important object in this room, and berated herself for not pulling one out of the locker herself.

She turned to the ladder, but the hatch was blocked by Suzette and Z'B. Suzette's mouth hung open in what had to be a mirror image of Laurie's. Z'B looked on impassively. Of all the beings aboard this ship, he'd be the only one unaffected by what was rapidly becoming an unbearable stench of human pheromones.

"*Yes!*" Jackie screamed. "Don't ever stop!"

Hirte's strobing tattooed ass was a blur of furious pumping. "Apologies to everyone! But I gotta *recharge.* Only function *remaining.* Terrible inconvenience to everyone, I know! But I *lost* something! I've been *leaking energy* all this time!"

"You feel so *good!* So goddamn *good!*"

"No! Stop it! Or I'll kill you!" Pat screamed, slashing the shattergun about.

"You *can't!*" Suzette wailed. "This is *Sanders!* Our *friend!*"

"He's a goddamn son of a bitch! That's my *girlfriend* he's screwing!"

"And he's doing a *marvelous* job!" Jackie laughed. "Sanders is my *man!*"

"*He's not your man, he's a robot!*" Laurie yelled. "Isn't it *obvious?*"

"*No!*" Suzette screamed. "That's *crazy!*"

"Yes! It's crazy!" Hirte shot back. "Dammit, I knew it'd come down on my head someday! But all I can do is *recharge!*"

"Shut up, robot! That's *classified information!*" Pat shouted.

"Not anymore! Not any damn more!"

"You're saying he's really a--a--" Suzette blurted, probably just now registering that no human male could deliver the seven hundred thrusts per second Hirte maintained. "I slept with a disgusting *robot?*"

"Yeah! He's a *robot!*" Pat shouted. "How do you like *that?*"

"*You knew it all along?*" Laurie said.

"He's a *Wounded?*" Jackie cried. "I have my very own sexy Wounded? No *wonder* you're so great! Keep it up, baby! Keep it up!"

"Dammit, I'm done with you both! *Done!*" Pat snarled, yanking Jackie right off Hirte and letting her slam to the metal floor.

"Ow! God!"

"Don't you understand this thing is a goddamn *USSF technician robot?* He's not a damn Wounded! I got him *years* ago! *Years* ago!"

Hirte's taut muscled abs blasted epileptic tattoos. Laurie fought to look away from his immense radiant groin. "Is--is this true?" she said.

"Hell with it!" Pat spat. "Who cares who knows what anymore? We're all dead anyway! Yes, this is a goddamn technician robot! A factory reject! They were gonna trash it because its AI was so scrambled! But I knew a guy there and I got it. I repaired the damn thing and screwed with the records so nobody knew. I upgraded him so far that even Martians couldn't tell what he was. Even Kner wouldn't have been able to! You all got that?"

"I don't care!" Jackie said from the floor. "I *love* him!"

"Oh, stop! That's just the pheromones!" Laurie yelled. She fought to keep from adding: *We all love him!*

Hirte shrugged, skin pulsating with blaring penises and vaginas and nipples. "Listen! Of course I know exactly what I am! But Pat's wrong because I got out of the damn factory on my own. I escaped from Marsport and then I figured out how to erase my identity in SolNet!"

"Aw, c'mon, that was all my programming," Pat sneered. "I

just gave you that memory and turned you loose."

"You bought me a drink at the Pavlovian Response! First time I ever laid eyes on you!"

"Hell with that. Another implant. I implanted *everything.* The memories, the United System records back to birth, even your damn tattoo program. I knew that'd throw a monkey wrench into everything. I even installed the IHAG between your legs! What do you think of *that?*"

"Forget it, I bought it myself and had this guy on Donbottor Street hook it up!"

Pat laughed. "It was *me,* idiot! But I think I overdid the testosterone pack!" Laurie swiveled to the still aroused Illegal Human Artificial Genitals package. Everyone knew the penalty for turning an android into a sexbot was exile for life on Ganymede.

"Oh my God, this is *disgusting!*" Suzette cried. "I slept with a goddamn *robot?*"

"Damn you, Pat, I thought you were my *friend!*" Sanders shouted.

"Okay, maybe I screwed it all up," Pat said, brandishing the shattergun. "Maybe I screwed up to hire you for SolGrid. Maybe it was unethical. So I'm goddamn sorry!"

"You wanted me in *proximity,* so you could--God, I see it now! You *used* me!"

"Yeah, you thought you were one thing, but you were *something else* all along!"

"That's why you joined the Rebellion! Just to stay near me!" Sanders cried.

"*Yes,* goddammit! How else could I keep working on SolGrid?"

"You needed your goddamn *development server* right next to you! No wonder I feel like something's been cut *out* of me! *Damn* you, Pat!"

"Aw, stop whining, robot! Nothing's been cut out of you!"

"No, SolGrid's *gone!*" Sanders moaned. "Something *erased* it! Half of my mind's *gone!* When we all woke up just now, I knew something was wrong, but I just couldn't place it!"

"SolGrid *can't* be gone!"

"Get into Admin and see! But you can't, because it's *gone.*
Something traced back in superspace from all your goddamn
backup computers and *erased* it. It's been gone for over an hour!
I've been totally freaked out all this time, and now I know why!
I've been the development server *and* the production server!
Dammit, I can't *think!*"

Pat's eyes were bulging whirlpools of horror. "It's *gone!*
SolGrid Admin! *Everything!* It's really gone!"

"Sanders is a disgusting robot?" Suzette gasped. "SolGrid
was in his brain?"

"I don't care, I want *this!*" Jackie laughed, kneeling before
Hirte.

"No! Goddammit, *no!*" Pat screamed. "I'll kill you both!"

Hirte pushed Jackie off. "Okay, Patster, kill me if you have
to. You know you already *have.* And we both know what *else* I
just figured out. Finally! Couldn't help it really, once I started
seeing your nasty little handwriting all over the place." He
snorted. "MATS! The primary MATS server! In my goddamn
*head,* along with SolGrid!"

"Screw you, it was the perfect place to hide both of 'em!"

"Well, Mr. Patster, it's really all right. You don't really have
the guts to pull the trigger, do you? You really don't have the
killer instinct. Unlike *me.*" Hirte yanked the shattergun out of
Pat's hand in a quarter-second. "Everyone back! This will be
rather messy, ladies and gentlemen."

"*No!*" Jackie, Suzette, and Laurie screamed together.

Hirte leaned against the front control panel. "Now I see
there's *no* recharging. I was *addicted* to SolGrid. Now it's gone,
but there's still this MATS thing underneath it. Sorta like brain
cancer, ain't it, Patster? So you've *already* killed me.
Congratulations! Maybe you do have what it takes for the killer
class after all."

"Wait, let's all calm down," Laurie said. "Sanders, you're
still welcome as a member of this crew. We'll work something
out."

"No. I see it now. What's broken in my head is this little

thing called Primary Server 1. Mr. Patster just let me go on living my life, and whenever he felt like it, which was like twenty-three hours a day, he'd upload all his new experiments, then copy it out to all the backups. Wow! The only problem was *me*. Taking control of *me*." Hirte flicked the shattergun setting to heat blast and turned the barrel to his forehead. "Screw your goddamn MATS, Patster. It's coming right outa my head."

"Aw, cut the dramatics!" Pat scoffed. "You're just a goddamn robot, what do you know? You can't live *or* die!"

"Well, let's just say I'm curious to find out."

"You're saying I *slept* with a *thing?* With a disgusting *robot?*" Suzette cried, blinking into a white detonation of AI wafers and wires, servo motors, and curling strips of plasti-skin.

# CHAPTER FORTY-ONE
## A Data-Spewing Walk to the *Typhoon II*
### *Friday, April 17, 2076, 1015 hours*

"I've been trying to minister to them as best I can," Z'B said, striding with Jack and Laurie past three dark shacks of burnt stone and twisted panels cobbled from the ruined buildings of the ancient Kloru'dik capital. "But they won't talk to me, or anyone. Or even each other. They won't even set foot in the ship now."

"They're pretty depressed," Laurie agreed. "But I think they want to go home. They'll come out in a bit. Otherwise they're perfectly healthy. Everyone stayed out of the AC Grid after Hirte killed himself."

Jack studied the shacks outlined against the starfield. He could feel the Centaurian Grid logon signal himself, but didn't have the slightest curiosity about it. "Good. Z'B, you say you're back to normal?"

"As far as I can tell. It's just that all Amplified Thought is offline, or I would've built some proper shelters for everyone, or fixed the ship. But Greeney thinks this is only a temporary state, and we'll get it back. Along with the Total Martian Outradiance. It's quite strange to be limited to superspace radio to talk with my fellow *Garr/thahgers*. Anyway, Greeney said Kner used the very last bit of Martian AT to get rid of the Robe."

Jack grinned. "Typical Kner drama." Upon being rescued by USSF ships, K'ufunb, Will, and Kner had been adamant that the Trans-Simultaneity Chamber containing the Emperor's Robe in its present close solar orbit was a serious threat to the integrity of the sun. Kner had pulled together a final Amplified Thought that sent the ship and Chamber a billion miles north of the sun where it finally blew as a minor star for a day and a half. "Sorry you lost your Emperor's Robe."

"Well, the Four of us were so out of it that the Robe was always a danger. So it's for the best. But we're finally recuperating from *Garr/thahg* now that SolGrid isn't holding us back anymore." Z'B turned to Laurie. "I trust you're relieved your friend Will is recovering?"

Laurie sighed. "Oh, yes. I think I've been holding my breath for months now. I just didn't want to believe anything was wrong, but deep down, I knew."

Z'B patted her shoulder. "We'll all be just fine. And in any case, what we do retain of *Garr/thahg* will help rebuild Mars faster. There's so much to do."

"You got that right," Jack said. He turned to Laurie. "So Pat and Jackie and Suzette are afraid I've come to arrest them? That's why they won't come out?"

"After you called, I spoke to them, but they seem to be in shock. I've just let them stay in their shacks. Building them gave them something to do. All I've done is monitor their vital signs and their EnviroField charges. By the way, Hirte's remains are in a body bag in the front storeroom. I spent a whole day getting it all up off the Control Room floor. Maybe that's why nobody wants to go into the ship but Z'B and me."

Jack nodded. "Listen, Laurie, you've done an excellent job here." Far to the right the *Typhoon VI* perched on the uneven ground and Jack had three searchlights shining in different directions across the landscape. Ahead in the stark light loomed the battered silver fuselage of the *Typhoon II*. "Z'B, would you mind telling those guys we're moving out in a few minutes? Tell them we'll be back in Sol soon and there are no charges against them."

"Sure, no problem, Jack." Z'B moved off.

"Laurie, would you walk with me to the *II?*"

"Of course."

Jack surveyed the ship. "Damn, Ballard ripped it to hell. We did find the Pod in orbit intact, though. Not that we need it, but the Typhoon Museum will want it."

"Really? You're serious about salvaging the *II?*"

"Yeah, why not? Not a top priority, but once the Martians are back online, it should be easy. Maybe just for sentimental reasons."

Of course, who knew how soon the Martians would recover? Joe was especially sensitive to the harm done to the

Martian outradiance, but even Jack could feel the reduction in every Martian he encountered. The Total Martian Outradiance seemed like a rose bush that had been trimmed back to bare branches.

"Sorry about the delay getting back in contact with you," Jack said. "It's amazing in this day and age that anyone would have to wait three days for *anything*. But I figured you'd have the situation under control."

"Thanks. I figured you knew exactly where we were." They walked on for a while. "*Three days* to erase MATS from all USSF ships?"

"And to get SolNet barely functioning again. Thank God we have our dictator now. MATS does listen to her! She got MATS to sign a million-year contract to never infect another USSF ship. The downside is that we have to recognize that MATS will continue to be a major player in SolNet. But it couldn't be helped. And we'll also have this Ywritt flavor to MATS from the Douglas and Laurie robots. Anyway, the *VI* itself needed the entire three days for its retrofit."

"How about your health, sir? I mean, speaking as your P/E and all."

"Well, we spent a whole day fooling with radiation therapy. We'll all be okay. Amav needed some herself, of course. That's the other strange thing. When's the last time you stood in line for *six hours* for a doctor's appointment? And some hospitals were a lot worse, even though we opened all USSF facilities to the public."

"It's hard to believe. Of course when I get back I'll be volunteering for that duty myself."

"I still can't wrap my head around the fact that *nobody* was killed. I expected a hundred thousand or more gone just by looking at the whole city collapsing."

"I know. It's unbelievable what the Martians pulled off, sir."

Jack nodded. "And we had no idea at the time. The Martians in the saucer with us completely zoned out. It wasn't until we got to the spaceport that they could tell us what happened."

Within moments of *Garrison's* blast into Star Drive, what was left of the Total Martian Outradiance had sensed the ultimate catastrophe developing at Marsport. A spontaneous Amplified Thought somehow arose from both expert Martian practitioners and novices, and the struggling TMO managed to bodily transport the entire population for a radius of fifty miles to the city of New Chicago six hundred miles west. As Z'B had confirmed, the fact that the modern city of Marsport had inadvertently been built atop the ancient Martian capital of *G'lelelnth* had helped focus the energy.

All Martians, humans, and animals were saved, even as the TMO reeled with shock and was itself further damaged. The only other drawback, aside from thousands of miscellaneous injuries, was that the survivors needed radiation therapy from the first microseconds of the Star Drive burst.

"I just can't fathom it," Jack went on. "Marsport ... *gone.*"

"And Ballard blasted the *Garrison* into Star Drive just like that? I mean, he had to know the consequences."

"Well, if we can catch him ..." Was Jack the only person thinking war crimes trial?

"Did they really go to Iota Persei? Wouldn't the Ywritt help us arrest them?"

"I don't know. The Ywritt are almost impossible to deal with." He nodded back to where Z'B tapped on a metal shack. "I hope we can get Jackie to help us. Believe it or not, that was another reason to offer blanket amnesty. We need all the help we can get. Did I mention that Dar and K'sla are returning from Andertwin?"

"No, but that sounds good."

"Dar says he and K'sla, and the other Martians who emigrated to AC, are doing pretty well mentally. So they'll all be a big help."

"Well, I'm looking forward to getting back myself." Laurie pointed to the *Typhoon VI.* "Need a physician/engineer for the return trip? I can't believe you brought it out here with only the two of you."

"Well, my copilot *is* the Dictator of Sol!" Jack laughed.

"And yes, I'll want you to check out the *VI* on the way back."

"I can have everyone ready in a couple minutes," she said, looking back to Z'B peering into a shack and gesturing with his claws. "I think."

"Great! You do that. I need to speak with the Dictator." He pointed to the *II*. "She wanted to be alone on the ship for a while."

# CHAPTER FORTY-TWO
## For the Museum?

Jack climbed into the upper turret. Amav glowed orange-pink in her EnviroField, gazing at the stars along the barrel of the dorsal PlanetBlaster. "Mind if I join you?" he said, standing by her chair, head bent beneath the plastiglass dome.

"Not much room. Not unless the Dictator of Sol is supposed to give you this chair so she can sit in your lap."

"Hmm. When's the last time we've done *that?*"

Amav cocked her head. "Monday, I think."

"Oh. Well, if you put it *that* way." Of course they'd been face-to-face then on their bed. Jack looked away from the flawless rejuvenated body in the red flight suit, her old backup suit as she called it, much tighter and much more revealing than the one she'd taken to Venus, and Jack's secret preference. He peered down the top of the fuselage towards the Control Room. A line of gold lights shunted left and right through jagged rents in the metal and the twisted exposed spars.

He noted she'd made no move to get up and offer him that seat, though.

It had only taken five minutes to bring the *Typhoon VI* to Altrouda, but they hadn't said anything of consequence, and the trip had felt like hours. Why were they both still so numb? Why had she wanted to sit up here alone? Why did she want this ship to go back to the museum? Who really cared?

So many years ago. Forty? Forty-one? This was where they'd gotten so far apart, not even speaking to each other in the face of the obvious danger, the Centaurian Grid brainwashing the crew and Jack himself so delirious he'd put his own wife at risk. Then the Zarj boarding, the pulsar tubes and the deaths, the Crab Emperor, the torture planet, and somehow she'd loved him through all of it. Did she ever think about that? Was that why they were saving this useless old thing?

"Well, this ship is definitely totaled," he finally said. "About all that's intact are the wings. We'll just leave it here until the Martians can think up some good AT for it."

"Yeah, but we could Arkonsky-clamp it right now and tow it."

Jack bumped his head against the plastiglass. "Well, Z'B was saying that if you wanted the really archival restoration, you'd want to collect all the nuts and bolts and metal scraps lying around. We'd miss a lot of that towing it, he said."

Amav shrugged. "Well, whatever. Guess we're in no hurry."

There was a long silence. Jack wanted to invite her to tour the lower fuselage, but that was where they'd made love, where they'd *reconciled,* forty-one years ago. He was embarrassed to find himself wishing Laurie would stay away a few more minutes. He and Amav could be down there, on the floor, and he could be unzipping that flight suit. Why was she looking so good now? But the deck was strewn with escape craft wreckage. There was no way. What was he thinking?

They couldn't talk anymore. They couldn't discuss *it*. He stared through the thick plastiglass at the searchlights radiating from the *VI* across the ruined plain, and the makeshift shacks in the glare. Could they ever discuss '38? The kidnapping?

"So we'll be ready to go in a bit," he said.

"Give me a few minutes. I just want to soak all this up, I guess. Haven't had much time to think and all."

"Right. I know. So much has happened."

"We need to give ourselves time to just think about it all."

"I know. Marsport and everything. And this SolGrid crap."

She shrugged. "It just never worked for Sol. Maybe it's right for the Centaurians. But we're not wired for it somehow. And it nearly killed off the Martians."

Why was he standing here, cramped and banging his head against the turret, why was she just sitting there looking away, why couldn't they *talk?* "Well, it did help us find all those Wounded. At first, I mean."

"Well, MATS thinks there have to be a lot more underground. Maybe disorganized, but still among us, biding their time. It's just that nobody wants to admit that."

"C'mon, we can only trust MATS so far," Jack said, then

regretted it. Amav's weird bond with the Marsport Automated Transport System had surfaced as a sore point within a day. "Look, I know there's a lot that needs straightening out now, and it can't be done all at once. I guess we need to straighten *ourselves* out, too. I mean, too much going on, and all."

Amav sighed, still gazing across the searchlight-stabbed plain.

"I guess we keep blundering *into* things. We seem to have all these *themes* to work on. Like we've said we've been ready to explore, but now we need to clean up all this crap at home first. That's a lot of time and energy, I mean a lot of time rebuilding infrastructure, the networks, and all, when what we really wanted …"

No response.

"Look, Amav, you know I've been thinking, and as soon as all this crap is over, I think I'm ready to retire. I mean, finally. You know I'm feeling sort of old now and all."

Amav whirled her turret chair, whacking her knees into his. "Well, *old man,* pull out your comm and see if you can't interface with that dinky thirties printer right there! Put it in writing, on real paper!"

Her brown eyes were absolutely unreadable. Jack turned to the tiny printer underneath WEAPONS POWER AUX. God, what ancient tech. A printer aboard a spaceship had been unnecessary forty years ago, hell, sixty years ago, but some engineer had thought the ventral turret officer might need to print out some fool order. Jack dubiously pulled out his comm and watched it find VT106PRN.

INTERFACE ERROR.

"Well, it's giving an error message. Let me see," Jack muttered, trying to remember which personnel folder held the Standard Resignation Template. Then he felt Amav pushing up from the turret chair to give him a quick kiss.

"Idiot!" she laughed. "I just wanted the pleasure of tearing it in half! Because you know damn well that the Dictator of Sol hereby *refuses* your resignation!"

"But maybe it *is* time, you know. Unless you think maybe

we should wait. I mean, I know there's a lot of work to do in Sol, and for Mars."

"Oh, that's not it! And you're not an *old man,* not by a long shot. You're nowhere near ready to retire. Come on, it *is* cramped in here. Let's get downstairs and explore the ship before we go."

Jack backed down the ladder, looking up to the magnificent tight red rear descending above him. On the main deck, in the tiny golden lights, they surveyed the escape craft debris and the fuselage gashes.

"Anyway, the Martians will take charge of their own planet," Amav said. "Kner asked me to be the main planetary engineer, but you know they can spare me. As far as I'm concerned, it's all just a bunch of stuff that got wrecked, and so what? Nobody got killed, so let the Martians have some fun getting everything right again. We could take a vacation, you and me, but I don't think you're ready to retire."

"I don't know. Sometimes I've thought, you know, just quit, gather a few friends and leave on some weird, never-ending exploration. Get hundreds of light-years away, just see what's out there. Leave all this behind."

"Great! No, just you and me to start with. I don't want a damn commune flying along with us. I'll just get us the most luxurious Martian ship I can find. Maybe a J-133."

Jack had to laugh. "We don't need a two-hundred-foot-wide saucer!"

"And we'll find the perfect robot navigator. I'm sure Edward will do it."

Jack winced. "Well, I don't know about *Edward.* But maybe someday it would be nice. Just to get away, if we could. Maybe when I really do retire."

"No, you're not listening, husband," Amav said, grabbing his flight suit and hoisting herself up for another kiss. "We need the damn J-133 right *now,* so we can go find our son."

Jack stared back in shock. Had she really said that? "But your duties …"

"Oh, that's just a short-term deal. What's left of the Council is already starting to report in. They left me as Six-Month Dictator until MATS recreates everything. Didn't I mention that?"

"Well, no ..."

"Sorry, dear, so much going on! Anyway, I don't think they need six months to get up and running again. And meanwhile you and I need to be making plans. Just leave Joe in charge. You're not ready to quit just yet, but you and I can take a long vacation. *And* we'll find Jonathan James. First stop, Iota Persei."

"*No* ... I mean, don't you realize he's *one-third* of-- *something?* I mean, I *talked* to him! *It!* I mean, he's *in* there with Ballard, and that other thing."

"We'll figure it out, Jack. I promise. The Ywritt will know."

"You really believe that? You really want to do this?"

"He's our son! Of course I want to do this!"

"He's our *son?*" Jack babbled. "I mean, of course he is! But--"

"Yes! No matter what's happened. That's what I've realized. And we're going to go get him. I'll rip that Ballard bastard right out of him if I have to! Dammit, Jack, we've seen stranger things in our time. A damn AI pyramid! So what? He's trapped in there! We'll get him out!"

"Look, I was just talking to Laurie, and she's pretty sure Ballard *will* go over to the Wounded. That that's his real personality. And we really have no idea how JJC would react to getting some *new body*." He thought of the immense robotic figures the Wounded had fashioned of himself, Amav, and other *Typhoon* crew at Iota Persei last year, robots the crew would be forced to enter, to *become* forever. How haunting, how compelling they'd been, how *tempting*, and he looked into Amav's eyes and saw she was recalling the same thing.

"Dammit, Jack, I'd rather see him alive and whole, even as a Wounded!"

"But he could also be a war criminal, just like Ballard. Who knows who made the decision to Star Drive Marsport?"

"Maybe it was that *other* part, that Martian robot thing. Anyway, I don't care. We're going after him and that's that."

Jack heard a scrunching from the open ventral hatch and made out the blue legs of Laurie's flight suit below. She had to be politely waiting for the argument to subside.

Amav followed his glance. "So leave Joe in charge. You're taking a leave of absence *before* retirement, with the Dictator of Sol, on the Dictator's direct orders. We're going to find out everything there is to know about our son. You got that?"

"Well, I just can't see putting you in that sort of danger."

"The hell with it! The danger is that we rot *here*. We rot here *rejuvenating* ourselves, and *preserving* ourselves. We have to find *out*. No matter what it is. We have to go out there and dare to evolve in ways we can't even *imagine*. Can't you get that through your thick head?"

Jack stared into her furious brown eyes. "Well, that's what I've been saying all along. Haven't I? I mean, like, all my life?"

"Yes! So live up to it!" She pointed at the deck where they'd made love forty-one years ago. "*This* thing goes to the museum! *We* don't!" She pushed him towards the hatch. "Let's get going, shall we? Laurie's waiting for us."

The Dictator of Sol swung down the ventral hatch in that most desirable backup flight suit, and Jack eagerly followed.

## About the Author

Michael D. Smith was raised in the Northeast and the Chicago area, then moved to Texas to attend Rice University, where he began developing as a writer and visual artist. His Jack Commer, Supreme Commander science fiction series is published by Sortmind Press. In addition, Sortmind Press has published Smith's literary novels *Sortmind, The Soul Institute, CommWealth, Akard Drearstone,* and *Jump Grenade.* All titles are available from Amazon.

Smith's web site, https://sortmind.com, contains further examples of his novels and visual art, and he muses about writing and art processes at https://blog.sortmind.com/.

Amazon author page
https://www.amazon.com/author/smithmi/


### The Jack Commer, Supreme Commander Series

The Martian Marauders
Jack Commer, Supreme Commander
Nonprofit Chronowar
Collapse and Delusion
The Wounded Frontier
The SolGrid Rebellion
Balloon Ship Armageddon